A LIFE
SPECTACULAR

ALSO BY EATON KRONE

LightSide Novels

Happy Meals: The Euwel (Book 1)

A LIFE SPECTACULAR

A LightSide Novel

Eaton Krone

A LIFE SPECTACULAR

In memory of Jacques.

PROLOGUE

What's been seen cannot be unseen, and what's been unseen cannot be seen.

Like The Nonexistent Observer. He hasn't been seen since the dawn of time, and he probably won't be seen after dusk either.

He calls himself The Nonexistent Observer because that's what he is and that's what he does. For him, there's just something about keeping one's identity straightforward that makes it feel more natural. More … authentic. It's something that none of the other nonexistent observers seem willing or able to comprehend, opting to stick with pretentious titles like The All-Seeing Eye, Icon737, or Gertrude.

Now, you'd think if you don't exist, neither does time, but you'd be wrong. You actually have quite a lot of it on your hands, and you have to pass it somehow. But while the rest of the nonexistent community generally keep themselves busy by observing major events such as supernovas, civil wars, or puppies chewing on a garden hose, The Nonexistent Observer prefers looking at the boring stuff. After billions of years experimenting with various observation techniques, he's come to the conclusion that it's far more satisfying to see something happening to the boring stuff than merely getting what you signed up for.

Which is why he'd spent a few months watching a half-eaten Vahltan pie orbiting a blue-and-green planet.

•••

Fortunately the pie – being a pie – didn't have that creepy feeling it was being watched, nor did it feel any pain or discomfort when it met a violent end against the viewport of a spaceship.

On the other side of the wide, curved glass, Captain Schuk Wozzel's brown-furred Stortian face carried an expression favoured by most people when a recently well-fed pigeon unburdened itself over their recently well-washed car.

The expression, in turn, carried a touch less annoyance than normal, because the captain had bigger problems on his hands – an odd power surge in Engineering had fried the ship's shields and sensors, leaving it vulnerable to threats bigger than discarded foodstuffs.

It wasn't the best situation to be in for the man in charge of the most important vessel in the Charted Universe.

While Captain Wozzel couldn't do anything about this technical predicament until the engineers located and repaired the cause of the surge, he *could* do something about the culinary mess staring him in the face.

He was on the verge of summoning a cleaning crew, when his eye caught a partial glimpse of something vaguely familiar in the distance. He leaned sideways to get a better look past the remnants of the now-two-dimensional pie. The object was a small, faint, greenish blur that mushroomed into a big, bright, greenish ball as it streaked towards the ship.

The middle-aged Stortian had often pondered how he'd die one day. Now he knew, and he also now knew which day *one day* was. But getting confirmation on the time and manner of his demise wasn't as fulfilling as he'd imagined it would be.

Despite knowing it was too late, Captain Wozzel spun around to scream an order to his crew, but didn't get further than "Take evasiv—" before he was silenced along with the rest of the souls on board. One of whom was the most important person in the Charted Universe. Or, at least, he *had* been.

•••

Of course, The Nonexistent Observer knew nothing about the ship or its occupants, nor did he really care. But as an enormous disc of green fire blasted debris far and wide into the cold vacuum of space, he couldn't help but think that this incident might just be the start of something … unpleasant. A more informed, caring observer would have thought that, in all probability, there would soon be hell to pay.

CHAPTER 1

Somewhere in Johannesburg, a mind felt something was wrong.

To assist the mind in shedding some light on the matter, a hand pulled down a duvet cover that looked like it'd been trampled by a herd of startled cows. The face unveiled wasn't handsome but, in fairness, it wasn't ugly either. On balance, it was pretty average-looking, albeit slightly more on the opposite side of pretty – the dishevelled brown hair and bloodshot brown eyes did little to tip the scales in the desired direction.

The eyes stared fixedly at the ceiling as the brain started to boot up. It was a slow process.

As awareness started trickling in, the first thing Guy Leatherman realised was that it was Tuesday, and even though no particular day of the week would have had him jumping out of bed with wild abandon, Tuesdays were lowest on his list of days to love. It wasn't just the fact that a Tuesday was the most unimpressive day of the week, with its wow-factor count of zero. No, it wasn't *just* that.

The big problem with Tuesdays was that, just over three decades ago, Guy's dreary existence had been inaugurated when his mother pushed him out on a Tuesday; five minutes before Wednesday. Wednesday was his least disliked day, mainly because it meant that Tuesday was over and he had the maximum number of days left before encountering the next one.

He tried to decide whether it was worth going to work, but he was just an employee, and employees like him weren't really entitled to make such decisions.[*]

This gave rise to the second thing Guy realised; something was indeed wrong. He glanced at his alarm clock and immediately identified the source of his unease. Leaping out of bed, he hurriedly performed the early morning rituals to make himself look and smell reasonably decent. Then, grabbing his keys from the kitchen counter, he locked the front door and rushed to his car. But despite his efforts, he was going to be late for work. Again.

● ● ●

Guy snuck into his cubicle, situated in the corner of the local newspaper's small editorial department, praying that his late arrival wouldn't be noticed. However, as with all his other hopes and prayers, this one received the DENIED! stamp. As soon as he sat down, a voice pierced the air with a firm "Guuuuy!!!", followed by the all-too-familiar sound of a door slamming.

Guy warily approached the door above which the letters E-D-I-T-O-R were displayed in white on a black Perspex sign that had seen better days as well as better editors. Jane Harding wasn't a woman to be trifled with. Not that Guy ever trifled with anyone, but Jane would look for trifle if there was any to be found and would make some if there wasn't.

Taking a deep breath, he slowly opened the door and stepped into the office with an awkward smile. This was a mistake; Jane hated smiles. The only times the editor ever smiled herself was when she was crushing someone's soul or privates. Although she had never physically done the latter to Guy, he still felt a pain in his mid-region whenever she chastised him for something. Which basically made it a chronic pain.

---

[*] Some employees entitle themselves nonetheless for various debatable reasons, although such debates are better suited for another day – preferably a day when the employees in question aren't there.

In contrast to her intimidating physical appearance, Jane had an extremely high-pitched voice, like a pig whose leg was being amputated with a cheese grater. Although, like Guy, a pig would probably rather have had its leg amputated with a cheese grater than listen to Jane's ranting.

"You'd better have a good explanation!" she squealed, tapping at her wristwatch.

Guy thought it better not to risk the merry "Hi there!" with which he usually greeted people to make himself sound more cheerful than he actually was.

"Hi," he said instead. "I … well, you see, traffic was a bit hectic this morning, and then my car overheated and—"

"Do you take me for a fool, Mr Leatherman?" Jane interjected with an eyebrow raised like the curve of a question mark, rounded off by the hairy-mole-dot below the eye.

"No," Guy muttered.

"I *thought* so. And do you know *why* I thought so?"

"Er … no."

"*Of course* you don't. You're *too stupid* to know *anything*. Your little brain will *never* be able to fathom why your *empty little life* isn't worth the paper your birth certificate is printed on. You're a *pathetic loser* who'll *never* achieve *anything* in life. And do you know *why*? *I'll* tell you *why* …"

Jane was a master at ripping people apart. For most people, this type of personal hammering would have been enough to knock them down a deep hole of depression, but not Guy. He was already at the bottom of that hole, and had been for some time.

However, while the majority of what Jane said was true, he didn't need reminding, so he simply let the words roll over him like lava off a duck's back.

When he eventually trudged out of the Devil Editor's office, Guy was waylaid by Jane's annoying nephew, Patrick, who had just found a potato in the bag of potato chips he'd bought. He looked really upset about it.

"I mean, a *whole* potato!" the young man griped at Guy's desk. "If a *whole* potato could slip through, *what else* have we been eating without knowing it?"

"Half potatoes?" Guy ventured flatly.

Patrick's eyes narrowed. "Are you mocking me?"

"No, er, of course not. I'm sorry, you have my full atten-tion," Guy said, and scribbled some boring notes on his note-pad while the man concluded his *horrible* ordeal.

"You will run it in this week's paper?" Patrick asked in a way that sounded more like a demand than a question.

Normally, Guy would never have considered publishing such drivel, but seeing as it was Jane's nephew, and seeing as his day with Jane had already started off on the wrong foot[*], he continued to write the best story he could about something that, for him, turned the word *trivial* into the un-derstatement of the year.

---

[*] No, the other foot wouldn't have made any difference.

CHAPTER 2

Traffic. No one living in the countryside could ever fully appreciate what it's like being stuck in heavy city traffic. Not that anyone living in the city appreciated it either.

Except maybe for Neville Andersman, Guy's traffic-cop friend who had a sick fascination with all things traffic. And the busier, the better. "Bumper to bumper is best," was Neville's motto. He excelled at upholding the laws of the road and punishing those who didn't. He truly enjoyed his work, and although Guy couldn't understand how someone could be so keen about *traffic*, he envied his friend for having such a passion for his career.

Along with many other things, passion was something that had never quite made it into Guy's emotional repertoire, and the little bit he possessed was barely enough to rival an eggplant's passion for quilting. Which was probably the main reason he didn't enjoy life as much as he should have.

A few months earlier, Guy had decided it was time for a change. Drunk and depressed, he'd sat outside a pub, looked up at the black canvas with the white dots above him, waited for the stars to stop swimming around, gave up on waiting and wished that he could experience something new in his life. Something … fun. Especially something he could share with Neville, as Guy was too skittish to experience fun on his own.

Not surprisingly, his wish hadn't come true, which was why he was now stuck in the same old car in the same old traffic with the same old worries. Thankfully, he'd soon be home to put this miserable day to bed along with himself. At least, that was the plan.

Glup ... glup ... glup ... blup ... blup ... blup ... blrrrrrr ... glup ... blrrrrrr ... bsssshhh!

Cars have a way of stating certain things in a way you don't want to hear.

"Great, just what I need!" Guy cried, punching the steering wheel with his fists, but not too hard, as his fists weren't used to punching.

Pulling to the side of the road in a cloud of steam, he got out and marched to the front of the tennis-ball-coloured jalopy. He lifted the hood and was greeted by a bigger cloud of steam. When it cleared a bit, he took a closer look.

Yep, it was just as he suspected: he still had no clue what went on in a car's engine.

Berating himself for becoming a second-rate journalist instead of a second-rate mechanic, Guy dropped the hood just as a marked traffic patrol car pulled up behind his stricken vehicle.

"Need a hand?" asked a familiar voice.

"Neville!"

"In the flesh," said the caramel-skinned traffic officer as he got out. Taking off his sunglasses, he strolled over to his stranded friend.

"How are you doing, bud?" he added, eyeing the steam wafting from the car's grill.

Guy shook Neville's hand. "Same as usual."

"That bad, eh?"

"Yeah."

"Want me to have a look at it?"

"I don't think it will help much. I could use a lift, though."

"No prob," Neville smiled. "Don't worry about your car. I'll take care of it."

"*And* I'll pick you up for work in the morning," he added before the expected question could be asked.

"Thanks," Guy said as Neville called in some favours on his handheld radio.

When he was done, the officer gestured towards his patrol car. "Shall we?"

Guy grinned. "Ladies first."

"Ooh, you're so kind, dear sir," Neville said in a *feminine* voice accompanied by a rough curtsy.

With a chuckle, Guy got in the passenger seat. "You're a good friend, Nev."

"Can I have that on paper?" Neville said as he settled behind the steering wheel.

"No."

"Thought so."

The patrol car sped off in the emergency lane with its lights flashing. Although Guy couldn't really complain about his turn of luck, he also couldn't trust it completely. As an ardent pessimist who knew that positive things never happened to him without him paying for it later, he wasn't looking forward to the immediate future.

CHAPTER 3

Back home, Guy donned his blue cartoon pyjamas depicting a familiar black-and-white cat chasing a small but clever yellow bird. In the kitchen, he constructed an impressive club sandwich that didn't have much time to bask in its own glory before being chased down by a cold beer.

There wasn't much on the tube, so Guy kept changing the channels relentlessly until he found something to watch, which turned out to be the things he always watched. He just started to drift off when a sudden flash of light, followed by a loud clap of thunder, left the house enveloped in darkness.

"Wonderful," he said glumly after ascertaining with relief that his heart was still beating inside his chest instead of his throat.

He got up and made his way to the kitchen using Braille navigation; a journey that included a stubbed toe and a blow to the shin. With all his hopes of immortality crushed by his furniture, Guy finally made it to the cupboard containing the candles and matches. After lighting one of the old-school sources of light, he tried flipping the circuit breaker's main switch back to the "On" position. After several failed attempts, he surrendered to the harsh reality that the power might be off indefinitely, which meant no more television.

This posed a problem, as the thunder had thwarted his plans to visit la-la land; a fact that was proven half an hour later after a bout of useless tossing and turning in bed.

Lighting the candle again, Guy picked up the used book he'd recently acquired from the flea market. It was the inspirational *The Best of Me*, written by a well-known banker who claimed that *anyone* could achieve the goals they set for themselves by tapping into the willpower lying dormant deep within them. It usually knocked Guy out fast.

It must have worked, because he was awoken from the world of dreams by a strange light. As he pried his eyes open, the book was lying cover-up on his chest, with the banker giving him an upside-down million-dollar smile. Guy squinted at his mechanical alarm clock, whose luminescent arms stated it was just before twelve. The power still seemed to be out, because no light filtered in through the drapes from the street lamps outside. But the light had to come from somewhere. He glanced at the candle, which wasn't producing any illumination either; only a thin wisp of smoke drifted up from the wick. But no draught could have killed the flame, seeing as all the doors and windows were shut.

He just started contemplating stopping at the pharmacy in the morning to pick up some flatulence medication, when the source of the illumination became evident: an eerie, pulsating white light with a soft blue hue framed the closed door of his walk-in closet. This was odd, as there had never been a light in the enclosure; at least not one that actually worked. He'd been meaning to replace the bulb but had never quite found the willpower to do so. If the banker had known how deep and dormant Guy's willpower actually was, his smile would have remained in a permanent state of upside-down-ness.

"What the …?" Guy said.

Putting the book aside, he got up for a closer inspection of the anomaly. He didn't learn much, and then realised he might learn more if he actually opened the door. Which, to his surprise, he did. On the face of it, the light that hit him seemed bright enough to blind a mole. But it was strangely pleasing to the eye, even hypnotically inviting. His mind tried to warn him that flames were also fatally inviting to moths, but he was too tired to listen properly.

He was about to walk in, but froze, thanks to his inherent inability to tamper with the status quo. Especially when the status quo was – like now – that he was still alive and well. He came to a mutual agreement with himself to return to the safety of his bed. Then a part of him, a part he never knew existed, broke the agreement by forcing him to shrug, grumble "Stuff it!", close his eyes and step forward.

The light enveloped him like a tingly cocoon.

It felt like a second.

It felt like a lifetime.

It felt … surreal.

When things started feeling real again, Guy pondered whether he should open his eyes. He did, and regretted it instantly as a yellow beast in a top hat grabbed him by the shoulders and hoisted him up, growling.

CHAPTER 4

With all the strength he could muster, Guy managed to struggle free from the creature's grip and stumbled backwards. Gravity lent a hand by pulling him down hard on his backside, sending up a cloud of blue dust. In normal circumstances, he might have found coloured dust strange, but the yellow-furred creature advancing on him with saliva dripping from its sharp fangs made any twists in his surroundings seem somewhat insignificant.

What wasn't insignificant, however, was the urge to get the hell out of there, wherever the hell *there* was. For a moment, Guy's legs didn't want to cooperate with his mind, but when the creature's large, hairy claw reached for him, cooperation was quickly re-established. Guy retreated hastily in semi-crab-like fashion and was on his feet, running, before he knew it.

Whatever the purpose was of the huge domed chamber he found himself in, he couldn't care less. The important thing was that there was an exit, and he made a run for it. Outside, it was dark, except for the light of the two moons shining brightly above. Again, his mind tried to tell him something, but adrenaline was blocking his ears as he quickly put some distance between himself and the now-roaring creature behind him.

Although surprised at the speed with which he bolted across the dark, unfamiliar terrain, Guy felt the energy rapidly seeping from his system. His lungs started to burn, but his legs refused to stop their forward momentum.

As he reached the top of a long, gradual incline, the outline of a building gave him hope. He doubled his efforts and dashed through a doorway in which a metal door hung open loosely. He would have kept running if it hadn't been for the dark shape he'd just run into, causing him to bounce back gracelessly. For the second time, Guy found himself on the floor. Exhausted, he barely managed to raise his head to identify the object that had brought him down. A pair of eyes opened, glowing amber in the low light.

"What are you doing out here?" he heard, or rather felt, a voice reverberating inside his head.

As the huge shape bent over him, Guy's mind and body ceased their newfound cooperation once more, and everything went dark.

•••

Guy opened his eyes and decided he should really stop doing so. Staring at him was an eight-foot-tall beetle-like monstrosity with four arms. Its dark-brown hide bore intricate beige patterns that curved and spiralled all over its body except for the bark-like shell on its back. The cone-shaped head, carrying two large, dark, bulging eyes on the sides, was quite small in relation to the rest of the body, and was nearly split in two by a wide, lipless mouth. There wasn't any sign of ears or a nose, although Guy fleetingly wondered if the two small, sunken holes beneath the mouth fulfilled the functions of the missing facial parts. As a matter of fact, *all* his thoughts came fleetingly, especially the ones relating to why the heck he was here and what the heck was looming over him.

"Firstly, I don't know why *you're here,"* a voice *said* in Guy's head as the creature folded both pairs of arms, *"since you're supposed to be training. Secondly, you must have hit your head pretty hard to forget your good pal, Cortex. And because I'm your pal, I suggest you get your butt back to the dome before Rimmy gets upset. You know what happens when he gets upset."*

"Er, you can … read my mind?" Guy said with a mixture of surprise, astonishment, fear, confusion and intrigue, as well as a mixture of other things that desperately wanted to escape the confines of his stomach.

"Of course *I can read your mind. You* know *I can ... oh yes, sorry, I forgot how much you hate it when I do that.*"

"Uh ..." Guy said.

"*It's just ... well, I just can't help myself sometimes, you know?*"

"I'm dreaming, right?" Guy breathed.

"*No, you're not,*" the creature named Cortex said with a feel of impatience. Seeing him speak was odd, especially as he did so without his lips moving. "*You* are, *however, supposed to be practising. Rimmy won't be happy that you're skipping a session.*"

Despite the bug's assurances to the contrary, Guy still wasn't sure if this was all part of a dream or in fact real. But he thought it best to go with the flow, as he didn't really have any options open either way.[*]

"Um ... what am I supposed to be practising again?" he said.

"*How about all those looking-to-break-your-neck stunts you're so proud of?*" Cortex said. "*You should really cut back on the heroics. You're becoming more ruthless and – dare I say – more egotistical by the day.*"

"Er, sure," Guy mumbled as he noticed a cracked mirror affixed to a nearby wall. Getting up, he nervously approached it, had a look, and gave himself a fright. While this had happened before, at least it had been in his own body, which *this* most certainly wasn't.

Staring back at him was a short creature with red skin, which was mostly covered by a tight, lime-green bodysuit that looked like a hideous cross between a wrestling suit and a wetsuit. It looked extra hideous on his scrawny body, and the elongated hands and feet didn't do his overall appearance any favours. At least the suit complemented his big, lime-

---

[*] When life hands you lemons, make lemonade. Or you can squirt them into your eyes to avoid seeing what's coming next. Applied correctly, both are fantastic options.

green eyes, which stood out like gems against the redness of the skin. His topknot of wiry, medium-length hair was green too, albeit a shade darker. It fountained up from the centre of his otherwise smooth scalp like the leaves atop an underfed, sunburnt pineapple.

Using the narrow mouth on his narrow face, Guy flashed himself a grin, but quickly unflashed it to hide teeth that would have been perfect for the *before* photo in a dental-reconstruction magazine. Above his thin lips, a long narrow nose flared out wide at the tip, and as he leaned a bit closer to the mirror, they appeared to have cigarette butts stuffed into them. When he tried to pull at the substance, his eyes started to water profusely. It clearly wasn't a good idea to do that – just like it wasn't a good idea to pull his nose hair, which apparently this was.

"What in Zolt's name are you doing, Bezam?" Cortex asked.

"Bezam?" Guy said with tear-filled eyes. *"That's* my name? Bezam? What a stupid name for—" he trailed off as he noticed Cortex's blank stare.

"You did *bump your head, didn't you?"* the bug said, now with a feel of concern.

"No … uh … I don't think so."

"Well, I'm not taking any chances. You're going to see Kola, just to be on the safe side."

Without warning, Cortex hoisted a protesting Guy onto his rough-textured back. *"Stop complaining, Bezam. You're in no condition to be on your feet. There's something wrong with your head. It's like you're not yourself. You feel … different. Kola will know what to do."*

Cortex was right about one thing; it didn't help to complain, because his tight grip held Guy firmly in place as he hauled him outside into the breaking morning light.

CHAPTER 5

Guy stopped struggling when his eyes got distracted by the odd surroundings. The bug carried him over a sea of neon-green grass and blue soil. At least the sky was blue too, but the clouds had a tint of green in them as they periodically passed in front of the three suns above. Such a landscape might have caused many people to fret a bit, but as Guy's alive-and-well status quo wasn't exactly threatened by blue soil and multiple suns, he forced himself to relax.

The flat terrain at the foot of the hill they descended was dotted with small, multicoloured domes surrounding a gigantic orange dome; very likely the same one he'd escaped from earlier. Except for the colours, the structures reminded him of those round parachutes he'd seen in old war movies.

Reaching one of the smaller domes on the outskirts of the settlement, or whatever it was, Cortex halted. The surface of the red dome seemed solid on the outside until it ripped into the shape of an arch big enough for them to pass through. Guy couldn't see a zip or any other kind of fastener as they entered through the flaps, which closed up and solidified again as soon as the bug carried him inside.

"Wa makeer *om*?" a voice said.

"Don't know," Cortex said as he lay Guy down atop one of the two gurney-looking beds in the middle of the room. *"But he's acting very ... strangely."*

A pink furry creature, similar to the one that had stormed at him earlier, suddenly bent over Guy. And because having a large, fanged creature in his face did *not* fall within acceptable status quo parameters, Guy started screaming in panic.

"Ho om vas!" the creature shrieked and hurried from view as Cortex pinned down Guy's squirming body.

When it returned, the pink beast pressed a gun-like device against Guy's right shoulder. After a brief *tsssh*, a sudden wave of euphoria swept Guy's panic off to another beach.

Cortex and the creature stepped back, staring at Guy in the same way art critics must have stared at the first Salvador Dalí painting. When their shapes started swimming before him, Guy's head fell back on the pillow, and it only took a few seconds for his eyelids to become too heavy to keep open. His mind took this as a sign that it wasn't needed at present and deemed it a good time to take a break.

• • •

Opening his eyes, Guy felt the ritual urge to relieve himself of certain bodily fluids. He also felt somewhat woozy.

Sitting up, he shook his heavy head. "What happened?"

"You have been sedated," a voice *said* in his head. It almost had the same feel to it as that of the bug mind-reader.

But as Guy looked up, he found himself facing a creature similar to those in that science-fiction television series about the two FBI agents investigating extraterrestrial phenomena – or in most similar shows and movies, for that matter. Neither agent would have been impressed by the yelp Guy gave as he stared into the large, black eyes staring back at him. They also wouldn't have been impressed by the volume of dark liquid streaming down Guy's leg. Or maybe they would have. Whichever, he didn't have to go anymore.

CHAPTER 6

"*That was* not *very polite,*" the creature *transmitted* as he/she/it shook his/her/its scrawny feet alternately to shake off the liquid that had formed a large, dark pool on the floor where he/she/it stood.

The classic-looking grey alien was quite short, and would barely have reached Guy's hip, had Guy been human and standing upright. But even in his new, shorter body, Guy was almost a head taller than the creature. It had big, dark eyes but only two small holes for a nose, and not much of a mouth either, with really thin lips that could have been used to slice ham really thin. It also had grey, hairless skin pulled tightly over the bones underneath, without much visible muscle to fill the spaces in between. It did, however, have a substantial belly; the type that should rather be covered by a loose shirt. The being, however, wasn't covered by *anything*. Fortunately, its naked body featured no visible genitalia, which was sure to be a huge advantage if its feet ever slipped off the pedals while riding a bicycle.

With a sour look, the creature stomped out the doorway, which was soon filled by another shape.

"What happened here?" bellowed the pink creature from earlier, eyeing the puddle on the floor in a way that could *not* be described as pleased.

"I, er … wait, I can understand you," Guy said, perplexed. Although, judging by the creature's tone, body language and scowl, he wasn't sure if this was a good thing.

"That's just *wonderful*!" it said. "Then understand *this*: if you *ever* take another leak on one of my medical beds, I'll make sure you're never able to take one again. Got it?"

With extensive Jane-training, Guy knew this was no time to argue, so he just nodded nervously. The creature looked at him sternly for another second before its face softened.

"Oh, yes, sorry," it said. "Apologies for snapping at you, Bezam ... I mean, um, *Guy*," it added, frowning. It seemed to roll the name around in its mouth, only to find that it tasted a bit off.

"Who are you?" Guy said.

"My name is Ms Kola," she said with a fanged smile that made Guy gulp. "But you can just call me Kola."

"Where am I ... Kola?"

"You're in *Rimmy's Magnificent Circus*, but I should rather let Mr Gray explain," she said, then noticed Guy's blank expression. "That's the Grey you ... uh ... decorated just now. But first you need to get out of those ruined clothes and into the shower." She gestured over her shoulder at a dark tube to one side of the tent.

"You have been potty-trained on your ... you know, the place you come from?" she asked.

"Uh ..."

"Well, I hope so, because I'm not going to keep on cleaning up after you."

She pointed at the tube again.

"Blue knob: water; white: soap; and crystal: air. Toggle the blue up for hotter water and down for colder. The same with the air-blower. Got it?"

"Er ..."

"Good. Now, here's a clean suit," she said, tossing a bundle onto the bed. "And please try to keep it clean this time."

With that, she walked out.

"But ..." Guy started, but realised that his aimless protestations at the now-resealed door would most probably be a waste of breath.

•••

Apart from getting the settings wrong a few times, which caused more than a bit of discomfort, it didn't take long for Guy to finish his shower, and he actually felt quite refreshed. Awkward too, after water, soap and air had sprayed and blown in from seemingly everywhere into places he hadn't known existed, but refreshed nonetheless.

The suit he donned was a replica of the previous one. He'd at least hoped for some variety. However, he didn't have time to ponder his fashion predicament, as the doorway went limp and the small grey figure from earlier entered warily.

"Are you ... empty?" it asked.

"Oh, uh, that," Guy replied with red-faced – or, rather, even more red-faced – embarrassment. "Yeah, well, er, sorry, um, Mr, uh, Gray, is it? I swear, it's never happened to me before, except maybe for when I was an infant and once during a concert when the queue—"

"Apology accepted, Mr Leatherman," the Grey stopped Guy before he could divulge any more information than needed, or wanted. *"Apparently many of your species that entered the programme have had the same response. I suppose I should have come better prepared."*

"What programme?" Guy frowned.

"Why, the Life Spectacular Life-Enrichment Programme, *of course,"* Mr Gray replied.

Guy blinked in a way that emphasised the fact that one person's "of course" wasn't necessarily the same as that of another.[*]

"Your Wish is Our Command?" Mr Gray tried, raising a querying eyebrow, or would have if he'd had one to raise. Instead, the skin above his eye scrunched up slightly, though not very far, as it already seemed stretched to its limits.

Not sure what was expected of him, Guy could only blink again.

"Live Your Dream?"

Not wanting to look repetitive, Guy resisted the urge to blink and merely stared at the Grey blankly.

---

[*] It isn't, but everyone knows that, of course.

"You don't know anything about the programme, do you?"

"Nope," Guy replied, happy to say something meaningful at last.

"Oh."

"What programme?"

Mr Gray closed his huge eyelids for a second and took a deep breath. *"Of course,"* he said, opening his eyes once more, *"how silly of me. I forgot you're from a Dumb Planet."*

"A dumb *what*?"

"Dumb Planet. It's what we call planets with civilisations that haven't yet developed the technologies required to make contact with other civilisations and determine their place in the cosmos."

This time it was Mr Gray's turn to blink as he noticed the scowl darkening Guy's face. *"Did I say something wrong?"*

"Hmm, let's see," Guy replied, trying to restrain himself without much effort. "What could it be? Oh, I know! Maybe it's the fact that the term '*Dumb* Planet' does *not* go down so well with the people inhabiting it!"

"Oh, I assure you, I did not mean to offend—"

"*Uninformed* Planets, *Unenlightened* Planets … or even *Planets Without a Clue* would have sufficed. But *Dumb* Planets?!"

"Okay, Mr Leatherman," the little Grey said, holding his hands up placatingly. *"I'm sorry if I came across as rude.* Uninformed *Planets, then?"*

After a pause, Guy gave his half-hearted approval by nodding half-heartedly.

"Marvellous," Mr Gray said, relieved to be able to continue without being raked over the coals – although his ashy appearance made it look as though someone had already done that to him, quite a few times. *"No, you wouldn't have heard about the* Life Spectacular Life-Enrichment Pro-gramme *on a Du— an Uninformed Planet. In short, by law, every person in the Unyun Federation, even those on Unin-formed Planets, must be given a fair opportunity to enter*

competitions, like the Life Spectacular Life-Enrichment Pro-gramme. "

Guy shook his head. "Why would I want to enter a com-petition where I get abducted by aliens?"

Laughter suddenly filled his head as the grey figure's shoulders started bouncing like unoiled pistons. *"Is* that *what you think happened to you, Mr Leatherman? That you were* abducted? "

"Yes, well—"

Mr Gray started laughing harder, and all Guy could do was to wait it out while making his annoyance as visible as pos-sible.

The Grey eventually regained his composure. *"No, Mr Leatherman, you were* not *abducted."*

"Well, *I* surely didn't ask to be here," Guy stated firmly.

"Oh, but you did. *We have everything on record. You en-tered; you won; you're in. "*

Guy folded his arms.

"How could I have entered something if I can't even re-member entering it in the first place?"

"Are you familiar with the concept of nanites? "

"Of course," Guy said, trying to look and sound surer than he was. "Small electronic bugs or some such."

"Or some such, yes, " Mr Gray said patiently. *"Nanites are microscopic robots. "*

"Yes," Guy said, clinging on to his vague certainty, "I knew that."

"I'm sure you did. But what you might not have known is that some nanites, called vernaculites, are programmed to attach themselves to the part of the brain that controls the linguistic functions of the individual, and translates any known language they encounter into the language or dialect the individual understands best. "

"So why couldn't I make out a word Kola said, until now? I understood Cortex just fine."

"Because Cortex, like me, is a telepath. We generally don't need translation to communicate with other species. As for Kola, your vernaculites were supposed to be reset before

you woke up in your new body, but they weren't. Which is why you couldn't understand her. Apologies for that. However, I just injected you with some fresh ones while you were sedated, so you shouldn't have any problems understanding anyone from now on."

Guy looked like he needed some nanites that could help him understand what the Grey was talking about.

"In any case," Mr Gray continued, oblivious to Guy's confusion, *"nanites are also used in the* Life Spectacular Life-Enrichment Programme. *Special nanites, similar to vernaculites, are added to randomly selected water sources on an Uninformed Planet, and can actually transmit thoughts to us when they pick up certain buzzwords."*

"You spiked our water?!"

"Well, uh, essentially, yes. It allows a randomised computer system to pick out lucky winners. Like you. You wished for a different life; a life filled with fun and excitement. So now you can have exactly that!"

Something gnawed at Guy. "Um, when exactly did I do that again; you know, enter the competition?"

"It was only a few months ago. Why wouldn't you remember something like that?"

"Uh, I think I might have been a bit drunk."

"Oh, er, yes, that would explain it."

"And that light in my closet – the one I saw before ending up here?"

"That would be a teleportation pocket; a cube designed to teleport a person from one location to another."

"Right. So you're telling me I was teleported to another galaxy or something in the blink of an eye?"

"Uh, something like that."

Guy felt the sudden need to sit, so he carefully took a seat on the bed, taking special care to avoid the damp spot he'd left earlier. "What happened to my body?"

"Don't worry, Mr Leatherman, your human body and your profile box are perfectly safe."

"Profile box?" Guy said, despite his mind's insistence that he stopped asking questions.

"It's a device that acts as a link between the bodies and minds of hosts and possessors. The nanites of the possessor's body – your human body – and the host's body – the one you're occupying now – communicate via these boxes through intergalactic communication relays. It basically controls the transfer of consciousness to keep things stable."

Guy rubbed his arm nervously. "And Bezam?"

"His consciousness is, for all intents and purposes, asleep. It's kept safe within the same profile box at our head office on Unyun along with your body. But don't worry, we'll reverse-transfer everything before degeneration kicks in."

"Degeneration!" Guy wailed before realising something. "Er …"

"It's when the mind starts losing its connection with the body, and degenerates, which usually leads to death shortly thereafter."

"That sounds terrible!"

"It is, but I can assure you we'll return you to your natural state long *before that happens."*

Guy, however, didn't feel very assured with the notion of falling apart. "So, how long can someone's body and consciousness remain separated before they start … degenerating?"

"In your case, I'd say about three to four months, as long as your human body and the profile box remain near one another."

"And if they don't?" Guy asked apprehensively.

"A few days."

"A few days!"

"Don't worry, Mr Leatherman," Mr Gray said, holding up his hands. *"I just have a quick stop to make, then I'll personally go check up on your body and the box. I'll be back before you know it, I promise."*

Mr Gray promptly walked towards the tent's exit.

"What am I supposed to do in the meantime?"

Without pausing, Mr Gray said, *"Practise, Mr Leatherman, practise. You* are *in the circus, after all!"*

•••

As days flowed into weeks and weeks flowed into months, Guy's anxiety started flowing into panic mode. Mr Gray hadn't delivered on his promise of a speedy return. Or *any* return, for that matter.

It wasn't as though Guy hated his new life. In fact, he'd been having some serious fun and adventure lately. Being in a circus, it was difficult not to, especially with him being one of the main acts. But the delay in the return of his body and consciousness to where they belonged weighed heavily on him. It's been almost three months already, without even a word from that blasted Grey!

As he sat outside his tent, looking up at the moons, Guy took a deep breath and decided to relax. He'd just have to wait a bit longer, as he didn't really have any other choice. For some reason, this realisation helped him to calm down a bit. But he knew this calmness was shaky at best, and wasn't going to last very long. He could only hope that something would happen, and soon.

CHAPTER 7

Gacko took the last slurp of his Clovarian shake before reluctantly letting go of the straw protruding from the tall glass.

The shake had been just the way he liked it; sweet, with a slightly bitter aftertaste. It was now also the way he didn't like it; finished. There wasn't any other place he knew of where Clovarian shakes tasted as refined as on Unyun; not even on Clovaria itself. Not that he knew what *refined* meant, but he'd heard someone say it about a drink once.

All the people with the best clothes, ships, cigars and cuisine – another fine word he'd picked up – were deemed refined. While Gacko desperately wanted to be refined, others considered him a bit dim. His nasal voice and poor language skills did nothing to alter this perception. But one day, when he was refined, everyone would regard him as smart.

He gazed through the window at the enormous Unyun Intergalactic Spaceport, UIS Alpha, which stretched as far as the eye could see to accommodate the vast number of mostly privately owned and corporate spaceships. Although it had happened on occasion, warships weren't allowed to land on Unyun, being neutral and all. The military planet, Unyun Beta, was however situated only a few million kilometres away, which always made Gacko slightly uncomfortable. He didn't like the Militorate. Too many rules and big words.

His partner, Kelp, on the other hand, never seemed too perturbed by it. Then again, Kelp never seemed too perturbed by anything. *He* was clever. He tried to help Gacko with his communication deficiencies from time to time, but it was a slow process, like rolling a concrete block up a steep hill.

Gacko stared at his partner standing by the window while talking to a client on his galphone. He nodded occasionally and, as always, seemed completely calm and in control.

Gacko had admired Kelp from the day they'd first met, although that had also been the day Kelp had shot Gacko and "appropriated" his ship. Hunting down Kelp had been fun, and Kelp had been impressed with Gacko's ability to track him down, despite his seemingly slow facade. Kelp had also been impressed that Gacko then offered the use of the ship that Kelp had stolen from him in the first place, to join his new bounty-hunting business as an equal partner. It'd been an easy decision. Of course, the fact that Kelp had been staring down the barrel of a fully charged flasher gun had been an important part of Gacko's sales pitch. Kelp had been calm and collected then, too. He knew how to keep his head in any situation, which was both a good trait and a practical goal for any bounty hunter hoping to reach retirement age.

Gacko and Kelp had lizard-like features, which made perfect sense, as they were both Monitaurs, with Kelp being bronze and Gacko dark-green in complexion. Of course, Gacko's tremendous appetite left him a bit slim-challenged, which quite a few marks had mistaken as slow; sometimes fatally. At the same time, people often mistook Kelp's wiry body as being weak, also with occasional consequences on the fatal side.

Kelp's black eyes turned to Gacko as he nodded in confirmation of something the client had said. He ended the call before slipping the thin galphone into the pocket of his long, black jacket, which draped just below his knees, and strode over to Gacko.

"You done?" the slim Monitaur said.

Gacko glanced at the empty glass, wishing he had more time to lick the little bubbles off the sides, but he knew that look in Kelp's eyes. They had something to do, and when they had something to do, Kelp wanted it done right away.

Besides, licking the sides of the glass was probably not a … *refined* thing to do.

"Yeah, I's finish," he said in a dopey tone – not that he had any other tone – and stared at the glass as if it would refill itself if he concentrated hard enough.

"Good," Kelp said, "because we have to go."

"I's finked so," Gacko said to the glass before looking up. "Who we's looking for?"

"Remember the mark we lost track of a few months ago?"

"De one dat Mr X look so badly for?"

"The one and only. We have a lead on his whereabouts."

"Dat are well news!"

"*Good* news."

"Dat are *good* news! So where we's going?"

"Grassi Nole."

Gacko's eyes lit up as he pushed the glass aside without a second thought. "Dat's so strange! I's being wanting to ask if we can go dere. You know how many I's love de circus. I's hear dere are a good one dere right now."

Kelp's mouth twisted into a sly grin, which blended in perfectly with the rest of his sly face.

"Precisely, Gacko," he said. "Precisely."

CHAPTER 8

Guy stood on the platform, which nearly touched the top of the dome. A cone-shaped network of pipes, ropes and nets under the platform crisscrossed its way downwards and outwards to the arena floor below. A spotlight that could roast pecan nuts was fixed on Guy while several others played across the crowd. He rotated slowly with his arms raised to the sides, his palms turned upwards to create a dramatic display as the beat of drums rolled through the enormous structure of the dome. Bezam was well known throughout the Charted Universe for his amazing stunts, most notably *The Plunge of Death*.

With a little help from muscle memory, Guy had quickly learnt to master the acrobatic skills of his host's body, and he'd even managed to keep his clothes dry after his first week of flying about. Apparently, Bezam belonged to a species called Salaman, whose arid homeworld of *Kilihiri* was riddled with mountains, canyons and chasms. Salamans tunnelled into the sides of these natural formations to create safe habitats for their families and tribes, so they were expert climbers and had a great affinity for heights.[*]

Kola, too, had a lot to do with Guy finding his feet so soon, as she'd quickly grown weary of washing his soaked clothes after every attempt to overcome his fear. In fact, it hadn't

---

[*] Except for Edgy Eddie, who wasn't named as such for having a love of edges. In fact, he was terrified of edges, ledges or standing on anything higher than his knees. Eddie wasn't very popular.

taken long for Guy to become even more terrified of Kola's wrath than of the terrifying heights he had to face.

Now, as he glanced down, he wasn't the least bit intimidated by the distance between himself and the blue arena floor, which had previously made his head and pants swim. He looked at the first bar fixed a few metres below the platform; a direct drop that, should he miss, would mean certain death. Hence the name of the act.

The drums suddenly stopped, and so did most of the normally useful respiratory functions of the onlookers, who stared up in quiet anticipation. All the lights went out, except for the spotlight on Guy. He slowly raised his arms farther until his fingers pointed directly towards the roof. Silence hung thick in the air.

And then it came.

After a small upwards leap, like he'd seen divers do at the Olympics, gravity took over to drag Guy back down to where he belonged. The sound of air rushing past his ears was complemented by the cumulative gasp of the audience, who followed it up with a cumulative shriek as he grabbed hold of the first bar and swung around it a couple of times before launching himself to the next one with a somersault. Bouncing off nets and swinging from vertical and horizontal poles and bars, he could feel life pumping through his veins.

As usual, Guy couldn't believe how quickly he'd made his way down to the arena floor. But there he was, after one final somersault, standing with both feet planted on terra firma as he gave the crowd a flamboyant bow. The lights came back on, and all around him people – yes, aliens are people too – were on their feet (or whatever the equivalent was), cheering, whistling and applauding (or whatever the equivalent was).

Not all were jumping with joy, though. Two reptile-like characters were watching him with a strange interest. No, it was more like a *keen* interest, like two cats watching a mouse rolling in catnip. They didn't applaud, whistle or cheer, although the shorter, chubby one seemed as if he had some pent-up excitement trying to burst out of his green skin. He stopped bobbing up and down when the taller, leaner one fixed him with a stern look. For some reason, the pair sent shivers down Guy's spine, even though he'd only caught a glimpse of them.

Oh well, not everyone could be expected to admire his newfound courage. There were bound to be people who thought he sucked.

After doing his customary round of appreciation for the audience, Guy left through the performers' exit. He felt amazing, and the two ungrateful fans were soon forgotten as he revelled in the aftermath of yet another satisfactory performance.

Backstage, Cortex caught up with him.

"By Zolt, Guy, you're becoming better by the day!" he emitted.

Cortex called Guy by his real name, as no one else could hear their conversations anyway. In the beginning, the bug had seemed a bit uncomfortable with the idea of someone possessing his Salaman friend's body. But he soon came around, and the two of them had become close friends. Even better friends than Cortex and Bezam had been, if Kola could be believed.

"If you keep this up," Cortex continued, *"you might even surpass Bezam. You stole the show!"*

"Well, stealing it back from you wasn't easy. You read the minds of more than ten people at the same time. And I thought your previous record of eight was impressive!"

"Thanks," the bug said modestly, but then his mood changed to one of concern. *"There was something wrong, though. I couldn't quite pinpoint it, but there were a couple of minds out there filled with ... less-than-honourable intentions."*

Guy immediately recalled the two figures he'd seen staring at him, but he was still too pumped with adrenaline to be bothered.

"Forget it, Cor," he said. "There are many less-than-honourable people out there, but at least some of them still enjoy a good show. Besides, couldn't reading so many minds at the same time cause some kind of ... interference?"

"It didn't feel *like telepathic exertion, but I suppose taking on ten people simultaneously could have put some strain on the system."*

Guy patted his friend's barky back. "Nothing that a quick beer can't fix."

Cortex eyed him suspiciously. *"I know how your* quick beer *usually ends up."*

"How?"

"Like that time I got knocked over by a bus on Unyun."

"Well, do you have a ticket?"

"A ticket for what?"

"For tonight's bus?"

"Kola's not *going to be happy about this."*

"How can she get mad at the two star attractions? And even if she does, she'll get over it. I promise."

Guy ended the debate by grabbing one of his friend's arms and escorting him out of the dome with minimal resistance.

•••

Two figures followed quietly, sticking to the shadows. They halted in a nearby alleyway as Guy and Cortex entered a bar. Covered by darkness, the shorter shadow turned to the taller one.

"You sure dat are him?" it said.

"Positive," the taller figure replied.

"But how we's get him and not get anyone sees us?"

"It'll be easier when they leave. I have the feeling they won't be too steady on their feet once they're done."

"Dat are if dey drink too many. But how we's be sure dey drink too many?"

"Don't worry, I've asked around. Apparently, they enjoy going out for *a quick beer.*"

"Oh, I's see," the shorter one said, nudging the other one. "And we's know what dat mean, does we not?"

"That we do," the other one said with an unseen grin.

CHAPTER 9

The thing about a *quick beer* after work is that, according to the Law of Social Physics, it usually isn't just limited to one. Guy knew it, Cortex knew it, and their two stalkers (whom Guy and Cortex admittedly didn't know about) knew it.[*]

Guy and Cortex had already gone through most of the main evening-out rituals and phases as they sat at the bar counter. They occasionally tested the empty peanut bowls with peckish fingers for the small, roundish, salty objects that were supposed to give these bowls their full name. And, for the umpteenth time, they debated the reason behind their existence.

"I shink," Guy philosophised with a slightly swaying body, "we're here … to have a few beersh … and … and to dishcush the reashon why we're here. Thash why we've been

---

[*] In fact, everyone in the Charted Universe knows it, and when factoring in the Law of Social Relativity, it's a good bet that everyone in the rest of the universe knows it too. Everyone in the universe also knows that this predominantly male exercise – although countless experiments conducted among female specimens have actually proved this wrong – leads to evenings of friendly banter, aggressive debate and/or depressing conversations about the same old problems, as well as the eventual swaying of participants' bodies as they focus hard on showing the world that they haven't lost control of their mental and mechanical functions. Usually without success – although they wouldn't believe you if you told them otherwise, which you probably have, quite a few times.

plaished on Earth … shorry, on the universh … shorry, *in* the universh. Ish it *in*? I can't sheem to recall. In any caish, I shink we're here to discush thingsh, like … like the reashon we're here … wait, I shaid that already, didn't I?"

He chuckled at his own stupidity and glanced at Cortex to see if his friend shared his amusement. He didn't. In fact, Cortex wasn't sharing anything with anyone. Sure, he was still sort of sitting up, but his snoring head was slumped forward and his four arms hung limply from his body as if they'd been sewn on by a four-year-old.

Guy leaned over to give the bug a shake, and after several – aka two – attempts, he gave up and took a little nap himself. A while later, he raised his head from the counter, which boasted an impressive puddle of saliva. The sticky stuff clung to his face and to the bar counter, refusing to let go of either and giving String Theory a whole new meaning. Again, he looked over at Cortex, who sat in exactly the same position as before, before noticing that the bar's other patrons had already left. The barman was still there, though, wiping a dirty glass with a dirty cloth. He stared at Guy with an expression that said it would have been better if *everyone* had left, so that he could go home instead of having to babysit two drunkards into the early hours of the morning. Although not exactly clearheaded, Guy caught the *hint*.

"I shink we'll be leaving now," he said, getting up unsteadily. "But I might need shome help with my friend here." After a killer-glare from the barman, he quickly added, "At leasht to the outshide, if thash not too mush to ashk?"

With the typical it-*is*-too-much-to-ask-but-if-that's-what-it-will-take-to-get-you-out-of-here expression, the barman slammed down the glass and ambled around the counter, grumbling. Despite being a big, blue block of a man – Guy assumed it was a man through all those birdlike features – he and Guy couldn't lift Cortex's enormous body. So they pushed him off his stool with a thud and dragged the bug out the door with a fair amount of effort. Of course, most of Guy's effort went into not tripping over his own feet, which paid off pretty well, except for two occasions that saw him taking tables and chairs with him on his way to the floor. Outside, the big, sweating barman dropped Cortex's feet and turned to walk back in. But when Guy tapped him on the shoulder, the man turned around with murder in his eyes.

"Thash for your trouble," Guy said innocently, stuffing a one-cred coin into the big man's hand. The man looked at the coin, looked back up at Guy, and showed his appreciation by slamming the door in his face. Well, had it been a good old-fashioned wooden door that didn't close electronically, Guy was sure it would have slammed in his face.

"How'sh that for rude?" he said to his unmoving friend. He stared at Cortex as if he would suddenly wake up to give Guy an answer. After about a minute, he hazily determined that this wasn't likely to happen. He however remained there, staring, while trying to figure out how to get the bug back to the circus.

"Well, I shure can't carry you," he said eventually, trying to focus his blurry vision. It was tricky, though, because his swaying body kept shifting the focal point.

"I shure can't drag you."

Cortex didn't respond.

"I shink I need shome help."

Cortex still didn't respond. So, not wanting to feel stupid, Guy took over the task.

"Yesh, thash a good idea. I'll get shome help."

That was indeed a good idea, he thought proudly, and then got another good idea, proving that he wasn't as drunk as he thought, because drunk people never had good ideas.

"*I* know! I'll go to … I'll go to the shircush and I'll … and I'll get the Shterkarm twins to help. Wishout Rimmy or Kola knowing, of coursh. Don't worry, Cortesh, our shecret'sh shafe wish me."

He held a skew finger on his lips for a few seconds to make sure the point was made.

"Don't go anywhere, okay? We'll be back before you can shay … before you can shay … anyshing."

Cortex didn't say anything, but Guy was sure his friend would comply with his wishes, because that's what a good friend would do. And seeing as Cortex was a good friend, he'd stay put.

"Okay," Guy said before stumbling in the general direction of the circus while focusing on his feet, which seemed to think that the general direction lay in whichever direction they chose to go.

Apart from bumping into a lamppost and stumbling over his left foot twice with what seemed to be his other left foot, he was making progress. He started to feel more confident in his amazing navigational abilities after managing a good ten metres. The dark alley in front of him, which in more-sober circumstances would have seemed like a bad idea to enter, suddenly looked quite inviting, especially with the confidence of his newfound footing spurring him on. He was sure the alley, despite its dark and dingy appearance, would make an excellent shortcut.

"No problem," Guy said with an assurance that nothing could go wrong as long as one foot could occasionally be placed in front of the other. "Piesh of cake."

As he staggered into the alley, he noticed something shiny on the ground; just before the border where the light from the street got swallowed by the darkness beyond. He shuffled forward and carefully squatted next to the object.

"How shtrange," he said to himself as he picked up the cred coin to examine it in the weak light. "I jusht gave shomeone shome money, and … and now I got shome money back."

Getting back up unsteadily, Guy leaned against the wall with one hand while bringing the coin as close as possible to his eyes to double-check if it was indeed what he thought it was. He wasn't disappointed.

"Thish musht be my lucky day!" he said, which were the last words to leave his lips before something knocked him over the head. Fortunately, the world had already gone dark by the time he hit the ground like a pudding-filled sock.

CHAPTER 10

As consciousness slowly crept back into Guy's mind, a sharp pain used the opportunity to creep in with it. This had to go down in the Leatherman records as the worst hangover ever, with patches of pain clinging to his brain tissue like an army of rabid koalas. How could a couple of beers have caused such agony?

He lay there for a few minutes with his eyes closed, trying to think the pain away, but it only intensified to unbearable proportions.

Guy realised that he'd have to open his eyes at some stage after vaguely remembering that he might have left Cortex outside the bar, and that he'd have to face the world in order to make sure his friend had reached the circus in one piece. He could, however, not remember having reached the circus himself.

Concern slowly forced Guy's eyes open, and he found himself squinting at a metal ceiling. Sitting upright was like lifting a horse with a pool noodle, but he finally succeeded with a fair amount of grunting. Rubbing the back of his head, he stopped when his hand encountered a lump.

"Ow!" he wailed, which sent a fresh flare of pain shooting through his skull, so he settled for a more subdued "Ooooww".

As enough consciousness crept in, it was accompanied by enough common sense to figure out that touching the lump wasn't something he should be doing.

For the umpteenth time in his life, he vowed never to drink that much again. Never, ever again!*

Looking up, Guy noticed he was sitting on a hard bed in a rectangular room of about five by ten metres. The room was divided by a transparent curtain of soft, blue light that hummed ever so gently; almost hypnotically.

He slowly swung his legs off the bed and squinted at the light as if at a crystal ball that might tell him where he was. It didn't, so he gingerly lowered himself to the floor with another grunt.

The world around him was spinning, but he inched himself forward, stopping just short of the flat blue surface. It made him think of electricity, which was odd because electricity wasn't supposed to look or feel inviting, was it? He'd never really given it much thought before now.

Extending a hesitant hand, Guy wondered what would happen if he touched the surface, but he was interrupted when a door on the other side of the light barrier slid open with a *whoosh*.

"I wouldn't do that if I were you," a voice oozed like gunky car oil.

Two lizardy figures entered. Although Guy didn't quite recognise either of them, a hint of familiarity tugged at his memory before it was slapped down by the pain that still dominated his head, refusing to relinquish its seat of power.

Guy eyed the newcomers warily. "Who are you? Where am I?"

The tall, thin lizard addressed his companion without taking his eyes off Guy. "Shall we tell him, Gacko?" he said.

"Why not, Kelp?" the shorter, fatter one called Gacko replied with a sharp-toothed grin. "It are not as if he can do anyfing about it."

"Indeed he can't," the one called Kelp said. "So in the spirit of good old-fashioned honesty, you are our prisoner. Hence the force field."

---

* While this has officially become *the* most overused yet futile vow in the universe, "I do" is still giving it a serious run for its money.

"Your *prisoner*?" Guy exclaimed. "Why?"

"That, my friend, is something I can't tell you," Kelp replied. "We're bounty hunters, and you're our mark. It was our job to track you down, detain you and deliver you to Mr X. So that's precisely what we're doing. What you've done is none of our business."

"Mr X?" Guy frowned. "Who's *Mr X*?"

"Who knows," Kelp shrugged. "People who call themselves Mr X usually don't go about revealing their identity to all and sundry. I just know that he's the person looking for you, and that he's the one who'll pay us the rest of our money once he gets you. I just came to check if you're still in a … sellable condition. Gacko can get a bit heavy-handed sometimes, and I wouldn't want Mr X to withhold payment due to damaged goods. You seem fine, though, but I suggest you get some rest before your meeting."

"But *why* is he looking for me?" Guy said. "Can you at least tell me *that*?"

"Unfortunately," Kelp replied, "that's something you'll find out for yourself, soon enough."

•••

After his two captors left, Guy sat back down on his bed and rested his chin on his hand. He dejectedly stared at the force field, which hummed along happily. Before they left, Kelp had said it was for Guy's own protection. When Guy had asked how that could be, the thin lizard said it was there to keep him safe, because if he tried to escape, he'd be shot. So Guy had to understand that it was there to keep him safe.

A tiny, black cockroach-like insect scurried across the floor until it collided with the force field, upon which it vanished in a puff of smoke and a sound like a gumdrop falling on a cushion. Guy kept staring at the small trail of smoke as it dissipated into nothingness.

Was that *his* fate too; his life ending in a puff for no good reason?

No, it couldn't be.

Although he'd never had the most exciting life on earth – or rather on Earth – Guy had always hoped that his life would amount to something more. Something bigger. Perhaps not something as big as saving the world, but at least something worthy of remembrance.

So, no, this couldn't be *it*.

It just ... *couldn't*.

CHAPTER 11

A *schwoop* jerked Guy from sleep's blissful embrace. His mind quickly severed the floating connection to the world of dreams and snapped him back to reality; a reality that excluded the group of bikini-clad supermodels who had moments ago been treating him like royalty. Instead, he was now treated to the unwelcome sight of the two bounty hunters entering his cell, hauling in a square metal container between them. Kelp touched a panel on the wall, and the force field vanished.

"I trust you had a good rest, Mr Bezam," he said. He gestured to Gacko, who in turn produced from his jacket what Guy could only presume was a gun of sorts, mostly because it looked like one, but also because Gacko looked quite ready and – to Guy's concern – eager to use it. "Our trip has nearly come to an end, but now comes the part you may not like."

Guy snorted. "Yeah, the rest of the trip's been *fantastic!*"

"Now, now, Mr Bezam," Kelp said. "No need to get so touchy. Touchy people upset Gacko, and I don't like it when he gets upset with a mark. Well, not when we need to deliver the mark *alive*. We lose money that way."

Guy glanced at the gun, which fit way too comfortably in Gacko's meaty hand.

He gulped. "So, er, now what?"

"Now we have to check you out of the executive suite."

Guy glanced about. "Can't be much worse than this."

"Oh, don't worry," said Kelp, rapping the metal box with his knuckles. "You'll be as snug as a bug."

...

Slinkie. She was tall, thin and the most flexible humanoid Guy had ever seen. She wasn't the prettiest humanoid he'd ever seen, but she had a certain gracefulness about her; if bending oneself backwards into the shape of a doorknob could be called graceful.

Slinkie was the circus contortionist, and could flex her body into almost any shape imaginable. She would have been impressed with how well Guy fit into such a small space, although it was easier to fit your head between your legs when there was a gun pressed to it.

"Comfy?" came Gacko's voice from above.

"Let me out of here!" Guy screamed at his buttocks. At least that's what his intentions screamed. What came out was "Mmm mm mmm mm mmmm!", which was what Gacko and Kelp heard, much to their satisfaction. Apart from patching gas leaks and holding some stuff together that should be held together on their ship, duct tape still remained the best way to keep a mark's yap shut.[*]

"Good," Gacko said, before slamming the container's lid shut.

---

[*] There was a time when humans thought Earth to be flat. However, after exploring the planet a bit more, they were surprised to find that it's actually quite round. A few people were really upset about this, especially the guys who'd invented parachutes for sailors who somehow managed to travel over the edge. Once Earthlings start flying to the outer reaches of space, they'll also be surprised to find that duct tape hadn't originated on Earth. In fact, its origin dates back thousands of years to the time when the androids on Bolton III got fed up with walking into walls due to leaky brake-fluid pipes, and developed a special band-aid to stop the "bleeding". Throughout the millennia, many species have used the tape for the repair of various things, such as ducts. Hence the name duct tape. The symbiotic undead Mortii of Ophal IV have since also found great use for the invention, which keeps the heads of their undead poultry from falling off whenever the wind blows too hard. Which is why they still insist on calling it duck tape, much to the annoyance of some people. Most other people don't really care, though.

...

It was dark. Perhaps not outside the box, but inside it was the type of dark that could make a grown man wet himself. The only reason Guy did not do so was because his bladder was too tangled up with his spine. It was also difficult to breathe with his calves pinching his nose. The fact that he swung about while being carried didn't help. He was glad that he hadn't had breakfast because, with the duct tape over his mouth, his nose would have been the only escape valve for anything pushing up from his stomach.

After what seemed like ages had passed – which would probably equate to only a few minutes for anyone not trapped inside a small, dark box – there was a sudden lifting-and-dropping sensation, and his whole body jerked as the container was plonked down hard. Shortly thereafter, the box started moving rapidly.

The movement included a lot of stops and turns, with Guy's body squishing against the container's sides with every change in speed and direction. It felt like he was being transported in the trunk of a mob guy's car, albeit a mob guy driving one of those small clown cars.

If a few minutes trapped inside a box were to pass like ages, an hour would take you back to the Big Bang … which, according to the theory, would have been accompanied by a big explosion … which, as far as big explosions go, would have been accompanied by a blinding light … which, as anyone who'd ever been locked up in a pitch-black box could tell you, was exactly what you saw when the box was finally opened in a well-lit area.

"Take him out," a voice said.

The voice wasn't familiar, but it *was* one of those voices that commanded respect. Not a voice that *demanded* respect like Jane's back on Earth. No, it was more of a calm voice, but calm like one of those rivers that, although seeming all tranquil on the surface, had undercurrents that would suck you down and drown you.

It was the type of voice that stamped its Authority with a capital A.

Four hands grabbed Guy by the arms and lifted him out of the box with a force that would likely have left his shoes behind, had he been wearing any.

"Come now, you two," The Voice soothed. "That's no way to treat our guest here, now is it?"

Yet the undertone hinted that the treatment could get worse whenever The Voice wished it so. It also hinted that The Voice had no problem making such wishes.

The manhandling Kelp and Gacko stepped away without a word.

Guy tried looking in the direction The Voice had come from, but the wall of searing bright lights directed at him and the lizards made this somewhat difficult. His eyelids frantically tried to climb over one another and called for assistance from his cuffed hands, which he promptly held up to shield his eyes.

"I trust you enjoyed your trip, Mr Bezam?" The Voice stated more than it enquired.

"I've … had better," Guy replied, squinting.

"You could have had worse."

"I …" Guy wanted to say something clever, but he recognised a threat when he heard one, having experienced quite a few of those during his lifetime. So, instead, he just finished it off with a cautious "… suppose so."

"Indeed," The Voice continued. "However, you are quite important to me, and I would not want you harmed for no reason."

"That's a relief."

"I'm sure it is, Mr Bezam. But you'll have to excuse me for my bluntness when I say that your *complete* wellbeing is not my primary concern."

"I'm not sure I follow," Guy said. He was also sure he didn't *want* to follow.

"My apologies for not being even more blunt, then. When I say that your *complete* wellbeing isn't my primary concern, I mean that I don't need you completely intact to get what I want. You see, I'm more concerned about what you *know*."

"What *I* know?"

"Yes, Mr Bezam, what *you* know. For instance, do you know *why* you are here?"

At first, Guy didn't know what to say, but then his nerves switched his brain to its default babbling mode when faced with situations where babbling seemed prudent.

"Well," he babbled, "when I was little, my parents told me this story about a stork dropping me down a chimney, which I said was strange because we didn't have a chimney. They then told me something about birds and bees, which also didn't sound right, seeing as we didn't have a garden. I later learned the truth from one of my friends, but I had to wait ten years before I finally got lucky with Debora Peterso—oooooffff!"

The blow had come from the side and, as his lungs were now too empty to say anything, Guy resorted to giving Kelp a was-that-really-necessary glare.

The bounty hunter replied with a yes-it-was stare and, with a satisfied smirk, added, "I suggest you cooperate. It will make life a lot easier for you, wouldn't you agree?"

Guy agreed with a pained nod, and wheezed as he addressed The Voice.

"No …" he managed to squeeze out. "I don't … know … why I'm here."

"Ooh, that will be a problem," The Voice said. "You see, it's like this: I *will* get the information I need from you. You have no control over whether this happens. You do, however, have a choice in *how* it happens: the easy way, or the hard way. I can tell you now that the easy way will be much more pleasant."

Guy felt as though he was caught up in some classic spy movie where the bad guy always had some body part made of steel; or laser eyes; and/or no hair. He glanced at Gacko, whose grin suggested that *he* liked the hard way much better, especially if someone else was on the receiving end of the hard way.

"But I really *don't know* why I'm here!" Guy protested.

"Let's see if I can refresh your memory," The Voice said calmly. "Where were you three months ago?"

Guy's eyes rolled up as he tried to calculate, but the flow of time had been a bit tricky since leaving Earth, and he didn't really keep proper track of it. [*]

"Uh, three months ago?" he muttered to himself, almost inaudibly, as he tried to work out the garbled calendar in his head. "Let me see, thr ws th circus … bt wt abt, wt … training nd thn, uh … no wait … uh—"

"Please stop mumbling, Mr Bezam," The Voice said less calmly. "I detest that. Look, it's simple. You tell me where you were and what you were doing, and *I'll* judge whether you're telling the truth."

"I have no reason to lie," Guy stated stiffly.

"People have all kinds of reasons to lie, and it seems to me you have something to hide."

"No, I don't."

"Oh, but I'm sure you *do*. Otherwise, it wouldn't have been this difficult to tell me what you were up to during that time."

"I just have difficulty remembering what happened when, really. I don't even have a watch— ooooffff!"

"Like I said," Kelp said, pulling back the fist that had just knocked the barely returned wind out of Guy, "I suggest you cooperate. We don't want Gacko here to start working on you. He sometimes forgets when to stop, or why he started in the first place."

Guy shot another glance at the grin on Gacko's face and wondered if it ever went away. However, *that* might be worse.

---

[*] The necessity of having Galactic Standard Time (GST) became evident soon after the start of intergalactic travel and colonisation, as problems were widespread. For instance, having to read twenty billion letters of complaint by mothers who had either had one Mother's Day call in twenty years, or twenty in one year, wasn't fun. Eventually, to end the constant bickering over which system's timekeeping methods would work the best, independent Earth time was adopted for GST. This kept everyone happy, or at least equally unhappy, which is sometimes just as important.

"Look," he said after regaining his breath, "all I'm saying is that I have a bit of trouble remembering things. Could you maybe ... *tell me* what I'm supposed to remember?"

"How about the day the Presidor of the Unyun Federation was assassinated along with the Vice-Presidor?" The Voice said after a brief pause.

Guy mulled the words over in his head before answering. "Uh, yes, it caused quite a political mess, and there's even talk of civil wars, if I understand correctly. I don't really follow the news lately. The assassin's ship crashed or something right after it blew up the Presidor's ship, didn't it?"

"*I'll* ask the questions," The Voice said patiently. "And what I want to know is what *you* were doing at that exact moment."

"Well, I was most likely covering another boring story for which I most certainly would have been crapped out by my editor, who I can definitely say has no love for me. At all."

"Your *editor*?" The Voice said with a palpable frown.

"Yes."

"At a *circus*?"

"Yes ... I mean, no. I mean, I wasn't actually *with* the circus at the time."

"Yes, you were," said The Voice, losing some of its patience. "We've confirmed it with various sources. You were, without a doubt, with the circus at the time of the assassination."

"No, I wasn't."

"Yes, you were!" The Voice said, with the touch of impatience turning into a wallop of anger.

Guy sensed that he'd reached a point where he had to say something to keep his head attached to his body, as he quite preferred its current location.

"Well, I *may* have been there ..."

"I thought so," The Voice said, shifting down a few gears in frustration.

"... but, at the same time, I ... *wasn't*."

"How in Zolt's name can that be?" The Voice bellowed, shifting right into top gear.

"Well," Guy said cautiously, "I'm actually … Guy."

"Who gives a blazing nova if you're gay?"

"No, I'm *Guy*."

"Yes, you're a guy, so what?"

"No, I mean *my name* is Guy. *Guy Leatherman*, to be precise."

"So your real name is Guy-whatever and your stage name is Bezam. Who cares?"

The Voice boiled; the lid of this pressure cooker was about to fly off.

Guy moved pointed fingers up and down to indicate his body. "You see, *this* is not really me," he said. "I'm actually … someone else."

There was a moment of silence.

"Mr Kelp," The Voice hissed, "are there any … psychological problems in his profile I need to be aware of?"

"No, Mr X," Kelp replied with a hint of uncertainty. "Not that I know of. It's one of the first things I check before we start hunting a mark. Can't be too careful with all the crazies out there. We even asked around at the circus before snatching him. Nothing much out of the ordinary, except for a problem with binge drinking now and again. Oh, and wetting his pants."

"*That's* a problem, isn't it?"

"Yes sir, but it stopped shortly after it started."

"Maybe he landed on his head during one of his performances?"

"I don't think so. No one mentioned any serious accidents besides the ones in his pants."

"Well, there *must* be an explanation, because if he's mentally unstable, he's no good to me. We might as well get rid of him now."

"What?" Guy exclaimed, feeling his bladder-control problems returning with a vengeance. "What do you mean, *get rid of?*"

"Believe me, Mr Bezam," Mr X said almost sympathetically, "it will be a way better alternative for you than falling into the hands of the others."

"The *others?* But …" Guy started, and then got a glimmer of hope. "Wait, wait! Why don't you just ask Mr Gray?"

"Mr Gray?" Mr X asked.

"Yes, Mr Gray," Guy said, clinging on to his newfound hope. "I'm sure *he'll* be able to explain what happened to Bezam's mind."

"What do you mean, *Bezam's* mind?" Mr X demanded.

"You know, *the competition?*" Guy said. "I'm sure *that's* what's causing the whole mix-up."

There was a moment of silence.

"*What* competition?" Mr X asked warily from behind the wall of light.

"I can't quite recall. It's the one in which I wished and won a prize."

"What prize?"

"This one," Guy said, indicating his body again. "I'm not really a Salaman. I'm actually a human. You know, from Earth?"

"A human?" Mr X said dubiously.

"Yes."

"From Earth?"

"Yep."

"Mr Bezam," Mr X said with a note of nervousness. "This is *very* important. You have to tell me *exactly* what competition you're talking about."

"Well, like I said, I really can't recall *exactly*—"

"Think, damn you, think!"

"Um, it had something to do with *live*. Live Glamorously, or something like that."

"*Life?*" Mr X asked, now with a slight tremble in his voice.

"Yes, Life Spectacles."

"Life *Spectacular?*" Mr X corrected reluctantly.

"Oh, yeah, that's it!" Guy said. "*Life Spectacular*. That's exactly it!"

There was another moment of silence before the voices of Mr X and Kelp harmonised in a frustrated chorus: "Oh fhark."

CHAPTER 12

It took a while for Guy to find his thoughts again along with his voice.

"What did they mean by 'oh fhark'?" he said to no one in particular.

Gacko, however, stopped whetting his wicked combat knife and squinted at the silhouette of Kelp, who shielded his eyes during his private discussion with the man behind the wall of light.

"It a bad word," he said. "Dat are what Muvver say. She not like de bad word and hit me wiff her hand if I's use de bad word."

"I know it's a *bad* word," Guy grated, feeling the frustration that Kelp must have felt all the time, "but why say it?"

"Oh, I's fink it mean you's in trouble. Or maybe Kelp are in trouble. Or maybe Mr X are in trouble. Or maybe we's all in tr—"

"No, that's not what I meant! I meant … well, I just … what does any of this have to do with *me*?"

"I's not sure. I's trying to fink, but it make my brain pain. Sometimes my brain pain when I's finks too many … much. Kelp say dat for me it are nurtural."

"You mean *natural*?"

"Dat are what I said."

Gacko's challenging glare stated that Guy should rather not press the point, so he didn't. As the lizard continued to sharpen his blade with a pained look on his face, Guy felt a little pain brewing between his own ears. He didn't have a problem with problems. His life had been full of those from the day he'd first opened his eyes, and he'd grown accustomed to it. He had learnt a long time ago to live with the disappointment of things not going the way he planned. As a matter of fact, he'd come to expect just about everything in his existence to turn pear-shaped or, for that matter, any shape that wasn't round. The times when things *did* work out for him were few and far between and, in some way, posed even more of a problem than not having problems; he didn't know how to handle *not* being disappointed. In any case, there was something much worse than problems: uncertainty.

Guy's problem with uncertainty was that it took the possible positives, mixed it up with the possible negatives and, subsequently, produced an even bigger negative. Until whatever was supposed to happen actually happened, uncertainty always led to a bigger problem in Guy's head, whether it eventually turned out to be a problem or not.

His current predicament planted a seed of uncertainty, and his vivid imagination watered it to such an extent that it made his nose run. However, there was nothing much he could do about it with his hands cuffed, so he resorted to wiping his nose on his sleeve.

"Wow!" Gacko said, pausing in his task. "Dat are a good one! Look at mine." He held up his knife-wielding arm and pointed at the sleeve, which featured a large patch of dried, silvery residue that Guy had previously mistaken for a piece of body armour.

Gacko's eyes gleamed with pride. "Muvver say I's must not do dis, because it gross her out. But I's not saw Muvver for long time, so I's working on mine for long time."

"And I've been telling you for a long time to stop doing that and clean up your attire."

Guy jumped at Kelp's voice behind him. He hadn't realised that the scrawny lizard had returned. There was no sign of the mysterious Mr X, though.

Gacko looked up defiantly. "And I's told you dat dis are my lucky shirt wiff my lucky patch!"

"It's snot!" Kelp said.

"It not what?"

"I mean, it … is … *snot*! It *is not* a lucky patch!"

"Well, Muvver say dat dis are my lucky shirt. And Muvver am always right. And I's make it more lucky wiff my lucky patch!"

Kelp opened his mouth to say something, but closed it again as if realising that he should rather save his breath for something more worthwhile; like breathing, or some sort of similar activity, like sighing, which he did. Guy had the impression that this was something that Kelp, when it came to Gacko, had gotten used to doing. A lot.

The thin lizard turned to Guy. "And what's *your* excuse?"

"*My* excuse?"

Kelp glanced at the wet streak on Guy's sleeve.

"Oh, that," Guy said and held up his cuffed hands. "It's a bit difficult being *proper* at the moment."

"I's fink it because he can't use his hands," Gacko volunteered, earning him two blank stares.

"Well, it are more easy making a lucky patch if your hands not tied," he retorted sulkily.

"Indeed," said Kelp. "Now stop feeling sorry for yourself and take off the magnocuffs."

This time, Kelp was on the receiving end of two blank stares.

It took a few seconds for the message to reach Gacko's brain. "Huh?"

"I said, take … off … the … mag- … no- … cuffs."

"Take off de magnocuffs?"

"Do … you … want … me … to … say … it … e- … ven … slow- … er?"

"Well—"

"Just take off the blazing cuffs, Gacko!"

"But he are our *prisoner*!"

"Not anymore," Kelp said, flashing a practised friendly smile that suggested he should practise some more.

"You're letting me go?" Guy said while the confused Gacko removed the cuffs. "I'm *free*?"

"Not exactly."

"But if I'm not your prisoner, why not just let me go?"

"Because we're now your … let's say, bodyguards."

"My *bodyguards*?" Guy exclaimed. "First you abduct me, then you threaten to torture and kill me, and now you want to protect me! Why? And from whom would someone like *me* need protection?"

"That," Kelp said, "is precisely what we plan to find out."

• • •

Guy rubbed his wrists where the magnocuffs had previously constricted the blood flow to his hands. Judging by the satisfied smirk on Gacko's face, he was sure that his captors, or bodyguards, or whatever they were currently supposed to be, had deliberately tightened the cuffs more than necessary. Kelp, however, didn't seem to be overly concerned with Guy's comfort. Which was no surprise, as he didn't seem like the type of person to be overly concerned with *anyone's* comfort other than his own.

"Does that mean I can go back to the circus?" Guy asked hopefully.

"No, Mr Bezam," Kelp replied. "Or do you prefer … um—"

"Guy! My name is *Guy*!"

Kelp gave him a warning look. "No need to get testy, Mr Guy."

Guy heeded the warning. "I'm sorry. I'm just a bit nervous. And it's Guy," he added with a sigh. "I'd prefer it if you just call me Guy, if you don't mind."

"No," Kelp said, "I don't mind at all. And I understand if your nerves are a bit frayed."

A *bit* frayed? Guy thought. A cheese-dipped ragdoll in a rat cage would be less frayed than his nerves!

"Still," the lizard continued, "I think for now it might be best to call you by the name that comes with the body. We wouldn't want the wrong people to find out that you're not really who you say you are, now would we?"

The wrong people? Guy wondered. How bad are the *wrong* people if these two are the *right* people?

"No," Guy said instead, "I suppose not. But I'd still like to know what's going on here. And where *is here*?"

"How about a little tour?" Kelp said as they walked towards a door, which Gacko opened to let in a stream of light.

Guy walked forward cautiously. For now, he would just play along with his so-called *bodyguards*. But the moment he knew where he was, he would start planning his escape. However, as soon as he stepped outside, all of his planned plans flew out the window with a squawk – even if the window had been closed, they would have smashed right through it. He gazed at the world around him with eyes that wobbled almost as much as his legs.

"Kelp, I's fink he are going to frow up or …" he heard Gacko say next to him. Or was that very far away? He wasn't sure, because his senses had faded along with Gacko's voice.

Shortly thereafter, Guy felt a sting on his face, and his eyes fluttered open just as Kelp was about to give him another slap. He must have fainted, because he found himself sitting on the ground, which was probably for the better as he looked up at the surroundings once more. He shook his head, just to ward off the dizziness that threatened to return with a vengeance.

Kelp helped Guy up. "I almost forgot you're from a Dumb Planet. You've never been here before, have you?"

"I think I would have remembered," Guy slurred, trying to steady his unsteady legs. "Where are we?"

Kelp waved his hand proudly at their surroundings. "This, my friend, is the greatest place in the universe! Welcome to Unyun."

CHAPTER 13

Everything was just so … big. Buildings of unimaginable sizes, colours and shapes towered all around them, with a stupendous number of odd, wheelless vehicles criss-crossing the structures at various altitudes like robotic bees. Instead of flying, however, they seemed to glide over unseen roads that ran along a vast network of spaced-out, square metal frames floating in the air, attached to nothing. At ground level, the streets' metallic sidewalks bustled with creatures from all walks of life, or rather all walks, hovers and crawls of life, to name but a few.

After ensuring that he was in a state to walk, the lizards escorted Guy down the street. They walked in silence for a while before Guy's curiosity overcame his initial shock and started scratching at the door to be let out.

As far as question-and-answer sessions go, this was more of a question-and-answer-followed-by-the-same-question-later-on-either-getting-ignored-or-earning-Guy-a-cold-glare type of session. While people in the know would understandably rather avoid going through the whole thing, others might like to know what was said. To appease everyone, you now have access to the abridged version of the Q&A along with some exclusive content but without the stupid questions in-between:

•••

Although classified as one, Unyun is not a planet per se. At least not in the natural sense.

Roughly two-thousand years ago, most species, systems and worlds in the Charted Universe started discussing the growing need to form a Federation – a central government to not only streamline trade but also to restore peace between warring species, or at least some semblance of peace. Of course, one of the major sticking points had been the location of said government, and this point got stuck worse than stickseed on wool socks.

Not only did each species feel that *their* home planet was better suited to host the Federal government, but they also had strong opinions over which planets were less worthy of doing so. Needless to say, things got a bit personal, which led to some bickering ... which led to the Ninety-nine-and-a-half-year War ... which led to the virtual destruction of Randuk ... which didn't really bother anyone except for the warmongering Randukians, whom no one liked much in any case.

Eventually, all parties left in the running realised they were getting nowhere and went back to the drawing board – on which someone had erased Randuk and replaced it with a smiley face – to see how the matter could be resolved without any further conflict.

This was greeted with dismay by the Vahltans, who'd just been about to propose invading a Dumb Planet like Earth and wiping out all the apes that ruled it, and repurposing it to serve as the new Federation's headquarters. They contended that it would be the most practical solution and, above all, the most fun.

But after a long period of brainstorming and storming out of conference rooms, the parties decided to build a new planet instead. It would be called Unyun, which (ironically) is the Randukian for "harmony". This provided the surviving Randukians with some solace, as well as a place to stay.

Albeit pricey, the construction of Unyun was deemed achievable if everyone involved clubbed in with resources and funding. The latter became a bigger burden on everyone else thanks to the Vahltans always conveniently forgetting their wallet at home.

With regard to Unyun's location, the Gamma Gamma system presented the perfect spot. The triple-star system was situated in a region of space with the highest concentration of wormholes in the Charted Universe. The precise reason for this had never been agreed on unanimously, but the most commonly accepted theory was that the system had intersected the earlier path of a supermassive black hole, causing sporadic gravitational vortices.

After another lengthy period of planning, Unyun was eventually constructed by placing a special shield-generator grid around the red dwarf star that orbited the binary stars at the centre of the system. The grid fed off the star's energy to create a self-sustaining shield – the greater the force exerted on the shield, the stronger it became; perfect for encasing the raging red dwarf, which was affectionately dubbed Little Red.

An inner shell was built around the shield to house the huge construction workforce and the first colonies. It now mainly housed the planet's vast utility and subway networks, as well as the people that refused – or couldn't afford – to move. This was followed by the surface level, which the bulk of Unyun's current mishmash of residents called home.

Due to an inherent need for separation, operational logistics, as well as the unique habitational environments required by certain species, Unyun was divided into thirty-two pentagonal and hexagonal sectors. Viewed from outside, Unyun strangely looked like a giant, multicoloured soccer ball – at least to those familiar with the sport.[*] Each sector featured its own slightly – and sometimes significantly – altered environment, including tailor-made landscapes, gravity, light, atmospheric pressure, and weather conditions. The latter gave rise to a staggering number of squabbles, as any person – even from the same species – working within an office environment can attest to. It usually goes something like this:

---

[*] For those not familiar with the sport, a soccer ball strangely looks like Unyun.

"I'm telling you, I'm freezing! Can we turn up the heat, please?" One would plead.

"Are you kidding me?" Two would say. "I'm melting here! Maybe you should try wearing a jacket."

"Well, maybe you shouldn't wear that thick layer of lard that's keeping you warm, you inconsiderate prat!" One would lash out at the overbearing Two, who usually gets his way, even with ordering the overly strong brand of coffee detested by everyone except him.

"Are you calling me fat?" Two would growl.

"No, I'd call your mom fat, but even her humongous body must have gone into shock trying to squeeze you out."

"Guys," Three would interject meekly. "Remember last month's workshop: A Happy Workplace is a Productive Workplace? Can't we just meet in the middle?"

Two red faces would slowly turn their attention towards the interjector.

"How about my fist meets your face?" Two would say through clenched teeth.

"Yes, Francis," One would add. "Don't you have other things to do?"

"Yeah, like carrying the boss's shoes after him," Two would contribute with a snort.

Upon which Three (aka Francis) would back away slowly before quietly returning to his cubicle, trying to remind himself why he'd gotten involved in the first place.

Initially, it was much the same on Unyun. No one was ever happy with the temperature or, for that matter, with the weather in general. Too hot, too cold, too dry, too wet, too cloudy, too windy, too … everything. So a decision was made to automate the weather conditions of each sector via an artificial-intelligence system called AERCON (Atmospheric and Environmental Regulation of the Climate of Natives), which mimicked the weather conditions that prevailed on species' respective home planets.

As for the powers that be, the headquarters of the Unyun Federal Government, as well as the headquarters of most of the governmental subdivisions and large corporations, were located in a sector called The Hub. It was the most densely populated and most heavily constructed sector on Unyun.

Apparently, this was the sector Guy now found himself in along with his new *bodyguards*.

•••

Guy's head spun, and not only from information overload. He looked at the surface under his feet and shivered. Sure, he'd always wanted underfloor heating in his apartment during winter, but this felt a tad extreme. He was walking on a *star*, for crying out loud!

His daze was dispelled when they finally arrived at a building that seemed as dark as the name that was supposed to be displayed in the broken lights above the entrance.

"T-h-e … W-o-r-m … h-o-l-e," Guy murmured, following the letters.

Kelp led Gacko out of earshot and, after a short discussion, the rounder lizard hurried back the way they'd come.

"Where's he going?" Guy asked hesitantly. He wasn't sure which bothered him more: seeing Gacko around or not seeing him around. Seeing him was like seeing a burglar in your house. Not seeing him was like knowing there was a burglar somewhere in your house. Neither of which would make anyone feel any better.

"He has an errand to run," Kelp clarified in a way that made it clear that this was all he was going to clarify.

"And what are *we* going to do?" Guy asked.

"We're just going to have a drink. Got a problem with that?"

"No," Guy muttered, "no problem."

However, eyeing the doorway suspiciously, he wasn't sure if he believed himself.

CHAPTER 14

There are places in the universe that are truly amazing. Places filled with wonder and beauty. Places where you can connect with everything around you, where love, peace and positive energy impart so much warmth and bliss that you never want to leave. Places where everything just feels … right.

The Wormhole was not such a place. As a matter of fact, *The Wormhole* was the complete opposite of such a place. It was possibly the closest thing you'd get to a warzone in the midst of civilisation. Not that Unyun was the most civilised place in the universe. It had a dark side. Even after more than a millennium since the first people started inhabiting the man-made planet, interspecies relations never quite fulfilled the expectations of Unyun's Founders. As the Federation grew, there were always new species joining it, and when new species were thrown into the mix, a new mould of civilisation was formed, with new allegiances and new enemies. Old habits die hard, while new ones can live forever.[*]

The Wormhole was the dark side of Unyun's dark side. It attracted the worst scum that drifted throughout space and clumped them together like a clogged shower trap. In *The Wormhole,* you could find anyone willing to do anything at any cost, from high-priced assassins to low-level thieves,

---

[*] The longest ongoing feud on record is the one between Faylins and Caynins, but apart from a noticeable difference in average height, they're not the only species that don't see eye to eye.

who'd steal their own dead mother's front teeth from her grave if it would pocket them a few creds – although, for a few creds extra, the whole dead-thing wouldn't necessarily be a deal-breaker.

The place was like a malevolent henhouse packed with broody, shifty-eyed characters waiting to hatch trouble. It was the perfect place for characters like Kelp, but not for Guy, who felt ready to hatch something else in his pants. He was sure he spotted a couple of humans in a corner. However, just like the rest of the patrons, they didn't seem like the type that enjoyed idle conversations with strangers about their favourite baseball team or flavour of cupcake.

Kelp studied the room, then herded Guy by the back of his collar towards a table where two long-faced, leathery, bird-like patrons were conversing. If pterodactyls had a topknot of long oily black hair instead of an upward-elongated skull, hadn't had wings under their arms, had a much shorter beak, wore mostly black leather, and could sit in a bar, they might have remotely looked something like these two.

The bird whose back was turned to Kelp and Guy, was deeply involved in telling his companion a story. "I was just about to blast a hole the size of my fist through his chest, when—"

"Excuse me, buddy," Kelp interrupted, "but it seems as though you might have taken the wrong table by mistake."

The storyteller froze mid-sentence but did not look away from his companion, who glared at the interrupters with black, beady eyes as he swirled the muddy drink in his glass.

"I don't think so, *buddy*," the storyteller said after a pause, before turning in his seat to face a lizard standing over him; hand resting nonchalantly upon the gun protruding from the flap of his jacket.

"I'm sure we can wait for another table," Guy said almost as hurriedly as his fleeing feet.

"That will not be necessary," Kelp said, tightening his grip to hold Guy's top half steady, which caused the bottom half to snap back into place involuntarily. The lizard hadn't taken his eyes off the brown, leathery creature sitting before him.

In turn, the bird's gaze flitted between Guy and Kelp, before finally settling on Guy. He stared so intently at Guy that it sent shivers down his spine and, almost, something else down his leg. What was he looking at? And was that a grin flashing across his face?

The bird turned back to his compatriot. "You know what, Doop? I think the Monitaur might be right."

"But Franki—" the other one started protesting, looking as confused as Guy felt.

"No, Doop," the storyteller said, getting up to face Kelp from a height. He was much taller than Guy had originally thought. Slim, but tall, with an exceptionally long, scrawny neck. "He's most certainly correct. This *definitely* is the wrong table. I'm sorry, sir. It was *our* humble mistake."

"No need to apologise," Kelp said, waving a hand dismissively. "Glad you understand."

The looming bird shot Guy another quick glance before ambling off, followed by a compatriot who shook his head in disbelief.

"What just happened?" Guy said through clenched teeth as Kelp took him by the shoulders and plonked him down in the seat vacated by the storyteller.

"Vahltans," the lizard said, taking the seat opposite Guy.

"Nasty bunch," he continued, and shrugged. "But I guess my reputation precedes me. Beer?"

Guy just nodded, noticing for the first time how thirsty he actually was, and how much he needed a beer to take the edge off his nerves.

"Wait," he breathed, "make that two."

"Two it is," Kelp said, and summoned over a pretty, blue barmaid in a sensual, red body suit to take their order.

Past the approaching barmaid, Guy noticed the Vahltan storyteller standing at the bar counter while his companion ranted on about something. The way the bird periodically glanced at him was disconcerting. There was something … *knowing* in the Vahltan's eyes, which were just as dead and black as those of Kelp. He oozed a reputation of his own; also not the good kind.

However, the – what was Kelp called again? – Monitaur *must* be right about his reputation driving away the two Vahltans, Guy thought. It's not as if guys like *that* would be scared off by someone like *me*. To validate this presumption, Guy jumped in his seat as the barmaid slammed three beers onto the table. He hadn't realised that Kelp had ordered already.

Pushing his confusion aside, Guy snatched the first beer and downed it with a few gulps. Yes, there was no doubt, he definitely needed more than one.

•••

While Doop voiced his displeasure at the way in which they'd just surrendered their table, Franki's head was filled with dark, restless joy. It hadn't been a particularly good period for the crew of the *Jolly Dodger*. More importantly, as he was part of the crew, it had not been a particularly good period for *him*. Franki didn't feel the least bit guilty about caring more for himself than the others. After all, he was a Vahltan, for whom selfishness came as natural as breathing. The only reason why any Vahltan crew member would be concerned about the others would be if the reason behind that concern could eventually concern himself.

When the Monitaur had interrupted him, Franki had initially been furious that anyone would have the audacity to do such a thing. Especially to *him*! And especially during such a great story. Sure, it was mostly made up, but it was a great story nonetheless! Doop had hung on his every word, and Franki was a sponge for attention. So, when his tale had been cut short, he'd instantly reached a state of readiness to dish out his best knuckle sandwich with extra meat. However, two things had made him change his mind.

Firstly, he had recognised Kelp. He'd seen him around *The Wormhole* a few times, and although he didn't know the Monitaur personally, he *did* know his rep. Not the type of guy to take on lightly. Still, Franki had his own reputation to consider and would, at the very least, have tried to give the lizard a run for his money, or taken it from his body – alive or otherwise. However, from what he'd heard – and once seen with his own eyes – the chances of him losing the fight were pretty good. But losing the fight would have been preferable to losing face among his peers. Running away from certain death or capture was one thing Vahltans could do, and have done, plenty of times.[*] But running away from a bar fight was something else. Wounds from a fist could heal, but wounds from cowardice rarely did.

The second thing was therefore the real reason why Franki hadn't gotten involved in a scrap with the Monitaur. At first, he'd ignored the Salaman hiding behind Kelp like a scared toddler behind his mother's apron. But when he'd gotten a better look at the small red figure, all thoughts of fighting had vanished in an instant. The crew would understand why he backed off from a punch-up.

"I mean c'mon, Franki. We could've taken them easily!"

Franki had nearly forgotten Doop standing next to him. His colleague was clearly still upset about the whole thing.

"Normally I'd agree with you, Doop, but do you know who that Monitaur is?" Franki asked his sulking mate, who only shook his head. "That there is Kelp."

"I don't care if his name is King Tu—" Doop started angrily before his voice trailed off. "That's *Kelp*?"

"Yep."

"*The* Kelp?"

"The one and only."

Doop shifted his feet uncomfortably. "Well, I still think we could've taken them," he muttered in the tone of someone who had a tremendously hard time believing himself. "We could've gotten rid of the little one quickly before giving the lizard a good pummelling, even if it is … Kelp." He dry-swallowed the name.

---

[*] Vahltans can be quite ferocious, especially when they're in a group and *know* they have the upper hand. If these two boxes aren't ticked, a fast retreat just makes more sense, because self-preservation is a commodity that Vahltans cherish above all else. They are ferocious, not stupid.

"Perhaps, but I'm not all that interested in Kelp, mate. It's the little one you're dismissing so offhandedly that's got my attention."

Doop glanced at the Salaman and then back at Franki, puzzled. Apparently, this was one of those puzzles he wouldn't be able to put together without being shown the picture. "The *little one*? Why would you be interested in *that* wimp?"

"You don't recognise him?"

"Nope, should I?"

Franki sighed. "Yes, Doop, you should. And that's why *I'm* the First Mate, and not you."

"Well, I don't know him, and I can't see any reason why I should," Doop muttered.

Ignoring him, Franki leaned over the bar. "Hey, Schuffle, could I use your galphone for a minute?"

The Stortian behind the counter, covered completely with curly black hair except for the top of his smooth scalp, scowled at him. "You haven't settled your bill for the month, Franki. Come to think of it, you still owe us for last month!"

"C'mon Schuff! We've just gone through a bit of a dip, but all that's about to change. I'll pay you back, *with* interest. I promise."

"Oh, believe me, Franki, the interest's already been added to your bill. And it's been a bad year for me too, but nobody's giving *me* anything for free. So I don't want to hear your sad story!"

Instead of trying to play the who's-been-having-the-worst-luck game, Franki opted to play on the bartender's ... well, tender side.

"Yeah, I heard about the bank turning down your loan for the farm," he said sympathetically. "Sorry it didn't work out for you, Schuff, but I'm sure you'll get it one of these days."

"Damn right I will!" Schuffle affirmed.

"Of course, mate. You're a *Stortian*. You guys are the best farmers in the gal— in the *universe*! They'd be crazy not to invest in you."

"You can say *that* again. One day I'll make it. One day. I just need to save up enough creds."

"Of course you will! And that's why I'm appealing to your good faith now. I'm in exactly the same position. But I've got this really big, uh, business opportunity that's just fallen into my lap, and I need to tell the boss about it right away. So, if I can just use your galphone for a minute, I'll be set for a while. Then I can settle my bills, along with the interest."

"*And* with some extra interest," Franki added quickly when he saw the dubious look on the hairy man's face. "Just for *you* … to help you secure that loan."

"What's wrong with *your* phone?" the bartender asked.

"It's been stolen."

This was met by the stare of someone who's heard that excuse more than a teacher heard the my-dog-ate-it line.

"No, really," Franki said. "You know how it goes in our business. You can't even trust your own mates with your stuff. *Especially* not your own mates. C'mon Schuffle, gimme a break, *please*."

"This had better not take long."

"Just a minute. Not even."

The bartender looked doubtful, but reached under the counter and handed his galphone over to a grateful Franki, who started dialling the number into the thin, transparent device.

As he waited for the call to connect, Franki couldn't help but grin. No, his crewmates *definitely* won't give his backing away from a fight a second thought after this. As a matter of fact, he was going to be their hero or, rather, one of the least unlikable people they knew. Which, in Vahltan terms, pretty much equated to being a hero.

The captain was going to like him even more upon hearing this. Especially, he hoped, come bonus time.

CHAPTER 15

Guy awoke with a hole in his memory. Sitting up slowly, he shook his head to reset his vision. The cell he found himself in was different from the previous one. Similar, but different.

It was strange, he couldn't remember having drunk all that much, and his head didn't have the usual hangover heaviness to it. Yes, he did feel a bit fuzzy, but nothing like when he'd had a good night out with his old friend Neville or his new friend Cortex. No, he hadn't drunk *that* much. He even admitted it out loud to himself.

"I did *not* drink that much," he groaned before doubting himself again. "Did I?"

"No, you probably didn't."

It was wonderful that he was in total agreement with himself. But something was a bit off. He couldn't, with any amount of certainty, remember answering his own question.

He tried again. "Did I just say that?"

"What, that you didn't have too much to drink?"

"No, that I *probably* didn't."

"Oh, no, that was me."

Guy's ears confirmed that they were, in fact, the ones that had heard the statement.

He got up and slogged over to the force field, but couldn't see most of the area beyond it. The voice had come from somewhere behind the wall to his right.

"Thank goodness," he said. "It's not that I never talk to myself, but this time I'm sure I hadn't."

The voice didn't reply, so after a while, Guy said, "So, uh, are you with *them*?"

"With whom?"

"You know, Gacko and Kelp?"

"Would I be locked up if I was *with them*?" the voice snapped.

"Hey, I didn't even know you were locked up. It's not as though I can see you or anything."

After a pause, the voice said, "Sorry. No, I suppose you wouldn't know. I saw them dragging you in here, out cold. I'm just peeved that I'm stuck here in who knows where with who knows who and for who knows what reason."

"Believe me, I know the feeling," Guy empathised softly.

"I mean, one moment I'm sweeping a street, and the next I'm cooped up in this box!"

"So, you don't know why you're here either?"

"What do you mean *either*? Surely *you* know why you're here."

"No, I don't. Those Monitaurs have locked me up for a second time now. And I thought they were supposed to *protect* me."

"Protect you? From whom?"

Guy realised he'd said more than he should have, and that he'd better be more careful about what he divulged to this stranger, even if he didn't really have anything worth divulging.

"I don't know," he said, "but I *do* know that you don't lock up someone you're supposed to protect!" That last part he screamed at the overhead camera on the other side of the force field.

"Not a lot of love lost there, eh?" said the voice.

"What? Oh, no, none at all. My life has been a bit more … bearable of late. But *those two* just had to come and ruin everything."

"What do you do?"

"I'm, uh, in entertainment."

"What kind of entertainment?"

"I … do tricks."

"Tricks? You mean like 'sit', 'roll over' and 'play dead'?"

Guy chortled. "No, just a few moves that people seem to enjoy."

It was weird, but for some reason he liked his fellow captive. While he hadn't seen him, there was just something in the way the stranger talked that resonated with Guy. Still, keeping his trust issues firmly in place, Guy refrained from playing open cards with his neighbour. He got the impression that the feeling was mutual, although he supposed being cordial wouldn't hurt. Besides, he might learn something useful along the way.

"By the way," he continued, "the name's Gu— Bezam."

"Well, hi there, Gu Bezam."

"Uh, you can call me Bezam. Just Bezam."

"Well, Bezam, you can call me Lenny. Just Lenny."

"Good to meet you, Lenny. Well, not that we've actually *met*-met, but you know what I mean."

"Right. But do you—"

The *schwoop* of the door cut Lenny off, and Kelp strolled in casually with his hands folded behind his back. "I take it you've acquainted yourselves with one another?"

Knowing full well that we had, Guy thought grumpily, glancing at the camera once more.

"Brilliant," said Kelp in answer to the silence, "because we're going on another little trip, and I wouldn't want the two of you to feel awkward or anything."

"What *trip*?" Guy asked warily.

"To see a man about a ship. Nothing to concern yourself over."

"What *ship*?"

"Relax, Mr Bezam. It's just an expression; one I like to use whenever I feel someone doesn't need or deserve an answer. So I use it a lot. I just came to make sure you two were feeling at home in your new lodgings. And you seem to be. Well, that's good. Enjoy your stay."

With that, the lizard walked out.

"Wait!" Guy started, but was cut off by another *schwoop*. "That's great! Just ... great!"

"Yep, great," added the voice next door.

Guy returned to the small, hard bed to lie down. He wasn't in the mood to chat anymore. His neighbour seemed to share his sentiments, because there was no further attempt at conversation from the other side of the wall. After a few minutes, there was a drone, followed shortly by a slight judder running through the ship as it undocked, or detached, or whatever ships did on Unyun. The drone intensified as the ship started moving.

Folding his hands behind his head, Guy stared up at the ceiling. He didn't know what was going on. He didn't know where they were going. And, honestly, he didn't know if he actually cared. He then thought about it a bit more honestly and realised that he did, which didn't help much.

CHAPTER 16

Guy must have dozed off at some stage, because he was awoken by a tremor passing through the ship. His awakening was expedited by the cold spot of drool that had accumulated between his face and the pillow. He rolled onto his back and rubbed the sticky saliva off his cheek before rubbing his eyes. He then groggily thought that it might have been better if he'd done that the other way around.

How long had he been sleeping?

Soft snoring emanated from the adjacent cell, where his co-captive seemed to be blissfully unaware of anything going on around him. Well, to be fair, the drone of the ship's engines *was* quite soothing, and almost drove Guy back to sleep with its humming lullaby. However, a loud clang, accompanied by a violent jerk that almost knocked him off the bed, erased any plans of returning to his slumber. The ship's engines suddenly died with a woeful *whoooommm*.

"What the…?" came the sleepy query from Lenny's cell. "What's going on?"

Guy got up and looked about.

"Not sure," he said. "I think we might have hit something."

"Like what?"

"How should *I* know?" Guy snapped. "Do I look like a rocket scientist to you?" He'd never been that great with the whole waking-up-feeling-refreshed thing, just like leopards weren't great with the whole having-someone-pulling-their-whiskers thing.

"How should *I* know what you look like?" Lenny said.

"Fair point," Guy conceded, rubbing his eyes again.

Another loud clang, followed by a shudder that nearly toppled him over, prompted Guy to grab the side of the bed.

"Well, whatever it is, it doesn't sound good," Lenny said.

Guy agreed; the noises did not sound good at all. He didn't know much about spacecraft, but he had a hunch that they weren't supposed to make such noises.

Nevertheless, he tried to stay optimistic.

"Maybe they're just engaging their hyperdrive or something," he ventured.

"You don't know a lot about space travel, do you?" Lenny said.

"No, I don't," Guy retorted irritably. "Like I said, I'm in the entertainment business."

"Don't entertainers travel a lot?"

"Fine!" Guy snapped for the second time in as many minutes. "I haven't been an entertainer for all that long, okay? And I mostly travelled on land!"

He took a deep breath to simmer down. "That is to say, I *only* travelled on land."

"I know the feeling," Lenny said empathetically.

"What, *you've* never travelled in a spaceship before? I would have thought that someone from Unyun would be a travel-hardened yahoo."

"The pay for street-sweeping is not as high as you might think."

Guy approached the force field. "Okay, so we're both not that knowledgeable about space travel. But I think we both know something's amiss with this ship."

"Agreed."

"But we don't know what it is."

"Right."

"So where does that leave us?"

Lenny's reply was interrupted by a series of soft thumps and thuds that gradually grew louder.

"I think," he said eventually, "we're about to find out."

•••

Thump, thud. Thump-thump, thud-thud. Thump-thump-thump, thud-thud-thud. Thump-thud ...

Guy was reminded of a few serious hangovers where even his heartbeat had been too loud for his aching head to take. Strange how he could always remember the hangover but not the night before.[*]

One particular morning-after, he'd been lying in front of the television, staring at a World War II documentary after a serious night out with Neville. That's all he remembered; it had been a serious night out. He could for the life of him not recall where they'd gone, or until what time, or even how they'd gotten back home.

Not that he'd been overly worried about that, because for some reason, no matter how much alcohol was involved, Neville always kept his wits about him. Guy always wondered how he managed that, and often suspected his friend of having normal soft drinks instead of mixes poured for himself at the bar when Guy wasn't looking. He'd never confronted Neville with his suspicions, though, because his friend always seemed to have a good time, with or without alcohol.

Guy, on the other hand, almost always ended up having too much. Alcohol didn't really agree with him, and he usually didn't agree with alcohol, as he often found himself hunched over a toilet where both his stomach and the alcohol would finally agree on something: they just didn't like each other. To lighten the mood, Guy would end up singing that classic death-metal song *"Whaaaaaaaaaah!"* into the porcelain bowl as his stomach and the alcohol parted ways not so amicably.

That particular morning-after, watching the World War II documentary, the sounds of bombs exploding echoed the throbbing in his head. The sounds now coming from outside

---

[*] This is generally a good thing. You've already done enough damage to your brain without having to worry about the damage done to your reputation, too. It's therefore advisable to err on the side of caution by staying off social media for the next few days or, in severe cases, permanently.

the holding area sounded like the mortar fire in that documentary; the thump of the mortar shell propelled from its tube, followed by the distant sound as it exploded. The sounds outside, however, were softer and more rapid, like muffled gunfire.

Thump-thump, thud-thud.

Yelling.

Guy couldn't discern anything from the raised voices beyond the door, although it might have been for the better.

Thump-thud.

Shouting.

Thump-thud. Thump-thump-thump, thud-thud-thud.

The sounds continued to increase in volume, but then started to grow fainter before eventually fading away completely. A strange odour, like welded metal, filled the air. All was quiet and, after the ruckus, the silence – which seemed to last forever – was even eerier than the preceding noise.

As Guy didn't like forever to last that long, he decided to break the stillness. "Was that ..."

"... gunfire?" Lenny completed the open question in an unfazed tone. "I'd say so."

"You don't sound very worried," Guy said, worrying about Lenny's lack of worry.

"My friend," Lenny replied calmly, "I'm as worried as I can be. Due to recent events, my worry threshold is nowhere near its normal level. So excuse me for not being as nervous as you'd like me to be."

Guy suddenly realised that his own ups weren't as high up and the downs not as low down as they'd been before everything had gone down the toilet like disagreeable liquor.

"I think I know what you mean," he conceded. "But I still don't like it."

"Believe me, neither do I."

Guy also didn't like what happened next as the door *schwooped* open. A cloud of smoke wafted into their small enclosure, causing him and Lenny to start coughing profusely. Through the smoke emerged a figure with *doof-clink-*

doof-clink footsteps. Another figure followed closely behind with normal spaceship footsteps.

"Ah, there he be!" said a deep, raspy voice. "*An'* the other one as well."

"See, I told you it would be worth it," a faintly familiar voice said.

"Aye, that ye did," the first voice said. "Ye did well, Franki. Very well indeed."

Still wheezing from the smoke, Guy rolled the name over his tongue along with any available oxygen. It didn't take long for his tongue to recognise the name and the second voice, and it tasted even worse than the fumes.

CHAPTER 17

The smoke cleared to reveal the two arrivals. Guy's watery eyes recognised one of them from *The Wormhole* back on Unyun.

The Vahltan's dark eyes gleamed with satisfaction as his gaze darted between the captives and the other Vahltan that had entered with him. While the spine-chilling presence of Franki still made Guy cringe, the feeling was like warm toffee pudding compared to the spine-freezing stare of Franki's compatriot.

Standing almost a head above the already-tall Franki, the other Vahltan had a lot more bulk than his companion. He wore a long black leather coat over a black shirt, with black breeches covering a big black boot on his right leg. In all likelihood, he also would have worn a big black boot on his left leg if he'd had one. Instead, protruding from the breeches was a silver robotic limb, complemented by a silver robotic right hand as well as a silver eyepatch over the left eye. The eyepatch partially covered a scar running all the way from his cheek before disappearing under the funny-looking wide-brimmed hat perched atop his narrow, elongated head. At least it *would* have looked funny if the rest of the Vahltan hadn't looked so terrifying.

The stare from the good eye didn't so much pierce Guy as it pulled him in like a black hole, absorbing everything, letting nothing escape. Guy felt trapped by its magnetism, and he only snapped out of his trance when another familiar figure entered the room.

"The ship is secure, Cap," said the entrant, whom Guy recognised as Franki's companion from the bar.

The semi-robotic hulk sneered. "Excellent, Doop. An' 'is two friends?"

"They're *not* my *friends*!" Guy protested, annoyed with the Vahltan despite his formidable appearance. "Do friends *kidnap* and *lock up* their friends? No, I don't think so! I don't even *know* them!"

"I'm with him on this," Lenny confirmed from next door. "I wouldn't classify them as friends either. Not even acquaintances."

Clasping his hands behind his back, the captain looked about the room before nodding. "Aye, I guess ye may be right," he said, fixing his eye on Guy. "But there be one thing I find strange. Maybe ye could help me out with that, Mr...?"

"Bezam," Guy said reluctantly.

"Mr Bezam," the Vahltan continued. "I be curious as ta the reason ye would be having drinks with that scum if ye weren't friends ...," he glanced briefly at Lenny's cell before adding, "... or *acquaintances*."

Guy wasn't very good at full-out lying, but he was pretty good at bending the truth into any shape that fit the hole he found himself in at any particular moment.

"Well," he said, picking his words carefully, "I'm not sure what *Kelp* wanted, but *I* like beer. Getting a free round or two didn't seem like such a bad idea at the time, until I woke up in here."

"Hey, the same happened to me!" Lenny exclaimed. "Except, it was the fat one that got me drunk. No, wait, maybe not drunk. He only got me one beer as far as I can remember. It was ... strange."

"Very strange," Guy said. "I only had two, I think. Do you think we were—"

"Drugged?" the big Vahltan interjected. "Aye, it be very possible with those two."

He turned to his colleague who had come in with the report. "Speaking o' *those two*. Doop, have ye secured 'em too?"

The one called Doop straightened, his eyes darting about nervously. "No, Cap. They, er, managed to escape in a speed shuttle. Shall we give chase?"

"That be very unfortunate, Doop," the captain said in a tone that barely hid his displeasure.

"We nay have the time ta chase after 'em weak-willed scum," he continued after a tense pause, and flashed a grin at Guy. "Besides, we got what we came for."

His gaze lingered a moment longer before he suddenly whirled around and started walking out with a *doof-clink-doof-clink*. "Get these two onta the *Dodger*. An' be quick about it! We do nay want ta attract any unwanted attention."

"Yes, sir!" Franki and Doop jumped to attention as the captain exited the room.

"And what about this ship?" Franki enquired, almost as an afterthought.

The captain halted, not looking back. "Maybe we *do* have a few minutes ta spare for a little fun. Once ye have loaded the commodities, get us inta safe firing range. Me hand's been itching for some target practice."

"Aye, Cap!" Franki affirmed as the captain continued down the passage.

As soon as the *doof-clink-doof-clink-doof-clink* faded, Franki turned towards his newly acquired prisoners. "Well, Doop, you heard Cap. Let's get these two in magnocuffs and off the ship. Start with that one."

He withdrew a gun from under his shaggy grey coat and pointed it towards Lenny's cell. As Doop lowered the force field, Franki cautioned his captives, "I hope I don't have to tell you not to try anything stupid."

Although he held the gun in a very relaxed way, Guy got the impression that the Vahltan knew how to handle the weapon, and he sincerely hoped Lenny saw this too. If Lenny knew that Guy's fighting skills were basically limited to whatever he could pick up and throw in the general direction of an opponent, he wouldn't try anything. In any case, Guy was sure – and hoped Lenny was also sure – that these two weren't the only members of the captain's crew.

Guy heard the click of magnocuffs, but when Franki motioned Lenny out of his cell, something also clicked in Guy's head. The source of the familiarity that had gnawed at Guy earlier suddenly became evident.

•••

Lenny looked exactly like Guy, or rather Bezam, and not just because they were of the same species. Lenny's features looked *precisely* like those of Bezam's, down to the lime-green eyes. The only differences were Lenny's hair, which was a tad longer, and his apparel. As opposed to Guy's tight, semi-clean lime-green outfit, Lenny wore loose, dark coveralls tucked into black rubber boots. Guy wasn't sure whether the coveralls were naturally dark, or if the outfit's natural colour was merely concealed by the layer of grime that seemed to have been permanently baked into the material. Strangely, Lenny's face and hands were squeaky clean, showing not a smudge of dirt.

Guy forced his mouth to un-gape just before Lenny did the same.

The grimily clad Salaman grinned. "Good to finally put a face to the name."

"Likewise," Guy replied.

"You're joking, right?" Franki said, leaning against the doorway.

Guy shot him an annoyed look. "What?"

"Please tell me you guys aren't seriously going to play the we-don't-know-each-other card?"

"We're not playing anything," Lenny said calmly, then nodded towards Guy. "Met him for the first time a few hours ago. And when I say *met*, I mean we *talked*. This is the first time I've actually *seen* him."

"Yes," Guy said, "we only just met."

Franki's beak twisted with amusement. "*That's* the story you're gonna tell the captain?"

Guy scowled. "It's not a story. It's the *truth*."

Franki's amusement intensified. "The truth, eh? What do you think, Doop? *You* think they're telling the truth?"

"Only one way to find out, Franki," Doop said.

Franki grabbed the detainees by the scruff of the neck and shoved them out the door.

"No, mate," he told his companion, "the fun part is that there are quite a few ways to find out."

CHAPTER 18

Guy glanced at the cuffed Salaman walking beside him as they were herded down a metal corridor. He was sure he'd met him before. At the circus, perhaps? Or maybe a bar? The latter sounded more probable. He tried to pinpoint the familiarity, but it kept evading him like those squiggly shapes on your eyeballs that keep moving along with your vision whenever you try to get a fix on them.

Driven forward by Franki, their footfalls rang out angrily on the metal open-mesh floor, echoing Guy's own anger. No matter what Mr Gray said, he hadn't wished *this* upon himself. It was like wishing you'd get a dead pony for your birthday. It was preposterous! He wished Bezam was here so that he could strangle some answers from the twerp. It had to be *his* fault. It *had to*. Not that his new captors would see it that way, especially that big one.

He shivered at the thought of the semi-robotic captain. The Vahltan seemed to be as cold and hard as his left leg. How could Guy convince *him* that he'd done nothing wrong? And even if he somehow managed to do so, the captain didn't seem like the type of person to offer you a hearty apology, slap you on the back and send you on your merry way with a basketful of brownies. No, whether or not the captain got the answers he wanted, Guy would most probably find himself drifting through space with a third eye blasted through his skull.

To fuel his fear, they walked past a large window that showcased the coldness of space up close and personal. It was the first time Guy had seen space like this. But what should have been a momentous occasion for any human was marred by thoughts of mortality.

He could just see his lifeless body floating outside without anyone knowing where he'd disappeared to, or why. Would anyone even care? Certainly not his cold-blooded editor back on Earth, who cared more for the wilted fern wedged in the corner of her office than for Guy. Certainly not his colleagues, who only seemed to realise he existed when they heard the editor screaming at him. And certainly not his family, with whom he's never quite gotten along. In fact, he hadn't seen or spoken to his parents since the previous year's New Year's fiasco. How was he supposed to know his mom's stupid cat would go chasing after the sparkling fuse of the Red Hot Rocket? He briefly wondered if the fur on Mr Cuddles's face had ever fully grown back. Nope, his family wouldn't miss him.

The only person that would give a rat's behind over Guy's disappearance would be Neville. If Neville had been here, he'd know what to do, although *he* would never have gotten himself into such a mess in the first place. Unlike Guy, who would step into dung the size of a bean bag even if it was hidden in the corner of a deserted bunker in the middle of the desert with a big flashing neon "CAUTION: DUNG!" sign stuck into it. Perhaps that's why he and Neville were such good friends; Neville always liked taking care of things, like injured birds and bonsai trees, while Guy always needed care. But now, when he needed him most, Guy's friend was on the other side of the galaxy, or the universe, for all he knew. There was no one around to help Guy this time.

•••

The procession reached a small mess hall with a few white tables and benches bolted to the floor. At least Guy thought they were white; it was quite difficult to see past the dirty dishes and discarded trash that tried their best to cover the stains of whatever was spilt over the grimy surfaces. Although Guy's knowledge of space travel was as nonexistent as his knowledge of the mating habits of the Tasmanian devil, he was convinced that mess halls weren't supposed to be this … messy. Even his kitchen on Earth, at its dirtiest, looked like a Michelin-starred restaurant in comparison. Something crawled across one of the tables using an empty wrapper as cover.

"Wait a second," Doop said, halting by a panel that slid up at a touch. A bright light revealed all kinds of foodstuffs amidst a white, gaseous substance cascading towards the floor. He rummaged through the contents of the fridge and emerged with a blue bottle.

"Stortian ale!" he beamed. "And there's a lot more in here. The boys are gonna love us for this!"

"Well done, Doop," Franki said. "Go get some help and haul this onto the *Dodger*. But make it quick – we don't want to keep the captain waiting."

Watching Doop storm off like a kid in a toy store, Guy noticed another big window in the opposite wall and, as he stared through the glass, he wasn't sure if what he was seeing was seen correctly. Lenny also stared out the window with a puzzled expression.

The space outside seemed … unnatural, almost warped. Guy rubbed his eyes vigorously and focused again, but the warpiness clung to his vision like syrup to a Husky's coat. He blinked a few times and glanced at Lenny, who cocked his head as if a different angle might help solve the mystery.

"Impressive, isn't it?" Franki suddenly said from behind, causing them to jump.

Lenny recovered first. "What? A smudged window? To be honest, as far as smudges go, I've seen better."

Franki spoke into a commlink on his wrist. "Hey, could you drop the cloak for a bit?" He nodded towards the window. "You might want to keep an eye on your … smudge."

"Still looks smudgy to me," Guy muttered to Lenny, but kept his eyes fixed on the spot.

The next moment, the smudge transformed into a still-dark-yet-solid spaceship. It sort of looked like an American football wrapped in perfectly smooth, highly reflective aluminium foil, with a sausage kebab, also wrapped in the same foil, stuck into its centre. Only, instead of sausages, the mast carried three engines ranging in size from big at the bottom near the hull to small at the top, with a big rotating sign affixed to the tip. The black sign boasted an elongated white skull that, upon closer inspection, bore a resemblance to Franki's head, with two crossed white bones below it.

"It sort of looks like a pirate ship," Lenny breathed.

"That's because it *is* a pirate ship," Franki beamed. "Behold the *Jolly Dodger*!"

They didn't really have much time to behold anything, however, as the ship went all warpy again.

"What happened to it?" Lenny asked.

"That, mate, is a secret," Franki said. "I can tell you, but then I'd have to kill you."

"Speaking of which," he added matter-of-factly as he shoved them towards the airlock.

CHAPTER 19

Aside from having their lives threatened, which would put most people in a rather un-jolly mood, the interior of the *Jolly Dodger* wasn't that jolly either.

Franki must have picked up on Guy and Lenny's repugnance at their surroundings, which couldn't have been too difficult, as their expressions were pretty self-explanatory.

"I'll admit," he said, looking about affectionately, "it might not be much to look at on the inside, but this baby's brought us through everything life could throw at us."

It looked more as if life had thrown up in the ship, with most surfaces covered by a layer of grime and, which Guy found surprising, rust. Again, space travel wasn't his forte, but one of the last things he ever expected to see inside a spaceship was rust. Sure, he never thought he'd see the inside of a spaceship to begin with, but still, *rust*? The section they found themselves in was also quite gloomy, as if light itself could only build up enough courage to peek around the corners, afraid to touch the surfaces of the filthy vessel.

Franki sighed. "Yep, they sure don't make them like this anymore."

Guy believed him wholeheartedly. In fact, he'd be willing to bet a month's salary – which, admittedly, wasn't that big of a wager – that *nothing* was supposed to be made like this. At least not anything made with the purpose of actually staying in one piece. Like spaceships. They were supposed to stay in one piece, weren't they? He sincerely hoped they were, especially this one, seeing as he was currently in it. He decided it best not to touch any rusty object, afraid that it would crumble and take the rest of the ship along with it.

Making up for the wretched condition of its interior, the ship's extraordinary hull was almost completely transparent. Despite his aversion to touching anything, Guy couldn't stop himself from running his fingers over the surface. Whatever material it was made of felt as cold and solid as steel.

"Neat, eh?" Franki said from behind.

"Uh, yes, but why would you want to see through it?"

"I'd have thought the benefits of being able to see all around you on a pirate ship would be quite obvious."

"Don't you have all kinds of sensor-thingies? You know, like radar?"

"Radar?" Franki said, perplexed.

"You've never heard of radar?" Guy said, sharing the Vahltan's perplexity.

"Of course I have," Franki snorted, "at the Unyun Museum of Technology. Using radar in intergalactic space travel would be like banging two rocks together to start a fire. Do *you* bang rocks together to make a fire?"

"No," Guy said. "I use matches."

"What are matches?"

"Never mind."

Franki aimed his attention at Lenny.

"And *you*?"

"What about me?" Lenny said with a jolt as his mesmerised stare through the hull got interrupted.

"Are *you* into banging rocks to start a fire?"

"What? Uh, no. I'm more of a *lighter* person."

"What's a lighter?"

"Never mind."

Franki rubbed his beak thoughtfully. "I'm not sure what to make of the two of you, but I think the captain might just find you amusing. *Very* amusing. Or not. You'd better hope, for your sake, it's not the latter."

CHAPTER 20

As their procession continued through the ship, Guy and Lenny tried fishing for information. But despite numerous efforts, they didn't have much success in finding out what the pirates wanted from them. Given, their efforts weren't really *efforts*. They were more like half-baked questions you knew you'd never get a proper answer to, like "How long is a piece of string?" or "Where has my left sock gone?"[*]

They did, however, achieve great success in getting manhandled into walls several times, so experience eventually started calling for a more subtle approach, namely to stop asking questions altogether.

The rest of the ship exhibited more or less – but mostly more – the same grimy surrounds as before, albeit with more Vahltans bustling about. They didn't seem to be doing much, although they did *appear* to be very busy doing it. Guy wasn't fooled by this beehive of activity, as he also had a knack for looking busy on his work computer while playing card games or looking for specials on used furniture.

They finally arrived in a room that sat like a bubble on top of the ship, affording spectacular views of the stars without any obstruction. What was even more spectacular was that the room, in contrast to the rest of the ship, was spotlessly clean, and completely white, except for the various panels

---

[*]For the sake of fairness and broader representation, this query is often raised about the right sock too.

and screens displaying data that wouldn't mean anything to anyone other than the people who knew what it meant. If Guy didn't know any better, he would have thought that this was some sort of bridge, but since he really didn't know any better, he wasn't sure.

"Welcome ta the bridge," said a familiar voice from a white chair suspended mid-air at the centre of the room. The chair rotated slowly to reveal the metal-legged captain lounging in it with a mobile monitor in his lap, looking very pleased in a very unpleasing way.

"Ye liked the tour o' the ship?" he said, with his good eye glinting like polished evil.

Guy wondered why he had, up till now, regarded it as the Vahltan's *good* eye.

"Uh, yes," he and Lenny said in unison.

"That be splendid!" said the one-eyed, one-legged hulk as he turned his attention to the screen in his lap and rotated away again.

"Hey, Franki," his voice continued from the back of the chair.

"Yes, Cap?" Franki said.

"Ye know ole Jeb from the *Masked Marauder*?"

"Yes, I know him. Not that well, but we've had a few drinks and bar fights together. Why?"

"It seems he be tying the knot again."

"So, who's he hanging *this time*?" Franki said flatly. "Surely not his sister. She's the only family he's kept alive."

"Nay, I mean he be getting married again," the captain said.

"*No* way!"

"*Aye* way."

"That's the *third* wife this year!"

"Arrr! With the last one, he really did tie the knot … round 'er wrists an' ankles."

"Could've been worse."

"Aye, but 'er wrists an' ankles were chained ta a metal ball."

"Still not bad."

"Before she was dropped off two miles above Ahkwah's Endless Ocean."

Franki winced. "Now *that* is bad. A bit extreme, though, I'd say."

"Think it had something ta do with 'im finding out that she be an undercover Federal Unyun Detector."

"He married a *Fud?*"

"Aye. Fourth one, in fact."

"You'd think he'd learn."

"Not ole Jeb. He be a hopeless romantic."

"At least you'd think *the Fuds* would learn."

"Aye, but the Fud who brings 'im down would be kicked up the ranks, so they keep on trying."

"But instead they get *dropped* two miles."

"Well, it be one way ta get rid o' the ole ball an' chain."

Franki sniggered. "You know, I sometimes forget you have a sense of humour, Cap."

"An' I sometimes forget ye have a bad memory."

"True, but at least *I* don't forget to put my eyepatch the right way up some mornings."

"Only because ye do nay have one."

"True again. Any other updates?"

"Sure, there be a pic here o' ole Andro dancing naked on a table at *The Wormhole* last night."

"That's horrible!" Franki said.

"Arrr, but stuff like that happens when ye get 'em sexy Minks waitresses pouring shooters down yer throat the whole night."

"No, I mean it's horrible to hear the words *Andro* and *naked* in the same sentence! I'm glad I missed it."

"Aye, I hear ye, but the photo did get 4 203 Loves an' … Arrr! What do we be having here? Jenne from the *Fire Breather* has left the ship ta become a swimsuit model for *Unyun Illustrated.*"

"No surprises there; she's a looker. But I *am* surprised Captain Shelk let her go. I thought he's smitten with her."

"I do believe that be exactly why he let 'er go. He always be giving 'er everything she asks for."

Franki shivered behind his captives. "Can't blame him. The things I would do for *that* woman. And the things I'd let her do *to me*—"

"Gentlemen," came a calm yet direct address from behind Franki, causing the startled Vahltan to dig his fingers into Guy and Lenny's shoulders, which elicited a pained yelp from the captives. "I hope I haven't interrupted anything … important?"

"No, sir!" replied Franki.

The captain spun his chair with lightning speed and sported an expression of someone who'd also just been struck by lightning.

A figure walked past Franki and his captives towards the captain, who rubbed his knees nervously. The newcomer was dressed in a tight-fitting black leather outfit, which hugged an outline that Guy hoped belonged to a female, otherwise there were a few things in his life that might need re-evaluation. The tip of a tail, which protruded above the round curves of the most perfect buttocks Guy had ever seen, swished from side to side.

A bead of sweat ran down the captain's temple as the sensual figure bent over to view the captain's screen. The pose also pushed some sweat from Guy's own forehead.

"Hmm," the figure said calmly. "Cap, I thought I had asked you to review the logs of the past week and report back to me. Am I mistaken, or is this *not* the report?"

"Nay… er, I mean *no*, sir, it's not," the Vahltan replied, suddenly appearing half his size as he tried to hide within himself.

"So what *is* this I'm looking at? *Surely* it's not that bothersome social network that's constantly keeping you from your duties, is it?"

The tone of the question made Guy feel safer on this side of the room in magnocuffs with a weapon pointed at him. He knew that tone pretty well; a tone his editor had frequently used when addressing him. The seated Vahltan cringed even more than had originally seemed possible and quietly stared at his twiddling thumbs.

The figure placed a firm hand on his shoulder. "Cap?"

"Sir?"

"What's the name of that social network?"

"Spbk, sr," he mumbled.

"Sorry, what was that? I couldn't hear you."

"*Spacebook*, sir," the Vahltan replied a little louder. But just a little.

"Ah, yes, *Spacebook*. So you *are* looking at the site I specifically *forbade* you from visiting when you have other tasks to perform?"[*]

Each emphasised word acted like a mini lightning bolt, causing the Vahltan to twitch every time one hit. "Er, yes, sir," he muttered to his thumbs.

"Hmm, interesting. If it's not *too much* of a bother, might I suggest you go to your quarters, Cap? We will discuss your punishment as soon as I'm done chatting with our guests here."

"But ..." came a slightly louder whine from the captain, who cut off any further protestation as if realising that this was an argument he wouldn't win. Or any other argument, for that matter, when the figure had that specific look on his/her-but-*hopefully*-her face.

"Yes, sir," he said sulkily. Getting up, he trudged past the captives, whom he glared at as though the whole thing was *their* fault.

---

[*] Similar networks have been causing similar problems across the universe, Dumb Planets included. And not just in the workplace. People who aren't active on these networks always find it strange how, for instance, a group of friends could sit around a table at a bar without talking to anyone who's there while talking to everyone who's not there. The people using these networks aren't completely oblivious to the irony of how unsociable social networks can be, and some will even admit it, as long as they can do so in written, electronic format just after they've watched the video of the singing cat they just downloaded ... and after they've shared it ... and read and replied to the comments on it ... and watched a similar video that Brenda just sent ... and commented on it, and ... well, they'll get around to it eventually. Really.

When the hulk disappeared from view with a dejected *doof-clink-doof-clink*, the figure swivelled the suspended chair and sat down with a sigh. Guy still hadn't had a good look at him/her, but the voice for some reason did *feel* female, although he wasn't sure if this was just him trying to convince himself.

"You know, Franki," the voice said from behind the back of the chair, "I sometimes loathe *Spacebook*. People tend to forget their responsibilities in here while they're trying to see what's happening out there."

"Uh-yes-sir-I-totally-agree-sir-But-what-shall-I-do-with-these-two-sir?" Franki jabbered, wanting to change the subject as fast as possible to prevent any further inquisition or scorn coming his way.

"Make sure they get cleaned up and fed, then take them to my quarters. There are some … things we need to discuss."

CHAPTER 21

After taking a shower in a bathroom that was surprisingly clean, Guy and Lenny dressed themselves in the fresh robes and slippers left for them. Franki escorted them back through the bridge before leading them down a corridor to the front of the ship. They halted at a door, where Franki announced their arrival via a panel.

"Enter," said a voice through the speaker. The door whispered open.

"Get in there," Franki said as he shoved his charges inside, causing Guy to stumble and sending Lenny sprawling on the floor. The Salaman took a moment to compose himself before getting up slowly. He gave the Vahltan a brief, unreadable look, then calmly stepped in next to Guy.

Guy couldn't see much in the dimly lit room other than the outline of the figure they'd encountered on the bridge earlier. Silhouetted against the starlight passing through the transparent hull, the perfect lines could *not* be mistaken for those of anyone else. Hands clasped behind its back, the figure watched the stars whizz by.

"Franki, Franki, must you always be so heavy-handed?" the figure said without turning around. "What are our guests to think of us?"

"It's not the first time I've been a *guest*," Guy grumbled, earning him a slap behind the head.

"Thank you, Franki, that will be all," the figure said with a wave of the hand.

"But—" Franki started.

"I said *that will be all*, Franki," the figure repeated, and although the voice was still soft and calm, the undertone suggested that it wouldn't repeat the order a third time without consequences.

"Yes, sir. I'll, uh … just wait outside, then."

"You do that, Franki," said the unmoving figure.

The Vahltan muttered something, but left the room without further objections. As the door *swished* shut behind him, the figure turned around.

"I have to apologise for Franki's behaviour," it said. "There are certain things Vahltans are good at; being well-mannered generally isn't one of them."

"You seem well-mannered … er … sir," Guy said hesitantly.

"You're quite a sweet one, aren't you?"

With heat spreading through his cheeks, Guy shifted uncomfortably on his slippered feet.

"Speaking of manners," the figure continued, "let's have a better look at you. JD, normal light."

The lights came on and, although quite bright, it was remarkably pleasant on the eye. But not as pleasant on the eye as the figure. Guy was relieved to see a female standing in front of him. Feline, but female.

Guy had seen two individuals of the same species before at the circus. Faylins, if he remembered correctly? However, they had been more muscular and had not featured any form of breasts. This Faylin, however, *definitely* was of the female persuasion, with bosoms that peeked out just enough to draw attention, but not so much as to make her look overly amorous. Although blue, they were the most perfectly formed bosoms he'd ever seen on any woman in a leather suit. Okay, this was the first leather-clad woman he'd ever seen in real life – those movies didn't count – but he suspected that, if he ever saw another, she'd pale in comparison to this angelic creature.

The rest of her figure didn't lack for perfection either, with curves that would have even the most docile artists ready to engage in a physical altercation for the honour of capturing her athletic lines on canvas. Her hair was tied in a long ponytail that draped down her back. The dark-blue strands melted into one another, looking as soft as velvet, and contrasted her light-blue yet equally velvety skin.

However, nothing could rival her face. It almost seemed human, but with a feline touch. Her high cheekbones were divided by a long, delicate nose, situated above lips that curved up slightly in a perpetual smile. The curve of her chin flowed upwards along the sleek lines of her jaw, which merged seamlessly with slightly pointy ears that reminded Guy of an elf.[*]

Her eyes were the coup de grâce, though, sending the butterflies in Guy's stomach into a flurry. Large, with a slight upward slant, Guy couldn't decide whether they were blue or green, or a combination of the two, or if the colour changed as the light hit them from different angles. They didn't bore through Guy, but rather sucked him in like hypnotic whirlpools of euphoria, like those cartoons where the swirling spiral left its victims in a deep trance in which they'd do anything the hypnotiser asked of them.

Something sharp in his side snapped Guy back to reality.

"I think she's talking to you," Lenny whispered from the side with another nudge.

"Huh, what?" Guy managed with a slur.

"I asked if they had punched you in the face or something," said the exquisite Faylin.

"Er, no," Guy said.

"So why is your jaw hanging like there's a rock tied to it?"

Only then did Guy realise he was gawking at her like a carp with a heavy lip, and snapped his mouth shut. "It must be, er, a lack of sleep or something," he said, blushing. He'd never have thought that his reddish skin could go even redder, but apparently it could; his cheeks felt on fire.

"Well, I'll keep this short, then you can have a good rest."

As Guy was clearly still somewhat slow, Lenny took over. "Sorry if I sound a bit blunt, but who are you?"

---

[*] No, not the ones who make toys. The other ones.

The Faylin studied Lenny with an amused smile. "I like bluntness … on occasion. I am Captain Phealix. As I'm sure you've gathered by now, you're aboard the *Jolly Dodger*, one of the most wanted pirate ships in the Federation."

Her eyes beamed as she said it.

Finding his tongue again, Guy was puzzled. "How, um, can *you* be the captain if the *other guy* is the captain?"

"What other guy?"

"The one with the missing body parts."

"Who, Cap?"

"Yes, the captain."

"No, that is *Cap*."

"Which is short for 'captain', isn't it?"

"Generally, you'd be correct, especially on *those* ships with limited discipline. Ships with captains who feel they have to be best buds with their fellow crewmen to remain popular. Captains who usually find themselves low down on the most-wanted list or floating out the airlock. But, no, we just *call* him Cap. It's short for Cappilanorani shon Shawali shon Bekamonsi shon Kalasmi."

They were silent for a moment.

"Cap's fine with me," Lenny said,

Guy nodded. "So, uh, *you're* the captain then?"

"Yes," the Faylin said. "Cap is my First Hand; my second in command."

"But he seems more … uh … well, no offence meant, more … um—"

"Scary? Intimidating? Imposing?" Captain Phealix said with the look of someone who'd had this conversation quite a few times before with doubters who had their doubt removed swiftly and decisively.

"I mean," Guy said, "he's just more what I'd always thought, uh, a pirate captain would, er, look like."

"You mean more *male*, don't you?"

"I guess," Guy said before realising he shouldn't have, and held his hands up placatingly. "It's not to say that women *can't* be bloodthirsty pirate captains—"

"Who said I'm bloodthirsty?"

"So you *don't kill* people?" Guy said hopefully.

"I didn't say that either."

The clashing messages caused a traffic jam in Guy's head, with negatives and positives hooting furiously at one another without willing to budge.

"So, uh, you *do* kill people?"

"Only those who ask for it."

"Like who?"

"Like people trying to kill *me*."

"I … uh, suppose that makes sense," Guy said.

"It would, to anyone who loves to live. Barring the Suicide Sect of Solstice, of course."

"The *who* now?"

Captain Phealix regarded Guy quizzically. "What's your name?"

"Bezam, Captain … sir … ma'am—"

"Captain's fine. You don't get out much, do you?"

Guy shrugged. "I'm kinda new to the whole … *travelling* thing."

"So it seems. And you?"

"Who, me?" Lenny said.

"Yes, you …"

"Lenny."

"Lenny, have *you* been around?"

"Around?"

"Have *you* travelled much?"

"Uh, well, I went to the shops a few times. A man's got to eat, you know? Oh, yes, I also went to the museum a few weeks ago during my lunch break. It was quite fascinating."

Clasping her hands behind her back again, the captain returned to the hull to gaze at the stars. She appeared deep in thought, so Guy deemed it better not to say anything.

After a long, uncomfortable interlude, the captain said, "So let me get this straight. You don't know anything, and you don't go anywhere."

After another long pause, Guy started to wonder if it had been a question rather than a statement, so he felt obligated to say something.

"Not much," he mumbled just as Lenny said, "Not really."

"Which makes me wonder," the captain continued, "why would the likes of Kelp and Gacko be interested in the two of you, then?"

Guy wasn't sure what she was after, or what possible use his previous humdrum life or his recent circus exploits could contribute, but again got the feeling that he had to offer her something.

"Well, I'm a great shot," he volunteered.

"You mean, like a sniper?" the captain asked in a hopeful tone, as if she was homing in on something.

"No, I get shot from a cannon. But I get shot *really* well. Rimmy says I fly farther than anyone he's ever seen. I just don't land that well, which is why he won't allow me to perform that act anymore."

The Faylin turned to Lenny. "And you?"

"I'm really good at cleaning the floor," Lenny said.

"I take it you're not talking about fighting?" the captain said flatly.

"No, I just sweep streets, on Unyun. But I'm very good at it too."

"A circus act and a street sweeper?" Captain Phealix said, not sounding pleased. "You're kidding, right?"

"Er ... uh ... well ... no ... sorry," came the mixed reply.

The Faylin sighed. "I wanted to make sure you were the right marks before taking you to your destination. I had hoped we could do this in a more civilised way, but you seem a bit vague; like there's something you're not telling me. I therefore have no choice but to take you to The Man."

"The man!" Guy exclaimed, before thinking about it again. "Um, *what* man?"

"*The* Man."

Guy and Lenny just stared at her.

"Mr Man?" she tried again.

Nothing.

"Mr Man – The Man of the criminal underworld?"

More nothing.

"Manni Karpachio?"

Nothing was all there was.

The captain sighed. "Suit yourselves. Franki, get in here!"

The door *swished* open, and Guy could feel the Vahltan looming behind them.

"The Man will get what he wants, one way or another," the captain said, now looking more terrifying than terrific. "He always does."

CHAPTER 22

Despite their protestations, Franki manhandled Guy and Lenny out of the captain's quarters. On the bridge, the Vahltan halted as if remembering something.

"Doop, keep an eye on these two," he said, taking a seat in the captain's chair. "Jakki, bring us into firing position."

One of the Vahltans sitting behind a panel tinkered with the screen in front of her, which brought the *Jolly Dodger* about to face a cigar-shaped ship. The decrepit vessel was pocked all over with uneven repair patches and stippled with botched paintwork.

"Not much to look at, is it?" Doop said.

"Not at all," Franki replied. "I expected more from Kelp. But I suppose we're not the only ones going through a rough patch. Or patches," he added after another look at the ship.

"I'm glad we never went into the bounty-hunting business like we'd originally planned," Doop said with a grimace.

"Me too, mate," Franki said. "I wouldn't want to be caught dead in a thing like that. Or alive, for that matter. I'm starting to think Kelp's reputation might have been slightly exaggerated, otherwise he'd have more creds to buy something decent. That thing is just ... embarrassing. So let's do poor Kelp a favour and put it out of its misery. Salli, power up the fore cannons and raise the shield."

"Yes, sir," said a Vahltan sitting at another panel.

There was a sound like an old ship's cannon being loaded. In answer to the baffled looks Guy and Lenny gave one another, Doop said, "That's just a little something we added to indicate that the cannons are charged. Cap likes to keep things traditional wherever possible."

"I must admit, Doop, so do I … up to a point," said Franki before addressing the captives. "Well, I hope you enjoyed your brief stay on that bucket, because here she blows."

He pushed a button on the chair, sending two huge balls of green energy racing to their target, which blew apart upon impact. Chunks of the ship flew in all directions. Something, which looked like the toilet in Guy's previous cell, bounced off the *Jolly Dodger's* shield like a skipping stone on water, producing a blue ripple that vanished within a fraction of a second.

"And that's how it's done, mate!" Franki said with a satisfied smirk.

His satisfaction didn't last long.

"Enjoy it while you can, Franki," Doop said. "Cap originally wanted to do the honours, remember?"

Franki's mouth tried to maintain its smirk, but his eyes lost interest in playing along.

"Well, I can't help it if the captain benched him," he muttered, knowing the excuse wouldn't matter later on. "In any case, it's … well … stop standing around, Doop! Take these two back to their hole!"

Doop did so, knowing full well that his friend would be sweating for the next couple of days. If there's one thing Vahltan friends were good at, it was making sure that you were never too happy for too long, because an unhappy Vahltan was a successful Vahltan.

As he glared at the prisoners being led away, Franki felt extremely successful.

•••

Guy and Lenny were chucked behind a force field in a cell that would make even the grimiest part of the ship look as clean as a germophobe's cutlery.

After donning the tight green suits shoved into their arms, they reluctantly parked themselves on bunkbeds. The mattresses looked like sheep who'd mud-wrestled before going for a roll on the floor of a hair salon. Apparently, Guy and

Lenny's lack of cooperation wasn't going to make their stay more bearable.

The meat left for them on the beds could only be described as edible. It tasted a bit like chicken. The more Guy thought about it, the more he realised that most of the meat he'd eaten since leaving Earth tasted like chicken.[*]

After finishing, he lay down, and his thoughts quickly jumped from food to Captain Phealix. Since possessing Bezam's body, Guy had seen a lot of females of various species, but none of them had ever affected him in the same way the Faylin had. She was mesmerising.

At school, Sarah Jenkins had been the first girl to steal Guy's heart. Unfortunately, she'd never returned it. Sure, much later on, he'd encountered a few women in his life; some of whom had left him weak-kneed. And a couple of them had even gone out with him long-term – which in his case was never more than a couple of months.

There was just something about Guy that women couldn't seem to connect with or, at best, stay connected with. He'd always blamed Sarah for this faulty connection. But now, as he lay there, he realised that the something had likely always been there. Ingrained in his psyche. No, his lack of romantic connection had never been Sarah's fault, nor that of the others. At least he could still lay some blame on his less-than-loving parents, so he didn't have to shoulder all of it himself.

Captain Phealix, however, aroused new feelings in Guy that had been dormant since, well, birth – just like his ability

---

[*] The Ja'nama cannibal tribes of Wahyoo VIII loves the taste of chicken, and since they also taste like chicken, they really love the taste of themselves. Many critics have slammed the Ja'naman slogan of *You Eat What You Are*, as it didn't go down well with them. One of the critics, however, did go down well with the Ja'namas, especially with a few cloves of garlic and a hint of basil.[#]

[#] Last-mentioned was also the name of the unfortunate critic who'd found himself stranded on Wahyoo VIII after his spaceship broke down. The Ja'namas loved Basil, and still speak of him fondly. He's even received a special mention in the new *How to Transform Foreign Foods into Local Delicacies* cookbook.

to participate in any kind of sport. In his experience, any ball thrown, kicked or hit in his direction was not a plaything but a weapon specially created to inflict the maximum amount of damage to his face, shin, groin, ego or, more often than not, all four.

The captain was an enigma, not only because he didn't know her, but also because she appeared to be as dangerous on the inside as she was stunning on the outside. As Lenny started snoring increasingly louder on the bunkbed above, Guy couldn't get the Faylin's image out of his head, even after he, too, eventually drifted off to sleep.

CHAPTER 23

Cap was in his study, which was "OFF LIMITS" to everyone "UPON PAIN O' DEATH!", as clearly stated on the sign he'd carefully handcrafted from wood and hung above the door. He'd even finger-painted the bold letters with ink that mimicked dried blood and added some "blood" splatters for extra effect.

He was surrounded by shelves stacked with books, mainly fictional, describing swashbuckling pirate captains braving deep seas, deep-sea monsters, naval fleets and other buccaneers in their quest for treasure, honour, revenge or love – the latter being his favourite motive for high-seas adventure.

Not that Cap ever wanted to be a captain himself. In fact, had he known how much real violence was involved in piracy, he'd never have joined the crew of his former ship, *The Annihilator*, whose captain and crew were the bad kind of pirate.

Most non-pirates wouldn't know, or wouldn't care, that there was a good kind of pirate and a bad kind. The good kind were those that lived by *The Code*, a set of rules drawn up at the Pirate Colloquium, an annual seminar attended by pirate captains and their senior officers to discuss the latest tactics, ships, technology, weapons and, more importantly, where to get the best deals on beer and rum.

The reasons for drawing up *The Code* were pretty straightforward.

Firstly, the more violent the pirates, the greater the effort and ferocity of authorities to catch and apprehend them, making the whole pirating thing much riskier than it needed to be.

Secondly, the use of lethal force really wasn't necessary. Knocking someone out with a stunner gun was just as effective as knocking a hole through them with a flasher gun.

And, thirdly, blowing up cargo and cruise ships – albeit fun – was completely uncalled for, which tied in with the all-encompassing reason: don't kill the goose that lays the golden eggs. Why destroy ships and kill people today if you could simply raid and rob them again tomorrow?

It took a few years, as well as countless Gee-mailed correspondence through the Galactic Electronic Express Mail system, but the final draft of *The Code* was put to the vote at the last Colloquium. Following a great deal of explaining and re-explaining, the majority of the crews had voted in favour of it, agreeing that the need to keep piracy alive and well coincided with their need to keep themselves alive and well. It also reduced the risk of having to stand in those ridiculously long queues at the unemployment office if all the geese were gone.

In any case, *The Code* was remarkably simple to follow, even for the more illiterate pirates[*], especially with the help of those nifty illustrated *How To* pamphlets and animated *All You Need to Know About Safe Pirating* training videos.

Of course, the crews who'd voted against *The Code* were a bit disgruntled with the outcome, and had shown their disgruntlement by blasting away at whatever ships they encountered en route to their respective hideouts.

The Annihilator had been one of those ships, but its commanding officer, Captain Nobeard, aka Babyface – which no one dared call him to his baby face – had made a vital mistake; he attacked the *Jolly Dodger*. Suffice it to say, it hadn't been long before *The Annihilator* found itself with a giant hole where its engines used to be and its Vahltan crew all unconscious from stunner blasts – which later on led them to

---

[*] Thus most of them.

the conclusion that the use of non-lethal force was perhaps not such a bad idea after all.

The only crew member that hadn't participated in the fighting was Cap, who in turn hadn't been too difficult to locate thanks to the muffled sobbing emanating from inside his locker. He remembered the locker door opening slowly and finding himself staring into the barrel of a stunner, which sent him bawling uncontrollably. As the gun lowered, a voice had said, "What in Zolt's name is wrong with you?" He'd looked up at the divine face of Captain Phealix, who eventually just sighed and offered him her hand. "Come on, big man, let's get you out of here."

She'd led him to one of the benches and listened as he explained how he had never really been a pirate – not at heart, anyway – but had dreamt of being one since he was little, and wouldn't know what to do with himself if he couldn't be one.

When he'd finished, Captain Phealix had given him a long, thoughtful look, before saying, "I actually might have some use for you, if you're willing to play the part."

The rest, as they say, was history. A history that included Cap being appointed First Hand of the *Jolly Dodger*. It was his job to keep control of the crew and to ensure that violence was kept to a minimum. The only way of doing that with a Vahltan crew was through a combination of fear and respect, which Vahltans basically viewed as synonyms. His imposing size wasn't enough, he'd felt, so he subjected himself to a series of surgical procedures to install the robotic leg and hand, as well as to create the carefully planned scar across his eye. The surgeon had done a magnificent job; it seemed so … authentic. However, the eyepatch was simply one he placed over a perfectly good eye. There'd been a couple of times when he'd forgotten to put it over the correct eye, causing some confusion among the crew, who'd thought they *must have* seen things wrong again.

With each procedure, the captain had told the crew that Cap had been wounded during a "special op". It wasn't as if she'd been lying – they just didn't need to know the *exact* details. The enigmatic special operations and their disfiguring outcomes had cemented Cap's reputation, and not just among the crew of the *Jolly Dodger*. His former crew soon started to think they might have underestimated the Big Wuss, the nickname they'd unaffectionately bestowed upon him aboard *The Annihilator*.

So yes, the *Jolly Dodger* and, more specifically, Captain Phealix, had given Cap a new purpose: to be a *good* pirate. And, for the most part, it had rubbed off on the crew too, although the one thing they seemed loath to incorporate was the new "pirate-speak" Cap was attempting to introduce. Admittedly, he'd been having trouble with it himself, but at least *he* was trying, and he was sure the others would eventually fall in line.

Cap was suddenly jerked from his trip down memory lane by the tone of someone banging on a wooden door. He had selected the tone in the spirit of traditional piracy, and he couldn't fathom why the others preferred farting and belching tones, which *they* found funny for some reason. Childish imps!

The knock-tone was repeated. He knew who the *someone* at the door was, and she didn't really require anyone's permission to enter any part of the ship. Yet she did so in any case, especially when it came to Cap's quarters. She respected him, and for that she had his undying loyalty, which he hoped would remain. Especially the undying part.

"Come in," he uttered as confidently as he could.

The door "creaked" open – another special touch – as Captain Phealix silently strode in. She took a seat behind the wooden desk that had been custom-made for Cap. The desk was complemented by the old lamp, feather pen and ink-pot he'd recently purchased at a pawn shop on Unyun.

"If this is about the *Spacebook* thing, Captain, I'm truly sorry and—" Cap started.

"No, no, Cap," Captain Phealix said, motioning towards the seat on the opposite side of the desk. "I'm sure you've had ample time to think about what you've done. Now, please, sit."

Cap carefully sat in the visitor's chair as the captain slid open the desk's top drawer, pulling out the bottle of whiskey and two tumblers he kept stashed in there.

"Hope you don't mind?" the Faylin asked after the fact. While she always showed respect, she also wasn't afraid to remind him who was in charge; in a respectful manner, of course.

"No, please, feel free," Cap said.

The captain poured a measure of the golden liquid into the tumblers and slid one across the table into the Vahltan's expectant hand. He however didn't take a sip, and watched the captain eyeing her own tumbler as she swirled its contents, immersed in her own thoughts.

She finally looked up. "We've known each other for a while now, Cap."

"Aye, Captain. I mean, *yes*, Captain," he corrected himself. She gave him leeway with his pirate-speak in front of the others, but not when it was just the two of them discussing serious matters behind closed doors. He got the distinct feeling that a serious matter was about to come up.

"And you know I trust your honesty," she continued. "So, do you think I'm doing the right thing?"

"You mean handing the marks over to The Man?"

She nodded.

"Well, Captain," he said, "I found it difficult getting a read on them. But I believe that *they* believe they're telling the truth about not knowing anything."

"That's the feeling I got too, which is why I didn't push them too much. I'm still not sure if we're doing the right thing, though."

Cap stared at the tumbler in his hand.

"Frankly, Captain," he said at length, "we don't have much of a choice. We cannot back out now. We need to finish what we started."

"I was afraid you'd say that," she said, before finishing her drink in a single shot.

Cap followed suit and placed the empty tumbler back on the desk.

"And I'm plain *afraid*, Captain," he said. "But I also know you're even more afraid of letting *him* down."

"I'm not afraid of anything, Cap," she said, putting her own tumbler down. "Not usually. But you're right; I cannot afford to disappoint him."

For a while, they just stared at the glasses standing emptily on the table, until the captain suddenly rose with a look of resolve.

"I should report in," she said, tugging at her ponytail. "Give the order, Cap. We're going to Irik."

As the *Jolly Dodger* set off shortly thereafter, another ship emerged from behind a nearby asteroid, following undetected.

CHAPTER 24

Guy and Lenny awoke as the ship landed with a jolt and the hum of the engines faded. Guy was a bit miffed at being woken up, as he'd been having a very … pleasant dream about the captain who, it turned out, was now lowering the cell's force field – which, coincidentally, was exactly the way the dream had started too. Hey, he thought, maybe it's one of those recurring dreams; one he had no problem recurring as often as possible.

"*Pleasant* dreams?" the captain asked, shifting her gaze to Guy's mid-region.

"Ye—" Guy started, then yelped. Sitting up quickly, he snatched his pillow to cover his lap. "That's, uh … that's completely natural where I come from."

The Faylin gave him an amused smile that didn't ease his discomfort. "I'm sure it is. I suggest you freshen up, gentlemen. This is going to be a long day."

With that, the Faylin exited the door, and another amused smile appeared over the edge of the bunk above. "You were dreaming about *her*, weren't you?" Lenny said.

"I don't know what you're talking about!" Guy snapped.

"Don't worry, Bezam, your secret's safe with me," Lenny said, before eyeing the pillow. "Although I think *you* could have done better at keeping it a secret yourself."

Clicking his tongue, Guy grasped the pillow tighter, causing Lenny to burst into laughter. All Guy could do was to wait it out.

"Hey, I can't blame you," Lenny said eventually, wiping away the tears. "I had a dream about her too."

"You did?" Guy asked.

"Yes, but mine was a bit more … hair-raising than self-raising."

The glare from below elicited another burst of laughter. Guy got up and turned towards the other Salaman.

"Well, I'm glad *you're* finding this funny," Guy said flatly. "Because you know we're about to be chucked from the frying pan into the fire."

All signs of jest faded from Lenny's face. "Yeah, I know. But sometimes it's just easier to laugh at the unknown instead of worrying about it, you know?"

Guy didn't. It was difficult to laugh in the face of uncertainty, especially if you felt fairly certain that things weren't going to end well.

•••

A dim, red emergency light illuminated the cargo hold of the *Jolly Dodger*, where strapped-down containers occupied most of the floor space. And, as with most other places in the universe, it was quite natural for it to be quiet down there when no one was around. So it would have been somewhat of a surprise to anyone within earshot to hear a voice breaking the silence from behind a crate in one of the room's dark corners.

"Dat were a good move dat you did," the voice said.

"Keep it down, you idiot," the other voice hissed, although the slap that came with it was louder than the comment that had provoked the slap in the first place.

"Sorry," the voice whispered miserably. "I's trying to be fewer of a idiot dese days, but I's find it hard sometimes." Then the voice cheered up a bit. "I's a lot gooder … better than before, are I not?"

This was followed by a loud *crunch*.

"Yes," the other voice said over the noise of more crunching, "but it would have been even better if you'd stop eating snack bars in the middle of an op. Put that thing away!"

The sound of a wrapper being scrunched up intermingled with a few more careful crunching noises, which were terminated by an unsuccessfully suppressed gulp.

"I's finish," came the proud whisper along with half a raisin skidding across the floor. "As I's saying, dat were a good move. And we was lucky dat dey found dat beer, or we wasn't have many time to get on board. But what if dey catch de ship and see we's not in dere?"

"They're not interested in us, Gacko," the other voice said. "They got what they wanted, so there's no need for them to go chasing after the shuttle."

"Well, dat ship were good decor, Kelp," Gacko said.

"*Decoy*," Kelp corrected with audible restraint.

"Dat are what I's *said*," Gacko said in a tone that dared his partner to take this new addition to his vocabulary away from him, as he'd thought about it long and hard – almost as hard as the unknown seed that went skipping across the floor in pursuit of the raisin as he emphasised the last word.

"Of course," Kelp said, before the ship started to shudder. "Turbulence. It seems we've reached our destination."

They looked through the transparent hull at a dark sky broken slightly by scattered clouds as the ship descended through a planet's atmosphere.

"We's going to bash a few heads?" Gacko asked.

"I don't think that will be necessary. It looks dark enough to slip out without being seen."

"It even more dark for someone if us bash dem over de head," Gacko tried hopefully.

"No, Gacko, we *cannot* be noticed. Mr X was adamant about that. And someone would *definitely* notice if they woke up with a lump on their head."

As soon as the ship landed and the engines died down, the slim figure of Kelp emerged from behind the container and made his way to the door. Standing to the side, the Monitaur peeked through a narrow glass viewing pane overlooking the corridor beyond, and ducked at the sound of approaching footsteps, one of which emitted an eerie *doof-clink-doof-clink.*

Waiting for the sounds to fade, Kelp peered through the pane again, just to make sure there weren't any slippered Vahltans following. There weren't.

"Okay, let's go," he whispered to Gacko, who joined him without making a sound. Kelp often wondered how his partner managed to move so stealthily at times and be so clumsy at others. Some mysteries, however, were better off being swept under the rug and covered by a bigger, heavier rug, and topped off by a billiard table for good measure. But despite seeming outright allergic to anything remotely intelligent, Gacko always did things right when it came to the crunch.[*]

Opening the door, the pair followed in the direction the procession had gone, and slipped out quietly to become one with the night.

---

[*] Snacks excluded.

CHAPTER 25

Behind Captain Phealix and Cap, Franki and Doop herded Guy and Lenny forward without regard for the occasional yelps of pain as bare feet met hard rock.

Thankfully, they didn't travel too far. Topping a hill, they were met by an impressive sight as a well-lit building came into view. The immense, pearly white structure looked like an observatory cum five-star resort, with a huge round domed structure in the middle, encircled by two lower buildings, one of which hugged the main building.

The premises, in turn, were encircled by a vast terraced garden that alternated perfectly level lawns with landscaped rings of exotic plants and footpaths. Every level was connected by circular steps that fanned down from one level to the next.

The building wasn't the only thing that was illuminated. Bright stationary lights dotted the lush gardens and lawns, which seemed out of place amidst the arid, rocky surroundings the group had just traversed. Other lights, however, weren't as stationary, swaying about as the guards holding them patrolled the area. A pair of these lights rushed towards the group as they reached the bottom of the hill, and one of them swung up to shine in the eyes of those who didn't appreciate it.

"Halt, who goes there?" shouted a high-pitched voice that clearly belonged to a body with at least one other hand holding a weapon.

"It is Mr Get-That-Light-Outa-My-Face-Before-You-Lose-The-Ability-To-Hold-One-Ever-Again," Cap growled, raising a hand to shield his eyes.

After a pause, the voice said, "Uh, can you spell that?" before the flashlight was slowly lowered by the hand of the inquisitor's partner.

"There won't be any need for that, Gabbi," the partner said composedly. "Please forgive her. It's her first day."

As Guy's eyes adjusted, a Vahltan that was almost as big as Cap waved away a shorter, rounder Vahltan.

"We've been expecting you," the taller Vahltan said with a smile. "Gabbi, why don't you run up so long to let the boss know that his visitors have arrived? And while you're on your way, be a dear and send some men to help escort our friends up to The Mansion. We wouldn't want them to get lost, now would we?"

"Can't I just call it in?" the other Vahltan asked hopefully.

"Gabbi, these are *important* friends, and the boss would *love* to hear of their arrival in person. Then, when you come back, I think it's *your* turn to take a round of coffee to the patrols, wouldn't you agree?"

"But I made *every* round tonight!" the shorter one objected. "Isn't it someone else's turn to—"

"No Gabbi, I'm *sure* it's your turn. And I'm *sure* you wouldn't be implying that there's something wrong with my memory, would you?"

"No, Andi, but—"

The taller Vahltan cleared his throat in an easily understandable manner.

"No, sir, of course not," the female Vahltan said, glancing dejectedly at the long way up. "I'll get on it right away."

She started up the stairs and was panting by the time she got halfway up the first set.

"Wouldn't your boss want to get the news without delay?" Cap asked.

"Of course he would," Andi said.

"So, why not just let her call it in?"

"It's her first day, and it's tradition to get someone into trouble on their first day."

"Isn't that a bit risky?"

"Yes, but not for me. Besides, those who survive come out stronger for it."

"And the others?"

"Don't you think the gardens look well-fertilised?"

"Oh, yes, I see."

"In any case, in our line of work, she needs the exercise."

"Yes, I saw."

"Ah, our escort has arrived," said Andi as four Vahltans rushed down the stairs and flanked the group on either side. Each of the new arrivals casually held some sort of rifle or handgun, ready to use it uncasually.

"Well, let's not keep the boss waiting," Andi said, motioning the group forward.

Guy glanced sideways at Captain Phealix, who hadn't said a word since leaving the ship, and seemed somewhat anxious amid her outer calm. This did nothing to boost Guy's confidence levels as the group ascended the stairs.

•••

When the party reached the top of the last set of stairs, a portcullis set in the smooth, seamless outside wall was raised with a series of clangs.

Two Vahltans stood guard by the entrance as the group made its way through a thick wall, which wasn't a building as Guy had originally thought. It was more like a modern wall encircling a modern castle, with armed guards patrolling the ramparts. Very retro.

They entered a courtyard that made the pristine gardens outside look like a city dump. The hedges looked like they'd been meticulously sculpted with a scalpel by a top-notch surgeon, which – although Guy wouldn't know – they were.[*]

Numerous gold and marble fountains of various designs and sizes were scattered everywhere, and one could easily be

---

[*] Mostly due to bad luck/habits, even successful surgeons sometimes borrow money from the wrong people.

found by a blindfolded person after being spun around a few times and tossing a coin over their shoulder in any direction.

They followed a pebbled path leading to a pair of large wooden doors set in the lower building encircling the main building. The doors creaked open as they arrived, and creaked shut with a dull thump once the party entered, adding to Guy's growing feeling of despair.

Two long, curved hallways ran off to the left and right along the circumference of the building. The group however continued straight up a wide hallway lined with old armour, statues, tapestries, as well as ornately framed paintings – one of which Guy recognised. He however quickly dismissed it as impossible, because the painting was supposed to be in some French museum or something. Nevertheless, the lady sat there, smiling placidly as he walked by. It *had to* be fake.

The hallway opened into a huge rotunda that looked more like the exhibition hall of a museum than anything else, and neither Guy nor Lenny could prevent gravity from tugging at their lower jaw. Guy calculated that the circus's main dome would easily fit within this space, which was filled with all kinds of historical and artistic items either affixed to the encircling wall, standing on the floor, or suspended mid-air. Some were small, while others were quite large, like the old, saucer-shaped ship hovering silently above. Most of the items appeared ancient, and Guy was fairly sure that some of the stony structures were the skeletal remains of various kinds of dinosaur, although none seemed familiar to him. Even more pieces of art hung or stood about, including statues of an array of creatures being ridden triumphantly by other creatures.

While the number of items was impressive, their arrangement wasn't. Everything seemed to have been dumped in any available space on or above the floor. Most of the pieces were displayed somewhat haphazardly, as if someone couldn't decide on a theme, or which piece was more prominent than the other.

Although the aisles crisscrossing the displays tried their best to create some semblance of order, the space felt like a warehouse for the richest yet most disorganised hoarder in the universe.

At the centre of the area, a hollow, circular glass column ran up through the floor and disappeared into the massive, gold-painted domed ceiling above. A shiny, opaque tube descended inside the column, which was clearly an elevator shaft. As the tube came to a silent stop, its doors slid open just as silently, revealing a light-brown Vahltan not much taller than Guy, although he was a lot … girthier.

The newcomer waddled out like a goose wearing tight underwear. Fortunately, it was difficult to tell how tight the Vahltan's underwear was, as his inflated body was mostly covered by white robes with gold embroidery. Another roundish shape followed quietly behind him to stand beside the elevator door, glowering at Andi, who didn't even try to hide his smirk.

"This one of the new ones, Andi?" the white-robed Vahltan enquired with a nod towards Gabbi.

"Yes, sir," Andi said, replacing the smirk with an overly serious expression.

"Well, see that she loses some weight, otherwise she'll find herself lost in the labyrinth, chased by my Le'us. You know I cannot stand the sight of people letting themselves go like that."

Looking at the robed meatball-shaped figure – which he assumed was the man known as *The Man* – logic dictated that Guy not say anything about the hypocritical nature of the comment, especially in the interest of self-preservation. Luckily, his mouth listened and remained shut.

The smirk returned to Andi's face as he glanced at the fast-paling Gabbi.

"No problem, sir," he said. "I'll see to it personally."

"Good, good," the boss nodded and turned to the new arrivals. "Now, where are my manners?"

As he walked over, he patted the golden curls perched on top of his head. It looked like real gold, although it didn't look like real hair, shifting slightly with each pat.

"Captain Phealix," he said in an overly friendly tone, "I trust you had a good trip, and that my men gave you a warm welcome?"

"Yes, thank you, Mr Man," the captain replied.

"Splendid! So that means our business is concluded?"

It was more of a statement than a question.

"Uh, yes, Mr Man, it would seem so," she replied hesitantly.

"Good, good. I wouldn't want to keep you from any other important business that might require your immediate attention."

"Well, Mr Man, we don't really have anything lined up at the mo—"

"Don't be silly now, Captain. I know how busy you and your crew must be, trying to pay off all those debts. I wouldn't want to feel responsible for anything *untoward* happening to you, should those debts suddenly be called in and you couldn't afford to pay up."

The underlying threat seemed evident to the Faylin.

"Of course, sir," she replied. "But we would be happy to assist in getting everything you need from these two. Especially if it would help in paying off some of the debts you so graciously took over. I insist."

"No one should *ever* insist I do anything," The Man hissed, then forced his rigid lips into a smile that didn't touch his eyes. "Besides, I just realised that these packages are *so* valuable that they *more than* cover any outstanding debts. As a matter of fact, it feels like *I* owe *you,* now."

"That's very generous of you, Mr Man. If you're sure?"

"Of course I'm sure. But I suggest you take this opportunity and run with it before I change my mind."

"Yes, certainly, Mr Man," Captain Phealix said with a slight bow. "We are extremely grateful for your generosity, and I'm sure the packages are in capable hands."

The Man turned his back on her to study a nearby statue.

"Don't worry, Captain," he said, "I'll be sure to take care of them."

"Well … then I guess … that's it then," Captain Phealix said to the Vahltan's back, seeming uncertain whether to stay or go.

"Yes, that's it," came the blunt reply, removing any doubt. "*Goodbye*, Captain Phealix."

The captain and her men turned and started walking off. She gave Guy and Lenny one last glance with a hard face but with eyes that seemed to say something different. Although Guy couldn't be *completely* sure, he was *almost* sure they said, "I'm sorry."

CHAPTER 26

When the footsteps of Captain Phealix's procession faded down the hall, Guy felt as though he'd been left standing against a wall to face a firing squad, without a blindfold.

The round figure of The Man continued to study the statue, which depicted an eight-legged creature bearing a muscular Vahltan triumphantly raising a staff or sceptre or some such above his head.

"So, what do you think?" The Man's voice suddenly pierced the silence. He turned around and walked up to the Salamans. "I said, what do you think?"

Guy and Lenny exchanged uncertain glances. "Er …" "Um …" they replied over each other.

"My collection. What do you think of my collection?"

Deciding to leave any references like "cluttered", "hoarder" or "a bit over the top" out of the equation, Guy opted to say something more suitable in the circumstances. "It's, uh, great."

"*Beyond* great," Lenny said in reaction to The Man's narrowing eyes. "Absolutely breathtaking."

The Man circled in place while holding up his hands to indicate his surroundings. "Yes, breathtaking. And do you know how many breaths I had to take from others to acquire some of these pieces?"

"Uh, no, Mr Sir Man … Mr Man," Guy said.

"Let's just say … a lot," said the robed Vahltan with a sinister air of nostalgia that made Guy shudder. "However, contrary to what some might think, I don't necessarily *like* killing; it's merely a means to an end, although the end is sometimes quite mean. Killing is a messy business but, unfortunately, it's also a necessary part of business. Especially in *my* business. It gets you what you need. Now, me – I don't really *need* things, but I do *want* things. Which brings me to the two of you. I understand you might have some … information I want."

Guy shifted under his gaze.

"Well," he said. "I, uh, *we* are not really sure what you need … er, *want* from us, Mr Man. Like I told Captain Phealix, we—"

"Oh, pish," said The Man, waving a hand irritably, and took a seat on a nearby bench. "I got the report, and I know exactly what you told her. It wasn't much. And what you *did* tell her sounded slightly fishy. I hate fish. The truth, however, is something I do like. It's also why I like circles. No matter how big or small a circle is, the end has to link up with where it started. Just like the truth. So why don't you tell me everything you know, then I'll decide whether it's true. Starting with you Mr … Bezam, if I'm correct?"

The Man motioned over two Vahltans, who started dragging Lenny away.

"Where are you taking him?" Guy demanded in a very undemanding tone.

"Don't fret, Mr Bezam," The Man said, leaning back. "Mr Lenny is just going to be shown some of my more gruesome pieces, to help him absorb the reality he's facing. This will also give us some alone time. I find it much easier to get to the truth when it's one on one, without anyone else clouding things, wouldn't you agree?"

"Uh, I guess so," Guy said.

"Good. Shall we begin?"

So, as he didn't really have a choice, Guy began.

•••

Guy wasn't about to tell The Man everything, especially as he didn't know everything, or anything for that matter. However, he had the feeling that The Man's long beak could sniff out a lie when he heard one. So he just told the Vahltan eve-rything from the time he was captured by Kelp and Gacko.

When he finished, The Man studied Guy in a way that made him feel like a lobster in a restaurant's selection tank. Then, with some effort, the Vahltan heaved himself up and strolled to the Salaman.

Although they stayed back, the guards' hands stiffened around their weapons. They appeared ready to strike at a moment's notice should Guy try anything funny, which he didn't, as he didn't know anything funny.

The Man stopped in front of Guy and leaned forward to loom over him with his slight height advantage.

"So," the Vahltan said, "you maintain that you don't know Mr Lenny?"

Guy swallowed hard. "Er, yes, Mr Man. I don't know him from a bar of soap."

The Man frowned. "Hmm. So why then would Kelp and Gacko capture you together?"

"I don't know. I don't even know if I can trust him."

"Trust him with *what*, exactly?"

"Well, just in general, you know? Nothing specific, really. No one seems to believe me when I say I don't know any-thing about anything."

"I want to believe you," The Man said, looming a tad far-ther over Guy, who got the impression that the short Vahltan enjoyed all this looming, not being able to do so with many other people, especially when they were standing. "Believe me, I do. But I get the feeling there's something you're not telling me."

"No, I promise you, there's nothing I can tell you … noth-ing of interest, that is."

"We'll see," the Vahltan said before returning to his seat on the bench and waving a hand. "Take him away, and bring me the other one."

Before Guy could say anything, a guard jammed a weapon into his back and led him away, passing a worried-looking Lenny who was being shoved by another guard towards his own inquisition.

Guy was forced to sit on the cold marble floor, from where he could only watch as The Man talked to the other Salaman about goodness knows what. He just hoped it wouldn't get them into more hot water, although he wasn't sure if that was possible.

At that same moment, on the bank of a river, an army of maggots feasted on the rotting carcass of a fish. For many, this would've been a nasty sight, but for Tina it was the home in which she'd been raised.

It wasn't a very happy home per se, especially seeing as Tina's mom and dad had never gotten her that dead puppy she'd always wanted when she was little. Given, "always" had only been a few days, but still, now it was too late; Tina was all grown up.

Not that Tina really knew who her mom or dad was, although she would have been shocked to learn that the two of them had been killed by George The Horrible, who had devoured them along with a few of her cousins and Uncle Greg. Killed for no good reason other than for George The Horrible to stay alive.

After moving out of her family home, Tina had gone underground as a rebellious teenager, not because she despised her parents for the whole puppy thing, but because it was just what flies were supposed to do.

Now, as she finally emerged from her pupa under the damp soil, she was, at last, a mature woman; an adult with her own wings, giving her the freedom and independence to do what she liked, whenever she liked.

She beat her wings to see if they worked.

They did.

Awesome.

She then looked about her at the mosaic of grass, soil, the sky, some other stuff, and the dead fish with the tiny maggots crawling over it.

"Aww, cute," she said, rubbing her hands excitedly. "I love babies!"

"Want some of your own?" buzzed another fly who had just emerged from a nearby pupa and ogled her expectantly.

At first she thought it would be a good idea; he was kinda cute with those big, green, compound eyes. But there was a world out there to explore, and she didn't want to be bogged down right now.

"Thanks, er …"

"Jeff."

"Yeah, thanks, Jeff, but I'm not looking for anything … permanent right now."

"Who said anything about *permanent?*" Jeff buzzed, rubbing his front legs vigorously.

Tina wasn't sure if she should be offended or flattered, although instinct preferred the latter.

"Don't get me wrong, Jeff," she said, "I think you're very handsome, but there's a big new world waiting for me out there. And for you. I hope you understand. I tell you what, though: in a few days, if I'm still single and you're still single, we can definitely hook up. Till later then!"

With that, Tina took off, leaving behind a flustered Jeff, who had just gotten his first taste of romantic rejection. She flew around for a while until she spotted a body of water surrounded by strange-looking shapes that attracted her attention.

As she flew closer, she instinctively recognised one of the shapes. It was a flower.

Pretty, she thought. And it smells good too.

She landed on a petal, intrigued by the welcoming rotten-flesh aroma that drew her closer. Little did she know that this was a carnivorous plant that would slowly digest her over the course of the next week were she to crawl inside.

Fortunately, she escaped this cruel fate as she was snatched by the lightning-fast tongue of a frog, who mercifully prevented Tina's drawn-out expiration by expiring her within a couple of seconds.

Unfortunately for George The Horrible (or just George, to his friends), as he hopped away, he was still feeling a bit peckish.

At that same moment, The Man gestured to Guy's guard, who yanked him up and led him back to the boss, still parked on the bench like a flabby cloud.

"It seems as though your stories are aligned, Mr Bezam," the Vahltan said. "At least parts of it."

"It's the truth," Guy stated with conviction. At least *he* was convinced of the authenticity of his own version of events. Lenny, on the other hand, was a different story.

"So you say," The Man said, this time getting up with the aid of two henchmen, and waddled closer. "But there's truth, and then there's *the* truth. You see, I'm very good at spotting a lie, and while I'm sure that what you told me was indeed true, you're definitely hiding something. Captain Phealix said you were a bit vague, and it seems she was right. But it doesn't really matter; over the years, I've developed certain techniques to act as a failsafe against fibbers and those un-willing to tell the whole truth."

"You're going to torture us?" Lenny said. "But we've told you everything we know!" This last part was accompanied by a nervous yet hopeful glance at an equally nervous yet less-hopeful Guy.

"Torture?" The Man mused. "Yes, that certainly is one way of getting to the bottom of things, especially if I lowered you into my snake pit."

He glared at them as if to give them some time to digest what he'd just said, which Guy did, leaving him with an up-set stomach.

"But no, gentlemen," the Vahltan continued, "fortunately – or maybe *un*fortunately – for you, I have recently devel-oped a specific technique that you might say is foolproof. As a matter of fact, I simply cannot wait to try it out on the two of you."

With a savage yet excited gleam in his eyes, The Man signalled for his guards, who manhandled the Salamans into the elevator behind their boss. The doors closed and the elevator started its descent into a place that probably was – according to Guy's overactive imagination – the pits of hell.

CHAPTER 27

Mind probes aren't fiction. They're perfectly real, like Santa[*] and those little grey men[†] that stole farmer Johnson's cow in Derbyshire last summer.

Mind probes don't work that well on cows. Firstly, you need a certain level of intelligence for the technology to work, which, ironically, also rules out a (not so) surprising number of politicians who were the initial targets of such probes. Secondly, the data gathered from the handful of intelligent cows out there never yielded the most interesting results, unless you're interested in their opinion on the size, shape and sound of different cowbells, or whether cud tastes better than grass.

Mind probes are also not a one-size-fits-all solution, not just because various species have various head shapes, sizes, and locations, but also because of the various brain patterns among various species and subspecies. And even if you had

---

[*] This is probably not the same Santa you're thinking of. The Santa mentioned here works as an accountant for one of Unyun's top accounting firms, Mor & Porely. He does have a beard, but he doesn't have a sleigh. He takes a bus to work. Apologies to those who got excited by the prospect of resubmitting your Christmas wish list and getting that four-decades-overdue BMX. You can try, but it's doubtful you'll get it. If you are indeed thinking of the Santa mentioned here, you're welcome to submit your tax returns during business hours, but please don't start your Gee-mail with "Dear Santa". He doesn't like that.

[†] These are exactly the ones you're thinking of.

two subjects from the same species or subspecies, the results could still vary significantly. So, to get the best results, you need three ingredients: lots of money, a brilliant doctor, and a fair amount of patience.

Manni Karpachio had two out of the three. Money wasn't a problem, and he'd had quite a few brilliant doctors who were no longer with him – or with anyone – mainly due to him running out of the third ingredient too quickly.

However, Manni *did* quite like Dr Snyer, not just because he was the best doctor he'd ever had, but also because of his sublime work on the hedges outside. He was a true artist. So Manni gave him a bit more rope than the others before him, whose ropes had not been quite long enough for their feet to touch the ground during their final moments.

A few months ago, Dr Snyer – who'd been a brain surgeon before filling the work-off-your-debts-or-die vacancy with The Man – had finally managed to get the probe working. And after extensive testing on people who owed Manni money as well as on underachieving henchmen, the machine was finally ready; just in time for the most important interrogation of Manni's life. Yes, Dr Snyer was a keeper, but Manni couldn't keep him. Although he'd miss the surgeon's steady hand in the garden, he knew too much. It was a shame, really.

•••

Guy didn't know the first thing about mind probes nor, for that matter, the second thing or anything after that. The only thing that had ever probed Guy's mind was the glare from his editor when she suspected him of not being truthful with her, which was most of the time. Oh, yes, and beer. His mind had been probed by copious amounts of beer on numerous occasions, quite successfully. Descending in the elevator, he wished he'd had one now to oil his nerves of steel, which were rusted beyond repair after a lifetime of neglect.

As the elevator came to a stop, he and Lenny were paraded out by a grinning Andi and a despondent Gabbi, who poked Guy extra hard in the back with her weapon, as if he was the source of her newfound despondency.

"Move it," she grated, using her weapon like a cattle prod to force the resistant Salamans out of the elevator.

Stretched out before them was a long, white hallway, down which they were herded unceremoniously, passing a few intersecting corridors and unmarked doors. Guy was convinced that he'd just heard a muffled yet agonising scream coming from behind one of the doors, and shivered. He tried to convince himself that it hadn't been a scream, but he didn't buy it, so he shivered some more as the procession moved on.

At the end of the hallway, they reached a door which slid open as Andi touched a panel, and they were jostled inside. Apart from a few armed Vahltans standing guard, the white room's walls were lined with counters and fridges, all neatly packed and stocked with medical equipment and containers. At the centre of the room, a computerised pedestal faced a half-circle of four chair-like beds that made Guy think of his last horrific visit to the dentist.[*]

A door opened to the side, revealing a dark Vahltan in white scrubs who entered with a sombre look. The Man waddled up to him and whispered something in his ear, which Guy could to some degree of certainty say was *not* sweet nothings.

The scrubbed Vahltan nodded, then motioned with his head towards the beds. The guards slammed the struggling Salamans onto the two central beds before strapping their limbs with built-in restraints.

The doctor's sombre expression deepened as he leaned over Guy. "My name is Dr Snyer," he whispered. "I know you're scared, but I'll try my best to make this as painless as possible. Just try to relax – it will all be over soon. Now, I recommend you keep still."

A guard enforced the recommendation by grabbing Guy's head and holding it in place. The doctor produced an injector and held it against Guy's neck. It went *tsssh* and Guy went

---

[*] If there's any other way of visiting a dentist, it is yet to be discovered.

"Aargh!" as pain flared at the injection site. He went limp for a moment before searing pain flashed through his body, causing it to spasm uncontrollably. After a few agonising seconds, the spasms subsided, leaving him panting and completely disorientated.

Through a haze of jumbled thoughts, Guy heard a cry of pain coming from somewhere else as his mind drifted off to a cloudy wonderland.

• • •

"Mr Bezam."

The voice, sounding familiar yet strange, echoed from some distant place, penetrating the soft mist surrounding Guy. A zebra-unicorn galloped past, carrying a clown that clung on to its mane for dear life with one hand; not because he was falling off, but because he was falling *up* thanks to the gigantic bunch of balloons held in the other hand. His happy-painted expression couldn't quite hide the panic that sent ripples of fear through the face underneath.

Stupid clown, Guy thought, why don't you just let go?

"Mr Bezam," the oddly familiar voice repeated, getting closer, or louder, or both. The zebra and clown were suddenly yanked upwards, disappearing into the mist above.

"Mr Bezam, can you hear me?" the voice now said from directly behind Guy's ear, and he swung around to see a terrifying amount of nothing. It would have been less terrifying if there actually *had* been something, because nothing shouldn't be saying anything. It simply wasn't natural.

"Wha … whe … wha …?" he tried with a mouthful of peanut butter, or what *felt* like a mouthful of peanut butter.

"I said, can you hear me?" the voice repeated, this time at a more respectable distance. Or so it seemed; distance is very difficult to judge when you're standing in a cloud.[*]

---

[*] Do not try this at home. Or above it. Or anywhere else, for that matter. Standing in a cloud should never be attempted without the aid of an experienced professional. However, if you *do* find a living, breathing professional with said experience, you'd be wise not to trust their CV.

"Yth," Guy said floatingly.

"Hold on," the voice said.

Guy heard buttons being pushed. Why were there buttons in a cloud?

"Can you try that again, Mr Bezam?" the voice returned.

"Yes," Guy repeated, with the peanut butter having magically melted away.

"Good," the voice said. "You're doing very well."

"Thanks, but what am I *supposed* to be doing?" Guy said, looking about hazily and, quite frankly, not really feeling like doing anything.

"You need to step outside, Mr Bezam."

"Outside where?"

"Outside that place."

"What place?"

"The place you're in now."

"But I don't even *know* where I am."

"You're inside your mind, Mr Bezam. I need you to step outside of it."

"You want me to go out of my mind?"

"In a manner of speaking, yes."

Guy's mind tried to process the peculiar instruction and came to the conclusion that it wasn't comfortable with the notion of leaving itself.

"I don't *like the sound of this,"* Guy's mind confirmed its stance on the issue from the opposite side of the voice.

"Neither do I," Guy said. "Sounds risky."

"Mr Bezam," the voice said in a serious tone from the other side, "the longer you stay in there, the more difficult it will be to get you out."

"That doesn't sound good," Guy said.

"No, it doesn't, Mr Bezam, and believe me, it *isn't*. If you don't come out soon, you may be trapped in there forever."

"That sounds even worse!"

"Don't listen to him," Guy's mind said offhandedly. *"You know doctors; always exaggerating. Remember that doctor who told you to stop binge-drinking?"*

"Yes."

"Well, you're still alive, aren't you? So why would you listen to Dr Know-It-All over there?"

"Hey!" the voice said indignantly from the other side, then forced itself into calmness. "Trust me, Mr Bezam, you do *not* want to be stuck inside your mind for the rest of your life."

"Good point," Guy agreed.

"No, it's not a good point," his mind argued. *"Who knows you better than me, eh? We'll have tons of fun! I have a whole itinerary drawn up. More clowns, more zebras, and pretty girls and ... ooh, yes, and beer. Lots and lots of beer!"*

After a contemplative pause, Guy gave a mental sigh. "As good as that sounds, it's not a good idea."

"Why not?"

"Because I get bored too easily, which is something *I* would have known."

"But if you just look at my itinerary, you'd see how much fun we'll have if you stick around."

"Well, that's another reason why I can't stay."

"What?"

"I *hate* itineraries! I would have known that too."

There was a moment of silence before his mind tried something else. *"I have freshly baked brownies in the oven and cold beers in the fridge."*

"They don't go well together. Come on, you're beginning to sound desperate, now."

"Of course I am! Do you know *how lonely it gets in here?"*

"Yes, and that's just the way I like it."

"But—"

"Okay," Guy said, holding up a mental hand to shush his mind. "How do I get out of here?"

"Just follow the sound of my voice," the voice said from the side. Guy turned that way and started walking, causing the top of his body to double over. Apparently, his legs hadn't received the memo about the whole walking thing.

"Hey, I can't move!" he cried.

"Just force yourself out, Mr Bezam," the voice said with a note of anxiousness.

Guy tried in vain to move his right leg forward.

"I can't!" he yelled as panic grabbed hold of him.

"You have to try, Mr Bezam!" the voice pleaded. "Don't give up!"

Guy jerked about as if he was stuck in waist-high mud.

"Fantastic!" his mind rejoiced from behind, accompanied by excited mental clapping. *"We're going to have a whale of a time, you and I. Just listen to what I've got planned."*

There was a mental rustle of paper behind Guy, which he could only assume was the dreaded itinerary. Transforming his panic into dogged determination, Guy forced his right leg to inch forward, followed by the left. Slowly but surely, he waded his way through the mental sludge.

"Hey, how did you do that?" said his mind, now with its own hint of panic. *"Wait, don't leave! We can be best friends, I promise!"*

This just forced Guy to wade faster in the direction the other voice had come from.

"Really, we'd be best buds!"

Guy almost turned around to say something, but then thought better of it. He didn't want to lose momentum and find himself unable to move again, perhaps permanently this time – especially as his legs seemed to grow heavier with every foot gained.

So he merely shouted over his shoulder, "No, we won't!"

"Why not?" his mind shouted back, growing fainter.

"Because if there's one thing I know, it's that I don't like myself that much!"

With that – before his legs gave out completely – he gave one final, hard push, and found himself falling out of the cloud and into darkness.

•••

"Mr Bezam," said the familiar voice from earlier. "Are you okay?"

Guy opened his eyes and squinted at a dark face hovering above him. His eyelids fluttered as a light was beamed into each of his pupils.

"I … um, yes, I'm … *great*," he said.

He was indeed feeling great, as if waking up from a bad dream and stepping into a more pleasant one. His mind seemed to float somewhere far away. Hopefully far enough, he thought dreamily.

"Where am I?" he asked in a daze.

"You're in a safe place, Mr Bezam," the voice said, sounding relieved.

With the light removed, Guy's eyes tried to readjust, but his vision kept swimming. He didn't mind that too much, though. It was strangely pleasant. He looked around at the blurry, white medical room he'd been in earlier. Or was he *still* there? Oh well, it didn't really matter. Everything felt great, which was a bit weird, because for some reason he was sure it shouldn't be feeling great. He couldn't recall why, though, as everything just felt so … great.

His blurry gaze took in a blurry figure lying on the bed next to him.

"Lenny?" he asked. His voice also sounded a bit blurry. "Lenny, is that you?"

"Yeah," came an equally blurry reply. "Yeah, it's me. At least I *think* it's me."

"You okay?"

"Yeah, I'm great. How are *you*?"

"I'm great too."

"That's great."

"I think they're ready, sir," said the blurry figure, whom Guy vaguely recognised as doctor Snyer. He stood back as a shorter, rounder blurry figure stepped forward.

"That's great, I mean good," said the figure, whom Guy vaguely recognised as The Man. Again, Guy had the feeling he should be afraid of this person, but he wasn't.

"Now, Mr Bezam, I'd like you to tell me everything about yourself," The Man said. He had a nice voice and seemed really nice. See, no reason to be afraid.

"Well," Guy said euphorically, "my mom and dad met in a pub, which is perhaps why I like pubs so much. Pubs are great. For long, my dad had tried to get into my mom's pants. Then, one evening, they got drunk and—"

"Not *everything*, you imbecile," The Man said irritably, although he still sounded very nice, no matter how mean he tried to sound.

"Oh, okay," Guy said happily. "What would you like to know? I'll tell you anything. You seem really nice."

The Man looked up at the doctor, who shrugged nervously.

"Apologies, sir," the physician said. "The dose might have been a bit strong. It's not an exact science. But at least he's cooperating."

Shaking his head, The Man proceeded. "Let's start with the assassination of the Presidor."

"Oh, that!" Guy said gleefully. "Yeah, I heard about that. Very sad."

"What do you mean you *heard* about it?"

"Well, I wasn't exactly around when it happened."

"What do you mean you *weren't around?*"

"Well, I wasn't exactly … *me*."

"What the fhark are you on about?" The Man exclaimed, looking up at the doctor, who was at a loss for words.

Guy giggled. "Weeeelll, I was kinda … someone else."

"What? Who *were* you?"

"I was actually *Guy*, and before you say anything, I know what you're going to say, but none of that is it. My *name* is Guy. Guy Leatherman. Nice to meet you. No, really, it is. You're a nice man."

"Hey!" Lenny interjected euphorically from the side. "*I* know a Guy Leatherman. He's a great guy." He giggled. "Excuse the pun … or not." He giggled again, and Guy felt so great that he joined in.

The Man walked over to Lenny's chair.

"I don't care what his real name is. I *know* you know each other, Mr Lenny."

"Oh, sorry, Lenny isn't *my* real name either. It's *Neville*."

CHAPTER 28

"Hey!" Guy semi-exclaimed semi-excitedly. "*I* know a Neville. Neville Andersman. Maybe your Guy and my Neville know each other."

"I don't think so," Lenny-Neville said. "*My* Guy is more of the human variety."

"Oh, yes," Guy said semi-sadly. "You're right. Sorry, I wasn't thinking."

"That's too bad," Lenny-Neville said. "I think we could have been great friends, especially seeing as we already have friend-names in common. It's a great start, though."

"Great indeed," Guy said. "But I don't think I have enough space in my life for more than one best friend at a time. Sorry."

"Yeah, *my* Guy is the same. Between his job and our nights out at the pub, there isn't much time for him to make any other friends either. Or so he says."

"Wow," Guy said. "He sounds like a bit of a loser."

"Hey," Lenny-Neville said semi-angrily, "don't talk about my friend like that. He *really* is a great guy, even if he doesn't know it himself. He just doesn't have much luck. The last time I saw him, his car had broken down, again, and I had to help him out, again."

"Wow," Guy repeated. "I have a car like that too. Fortunately, *my* friend Neville is a traffic cop, so he helps me out plenty."

"What a coincidence, *I'm* a traffic officer too!"

"My word, that *is* a coincidence! No wait, I thought you were a street sweeper."

"No … I mean, yes, but originally I was a traffic officer."

"On Unyun?"

"No, in Johannesburg."

Guy wished he could scratch his head to emphasise his confusion.

"That can't be right," he said. "There aren't any Salamans in Joburg. At least not that I know of."

"True, but I'm not really a Salaman," Lenny-Neville said. "Well, I am now … but not originally. I am, originally, a human."

"Hey, I'm originally a human too!"

There was a moment of silence, for which The Man was extremely grateful. He rubbed his neck from trying to follow the tennis-match conversation, which he'd wanted to stop but didn't, mainly because he had hoped something useful would slip out.

Something clicked somewhere in the haze of Guy's mind, which had given up in trying to make friends with him and reverted to its normal role of Technical Support.

"Neville?" he said.

"Guy?" came the reply.

"Great to see you again."

"Yep, great. Really great."

"Enough!" The Man exclaimed, rubbing his neck some more. "What's going on here?"

"That's Neville," Guy said.

"That's Guy," just-Neville said almost at the same time.

"I don't care!" The Man screamed. "What does this have to do with anything?"

"Well, I'm a human called Guy," Guy said happily.

"And I'm a human called Neville," Neville added happily.

The man tugged hard at his golden curls, sending some dislodged gold flakes flying in all directions. "But you are *Salamans!*"

"Yes, but we're *originally* human," Guy said. "I just recently became a Salaman."

"What the fhark do you mean?" The Man said as more shiny flakes drifted to the floor.

"Well," Guy said, unfazed by the Vahltan's frustration, "I was placed in this body by Mr Gray."

"Mr Gray?" said The Man, whose wig was very close to joining the gold flakes on the floor. "Who the fhark is *Mr Gray*?"

"Oh, yes, sorry, you wouldn't know him," Guy said. "He works for the, uh, *Life Spectacular* company."

The Man suddenly stopped his hair-pulling and looked at Guy like a cat spotting a mouse twice his size.

"What did you say?" he asked.

"The *Life Spectacular* company. They take people and put them in others and then they—"

"I *know* what the *Life Spectacular Life-enrichment Programme* is about, you twat!" The Man snapped.

That wasn't so nice, Guy thought. However, The Man was so nice that he immediately decided to forgive him.

"I'm in the circus, you know," he continued dreamily, despite the rude command. "It's a really great circus. They're on Grassi Nole now. It's a nice place. Nice people. You'd like it. And I didn't even have to run away from home to join the circus. Although, when I was little, I'd always thought about it, but—"

"Shut up!"

"Okay."

"And what about you?" The Man asked Neville.

"I'm not in the circus," Neville replied. "It would have been great, though."

"I mean, are you also in the programme?" The Man grated.

Despite his confinement, Neville managed a small shrug.

"Not sure," he said cheerfully. "The one moment I was Neville, the next I was Lenny. I'm not in the circus. Did I say that already? In any case, I sweep streets now. It's nothing fancy, but it's great."

The Man whirled and started to pace the room, muttering to himself, before he suddenly stopped.

"Could it have been *him*?" he said to himself.

"No, it *couldn't* have," he rejected it hopefully.

"Or *could* it?" he second-guessed his rejection.

His self-conversation went on, which might have seemed strange to anyone not floating around in a world of drugged-up bliss, where *strange* is the norm.

"Who else?"

"There aren't a lot of people who could pull this off without *me* knowing."

"It *cannot* be a coincidence."

"No, it can't. It *must* be him."

"Yes," he finally seemed to convince himself.

"It's *definitely* him."

•••

"Aargh!"

Guy wondered why Neville sounded so pained, as he himself still felt great.

Shortly after that, the doctor bent over Guy with an injector. No one had to hold Guy's head steady this time, as he felt very compliant. And as the device went *tsssh*, Guy didn't go *aargh!* Neville should really stop being such a ba—

"Aargh!" he went when full consciousness suddenly flooded his mind and informed him that the injection had in fact been quite painful. He then calmed down a bit. But just a bit, because other things started flooding back into his mind, like where he was, and with whom.

The doctor produced another injector.

"Apologies in advance for this," he said, depressing the device on Guy's arm, "but it's necessary to facilitate your transition. But don't worry, this one isn't going to hurt a bit."

The doctor was right. It didn't hurt at all. Guy tried to say as much, but his mouth suddenly went from peanut-buttery to rubbery to completely numb, followed by the rest of his body and mind.

•••

When Guy's consciousness returned, he found himself staring at the bottom of a white bunk. He felt somewhat groggy, but he supposed it could have been worse. He sat up slowly, facing an entirely familiar scene. However, apart from the now-tiresome sight of a cell, at least this one was immaculate; completely white, without a speck of dirt.

Nevertheless, he was fuming.

"Fhark!" he exclaimed, just to drive the point home.

"As I recall, you usually don't swear much," came a voice from the bed above, followed by a face that didn't belong to his friend. Not really.

"Neville!" Guy said, all anger forgotten for the moment. "I … what … how—"

Neville held up his hands. "Whoa, slow down, bud! This is news to me too."

"Come down here!" Guy said, getting up as his friend dropped down.

"I'd love to say it's good to see you, but this is a bit weird," Neville said, looking Guy up and down.

"*Everything's* a bit weird, Nev. But if that's truly you, things just got a lot more bearable."

"Same here, Bez— Guy. Sorry, it's just strange to call you by your real name while you're looking like … *that*."

"Well, you don't look much better."

There was a moment of awkward silence, which was broken by Neville.

"Come here, you!" he said and pulled Guy closer for a long hug, which was followed by another moment of awkwardness.

"This is getting a bit awkward," Guy said, pulling back. "Don't get me wrong, I'm over the moon to see you, and maybe over a few galaxies and what not. But you know the rule of bro-hug."

"I know, I know, never longer than two seconds," Neville said, pulling him back again. "But how often do I actually listen to you?"

"Good point," Guy said, enjoying the next few seconds before they parted.

"Okay," Neville said, smiling, "awkwardness attained. But I thought I'd never see you again, bud, or Earth for that matter."

"I'm glad I could be of service on the first," Guy said. "But I'm afraid we cannot bank on the second. Things aren't looking too rosy for us making it back home … or out of here alive, for that matter."

"I'd put money on it," a voice said from the other side of the force field, making them jump.

The swimsuit-model-challenged Vahltan, Gabbi, put a tray into a slot in the wall. She pushed a button, upon which the tray was transferred to a slot inside the cell. She did the same with another tray.

"I haven't been here long," she continued, "but from what I hear, not many who are brought down here make it out alive. Sorry."

She didn't look sorry.

"Now take your grub and eat it!" she added, before walking out.

"Well, I'm not hungry!" Guy shouted after her as the door closed.

"I bet *she* is, though," Neville said drily, which caused both of them to burst out laughing, possibly more than they would have in normal circumstances.

After calming down, Guy said, "I'm serious, though. I'm not in the mood to eat anything. Besides, they might have poisoned our food."

Neville shook his head.

"If they wanted to kill us," he said, "I doubt this is the way they would do it. I get the feeling The Man is more of the hands-on type, or at least the type that likes watching his men get hands-on. Besides, whether you want to or not, you really *should* eat something. We don't know what's lying ahead of us, and we may need all the strength we can get."

Guy knew his friend was right. He walked up to the slot to collect a plate and cup made from rubber, presumably to prevent prisoners from using them as tools or weapons. Sitting down at the head of the bed, he started eating without putting too much effort into it. Having collected his own food, Neville joined him.

Guy got about halfway through his meal, but couldn't stomach any more of the dry bread and the vile brown-green slop. Even the water – if that's what it was – had an oily aftertaste. He pushed his tray aside.

"Well," he sighed, "we heard it from the horse's mouth – we're done for."

"Hey, *that* horse wouldn't make it out of the gates at the July."

Guy would have laughed if it hadn't been for reality leaving an even worse taste in his mouth than the food.

"I suppose there's nothing much we can do about it now, huh?" he said solemnly.

"No," Neville replied, "but that's why I'm not going to let it bother me too much. It's not over till the fat lady sings."

In Guy's head, he could however hear her backstage doing the whole *do-re-mi* thing, or whatever it was that opera singers did to warm up before a performance. But he didn't say it out loud, because Neville deserved to cling on to his hope. In any case, with his friend's usual glass-half-full attitude, he wasn't sure he'd be able to bring Nev down even if he tried.

So he decided to change the subject. "What are the odds of us both winning that competition?"

"Wouldn't know," Neville shrugged. "I don't even know what competition you're talking about."

Guy was a bit baffled by this, but explained it to Neville as best he could from what he could remember. Once done, Neville took a moment to contemplate.

"By the sound of it," he finally said, "I'd say our chances were slim to none to insanely impossible. But why don't *I* know about any of this?"

"Not sure," Guy said. "Didn't Mr Gray explain it to you?"

"Never met a Mr Gray. I just know that, on the last day I saw you, I woke up to a bright light coming from my bathroom. I opened the door, walked in, and the next moment I woke up in a dirty little apartment on Unyun, not knowing where I was, or why I'd shrunk, or how I'd received such a bad sunburn along with some … other strange features."

"Yeah," Guy said with a wry smile, "it's odd for me to be able to look you in the eye. In fact, I think I might be half an inch taller than you, now."

"You wish."

"Don't have to, for a change. But how did you become a street sweeper?"

Neville shrugged. "Hey, you know me. If you don't know something, find out. I started with my neighbour, a hairy fellow who couldn't understand me. And I couldn't understand him. He must have figured out that something was wrong, because he called some sort of ambulance service. After more communication failures, they injected me with something, after which I could understand them."

"Yeah, that would be the *vernaculites*," Guy said, proud to know something. "They're like tiny little robots that translate stuff."

"So I gathered, although it didn't help much in understanding anything else. I went back to the neighbour, and told him I'd bumped my head and couldn't remember anything, which is why I'd acted so strangely before. He said my name was Lenny, and that I worked for the local municipality. He was nice enough to hail me a taxi and told the driver where to take me. So that's how I became a street sweeper. Oh, and apparently I – or rather Lenny – is from a planet called Kilihiri."

"Hey, me too!" Guy said. "Or at least that's what Cortex told me."

"Cortex?"

"He's a new friend. You'd like him."

"I don't think I trust him."

"Why not?"

"Well, he's friends with you, isn't he?" Neville grinned. "Besides, since when do you have friends other than me?"

"Since I joined the circus."

Neville shook his head. "I still can't believe it. The circus! Tell me everything."

So Guy told him everything, and Neville squeezed out every bit of detail he could. They also spoke at length about their new lives as well as their old ones. Eventually, when fatigue finally demanded action, Neville snailed back onto the top bunk.

"Think we'll make it out of this in one piece?" Guy asked, and punctuated it with a big yawn.

"I can't see any other way for us to make it," Neville said, adding a drawn-out yawn of his own.[*]

I wish I could share Neville's optimism, Guy thought, because he sure didn't believe it himself. But as he drifted off to sleep, he also kept this thought to himself.

---

[*] Contrary to the belief that contagious yawning is a result of empathy or social harmony, Unyun's psychological fraternity have recently started speculating that it's actually an inherent form of highly competitive, subconscious dominance found in many species, including hippos. Just reading about it can instinctively send you into a fierce bout of yawning, which is why about half of you are yawning right now. But rest assured, the symptoms should abate shortly. Warning: If you are highly susceptible to contagious/competitive yawning, please refrain from reading about it again.

CHAPTER 29

Somewhere during the night, Guy got up to relieve his bladder of some excess pressure. Everything was dark except for the glow of the force field, which emitted a soft light along with its soft hum.

As he plodded to the loo, the corner of his eye caught movement where the guard was standing guard. His mind, however, was too tired to focus on anything other than his immediate goal, so he proceeded to perform an impressively long emptying process, although he didn't seem too impressed by it himself, judging by the deep yawn he gave.[*] Once done, he shuffled over to the basin to wash his hands to the sound of a soft *whack* and *thud*, before making his way back to the bed. This time, the corner of his eye caught sight of the guard on the floor, and he dropped back onto his bed.

Guy's eyes kept trying to tell him something about something their corners had seen, and kept prodding him until he forced them open to see what all the fuss was about. At first, his dry gaze didn't see much. Things were suddenly darker

---

[*] You've been warned about the dangers of competitive yawning, so no liability will be accepted for any past, present or future yawning, nor for any loss, damage or injury that may (or may have) occur(ed) from said activity. The full disclaimer can be obtained from the Unyun Bar Association, who will provide you with a free copy. If you'd rather forget about the whole thing, you can also contact the other Unyun Bar Association, who will provide you with a free drink. Not to try and sway you or anything, but most people go for the second option.

than a minute earlier, presumably because the force field was now down for some reason. Next to him, an even darker shape moved slightly.

A chill passed through Guy as his eyes swivelled to the side of the bed, over which a big, dark figure now loomed. He pulled in a breath, but a shadowy hand shot out and clamped itself over his mouth, trapping the scream that had been planning its desperate escape a second ago.

•••

"Shhh!" a voice commanded.

So Guy did the opposite. "Mmm mmm mmmm!" he yelled into the hand holding his mouth shut and kicked about wildly in an attempt to free himself.

"Shhhhhh!" the voice hissed with a bit more vigour. "You're going to get us killed."

Joining his kicking legs, Guy's instinct kicked in. He bit down hard on the hand, which was promptly snatched away with a restrained yelp, followed by a dull smack as a rearing head struck the top bunk. The dark figure jumped back and took a moment to rub its head before advancing again. However, the pause had given Guy enough time to flop off the bunk and roll underneath it.

Guy watched the figure's feet approaching, and then saw the rest of the dark shape dropping to the floor, grappling at his flailing limbs. A hand caught one of Guy's legs and started dragging him out before suddenly letting go with muted curses.

All Guy could see was the figure's feet shuffling about in all directions, and he took the opportunity to scramble out from under the bunk. He sprung to his feet and was about to start running when realisation hit him that Neville was still trapped on the top bunk.

Self-preservation and friendship had a very quick debate over the pros and cons of sticking around. Self-preservation soon realised it had forgotten its notes at home, and that it didn't stand a chance of winning the debate in any case. Which is why Guy's self-preservation just sighed and waited with apprehension for him to jump onto the dark figure's back. Guy was about to do exactly that, when he noticed the space was already occupied by another, smaller dark shape, which was frantically trying to hold on while landing small but painful punches.

With a quick glance at the empty bunk above, Guy concluded that the smaller shape had to be Neville. His friend wasn't even remotely as big and strong as he was in his human form, but from the looks of it, he was giving it a good go regardless. Without anything else to latch onto, Guy lunged forward to hug the bigger figure's legs, pulling them together with all this strength.

The intruder toppled over with an "Oooomf!"

Neville let go as soon as the figure struck the floor and took position on its chest. "Don't make a move," he grated, "or I'll pop your eyes out."

Guy let go of the legs and inched himself closer to the attacker's head, which Neville now gripped with both hands, thumbs on eyes.

"Yeah, he'll pop them *right out*," Guy said determinedly, although he was also determined to throw up should this actually happen. He had to force down the sick feeling rising in his throat as he added, "Who are you?"

"I'll tell you," the figure said, "but can you *please* keep it down?"

"Why?" Neville said. "Afraid your Vahltan brothers will come down here and see that you've been overpowered by two tiny Salamans?"

"They're *not* my brothers!" the figure hissed. "I'm not a Vahltan!"

"I don't care what you are," Neville said. "Scum like you come in all shapes and sizes. If you were sent to kill us, I'd suggest they send someone else to finish the job."

"I don't think you should *suggest* that!" Guy said in exasperation.

"Neither do I," the figure on the floor agreed.

"That's good, you filth …" Guy began, glad to have someone in his corner, before the corner became crowded with confusion. "Uh, what?"

Avoiding any sudden movements that might get his eyes popped accidentally, the figure pointed to the guard lying next to the door. "If I was *with them*, why would I have taken *him* out?" he said.

Neville looked at where he was pointing.

"Oh," he said.

"Oh," Guy echoed. "Er, yes, I forgot about that."

"You mean you *saw* that?" Neville asked incredulously.

"Well, yes," Guy replied, "but in my defence, I was virtually asleep. And besides, this can just be some ruse to catch us off guard and kill us in any case."

"Why in Zolt's name would I do that?" the figure grated. "If The Man wanted to kill you, you'd be dead already. And he'd want you to *know* what was coming before it came so you could see it coming."

Guy thought about what he'd seen and heard of The Man, and couldn't come up with a viable argument.

"If you're not here to kill us," Neville said, "then why *are* you here?"

"To … rescue … you," the figure wheezed, because that's the type of thing that happens when your windpipe is suddenly obstructed by a Salaman knee pressing into it.[*]

"And why should we believe you?" Neville said, putting a little more force into his knee-choke.

"Do you … mind?" the figure wheezed harder, tapping Neville's leg. "It's a bit … difficult … to talk … without … oxy- … -gen."

"Fine," Neville said calmly, "but if you try to call for help, I'll still crush your eyes like grapes. Got it?"

The figure coughed as the Salaman removed his knee.

"So, why should we believe you?" Neville repeated.

"The short answer is that you *don't* have to believe me," the figure said, taking a deep breath. "But what if you don't? You want to stay *here*?"

---

[*] Non-Salaman knees may yield the same result, but please don't test this on anyone, especially not anyone you actually like. It's bad manners.

"Well, I was just getting cosy," Neville said stubbornly. "That bed isn't so bad."

"Well," the figure countered, "the bed about three doors down the hall is anything but cosy, and I'm sure there's still some blood left on it from its previous occupant."

Guy gulped, recalling the screaming he'd heard from behind one of the doors earlier on.

"And *I'm* sure you're exaggerating," Neville said, sounding as if he was trying to convince himself more than anyone else. He must have heard the screams too.

"Wish I was," the figure said. "People who've had first-hand experience with The Man usually don't have a second hand any longer. And those are the ones lucky enough to have made it out alive. But I take it you've met The Man by now, haven't you? What's your gut feeling about him?"

After a moment's silence, Guy sighed. "That we may not have guts left by tomorrow."

"Don't listen to this guy!" Neville hissed at his friend.

"The Man is pure evil rolled into a bad-guy bun," Guy said. "But you've always had an instinct when it comes to the true nature of people, Nev. What's it telling you?"

After a pause, Neville relented, "You're right, we're screwed."

"Yep. Our chances of getting out of here alive are basically nonexistent. Even the guard said as much."

Neville looked at his friend's shadowy shape. He knew that Guy, with his lifelong experience in bad luck, was an expert in worse-case scenarios. If a bad option was better than a worse option, it was still better, albeit still bad. With that in mind, he merely nodded.

"Would you mind getting off me, now?" the figure said.

Neville got up reluctantly and stepped over to where Guy was standing, which was now – due to self-preservation taking its rightful place on the throne again – a couple of steps farther back from where he'd been standing earlier.

"Thanks," the figure said, rubbing his throat tenderly. "Now can we *please* get out of here?"

"We still don't know who you are or what you want," Neville said. "So forgive us for not being all that eager to follow your orders."

The stranger seemed to measure them for a moment before reaching a decision with a slight nod. He crouched down, causing Guy and Neville to rear back against the cell's wall.

"Sorry," the now-eye-level figure said, holding out a hand that was only stared at, so he pulled it back. "My name is Max. As for exactly who I am and why I'm here, we don't have time. Other guards will be doing the rounds, so we'd better get going. Just do what I say and we might just make it out of here with all our guts and limbs intact. Got it?"

Guy and Neville nodded and watched as the figure of the man called Max slipped out the door.

A moment later, the figure of the man called Max slipped back in. "Are … you … coming?" he grated impatiently.

Only after Neville started moving did Guy manage to force himself forward.

The dark figure of Max shook his head and mumbled something that had the air of a curse, before he slipped out once more, followed by two smaller dark figures that moved with the grace and courage of tin men approaching a trash compactor.

CHAPTER 30

The hallway was dark too, and Guy nearly tripped over the legs of another guard slumped against a wall. Biting back a yelp, he continued on. At the elevator, Max pressed the panel to open the doors.

"Wait here," he whispered, before stepping in. The interior light illuminated him as he turned around.

Guy had seen his kind before; a Caynin. He was about as tall as a not-so-tall human; just a tad shorter than the average man[*] but a lot more muscular.[†] His dark-grey coat had probably been in better condition once upon a time … a time that had long since passed; the same with his washed-out black pants and heavily scuffed black boots. His bulldog-like face was covered with short, light-grey hair, and his light-brown eyes were framed at the top by thick, black eyebrows.

Guy resisted the urge to walk over and scratch his head. Thankfully, the elevator doors closed before the urge got too strong for self-restraint to hold it at bay.

Apparently, Neville had the same thoughts. "Is it just me," he said, staring at the closed doors, "or did you also want to take him for a walk in the park?"

"Thank goodness it wasn't just me," Guy said. "I can easily see myself doing that. But not without taking a tennis ball along."

"And a juicy bone."

---

[*] Most average men will feel pretty good about this.

[†] Most average men will conveniently ignore this.

"And a little scoop."

"I'd say a big scoop, with a big bag."

They had to muffle their nervous giggles with their hands.

Guy forced himself to calm down. "I must say, now that I've had a better look at him, he doesn't *seem* all that bad."

"Yep, I'd say he's a *good boy*."

As the doors slid open again, Max found two Salamans covering their mouths, crying.

"What happened?" he hissed, yanking out a gun from under his coat and holding it at the ready. He eyed the dark hallway suspiciously.

Neville finally bit back the tears and removed his hand from his mouth. "Whoo!" he exhaled. "Nothing, nothing; just nerves."

"Yes," Guy said, "just nerves."

"Well, we have to go," Max said as he ushered them into the elevator.

"Aren't *you* nervous?" Neville asked innocently, avoiding looking at Guy.

"No, I'm too focused to be nervous," Max said, touching the panel.

"Come on," Guy said, biting his lip, "not even a nervous tic?"

The doors closed silently as Max stared confusedly at the small Salamans, whose bodies almost went into spasm.

• • •

As the elevator doors opened, the Caynin's hands were clamped over the mouths of the two Salamans, who had tears streaming down their face. They however quickly regained their composure after spotting two guards lying still on either side of the doors.

"We have to move," Max said with a note of urgency. "Stay close and keep quiet."

Nervous humour quickly made way for bona fide nervousness as Guy and Neville stayed both close and quiet. They were in the rotunda with its extensive range of exhibits. Apart from the guards who had taken a vacation from the land of the conscious, no one else was around.

Max moved forward in a crouch, holding his weapon at the ready. Guy and Neville followed, snaking their way between the exhibition pieces until they got to the hallway leading to the exit doors. Standing with his back against the wall, Max quickly glanced around the corner. He started moving forward, but quickly stepped back again, pressing Guy and Neville flat against the wall with his free arm. Some voices and footsteps slowly became louder before slowly fading again.

"Okay, move," the Caynin whispered, gliding forward silently with his weapon pointed down the hallway. He paused at the intersecting hallway running along the inside of the round building, looking both ways to check for guards.

Satisfied that all was clear, he approached the big, wooden exit doors and tested one of the handles. It wasn't locked. He pushed the door slightly ajar with a creak that made them all freeze in place. They stood like that for a while, waiting for someone to come running and yelling. But no one came, and no one yelled. Max peered through the opening, then squeezed through sideways to avoid making any more noise. He surveyed the dimly lit courtyard before signalling for Guy and Neville to follow.

Outside, the running water of the fountains aided in masking their footsteps. This would have been perfect if it didn't also have the potential to mask the sound of someone else's footsteps. Max listened intently and, once satisfied that no one was approaching, they moved forward, staying as low as possible to keep themselves hidden among the fountains and foliage.

They came to a halt at the portcullis. It was open. Max stared at the raised gate, then looked around with a worried frown.

"What's wrong?" Neville whispered.

"Nothing," Max breathed after a pause. "Let's go."

Quickly yet quietly, they descended the long series of stairs and terraces. Despite the low light, Guy felt as exposed as that time during the office's year-end function when he'd drunkenly neglected to fasten his pants properly after a visit to the bathroom. The fact that he'd been left somewhat exposed when his pants dropped to his ankles on the dance floor hadn't bothered him that much at the time, but he *had* felt pretty exposed that Monday when he walked back into the office amid looks of disgust and amusement.[*]

Reaching the fringe of the gardens, Max turned to frown at the structure once more. Shaking his head, he continued on, and the night soon swallowed the three figures without a sound.

---

[*] Yes, a headache is an excellent short-term reminder of a good night out, but the memories written on the faces of those you went out with tend to last a bit longer and, unfortunately, don't go away with a handful of aspirin. And yes, many people would know that feeling. Also, yes, those who don't know that feeling have never really had *a good night out*.

CHAPTER 31

The trio headed in the opposite direction from where Guy and Neville had been dropped off by the *Jolly Dodger*. Rounding a small rocky outcropping, Max suddenly stopped, causing a mini-pileup behind him. Startled, an already jumpy Guy was about to utter a word that was better suited for utterance in *The Wormhole*, but bit it back as Max dropped to a crouch and held up a hand.

Peering over the Caynin's shoulder, Guy couldn't see much at first, but a moment later the beams from a pair of flashlights appeared from seemingly nowhere. One of the beams searched over the dry landscape while the other was directed at some kind of metal object. As the beam played over the object, it revealed what looked like a spaceship's window, then what looked like a spaceship's wings, followed by what looked like a spaceship's engines. Guy felt confident that he had gathered enough evidence to identify the object as a spaceship.

"That's my ship," Max whispered, sounding annoyed. "I thought I'd landed far enough from The Mansion to avoid detection."

"Seems you hadn't," Guy stated, earning him a glare.

"Hey, you brought it up," he added, holding his hands up defensively. "Are those The Man's cronies?"

"I'd bet on it," Max said, apparently deciding it best to leave well enough alone.

"How do we get past them?" Neville asked.

"*We* don't," Max said. "You two stay here and keep a lookout while I take care of it."

"But—" Neville started, peering into the darkness, but he was silenced as Max rounded on him.

"It was *not* a suggestion," the Caynin scolded, as much as one could scold softly. "Do not move from this spot until I come back, okay?"

"*Okay?*" he repeated to the blank expressions.

"Okay," Guy and Neville whispered with a respective nod and shrug.

Max glared at them a second longer before he crept towards the two flashlights, crouching whenever a beam was directed in his general direction. He came so close to the nearest target that the figure only managed to spin around at the last moment. The Vahltan was too late. One of the Caynin's stocky arms blocked the thug's weapon-holding hand, which wasn't holding a weapon a fraction of a second later, and an instant after that another stocky arm snaked around his scrawny neck in a chokehold.

The other guard, standing a few metres away, was caught off guard and didn't even have enough time to raise his weapon before a light streaked from Max's gun with a soft *tshoop* and dissipated on impact. The guard's body stiffened, then dropped to the ground in a puff of dust. The feeble struggles of the guard in Max's arm subsided as consciousness drained from his eyes, and the Caynin laid him down none too gently.

As Max got up, he was surprised to find himself facing yet another guard who'd come from nowhere and whose flashlight, mounted on the rifle he was carrying, was blinding the two eyes that would soon sport a hole between them. The guard seemed on the verge of saying something when a crunching *thud* sent him plopping onto the dust like a meaty raindrop.

Neville stood over the fallen body with a bloody rock raised in his hand, ready to bring it down again at the slightest sign of movement, of which there was none. Satisfied, he dropped the rock onto the guard's chest, which was already struggling to rise and fall without the added pressure.

"I tried to warn you that I'd seen another flashlight," he said, looking down at the unmoving shape at his feet.

"You could have tried harder," Max grumbled.

"Yes, but then I wouldn't have been able to do *this*," Neville said, giving the shape a good kick.

"How did anyone manage to capture you in the first place?" Max said, astounded.

Neville shrugged and glanced at Guy approaching cautiously. "We're learning as we go along."

"Not bad, but next ti—" Max started, but was silenced by the sound of a distant alarm piercing the tranquil night air.

The Caynin hurried to the back of the blocky ship to lower a ramp. "That's our cue," he said, motioning the Salamans aboard.

"I don't think so," Guy said.

Halfway up the ramp, Neville swung about to frown at his friend, who returned it with interest.

"Hey, we don't even know this guy," Guy said, as his worse-case-scenario senses made allowances for ... well, a worse scenario. "I know I wanted to get out of there, but we can't just go flying off with him to who knows where. For all we know, he could be taking us someplace *worse* than this!"

"You mean a place where we'd also definitely be killed in a myriad of artistically brutal ways?" Neville countered.

Guy's worse-case-scenario senses insisted that Neville had a point.

"Well, yes ... no ... I don't know!" he stammered, then turned to Max. "All I know is that I don't know *you* or what your intentions are, so excuse me for being a tad skeptical!"

"You're excused, but unless you want *that*," the Caynin said, pointing in the direction of the blaring alarm, "to become a real problem real soon, I suggest you get on the ship so that we can get the heck out of here!"

"He's right, Guy," Neville said. "We can't stay here. We need to get going, now!"

"Fine," Guy snapped, traipsing up the ramp, "but I want some *answers!*"

"And you'll get them," Max said as he made his way inside before raising the ramp.

When the metal clanged shut, it instantly cut off the noise of the alarms outside, although it did nothing to silence the alarm of paranoia still ringing out loudly in Guy's head.

CHAPTER 32

In the cockpit, Max jumped into the pilot's seat and fired up the engines, which came alive with a roar accompanied by blue-white light.

Outside, vehicle-mounted lights bounced as the vehicles they were mounted on raced towards the ship over the rough terrain. A green ball of energy was fired wildly from the lead vehicle but fortunately also missed wildly.

After buckling himself in and punching some buttons and panels, Max looked back. "I suggest you strap yourselves in, unless you want to spend the next few months in a body cast!"

Guy didn't want to, so he plonked himself in the nearest seat and frantically tried to strap himself in. Neville had the same idea, but first leaned over to help Guy with his buckles before fastening his own restraints with a few loud clicks.

As another green shot flashed by the cockpit window, Max grabbed the ship's control stick with his one hand and a lever with the other.

"Hold on tight!" he yelled as he pulled back on both the stick and the lever, causing the ship to lurch into the air. He pushed forward on another lever, which in turn pushed the ship forward with a violent shudder. They picked up speed as they rose higher into the night sky. More shots streaked past the window from below, and Guy hoped that the ship would be able to withstand a direct hit. Fortunately, his hope wasn't tested, because they soon rose high enough to make a hit either unlikely or ineffective.

Max flipped another switch and pushed forward on the lever, pressing Guy hard into his seat, with his innards vying for new positions in his abdomen.

It didn't take long for the dark, lightly clouded sky to clear completely and the stars to shine brighter as the vessel exited the confines of the planet's atmosphere. The engines also changed from a roar to a hum as the silent vacuum of space enveloped the ship, whose occupants remained quiet for a while.

"Geez, that was close!" Neville finally exhaled. "I can't believe we made it!"

"Don't get your hopes up just yet," Max said, eyeing the screen in front of him.

"Why?" Guy asked, not quite sure if he wanted to know the answer.

"*That's* why," Max said, pointing at the screen.

Guy tried leaning forward to get a better look, but had to settle for craning his neck, as he was strapped tight in his seat. The screen showed two dots behind another dot, which didn't mean much to him.

"What's that?" he said.

"*That* is us," Max said, pointing at the centre dot.

"And *those*," he added, indicating the other two dots below the first dot, "are most likely the ships that have been sent to blow us to bits."

As if to prove this point, some white balls flashed by the window. One must have hit, because a tremor passed through the vessel, accompanied by an alarm.

"But I'd like my bits to stay together!" Guy cried, grabbing his straps until his red knuckles turned pink. Eyes wide, he glanced at Neville, who seemed undecided between looking ecstatic or terrified.

Max coolly yanked the stick sideways, sending them into a roll, before dipping it forward, which sent them spiralling downwards. Adjusting controls and deftly steering the ship in all directions, he continued employing an array of evasive manoeuvres. At one point, a small arrowhead-shaped ship whizzed by, followed shortly by some more blasts. Most missed their mark, except for one that caused the ship to jerk. Sparks flew from a panel near Guy's head.

"What was *that?*" he screamed, turning his head away from the ball of smoke drifting towards his face.

"Don't worry," Max yelled back, "it's a non-essential system!"

"Meaning what?!"

"Meaning we won't be having toast tomorrow morning!"

"Oh!" Guy said after a relieved pause.

His relief lasted only a moment, though, as a sudden craving for toast overwhelmed him.[*] Nothing fancy; just plain toast with a dollop of butter. However, when Max sent them into another violent spin, all further thoughts of eating were expelled along with the contents of Guy's stomach and were replaced by thoughts on how to get the puddle of well-digested food off his lap. Max provided a solution by spinning the ship in the other direction, which resolved the puddle-problem by sending it spiralling outwards.

During their long friendship, Neville had helped to carry a lot of Guy's emotional burdens, but a friend should *never* have to carry one's intestinal burdens. Which is why Neville's queasy scowl was perfectly understandable as he tried to wipe a glob of Guy's now-unburdened burden from his cheek.

"Was that really necess—" he started, before another plunging spin caused him to share some of his own burdens with Guy, who tried to avert his face without much success.

Guy shot Neville a disgusted look, which was returned with interest along with a tinge of justice.

For a moment, Guy forgot they were being hunted by murderous Vahltans, partly because of the unpleasant episode he

---

[*] Cravings for things you suddenly cannot – or aren't allowed to – have any longer is entirely natural. People who have never experienced this themselves can still experience its side-effects by having a nice big glass of wine in front of any pregnant female/male of just about any species anywhere.

and Neville had just shared, and partly because the ship had suddenly ceased its erratic manoeuvres.

"Why aren't you flying like a lunatic anymore?" he asked, and immediately wished he hadn't when something took the opportunity to slip into his mouth. He wasn't sure whether it belonged to him or Neville.

He was just starting to feel sick again when Max said something sobering. "Because they stopped following us."

Glancing at Neville, who now looked just as disgustedly confused as him, Guy said, "Why would they do that?"

"Don't know," said Max, shaking his head. "One of the blips on the screen just vanished."

"And the other one?" Neville asked.

"See for yourself."

They craned their necks just in time to see one of the dots disappearing off the screen's edge.

"So, we're safe?" Guy said.

"It would seem so," Max said pensively. "For now."

He adjusted some instruments and worked on the screen for a bit before unbuckling himself and getting up. He froze in place as his eyes absorbed the scene before him.

"What in Zolt's name happened to *you?*" he asked as shock and revulsion battled for control over his face.

This was met by silent stares and something clumpy oozing off Guy's chin.

After a self-composing pause, Max sighed deeply. "Okay, let's get you cleaned up."

As he walked off, Guy struggled with his buckles, but he could swear he heard the Caynin grumbling something about "bloody rookies" as he marched off, grumbling some more.

CHAPTER 33

The ship wasn't very big, and neither was its bathroom, which probably accounted for the absence of a shower or a bath.

The room was fine for a number one or two or – if you've just been spun about in a spaceship – a number three, or – for certain species – a number four or higher. At least it had a washing basin.

After cleaning themselves as best they could, Guy and Neville also washed their clothes before hanging them up to dry near a heating vent. They then went to the kitchen, where they sat down next to each other on a bench at the small table. They were now only dressed in underwear that would have most fashion designers wailing in agony before gulping down a few glasses of sparkling wine to help them forget the horror they'd just witnessed.[*]

Sitting opposite them, Max stared pensively at the empty coffee mug he kept revolving slowly on the tabletop with dull scraping sounds. Guy and Neville weren't sure what to do except for feeling a bit … bare. But after a while, Guy couldn't stand the scraping any longer.

"Would you mind stopping that, please?" he said, bending his lips into a failed smile.

---

[*] In all likelihood, they would have gulped down the sparkling wine regardless. It's a universally known fact that fashion designers really like sparkling wine.

"What?" Max said, snapping back from wherever he'd been in his head, and looked at the mug as if seeing it for the first time. "Oh, sorry."

The Caynin pushed the mug away but didn't take his eyes off it.

"What's going on?" Guy asked suspiciously.

"We got away easily," Max said.

"So?" Guy said. "That's good, isn't it?"

"It was *too* easy."

"*Too easy?*" Neville jumped in. "How was *that* too easy? We almost got blown up and scattered in a million directions back there!"

"That's the thing," Max said. "We *should have* been blown up. Don't get me wrong, I'm good, but I'm not *that* good. This ship wasn't built for battle against combat fighters. Any pilot worth his salt, or even just a grain of salt, should have been able to destroy us with ease in a fighter like that."

"But one of them disappeared off the screen," Neville said. "So maybe, with all your flying about, one accidentally blew up the other."

"Not impossible. But why would the other one just take off like that? Those guys work for The Man, and The Man doesn't accept failure. They'd be better off being blown up than return empty-handed."

"Maybe they had an emergency, or maybe they collided."

"Maybe," Max said, not sounding convinced. "But then there's also The Mansion."

"What about it?" Guy frowned.

"I take it you saw the security around the premises when you arrived?"

Guy nodded.

"And what did you see when we left?" Max continued.

"Not much," Neville pondered, seeming to catch the Caynin's drift.

"Exactly. Where were all the guards?"

"Well, *you* took out quite a few," Guy ventured, not feeling comfortable with the direction of the drift.

"I did, but Manni Karpachio is usually surrounded by a small army of guards. There were only a handful inside The Mansion, and hardly any outside."

"Yes," Guy admitted, "there definitely were more when we arrived. But we *did* run into a few of them when we got to your ship."

"True," Max said, "but I'll get to that in a moment. What else did you notice that was strange?"

"The doors and the portcullis," Neville said. "They were unlocked, and open."

"Precisely," Max said. "There's no way someone like Karpachio would leave his precious collection unprotected and unguarded like that. And don't forget the lights outside. They were quite dim."

"Well, maybe they keep him awake at night when they're too bright," Guy tried. "Or maybe he is trying to save electricity."

"Does he strike you as the type of person that needs to save electricity?"

"Er ... no."

"So what are you trying to say?" Neville said. "That they just *let* us leave?"

"That's precisely what I'm saying," Max said, staring at them, but not too hard, because he seemed a bit uncomfortable with the two sitting across from him in nothing but their underwear. "They put up just enough of a show to make most people think they'd escaped. But I'm not most people. It's obvious that they let us get away."

"Okay," Guy said. "Let us, for the sake of argument, say you're right. Why would they do that?"

"To track us," Max replied. "Those Vahltans at the ship; I think we caught them just after they'd disembarked. If they had simply found the ship, they would have called it in immediately. The place would have been swarming with The Man's cronies within minutes, and we wouldn't have been able to get anywhere near the ship."

"All in all, it *does* make sense," Neville said. "But how can we be sure?"

"Because of this," Max said, picking up something from the floor next to him and dropping it on the table with a *bang* that made both Salamans jump.

"What's *that?*" Guy exclaimed, looking at the little box like it was a dog-sized spider-snake.

"That," Max said matter-of-factly, "is a tracking device."

"A tracking device?" Guy cried, now looking at the box like it was a horse-sized spider-snake.

"You mean you *knew* about it this whole time?" Neville bellowed, perplexed.

"Yep," Max said.

"When did you find it?"

"While you were busy cleaning up."

"Then why talk everything through if you knew?"

"Because I need *you* to start thinking," Max said, tapping his temple. "We're going to need a lot more than just *my* skills if we're going to survive this. A Michin chain is only as strong as its weakest link." [*]

Neville composed himself by taking a deep breath. "Okay, so we're being tracked—" he started.

"*Were* being tracked," Max corrected. "I disabled it."

"Fine, so we *were* being tracked," Neville continued. "But it still begs the question as to *why* The Man would let us go, even with a tracker in place. Why not just kill us and get it over and done with?"

"Why indeed?" Max said. "Maybe it was just a backup, or maybe there's some other motive. At this stage, we can only guess."

---

[*] In order to get to the fruit hanging from hard-to-reach plants growing out of the cliff faces on Kilihiri, Michin monkeys form a chain, starting with the strongest monkey hanging from the top to the weakest at the bottom. The problem comes in when the fruit gets too heavy for the chain to hold. Whole Michin families have been lost this way, which is probably why Michins have lost their appetite for the otherwise delicious Kilihiri giant mountain watermelon.

Guy was good at guessing, which was the only way he'd managed to scrape through school. But he didn't like guessing all that much when his life was hanging in the balance. That said, they were still alive, so he guessed he could live with it, for the moment.

CHAPTER 34

People who knew Manni Karpachio also knew he didn't like bad news that much or, more specifically, at all. This is precisely the reason why Andi never gave The Man any bad news himself. Why put yourself in the line of fire – often literally – unless absolutely necessary? Giving The Man bad news wasn't the best career move, nor was it a good life choice. It was also the main reason why The Changing of the Guard had a slightly different meaning for those in the employ of The Man.

Fortunately for Andi, bad news wasn't on the cards today, so he opted to deliver the news himself instead of sending one of his subordinates. You had to know when to delegate blame and when to take praise for yourself. That's what good management was all about.

Feeling like Manager of the Year, Andi exited the elevator and strutted into The Man's luxury quarters – a smaller dome perched atop the main dome. It was cluttered with more pieces of art and history to tie in with the hoarder motif downstairs.

"Sir," he said proudly to the back of The Man, who stood staring out the window overlooking the lush gardens. "The prisoners got away."

The Man sighed.

"Any other time, Andi," he said to the night air outside, "that would have been … unfortunate. But this isn't one of those times, now is it?"

"No, sir," Andi said with a happy bounce in his voice.

The Man turned around. "So you managed to place the tracker on the ship?"

"Yes, sir," Andi said. "The signal is up and running. We barely got it in place before *he* came along and took our guys out."

The Man's eyes narrowed. "You're sure it was him?"

"It was a Caynin. So, yes, I'm pretty sure." Andi almost added that he'd bet his life on it, but stopped himself short. You just didn't tempt fate like that with Manni Karpachio. So he merely added, "Who else could it be?"

The Man pondered for a moment before nodding. "That's what I thought too. It *must* be Max. I trust you put up a good show in preventing their escape?"

Andi nodded. "We made it look like an accident – one of the Arrowheads destroyed the other and retreated."

"An acceptable loss," The Man said. "Just make sure you get another fighter and pilot in place. We might need them soon."

"Will do, sir," Andi said, then hesitated. "Er, sir?"

"What is it, Andi? Speak freely."

While Andi was the only one allowed to speak freely to The Man, he also knew the term *freely* was used loosely, and didn't always mean what it was supposed to mean when it came to the boss. He generally wouldn't even have asked this question, but his curiosity had gotten the better of him, and while he knew it had killed more cats than anything else in the universe, he just couldn't help himself.

"Uh," he said hesitantly, "you know I'd never question your motives or tactics, but it seems a bit … er … uncharacteristic of you to have let them go in the first place."

He had rambled off that last part, just to get it over and done with.

The Man didn't look upset, which Andi took as a good sign, although it didn't feel that good when The Man slowly walked up to him. He stopped just short of Andi, looking the taller Vahltan up and down.

"Oh, yes, sorry, sir," Andi said, bending a knee so that the short Vahltan could (almost) look him in the eye.

"Well," The Man said, "if it were up to me, the lot of them would be feeding the garden right now. But it's not up to me. The client seems bent on playing games."

"But, er, sir, I thought you liked games too."

"Oh, I do, Andi. Believe me, I do. But there's one problem with games, and do you know what that is?"

"No, sir."

"They have rules. And do you know what the problem is with rules?"

"No, sir."

"Nothing, Andi. Absolutely nothing. As long as *I* am the one making them."

"So, uh, why let the client dictate the rules then, sir?"

"Because I *am*, first and foremost, a businessman. And, as a businessman, I like to keep my clients happy, especially when they're paying me well. Which is precisely what this client is doing, on top of providing me with a business opportunity that will make me the most successful crim— businessman of all time. Besides, with the tracking device in place, I'm still in control of the game."

The elevator doors opened and a Vahltan – one of the new recruits – stumbled out unsteadily, holding the back of his head where a rock had nearly crushed his skull earlier. He came to a standstill a few metres past The Man, although the top of his body wasn't very still. Things were a bit hazy.

"Sir," he said, swaying heavily and, with a rubbery arm, saluted a statue. Andi turned him in the right direction before taking a few steps back. The higher-ranking Vahltan had a keen sense of impending trouble.

"Sir …" the unsteady Vahltan saluted again. He appeared on the verge of passing out from a combination of injury and fear. "… the boys sent me in to tell you …" he caught himself before falling over, "… to tell you that … the tracker has stopped transmitting."

The Man just stood there, looking surprisingly calm, especially from the viewpoint of the guard, who suddenly felt hopeful that he might actually walk away from this, mostly intact. He was partly right, as a moment later there was a blurry movement and a flash, which took out a small part of the front of his forehead and a considerably larger part at the back. So yes, he was *mostly* intact, but he just hadn't managed to get the whole walking-out-of-there part right.

The Man returned the flasher gun to its designated place in the folds of his robe. "Who was responsible for the tracker?" he grated.

Thinking fast, Andi pointed at the mostly intact guard's lifeless body. "*He* was, sir."

The Man cast Andi a suspicious glare, glanced at the fallen Vahltan, then started pacing the floor, muttering to himself.

Andi couldn't hear most of it, but the last words he could discern were "… will *not* be outdone by a fharking street sweeper and his nitwit …"

The Man abruptly stopped pacing. Andi's eyes swivelled in all directions in search of good cover to duck behind in case the flasher made a return. But his anxiousness seemed unwarranted, as a malicious grin split the boss's face.

"You know what, Andi?"

"Er … no, sir," Andi replied, struggling to keep the quiver from his voice.

"Maybe all is not lost. In fact, it might even be for the better."

"I'm sorry, sir, but I'm not sure I follow."

"You will, Andi, you will. Assemble a team to go after them."

"Er, sir," Andi said carefully, "they'll be long gone by now. We'll never catch up."

The Man's grin deepened. "You won't have to catch up, Andi, because I think I know exactly where they're going."

CHAPTER 35

As far as understatements go, Max wasn't the best cook on Earth, or whatever planet he called home.[*] Guy and Neville didn't have to say so; their expressions said it all. However, actual words would have conveyed their … gratitude in a more diplomatic manner, which is why Guy mumbled something that had the words "thanks" and "good" in it.

Neville also seemed to find it difficult to replace the lost saliva in his mouth. "Thangns," he managed to squeeze out, and took another big swig of water to wash the dry lump down his throat.

Max gave them an appreciative smile, then eyed them hopefully. "Had enough? There's more."

"No!" Guy and Neville stated firmly.

"We've, er, had *more than* enough, thank you," Guy added with absolute honesty.

"I couldn't get another bite in, even if I wanted to," Neville said, knowing that neither of them wanted to.

---

[*] It's called Hok, and it's the only place in the Charted Universe where Caynin restaurants remain open for more than a day without being closed down by the Health Inspectorate. Caynins can eat just about anything, and cannot understand why so many other species aren't able to do so too. Not that this bothers Caynins all that much, especially when it means more leftovers for them. As a general rule, Caynins regard any food left unattended for longer than five minutes as leftovers. So if you ever have dinner with one, keep your bathroom breaks short.

"Great!" Max said happily, taking their plates and scraping the leftovers into his own. "There's nothing like a home-cooked meal."

Guy and Neville silently stared at him munching away, praying for another few flips in the ship to get rid of whatever they'd just eaten.

Finishing the plate, Max sighed as he longingly eyed the pot containing the rest of the food. "I really shouldn't overdo it," he said as if to convince himself.

"No, please, go ahead," Guy pleaded. "Don't mind us."

"Yes," Neville affirmed in a hopeful tone, "don't mind us at all, *please*."

"Well, if you insist," Max said with a grin, gathering his plate and dumping the last of the so-called food into it, before sitting down and finishing it all without any sign of struggle. He finally licked off the residue plastered around his mouth.

Guy and Neville watched him with horrified fascination, before Guy finally gathered himself and took another sip of water.

"I ..." he said, "uh, *we* are really grateful for the meal you've prepared for us ..."

"And for saving us back there, of course," Neville added.

Max stared at them for a moment. Guy wasn't sure if this was to gather his thoughts or to savour the aftertaste of the food, which Guy was desperately trying to unsavour.

"And now you want answers?" the Caynin said.

"Yes," Guy replied.

"I'd like a few answers of my own."

"You first," Guy countered resolutely.

Max measured him for a moment, causing Guy to shift on the bench, but he wasn't about to budge.

"Fine," the Caynin said at length, "I'll tell you what I can. What would you like to know?"

Expecting more of an argument, Max's sudden compliance sent Guy's carefully prepared queries into disarray. "Well, I, er, firstly, um ..."

Neville, on the other hand, seemed ready to start his own talk show, and plunged right into it.

"Who are you?" he began.

"Like I said," the Caynin said, "I'm Max."

"We know that!" Neville said. "Max *who*?"

"That, my friend, I cannot tell you."

"You said you'd answer our questions!"

"I said I'd tell you what I *can*."

"So why can't you tell us who you are?"

"Because I'm not allowed to reveal my true identity."

"Says who?"

"The Infiltratorate."

"The *what*?"

"The Clandestine Infiltratorate of Unyun. The CIU, if you like."

"I don't know if I like," Guy said, "because I don't know what that is."

"It's a Federal division responsible for clandestine operations and intelligence gathering."

"Like ... a spy?" Neville asked.

"Yes."

Guy and Neville were quiet for a while, letting it sink in, while Max waited patiently for this to happen.

"Hey," Guy said after a while, his spirits lifting slightly, "that's good, isn't it?"

"It would have been," Max replied, "except for one tiny problem."

"What kind of problem?" Guy said, his spirits sagging back to their original position.

"I'm kind of ... on the run," Max said uneasily.

"From whom?"

"From the CIU ... and from the law ... and, you could say, from everyone else."

"Uh ... okay. Do we want to know why?"

"No, but you *should* know why."

When Max didn't provide an answer, Neville reluctantly asked the question, "Why?"

Taking a deep breath, Max said, "Because I'm wanted for the assassination of the Presidor."

• • •

Whatever hopes Guy had left in him did not stay long and left without saying goodbye. A wave of nausea suddenly overwhelmed him, and the only reason the food remained in his body was because it was too dry and lumpy to escape without the assistance of a crowbar.

He shot a look of alarm at Neville, who in turn looked at the Caynin like he was a vegetarian eating a steak.

"Wait," Neville said with a dry gulp, seeming ready to leap from his seat at any moment, following Guy, who had already done so and was standing a few metres away, swivelling his head in every direction in search of an exit he knew wasn't there. He searched in any case.

"No," Neville said, and gulped even harder to gulp down the previous gulp. "That can't be right. The news said the assassin was killed after the attack."

"I don't know about the assassin, but *I* survived."

"But you said *you* were the assassin!"

"No, I said I'm *wanted* for the assassination. I didn't say I *was* the assassin. At least I don't believe so."

"How could you *not* know whether you've assassinated a Presidor, or anyone else for that matter?" Guy exclaimed, pausing his futile search.

Max looked at him and motioned for him to take a seat again.

"Are you kidding me?" Guy said, taking another step back. "You expect me to sit down with … with a *murderer?*"

"No," Max said, "I expect you to sit down and listen to what I have to say."

"And why would I do that?" Guy said, adding his stare to that of Neville, who had overcome his initial shock and now looked ready to pounce at a moment's notice.

Max looked at Neville and sighed. "I know what you're thinking, but I'd advise against it."

"And why would that be?" Neville hissed.

"Three reasons. Firstly, I'm well trained in combat. And, secondly, even if you somehow managed to overpower me, who will fly the ship?"

Guy and Neville shot one another uncertain glances, before Neville snapped his head back.

"I'm sure I'd be able to figure it out," he grated with conviction.

Guy believed this completely. Neville was a natural when it came to mastering any mode of transport.

"Even if you do, how much do you know about space navigation?" Max said, raising a querying eyebrow.

"I'll figure *that* out too," Neville said.

Despite wanting to, Guy didn't quite believe *this*. And, apparently, neither did Neville, as he'd said it with all the confidence of a school chess champion threatening to beat up the school rugby team by himself, and punctuated it with yet another gulp.

"Okay, fine," Neville conceded after a pause, "what was the other thing?"

"What other thing?" Max asked.

"You said there were *three* reasons."

"Oh, yes, and this is the most important one: *you* were involved too."

"What?" Guy and Neville exclaimed.

"That's ludicrous!" Guy added.

"Yeah," Neville said, "that's completely insane! Why would *we* be involved, and how? I mean, just *look* at us! I seriously doubt *we'd* be involved in killing a Presidor!"

"I didn't say you were the assassins," Max said, "but I *do* believe you're witnesses."

Guy eyed him apprehensively. "And *why* would you believe that?"

"Because that's what *you* told me."

CHAPTER 36

Guy was cautiously relieved, because now he was sure there'd been some kind of mistake.

"There's been some kind of mistake," he said, backing himself.

"Ditto," Neville said. "We've never met you before, so there's *definitely* been some kind of misunderstanding. So you can drop us off anywhere and continue your … whatever it is you're doing. We wish you all the best."

Max looked at them sadly for a while, and Guy suddenly wished he had a biscuit he could toss to the Caynin to make him feel better.

The Infiltrator eventually gave a heavy sigh. "Gentlemen, I wish it was that simple. But how about this? I'll tell you *my* side of the story, and if you still want to go, I'll drop you off at the nearest settlement or wherever you prefer."

Guy looked at his friend for guidance.

"Deal," Neville said. Folding his arms, he sat back, staring at the Caynin expectantly.

Guy shrugged and sat down. "Fire away."

"Thank you," Max said. "But please let me finish without any interruptions, okay?"

Guy supported Neville's nod with another shrug.

"Good. I'll try to keep this brief, but it shouldn't be difficult, because I, well … I cannot remember the time leading up to the assassination."

"Oh, come on!" Neville exclaimed. "Are you seriously telling us you *conveniently* don't remember anything?"

"I asked not to be interrupted," the Caynin grated. "Think you can manage that?"

This time, it was Neville who shrugged.

"As I was *trying* to say," Max continued, "I have a gap in my memory. The year leading up to the assassination is completely blank. The first thing I remember was waking up in a crashed gunship on Grassi Nole. Physically, apart from a few scrapes, bruises, and a bump to the head, I was okay. But I didn't know where I was or why I was there. The only thing I could think of was that I must have been on a mission, and that I simply couldn't remember because I'd knocked my head too hard in the crash. So I switched the ship's comm system to a CIU channel to find out what was going on.

"Before I could speak, however, I heard frantic exchanges about the Presidor's ship having been attacked by a gunship on Grassi Nole, and that all available law-enforcement and Militor units were being dispatched to the scene. It didn't take much to figure out that the gunship mentioned was the one I was sitting in. It also wasn't difficult to figure out that something sinister was afoot, and that I was smack dab in the middle of it. I knew I had to get out of there before anyone discovered the crash site. As I got out of the ship, I noticed a town in the distance and headed for it.

"Once there, I stuck to the backstreets and alleys to avoid attention, until I found a bar. It seemed as good a place as any to lie low while trying to plan my next move. But I didn't have any creds on me, or anything else for that matter. So I waited for the first drunk guy to stumble out of the bar and lifted his wallet.

"Inside, I ordered a drink to numb the pain in my head. Shortly thereafter, two Salamans came stumbling in, looking both drunk and nervous. They took the table next to mine, but didn't seem to have noticed me, because they didn't look in my direction once. But their conversation immediately caught my attention.

"I overheard them talking about having a close call with a gunship, and they seemed highly upset over whatever had transpired. So I approached their table and asked them if they'd like to join me for a drink. They said they didn't have any money on them, but I insisted I would pay.

"After getting their drinks, I asked them what had them so riled up. They told me they'd gone AWOL from the circus and had 'borrowed' one of the circus's shuttles to have some fun at a spacebar orbiting Grassi Nole.[*] When they ran out of creds, they flew back towards the planet, but got into an argument over a girl they'd met at the spacebar; about which one of them she'd actually been interested in.[†] So they weren't really paying attention to where they were flying, and the next moment they were almost on top of a gunship. They pulled up at the last moment, but the bottom of their hull still scraped the top of the gunship. Shaken, they decided to stop at the nearest bar. They were hoping to score a free drink for the famous Bezam, and were lucky enough to find me.

"I was just about to ask them if they could identify the ship they'd collided with, as I was sure it couldn't have been the one I'd been in. There *had to* have been another ship involved. However, I noticed Protectors searching the buildings across the street. While I desperately needed the info from the Salamans, I knew I wouldn't be able to do anything from behind bars. I had to get out of there, but I also needed *some way* of keeping them safe somewhere; somewhere I could easily find them again once things cooled down a bit. I remembered someone who might be able to help me, and

---

[*] Spacebars are popular hangouts, offering magnificent views of planets, moons, suns and stars while enjoying a cold beer or a tall cocktail. The only problem with spacebars is that you should behave yourself, as you never know when a peeved bouncer might "accidentally" chuck you out the wrong door (aka the airlock).

[†] An argument that would've been settled had they put two and two together to figure out that the girl had disappeared as soon as their money had. So yes, guys, you get girls like that all across the universe. Don't fall for it. And yes, girls, it's perfectly okay to exploit guys who are gullible enough to fall for it. It's just one of those things.

asked the Salamans if they were up for making a good sum of money for basically no effort whatsoever. They were, so I said that someone would contact them, and that this person would identify himself as a friend of Max. I spotted two Protectors coming towards the bar, so before the Salamans could ask me anything else, I left money for the drinks and slipped out the back.

"I found a nondescript ship that was easy to jack and managed to escape Grassi Nole before the authorities could lock it down. I got the location of the person who could keep you off the grid for a while, and tracked him down before he could return to his offices at the *Life Spectacular Corporation* on Unyun."

"Wait," Guy said, who'd been listening with increased boredom. "Did you say *Life Spectacular?*"

"Yes," Max said, seeming to have expected this particular interruption. "That's where my contact works – Mr Gray. I presume you've met him by now."

"Yes," Guy replied, "I met him once."

"What do you mean *once*?" Max asked, frowning.

"Well, he came to the circus one day, told me all about the prize I'd won, and left. He said he'd return, but never did."

Neville just shrugged. "I never even met the guy."

The Caynin eyed them nervously. "You need to tell me *everything*."

So Guy and Neville told him everything. When they were done, Max appeared stumped.

"So, you never saw him again after that?" the Caynin said, his nervousness now palpable enough to take a seat at the table.

Guy shook his head.

"And your bodies have *not* been switched back yet?" Max asked, his nervousness shifting over to make space for full-blown panic, which prepared to make itself at home on the bench.

"No, and I must say it's a bit worrying. Apparently, we can only occupy these bodies for a certain period before they disintegrate or something."

Panic took a seat and bumped off Max, who jumped up and walked away. He then walked back as if to say something that got stuck behind his clenched teeth, before walking away again. He stood stationary for a while with his back turned, scratching his head and muttering to himself; something about "fhark", "humans", "what was he thinking?" and some more "fhark".

After a while, the Caynin took a deep breath as if to compose himself, then shouted "Fhaaaark!!!" so loudly that it would have warranted three exclamation marks had it ever been written down for someone – who hadn't been there – to read, just so that they could also experience the true spirit in which the message had been conveyed.

Having been there, however, Guy got the message. It left him a little shaken, while Neville looked ready to engage in hand-to-smaller-hand combat.

Max, however, took another deep breath before sitting back down.

"I apologise for that, gentlemen," he said, still looking troubled. "But it appears as though things haven't turned out the way I'd planned."

"You can say *that* again," Guy grated. "It's not like *we* planned to be ripped away from our homes … or our planet. We didn't *plan* to be stuck in bodies that don't belong to us. We didn't *plan* on running from the law and outlaws and who knows whom else, only to be cooped up in a ship with some spy who had *planned* everything but doesn't seem to have a clue what he's doing!"

They sat there staring at one another, with Guy's chest rising and falling heavily as he tried to get his breath back after his marathon outburst.

It was hard to tell whether the Caynin was angry or humiliated. Eventually, he just sighed. "You're right. I never meant for you to get involved. But you *must* understand the impossible situation I was facing. It's not every day that you wake up wanted for the assassination of the Presidor of the Unyun Federation."

"Well, that's another thing," Neville said, eyeing the Caynin suspiciously. "We don't even know you *didn't* do it. Heck, *you* don't even know that you didn't do it."

"I *know* I didn't," Max growled, leering at Neville.

"How? Even if there *was* a second gunship at Grassi Nole, how do you know that *you* weren't the one who pulled the trigger?"

"Because Harild Dooka was my friend!" Max cried, jumping up again to pace the floor. "I couldn't ... no, I *wouldn't* ... I would *never* do that!"

"In my experience, *never* is a strong word," Neville said. "On Earth, I too was an officer of the law. Not a detective or a spy or anything, but law-enforcement nonetheless. I've seen what people can do to others, even to those close to them – *especially* those close to them. Maybe you had a falling out with the Presidor about money, or a girl, or the lawnmower you never returned. It could have been anything. So, again, how do you *know* it wasn't you who killed him?"

"Because I *do*," Max said, disturbed.

"But *how?*" Neville prodded unrelentingly.

Not taking his eyes off Neville, Max suddenly slammed his hands down on the table. "Because I *just do*, okay?"

"Geez, okay!" Guy yelped, as his hand was unfortunate enough to have been caught between the Caynin's hand and the tabletop. "Was that really necessary?"

"I'm sorry," Max said, looking shocked at his own behaviour. He got up to check on the little Salaman, who recoiled when the Caynin reached out to him.

"I'm sorry," Max repeated, shoulders sagging and ears drooping. Despite the volatile situation, Guy had the sudden urge to pat him on the head. But he didn't.

The Infiltrator finally shook his head and sat down once more.

"I don't know," he said. "Maybe I did ... maybe I didn't. If I did, I must pay for what I've done. And if I didn't, the bastards behind this had better hope I don't find them. The question is, though: will you help me?"

CHAPTER 37

Neville glanced at Guy before locking eyes with the Caynin.

"Well, I'm always up for some justice," he said, "even if the assassin turns out to be you. What do you say, Guy? You in?"

Guy stared at him in disbelief. "What? No! You *know* I can't do this, Neville. I'm not like you, or him. I don't have it in me!"

"Did you have it in you to take on *The Plunge of Death* that first time?" Neville said, now looking his friend in the eye.

"Er … no, but—"

"But nothing. You still did it, and from what you've told me, you've come to excel at it. You wouldn't have embellished your newfound talents, now would you?"

"Of course not! But this is *different!*"

"I don't think so, bud. I've always said you have more in you than even *you* would like to admit. And I still believe it."

Under pressure from Neville's stare and Max's sad face, Guy finally relented.[*]

---

[*] Caynins are widely regarded as some of the best natural fighters in the Charted Universe, and they're quick studies when it comes to all forms of combat, with or without weapons. However, it is also widely agreed that the most dangerous weapon in a Caynin's arsenal is the sad face. It's nearly impossible to fight a Caynin if you can't stay mad at them.

"Fine," he said with a tone of irritation to mask his disbelief at what he was about to say. "I'll do it … if only to get you to shut up!"

"I'll take that," Neville grinned, before turning his attention back to Max. "So, what's the next step?"

Max eyed them respectively. "Well, I know how you're going to react to this, but … I'm not completely sure yet."

"Oh, for goodness' sake!" Guy said, throwing his hands in the air. "What a surprise!"

Neville looked a bit irritated himself.

Max held up his hands. "No, you don't understand. I know *what* we need to do, but I'm just not sure *how* to go about doing it. Not yet, anyway."

"What do you mean?" Guy said.

"Well, in order to identify the gunship, we need to get you reverse-transferred with Bezam and Lenny. And for that, we need to find Mr Gray."

"So what's the problem?" Neville said flatly. "We go to Unyun, we go to his offices, and we find him."

"The problem," Max said with a concerned expression, "is that we should avoid Unyun as far as possible."

"Why?"

"Because it's a hot zone for all kinds of scum who'll be out looking for us. The Man has eyes everywhere, especially on Unyun. Besides, I contacted the *Life Spectacular* offices to organise an off-planet meeting with Mr Gray, but it seems he isn't there anymore."

"What do you mean he isn't there anymore?" Guy said anxiously. "Maybe try calling him outside his lunch break."

"Well, unless his lunch break is longer than that of the average office worker, I don't think it's the problem. He hasn't been in for months now."

"Months!" Guy and Neville exclaimed, looking at one another in alarm and then at Max in some more alarm.

"*How many* months?" Guy demanded.

"Well, judging by what you've told me, I'd say round about the time he last saw you, Mr Leatherman."

•••

Cholesterol builds up over time. It can clog arteries and subsequently block blood flow. It usually stems from bad habits such as bad diets; a fact that's continually drilled into humans by Earth's healthcare professionals.

However, after extensive research in other parts of the universe, healthcare professionals were shocked to discover that, while bad habits definitely contribute to high cholesterol and its subsequent undesirable effects on the body, other blockages might be the main cause of high cholesterol and many more medical conditions. They ascertained that these blockages are generally found between the ears and the brain of most individuals across various species, preventing certain messages from reaching the body's central processing unit. The medical fraternity have, however, not been able to pinpoint the exact location, nature or cause of these blockages. So, for now, they've settled on calling it SHS, otherwise known as Selective Hearing Syndrome.

Bad news can be like cholesterol, although it doesn't gradually build up but rather manifests itself instantaneously. And while it can easily break through the blockages of SHS, it also tends to form its own blockages that restrict blood flow, causing the subject to feel faint. Which, coincidently, is what Guy was suddenly feeling.

"Mr Gray is missing?" he said, sounding like he felt. "Did he just leave? How could he *do* that?" Then hysteria crashed the party. "Do you think he's dead?! You think he's dead, don't you?!! Oh, geez, he's *dead!!!*"

Neville gave Guy's face a concerned slap.

Hysteria can be another side-effect of bad news, and while slap-in-the-face treatment is highly effective in providing immediate relief, it has its own side-effects, which often includes sobbing, scowling, grimacing or, in severe cases, all of these symptoms simultaneously.

"What was that for?" Guy said, rubbing his cheek as tears impeded the intended effect of his grimacing scowl.

"Getting hysterical isn't going to help anyone right now," Neville said, not sure whether he was trying to convince Guy or himself.

"He's right," Max said. "You cannot fall apart now."

"Sorry," Neville said, flashing Guy a guilty look.

"Mf," Guy grunted sourly.

"We need to figure out what our next step is going to be," Max said. "We don't know where Mr Gray is, but we cannot let that stop us."

Guy suddenly paused his face-rubbing.

"That's it!" he said, all sulkiness disappearing.

"*What's* it?" Neville asked.

"We don't know where Mr Gray *is*, right?"

The other two nodded in confirmation.

"But we *do* know where he *would have* been," Guy continued with sparkling eyes, only partly due to some residual tears.

The other two stared at him in confusion.

"I'm not sure I—" Max started. "Ah, yes, of course!"

"What are you two on about?" Neville asked, alternating confused glances between Guy and Max.

"The circus, Nev," Guy said excitedly.

"What about it?" Neville said, still feeling lost.

"We need to go to the circus."

"Why, do you need to pick up clean underwear?"

"No," Guy said. Although, come to think of it, he *did* have a lot of clean underwear there. Kola had made sure of it. And, he thought as he glanced down at his current undergarments, it might come in handy.

"It's the last place I saw Mr Gray," he continued, "and that's where he would have gone to check in on me. So maybe he's there, or maybe he left me a message."

Neville rubbed his chin. "Hmm, yeah, I suppose it's worth checking out."

"Yes," Max said, getting up. "It's our best possible course of action at this stage. Gentlemen, I suggest you get some sleep because – and I can't believe I'm saying this – we're going to the circus."

CHAPTER 38

Guy was embroiled in a heated argument with a zebra-unicorn that had popped Guy's balloon. They were mostly arguing over the creature's refusal to buy him a new one. They got into a scuffle, with the black-and-white-striped beast shaking Guy and telling him to wake up. Which was strange, as this had nothing to do with the balloon. Why couldn't people just stick to the issue at hand?

"Wake up, Mr Leatherman," a familiar voice repeated.

Guy awoke with a start and gave the Caynin shaking him a startled look while trying to escape into the seat he'd fallen asleep on.

"By Zolt, you're a deep sleeper," Max said. "I almost thought I'd have to give you another slap. It seems to work well on you."

"You try that, then we'll see how well it works on a Caynin," Guy growled groggily, before realising what he'd just said to a trained fighter.

"Sorry," he added quickly, "I don't wake up well.[*] Where are we?"

"We've arrived," Max said.

Guy got up unsteadily and joined Neville, who gawked at the window like a hobo in a bank vault.

"Look at *that*, bud," he breathed. "Amazing, isn't it?"

---

[*] In fairness, this is true of most people. But if you're not most people, good for you.

"Yeah, amazing," Guy said offhandedly, rubbing his eyes, then rubbed them some more after taking a second look at the planet growing bigger before them. The sight instantly washed away the remaining sleepiness that stubbornly tried to hold on.

"Wow!" he said less offhandedly.

As the first planet he ever personally observed from orbit, Grassi Nole was indeed impressive. It was pretty big, and just plain pretty. With its blue soil, it boasted a lot more blue than Earth, with vast cloud formations hanging peacefully above the landscape – or at least they seemed peaceful from up here. Guy wasn't fooled, though. He'd experienced quite a few storms on the planet's surface, some of which could be outright scary, especially if you were trying to erect a circus dome.

Neville nudged Guy in the side. "So *this* is where you spent most of your time hiding from me."

"Yes," Guy said, "pretty much."

"Any places of interest?"

"They've got some awesome pubs."

"You really should get out more."

Guy opened his mouth, but Neville interrupted him.

"Pubs don't count," he said flatly.

Guy closed his mouth.

"Sorry to interrupt, gentlemen," Max said, pushing through to take a seat behind the ship's controls. "Where were you last, Mr Leatherman?"

"I think it was Mashin. Yes, Mashin."

Max entered the name into some kind of planetary map.

"It seems the circus has moved on to another town not too far from there," he said, before continuing the search.

"Perfect," he added. "It seems it will be night there soon. We can use the darkness as cover."

Guy felt excitedly anxious: excited to see his circus friends, but also anxious to get some good news. He could *really* do with some good news. Too bad he didn't get any.

•••

Boredom, like bad news and high cholesterol, is a terrible condition to be stuck with. Boredom has led to almost as much destruction and chaos in the universe than stupidity, which is why these two forces have officially been added to the Charted Universe's Top Ten Destructive Forces. They rank right up there with magnetars, quasars, hypernovas, gamma rays and the collision of two supermassive black holes, which is currently ranked second. The only thing more destructive than two supermassive black holes colliding is when boredom and stupidity collide and merge.

Many bored people have stupidly questioned this fact. On the face of it, their arguments had merit, as many of the other destructive forces listed would occasionally come along and make a huge mess of things. However, boredom and stupidity are constant, and everywhere.[*] Every skeptic that's ever argued against bored-stupidity's position at the top of the list

---

[*] For his remark about the infiniteness of human stupidity, Albert Einstein had almost received a Posthumous Award for the Most Valuable Contribution by an Individual of a Dumb Planet from the Unyun Institute of Science. But three things had counted against him. Firstly, he hadn't properly considered the probability of how prolific stupidity actually is among *all* species across the universe – not just humans. So, some points had been deducted. Secondly, he hadn't factored in the addition of boredom, as well as the exponential effect of each person added in doing something collectively stupid. However, thirdly, and most importantly, Judge Three hadn't liked Einstein's hairstyle. Which is why Albert got edged out by Lester Schnik from Gloob, who'd died in a mountain-climbing accident. Lester had broadcast taunting, derogatory remarks about aliens in the hope that his messages would one day reach as many species out there as possible. The only reason the Unyun Federation decided not to break its own laws on attacking a Dumb Planet – just that one time, as an exception, of course – was because Lester had died in the mountain-climbing accident. This in itself was seen by all as the Most Valuable Contribution by an Individual of a Dumb Planet, especially in preserving that planet. Now, getting an award for dying might sound horrible, but it should be made clear that Lester had been a truly horrible man. Getting an award for dying should be proof enough of that.

has been silenced, usually by themselves after less than a minute of actually thinking about it.

•••

Samba and Safamu were lying in their cage, feeling as bored as they looked.

Le'us, just like other beta species such as cows, sheep, dogs and cats, cannot be understood by alpha species. Scientists and engineers had tried to rectify this by trying to tweak vernaculites in countless combinations, but even the best results hadn't yielded anything worthwhile. So, eventually, everybody just gave up on the project, reckoning it probably was a stupid idea in any case. However, most beta species have a good form of communication among their own, and they're generally quite happy with the idea of not being understood by those who *think* they're better than them.

"Mmmmf," Safamu moaned.

Now "mmmmf" is a very understandable sound for "I'm bored" among most species – including alpha and beta – throughout the universe. But because of their general lack of understanding beta species' vocabulary, alpha species usually see the sound as just that; a sound. For the benefit of individuals from alpha species, the rest of the conversation might therefore need some translation.

"Yeah," Samba moaned in reply. "Me too."

He yawned, baring enormous fangs, then stretched his long, scaly body, which ended in a long, scaly tail. He got up and padded lazily to the side of the cage, resting his head on a crossbar with his snout protruding outside.

Not to be outdone, Safamu also yawned.

"Mmmmf," he moaned again.

"I know, I know," grunted Samba, staring longingly at the circus dome. "Why can't they just let us eat someone? I mean, they always fill that place with all kinds of tidbits, yet we aren't allowed *any*. All they do is bring us food in buckets. That's *so* boring. Why can't we just hunt down some live ones? It's been *so* long."

Behind him, Safamu got up with a grunt and made his way over to rest his head beside that of Samba.

"I know what you mean," Safamu puffed. "It's like something's *calling* me to catch and rip something else apart. Preferably something tasty."

"Exactly!" Samba roared. "Is that too much to ask?"

"Yeah, all this routine and lying around is just *so* boring. I need a *fix*!"

"Please don't use that word," Samba moaned, with a feeling of discomfort manifesting itself between his hind legs.

"Oh, yes, sorry," Safamu grunted apologetically. "But we need to do something … exciting, and soon."

"But what?'

"I don't know."

They both just stared at the dome for a while.

"*I* know," Samba growled. "Let's play Swallow the Leader."

"Mmm," Safamu purred, licking his lips.[*] "Our new tamer *does* look quite yummy, doesn't he?"

"That he does! It won't be difficult getting the whip and that little chair away from him. Too bad he won't be able to run very far with all that fat around his waist. But if we run *really* slowly, I'm sure we can stretch it out a bit."

They stared at the dome again in silence, saliva dripping from their fangs.

"It's a good suggestion," Safamu sighed, "but a bad idea."

"Why?" Samba grunted.

"Because we've already attacked the tamer before him."

"Oh, yeah. Remember how I clawed his fleeing rump just before we got stunned?"

"How could I forget? That was epic! But we can't do it again. We were lucky to have gotten away with it the first time. I think a second time, and we're out, or worse."

---

[*] "Mmm", or its shorter cousin, "mm", is another universal cross-species term that can be used to express contentment, pleasure, agreement, approval, uncertainty or reflection. Unless of course you have duct/duck tape over your mouth, in which case it could mean anything.

"Yeah," Samba moaned. "We'd be stupid to do it."[*]

"*Really* stupid," Safamu agreed. "Never bite the hand that feeds you."

"What about a hand that doesn't feed you?" Samba purred as he lifted his head with an air of hope.

"What do you mean?"

"Look over there."

Safamu looked where Samba was looking and spotted three shadowy figures approaching.

"Hey, I haven't had the scent of *that one* in my nostrils for a while," he purred. "I've always thought he'd make an excellent snack. And look, the one next to him is bite-size too."

"Mmm, yes," Samba moaned, "I'd love to sink my teeth into *that*."

They stared at the three figures passing the cage. Although they'd been fed quite recently, Samba and Safamu were suddenly hungry again. Blast those annoying iron bars!

•••

After satisfying himself that the circus grounds were clear, Max signalled for the other two to follow. Staying low, they used tents, a-grav trailers, containers and other objects as cover to avoid being spotted. The fewer the people who knew they were there, the better.

Neville glanced uneasily at the two big, scaly cat-like creatures staring at the trio as they passed their cage. It wasn't the fact that they were staring, but more *the way* in which they were staring while licking their chops that had him on edge.

"What's wrong?" Guy whispered.

"Those things," Neville said, pointing a thumb at the cage.

"Oh, the Le'us. What about them?"

"I don't like the way they're looking at me."

"Looking at you like what?"

"Like a cheeseburger."

"Ah, that's the way they look at everyone," Guy said semi-nonchalantly. "Don't mind them, they're quite tame."

---

[*] There's a lot that alpha species can learn from beta species.

As Guy didn't look like he truly believed himself, Neville didn't either, and he was quite relieved when they eventually put some distance between themselves and the beasts.

Max halted. "Which way now?"

Fortunately, the circus was almost always set up in the same configuration to make it easier for circus folk to navigate, and for them to feel at home wherever they set up shop.

"We're almost there," Guy said. "Left here; third tent on the right."

They made their way to the tent indicated by Guy and slipped in without a sound.

•••

Cortex was asleep, which meant the Wispin was asleep too. Those not familiar with Veagins might like to know that every Veagin comprises two parts.

Part one is the Veagat that, on its own, is basically a large beetle-like creature that grazes on grass and tree leaves. Two of its three pairs of legs double as arms, which is particularly useful for climbing and even more useful – as was later discovered – for flipping burgers. Which is why, thanks to the massive fast-food industry, there's no such thing as an unemployed Veagin.

Part two is the Wispin, a race that had long ago transcended their physical form, which wasn't the biggest loss to the universe, as they weren't much to look at. However, after hanging around for a few millennia in their metaphysical form, playing various mind games and telling the same knock-knock jokes over and over … and over … and not being able to interact with the physical world, they had become bored. And, being highly intelligent, Wispins knew the dangers associated with boredom, and opted to enter symbiotic agreements with individuals of certain beta species.

It was simple. Wispins would invade the mind of the subject for a while. If the individual enjoyed their newfound transcendence to a higher level of consciousness and consented to a more permanent arrangement, the Wispin stayed on, forming a new species. Which, in Veagats' case, was called a Veagin.

However, while giving beta species the ability to function normally in society through higher intelligence and telepathic communication, occupying the minds of such species has its drawbacks. Wispins know just about everything there is to know about anything, but they cannot hold all that information in the symbiotic relationship, which leads to them dumbing down quite extensively – the extent of which also depends on the species and the individual. But what is all that knowledge worth if you cannot share it, right? Besides, being able to enjoy nachos and mojitos again is totally worth dropping a few hundred IQ points.

Waking up a Veagin also involves two parts, as you first have to wake up the Veagat, who in turn has to wake up the Wispin. Which is why it took a second longer for Cortex to awaken.

"Come on, Cor, wake up," Cortex heard as he awoke to a finger poking him in the side.

With a murmur, he opened his eyes and saw a familiar face staring down at him. *"What ... oh, Bezam, leave me alone. I'm trying to sleep."*

He turned over to resume his slumber, but the Wispin in his head kept nagging at him about something. When the message finally hit home, he sat bolt upright and looked at the face again.

"Bezam!" he exclaimed. *"I mean, Guy! What are you doing here? And what weren't you doing here? Where did you go? What's your brother doing here, and who's the other guy?"*

Guy looked at him, befuddled. "My *what?*"

"Your brother," Cortex said, pointing at Neville. *"Or Bezam's brother, I should say. Did Lenny get you into trouble again? Or did you get him into trouble? Sorry, I should have warned you about him ... or I should rather have warned you about the two of you being together."*

Guy stared at Neville, who just stared back at him along with Max.

"We're *brothers?*" Guy said.

Neville mirrored Guy's befuddlement. "What?"

"Oh, sorry, I forgot I was still in one-on-one mode," Cortex said. *"Is that better?"*

"Is what better?" Neville said, then looked around warily. "Wait, who said that?"

"*He* did," Guy said, pointing at Cortex.

"But his lips didn't move!" Neville said.

"Telepath," Guy said matter-of-factly.

"Oh … er … yes, of course," Neville tried to say matter-of-factly without the desired effect.

"This is Cortex," Guy said. "Remember, the friend I told you about?"

"Yes, quite a few times."

"And this," Guy addressed Cortex, throwing a thumb at Neville, "is Neville. Remember, the friend I told *you* about?"

"More than a few times," Cortex said.

"*Glad* to *meet* you," Neville and Cortex spoke over one another, although Neville had spoken it out quite loudly.

There was an awkward moment of silence.

"You don't have to shout, Nev," Guy said. "He's telepathic, not deaf."

"Oh," Neville said, embarrassed. "Er, sorry."

Cortex shrugged. *"No problem. It happens to most people the first time."*

He then nodded towards Max. *"And this one?"*

"That's Max," Guy said, and held up a hand as Cortex was about to ask something else. "Listen, Cor, I'd love to tell you everything, but we don't have much time."

"Not even for a couple of cold ones?"

"No, not ev— you've got *beer*?"

"Of course," Cortex replied, nodding towards his small fridge. *"I kept it stocked in case you returned."*

Guy grinned.

"Well," he said, "I guess we have some time after all."

●●●

Sitting at the small table in Cortex's tent, Guy recounted the events that had transpired since the last time they'd seen each other.

When he finished, the bug gave a mental whistle. *"Geez, that's intense!"*

"Yep, and you don't even know half of it," Guy said, trying to sound enigmatic.

"Heck, *we* don't even know the half of it," Neville said, spoiling the effect.

Guy glowered at Neville. "No, we don't."

He turned his attention back to his Veagin friend. "Which is why we're here," he said hopefully. "Has Mr Gray been around?"

"No, I'm afraid not," Cortex said.

Guy's hopes took a knock before rising again.

"Did he maybe leave a message?"

"Nope, sorry."

This time, Guy's hopes were knocked to the ground and seemed to be out for the count.

"So we've got nothing," he moaned. "All of this … for nothing."

He took a swig of beer, hoping someone else would come up with a solution. No one did.

After a long period of silence, during which everyone just sat there staring at their bottles, Max eventually gave a sigh. They all stared at him expectantly, so he gave another sigh, took a sip of beer, and continued staring at his bottle.

"Oh, come on!" Neville said, looking at him. "Is this *it?*"

The Caynin sighed again, but this time he followed it up by saying, "For now."

"What do you mean for now? We can't just sit around. We've got to do… *something!*"

Max's attempt at a reply was waylaid by a distant scream, followed by more screams and the *thumps* of weapons being discharged.

"Well," the Caynin said, placing his bottle on the table, "it seems we've got something to do after all."

CHAPTER 39

Panic filled the air outside as the four peered through the tent's exit to witness a scene of chaos. Circus folk ran helter-skelter, trying to avoid the Vahltans walking about, shooting at anything that moved. Fortunately, because it was dark and Vahltans generally cannot see that well in the low light, they weren't successful in hitting anyone. They were however successful in hitting everything else, which was why parts of the circus grounds were now on fire.

Max looked about cautiously until he found something that caught his attention.

"Over there!" he said, indicating a stack of small metal containers nearby.

With Max leading the way, they made a run for it, ducking and weaving to avoid the stray shots fired in all directions. Reaching the stack, the group took cover with their backs pressed against the metal boxes.

"What do we do now?" Guy yelled at Max over the din of weapons fire and screaming.

"We need to get back to the ship!" Max yelled back. "Just give me a minute's head start to make sure the way is clear, then follow at a safe distance!"

Guy and Neville nodded, while Cortex looked too shell-shocked to do anything other than looking shell-shocked.

"And don't do anything stupid," Max added with a serious glare before rushing off, leaving behind three figures who tried to make as small a target of themselves as they could.

Two of them succeeded, while the third still had several Veagin parts protruding from behind the cover.

"Okay!" Neville shouted after what he estimated to be a minute, "you heard Max. On my three, we start moving, alright?"

Despite the lack of any kind of response from the other two, he started counting. "One, two, three!"

He was about to take off when he noticed that his companions remained fixed in place.

"Three," he repeated.

"What are you *doing*?" he hissed, seeing a look of uncharacteristic resolve crossing his friend's face.

"We can't leave, Neville," Guy answered the puzzled frown directed at him.

"What about the whole Presidor-assassination-big-picture thing?" Neville said.

"That will have to wait," Guy said firmly. "These are *my* people, Nev. Bezam's people, yes, but *my* people too."

Neville looked at Guy pleadingly. "They're after *us*. You know that, right? So if we go, they might follow us."

"They *might*, yes, but we cannot take that chance. We need to help."

"How, Guy? We have no weapons, and the last time I checked you weren't exactly king of the boxing ring."

Guy gave him a resolute stare; fearful, but resolute.

"I cannot keep you safe here," Neville said, "and … I *have* to keep you safe. *You* are my people."

"I know, Nev," Guy said, looking around at the panicked circus folk running about. "But I need to keep *them* safe. They're in this mess because of me."

Neville had seen the look on Guy's face a couple of times before, but it had usually been when his friend was trying to down a drink on a dare, knowing full well what the messy outcome would be. So he just took a deep breath and resigned himself to the fact that, despite strict instructions not to do so, they were about to do something stupid.

He sighed. "So, what do you propose?"

Guy gave a grin that Neville had never seen before on Guy's face. He wasn't sure he liked it.

"It's simple, really," Guy said mischievously. "We'll just do what we do best."

•••

Guy, Neville and Cortex had a quick huddle. With a nod, the bug ran off from cover to cover before finally disappearing between two tents.

"Are you sure this is going to work?" Neville said, peering around the corner of the container at two trigger-happy Vahltans advancing on their position.

"No," Guy admitted. He left out the fact that he'd never really been sure of anything in his life, and was therefore not quite sure what it should feel like.

"But this is our only play," he continued, "so we just have to *make sure* it works."

Realising that time was of the essence, Neville abandoned all attempts at arguing the matter further. He looked around and picked up a short yet sturdy pipe lying atop one of the containers.

He clenched the weapon almost as firmly as his teeth. "I'll do my best."

"Here goes," Guy said and stormed off towards the two approaching Vahltans, who jumped back in surprise at the small figure suddenly rushing past between them.

In fact, their surprise was so severe that one of them accidentally fired off a shot. He swung around and watched as the figure sprinted towards the big dome. He fired a couple more shots in the general direction of the rapidly dwindling figure before it disappeared from sight.

He squinted into the darkness.

"Hey, Jeffi," he said, "isn't that the bugger we're looking for?"

Receiving no answer, he turned around. At first he thought his fellow Vahltan had bolted, but after a brief search – by looking down – he was relieved to see that his partner wasn't gone. He was however quite distraught to find that most of his colleague's head was gone.

"Fhark," he breathed, looking in horror at the weapon in his hand. The others weren't going to like this, especially Andi. He then got an idea and whipped out his commlink.

"Guys," he yelled into the device, "it's Ricki! They got Jeffi! I found one of the marks. He's heading to the dome. Meet me there!"

Putting back the commlink, Ricki quietly praised himself for his quick thinking and hurried towards the dome. That little red jerk was going to pay for almost getting him into trouble.

• • •

Guy had heard the shots behind him, prompting his legs to pump even harder. Without stopping, he ran through the dome's entrance and stopped at the edge of the arena floor.

Under the dome's dim interior night lights, all was quiet except for the weapons fire outside, which seemed to have diminished somewhat. The screams were quieting down too. There wasn't any sign of people in the dimly lit interior. The silent, empty stands looked ominous, as if a crowd of unseen ghosts were seated to witness the final big act of the great Bezam. The only sign of life was a furry blue rodent that sent up small puffs of blue dust as it scurried across the arena floor to take shelter under *The Plunge of Death*.

Guy wasn't sure why the towering structure was still there. Had they expected him to return, or had they already replaced him? There wasn't any time to contemplate it, though, as he heard another shot from outside, this time a bit louder. They were getting closer.

He hurried over to *The Plunge of Death* and nimbly started clambering up it without a thought, except for one, which gave him goosebumps – he sincerely hoped the structure wasn't going to live up to its name tonight.

• • •

Assembling outside one of the dome's entrances, the Vahltans were quite agitated. Ricki had just finished telling them how he and Jeffi had been ambushed, and how Jeffi had been brutally murdered despite Ricki's valiant attempt to save him.

Notwithstanding Vahltans' natural feeling of apathy towards one another, Jeffi had generally sort of been liked by most of The Man's crew, which in Vahltan terms meant he was quite popular – or had been. The now-deceased Jeffi had in fact been quite a good bad guy, who'd always joked around as other people were being tortured. And he had never stabbed any of his colleagues in the back, having enough decency to do it from the front when they weren't looking. Yes, Jeffi would sort of be missed.

"Remember," Ricki said, "we need him alive, so stunners only."

When none of the others appeared pleased with this, he added, "I'm sure the boss will let us have the maggot after he's done with him."

This had the desired effect, with all nodding and grunting in agreement, for which Ricki was extremely grateful. He didn't want anything to go wrong due to a stupid act of vengeance.

"Now, let's go get the bastard!" he yelled as he ran into the main circus dome with a bunch of yelling Vahltans right on his heels.

CHAPTER 40

Guy was almost at the top of *The Plunge of Death* when he heard the blood-curdling yells coming from below. He paused briefly to glance down at the large group of Vahltans charging in through the dome's entrance, before resuming his swift ascent.

"Up there!" he heard someone shouting. "Get him!"

Reaching the top, Guy heaved himself onto the platform and peered down as a dozen or so Vahltans came rushing towards the structure. Holstering their weapons, they started climbing clumsily yet steadily. He waited until the first Vahltans were about halfway up.

"Here goes nothing," he said, straightening his back. He took a moment to compose himself, then inhaled deeply before taking the plunge.

As air rushed past his ears, he heard someone shout "Hs cmn dwn!", but blocked it from his thoughts as he grabbed the first bar and started his swift descent. He gracefully swung, pivoted and somersaulted his way down, occasionally using his feet to kick a face that barely had time to gasp before plummeting to the ground below, sending up a small cloud of dust each time. The lucky ones swore under their breath before starting the climb back down. With one final somersault, Guy stuck his landing perfectly atop a Vahltan who'd been trying to get up after a painful fall.

Forgetting himself for a moment, Guy stood up straight and raised his arms in acceptance of the applause that didn't come. When he stopped forgetting, he glanced about at the few dazed Vahltans who'd managed to get up, as well as the others still making their way down *The Plunge of Death*. Two of them made the last bit down very quickly, landing on the blue arena floor with groans.

"Thought you were clever, didn't you?" said one of the Vahltans who had remained on terra firma the whole time. "What did you think was going to happen; that you'd take us all on by your lonesome self?"

"No ..." Guy said, catching his breath, "... I was just ... buying some time."

"Time for what?" the Vahltan sneered.

"For not ... being ... by my lonesome self," Guy said, before the lights suddenly dimmed to near darkness.

•••

The Vahltans swung about warily in all directions, as they were now almost completely blind. They *had* brought their flashlights, but apparently that good-for-nothing rookie Gabbi hadn't charged them like she was supposed to.[*]

"This won't stop us, you little—" Ricki started, and spun to aim his weapon at the now-empty space where the Salaman had stood before.

The Vahltan heard a growl somewhere distant. Or was it close? He and his colleagues pivoted in that direction but couldn't make out anything. Another growl, closer than the first, came from behind, and they spun back. They still couldn't see a thing, so they strained their ears tensely, but could also not hear anything aside from their own heavy breathing.

For what seemed like ages, nothing continued to happen, but it happened in a way that made Ricki's skin crawl.

"Uh—" the Vahltan next to Ricki finally broke the silence, but he didn't get any further, as a roaring, scaly blur suddenly leapt from nowhere, toppling the Vahltan over and dragging him off, kicking and screaming, before anyone could react.

---

[*] It's easy to judge if you aren't the one who has to make coffee for everyone else the whole time. Multitasking has its limits.

All Vahltan eyes stared in horror in the direction their compatriot had vanished.

"What the fhark was that?" the other Vahltan next to Ricky yelled before he found out himself. He was wrenched from the group from behind by another blurry shape that dragged the henchman off with a satisfied snarl. Ricki now recognised the sound, and his blood turned to ice.

All Vahltan heads in the group now swivelled in multiple directions along with their respective bodies.

"We need to get out of here, Ricki," one of the Vahltans said anxiously, looking about him with eyes that seemed tired of the confines of their sockets and were planning on doing something about it.

"Right," Ricki said in what he hoped was a passable tone of courage. It wasn't.

"Retreat," he added with a shaky voice, "in an orderly fashion, on my go."

He took a deep breath to give the order, which the others conveniently took as the order and scattered in whichever direction they'd been facing. This made Ricki momentarily angry, because he'd been hoping to get a head start, but then survival instinct took over and sent him running towards – which he sincerely hoped – was the nearest exit. His hopes were however quickly dashed as he ran into an average-sized figure with beyond-average strength. Ricki knew the figure's strength was beyond average, because it grabbed him by the neck and lifted him up effortlessly.

"What do we have here?" the figure said, and flung the Vahltan aside like a shrieking pillow.

Ricki crashed headfirst into the arena barrier, which instantly caused his vision to swim. Before him swam a vision of the figure grabbing another Vahltan by the chest and bashing him over the head. The henchman crumpled to the ground. Other visions also swam across Ricki's dazed field of view, like a Salaman riding the back of a staggering Vahltan, beating his ride repeatedly over the head with a metal pipe while another Salaman clung to one of the henchman's legs. Like a woman spewing fire, setting a Vahltan's coat ablaze, causing him to drop to the ground and roll around to douse the flames engulfing him. Like the knife-thrower who turned a fleeing Vahltan into a porcupine, sending him sprawling face-down in the dust. Like the fierce-looking clowns who were chasing down two Vahltans with hammers that did *not* go *squeak* when they hit. Like the figure straddling two long-necked camelhorses that knocked down a Vahltan who'd nearly made it off the arena floor. Like the Le'u tearing out the throat of another Vahltan before looking around for its next victim, panting happily.

Like, like, like.

The overload of visions finally managed to meet up with the blow to Ricki's head, and they both agreed it might be a good idea for his consciousness to close up shop for a while, because things were getting a bit crowded. The Vahltan's consciousness was all too happy to oblige, especially as the last thing it noticed was the Le'u noticing him. As the creature closed in on him, Ricki's consciousness was glad that it wouldn't be around for what came next. It did, however, feel slightly guilty about leaving the rest of the body behind as it drifted off into ignorant bliss for the last time.

•••

Guy stared at the gory scene around him, which was now well-illuminated by the lights that had been turned back on, full blast. He felt the weight of remorse pressing down on him. Not because of what they'd done – it *had to* be done – but because it was *his* presence that had led to this mess in the first place. As adrenaline faded, the weight became too much to bear, causing his legs to buckle and his backside to hit the ground hard. He didn't even notice the pain.

He buried his face in his hands. "I'm sorry. I'm so, so sorry."

"Sorry for what?" said a voice from behind.

Guy recognised the voice as that of the yellow-furred circus boss, Rimmy, who walked over to sit next to him. Kola was his wife, and apart from his broader face and shorter yellow hair, they looked pretty similar.

Guy pulled up his legs, crossed his arms over his knees and rested his head on his forearms. He stared at the blue grains of sand between his feet as tears welled up in his eyes.

"It's all my fault," he said softly.

"Why?" Rimmy said, taking off his black top hat. "Because you got snatched from your life and shoved into a nightmare? It sure doesn't sound like *your* fault to me."

Guy's head jerked towards his former boss. "You mean you *know?*" he said.

"Well, Kola told me, of course. I was almost as surprised as the others."

"*They* know too?" Guy looked around at the figures walking about. A few paused at the unmoving shapes on the ground, kicking them to make sure they remained unmoving.

"Of course," Rimmy said in a gentle tone. "We're family, you know? What happens to one of us happens to all of us."

Guy stared at the yellow man in amazement. "But I'm not even part of your family. Bezam is. Why would you risk your lives for *me?*"

"Because, even if it was only for a while, you *were* part of the family too, which makes you a lifetime member. Also, Bezam would never have forgiven us if we'd let anything happen to his precious little body."

"I suspect you might be right," Guy said gratefully, wiping his eyes.

"Besides," Rimmy said, his expression growing stern, "we didn't just do it for you. *No one* attacks our home and gets away with it."

Somewhere distant, sirens started wailing, and Max came storming in through the entrance with his weapon drawn. He stopped just inside the arena floor, glancing about him, bewildered, then walked over to Guy.

"I told you to follow me to the ship and *not* to do anything stupid!" the Caynin said, then had a proper look around. "What in Zolt's name happened here?"

"Something … stupid," Guy said, getting up slowly as Neville and Cortex joined them.

"I can see that," Max hissed, and then listened as the wail of the sirens grew louder. "But we don't have time to discuss it now. You hear that?"

They nodded.

"*That*, my friends," Max continued, "is the sound of the Central Unyun Protectorate coming to find out what's going on, and you'd better pray they don't find us."

"Trouble with the Cups?" Rimmy asked in a way that stated this wasn't the first time the long arm of the law has come looking for his folk.

"Yes," Max said. "We need somewhere to hide."

"No problem, " Cortex volunteered, motioning for them to follow as he trotted towards the dome's exit. *"I know* just *the place. "*

CHAPTER 41

As the first light of the first sun crowned the dome of the circus, three figures huddled in a big metal container with **CAUTION: FAECAL MATTER** written in bold, red letters on the side.

Six eyes peered out from behind metal drums containing material that didn't really need the words outside to identify their contents. The eyes watched tensely as Protectors in tight-fitting, dark-navy uniforms searched the area. The lawmen popped in and out of tents, looking behind equipment and everywhere else a good Protector should look. They however seemed to turn a blind eye to the container in which the three figures were hiding, each probably hoping that one of their colleagues had done their due diligence in inspecting the repulsive structure.

Guy and Neville exchanged sour looks that echoed the smell filling their nostrils, while Max looked quite pleased for some reason.

Guy redirected his sour look at the Caynin. "Why are you looking so chipper?"

Ignoring the question, the Infiltrator took a deep whiff that he rounded off with a satisfied sigh. "Your friend's quite clever. Those Protectors will avoid this area like the plague."

Neville's face turned pink. "Maybe because it *is* filled with the plague."

"Oh, nonsense," Max said, taking another whiff, triggering the automatic lurch reaction in Guy's stomach.

"That's just sick," Guy hissed, covering his mouth and nose. "*I'm* going to be sick."

"Keep it in," Max warned. "We don't want to draw attention to ourselves."

"How long is this going to take?" Guy managed without something other than words spilling out.

"Quite a while," Max said, peering between two drums. "In a case like this, I'd say the whole day."

"The whole day?" Guy gasped, then wished he hadn't.

"At the very least," Max said. "They have to process the scene and, judging by the severity of the scene in the dome, it's going to take some time. They then have to …"

Guy and Neville waited for the rest, which didn't come.

"They then have to *what?*" Neville said.

Max held a finger to his lips.

"What—" Neville started again.

"Shh," Max said, clamping a hand over Neville's mouth while peering through the barrels.

"Is that …?" he said, shaking his head before looking again. "Yep, that's him alright."

Guy and Neville tried to see what Max was seeing and tensed up even more when they succeeded. A man, who appeared to be human, was closing in on the container. While dressed in the same tight-fitting uniform as the other Protectors, he also sported a navy, knee-length coat.

They held their breath as the uniformed man came closer with cautious interest, reaching a hand inside his coat and keeping it there as he advanced slowly.

•••

The man, using his free hand to cover his mouth and nose, came to a halt. He squinted as he carefully scanned the shadowy interior of the container from a reasonably safe distance. Guy and Neville reluctantly took a deep breath and held it until they felt like passing out, but were afraid to take another one, and not just out of fear of making a sound.

"Looking for me?" Max said suddenly.

Neville and Guy would have gasped if they'd had air left in their lungs, so they settled for wheezes instead.

The man whipped out a gun faster than the blink of an eye[*] and pointed it towards the drums.

"I suggest you get up slowly," he commanded coolly yet firmly. "Hands first, if you please?"

Two pairs of hands, as well as a pair of hands and arms, rose slowly from behind the drums.

"Now keep it there and get up," the man ordered. "Slowly. No funny business."

Three figures got up, and the biggest one made its way around the drums.

"Oh, come now," it said from the shadows. "If you cannot have funny business at a circus, this universe is just not worth living in."

"What …" the man started, sounding as astonished as he appeared all of a sudden. "Max?"

"In the flesh," the Infiltrator responded as he stepped into the light. "Speaking of which, I'd appreciate it if you don't shoot any holes in it."

"If I were to shoot you, it would be for making bad jokes."

"If that were the case, I'd have been dead long ago."

"Ain't that the truth," the man chuckled, holstering his weapon. He however kept his distance from the container, so Max instead walked over to give him a quick embrace. As they exchanged pats on the back, the Caynin's leg twitched involuntarily. Parting, the man stepped back.

"Well, *you've* looked better," he said, looking the Infiltrator up and down.

"So have you," Max replied, flashing a grin.

"What in the name of Zolt's two dogs are you doing here?"

Max's grin faded.

"We have to talk," he said, and pointed at a nearby tent that had already been searched earlier by two Protectors; very hastily for some reason. "In there."

"And those?" the man said, nodding towards the four arms still silhouetted above the drums.

---

[*] For those who aren't sure, this is pretty fast.

"What?" Max frowned. "Oh, yes – Guy, Neville, it's okay, you can come out."

"It's okay," he repeated, but the hands remained where they were. "Really, everything's fine."

The four hands turned sideways and made their way around the drums, revealing two nervous-looking Salamans.

"And put those down," Max said brusquely, so Guy and Neville lowered their arms, but kept their nervous looks right where they belonged, fixed on the Protector.

Max ushered them into the tent. The interior was filled with unwashed clothes, empty liquor bottles, leftover food and all sorts of junk. Small red balls and hairy bundles lay scattered over a filthy vanity table amidst several jars of makeup.

Guy tripped over a pair of exceptionally big shoes and stepped onto a red ball-like object that went *whaaahk*. Great, he thought, Max just *had to* pick a clown's tent. There's a reason why their tents were always situated nearest the Poop Box, and the reason undoubtedly had something to do with the fact that the tents themselves didn't smell much better than the container outside. In *Rimmy's Magnificent Circus*, the clowns weren't exactly known for their high levels of hygiene.[*]

Max motioned for Guy and Neville to take a seat on what appeared to be the clown's bed, so they didn't.

Shrugging, the Infiltrator indicated the lawman.

"This, gentlemen," he said, "is Nelis Matters. We were in the Academy together and have been best friends ever since."

"*One* of my best friends," Nelis corrected over the collective mumbled "Hi" from Guy and Neville.

---

[*] Nor in most of the universe. However, to be fair, there *are* clowns out there who pride themselves on setting the bar high when it comes to personal hygiene. Some of them had even started a concerted, organised, non-profit movement called Clean Up Your Act. The other clowns took it as a joke – a funny one at that – and kept going about their business in the usual way.

"*My* best friend, then," Max said.

"Fine, but that's just because you don't have any other friends."

"After the Academy," Max continued, ignoring the comment, "Nelis here took the easy way out and became a Protector."

"Says the scaredy-cat that hides in the shadows."

"Hey, no one calls me a cat."

"Well, I could have called you something else that equates to a cat, but because my mom raised me with manners, I'll leave it at that. Besides, I wouldn't want to hurt your feelings."

Max gave him a nostalgic smile. "Man, it's good to see you again! I'm just glad it was *you* who saw us. If any of your fellow Protectors had spotted me, I'd most likely be hauled away, or worse."

"They're not really my *fellow Protectors* anymore," Nelis corrected. "I've recently been promoted to Federal Unyun Detector."

"A Fud? So they finally realised their mistake and made an even bigger one," Max said, trying to get his mirth back, without success.

"What are you doing here, Nelis?" he continued after a quiet moment. "Last I heard, you were stationed on Unyun."

"Still am," Nelis replied. "My mom finally retired a while back and moved here, to Grassi Nole. She's always liked the countryside. But that old piece of junk she'd been flying finally broke down permanently last month. So, with my bump in salary, I could finally afford to buy a small used ship with better sensors for the old gal. Nothing much, but dependable. I was on my way to surprise her with it when I heard the call about an attack on this circus. It's not something you hear of every day, so I thought I'd check it out."

"It's a bit far out of your jurisdiction, though, isn't it?" Max said, with a hint of suspicion breaking through.

"What can I say, I just couldn't resist," Nelis said, before seeming to pick up on Max's undertone. "What's eating you?"

Max eyed his friend firmly for a second or so, then gave a deep sigh. "Nothing. It's just … sorry, I've been on the run for some time, which hasn't done my normal levels of paranoia any favours."

"Yes, I know," Nelis said. "A while back we received an InterCup bulletin that you were wanted for questioning. Nothing about *what* you were wanted for, though. I just assumed it was part of some cover or something to help you infiltrate some organisation. I take it that's not the case?"

The human stared at the Caynin expectantly.

"Believe me," Max said glumly, "the less you know, the better."

Nelis kept staring at Max expectantly.

"No, *really*," Max tried again, "you don't want to know."

After another look at the Detector's unwavering stare, Max relented. "Okay, fine, but don't say I didn't warn you. I, er … I'm sort of … sought for … well … the assassination of the Presidor."

Nelis gave him a look which clearly stated that, in retrospect, he would have been better off not knowing.

•••

Nelis was the first human Guy had actually talked to since leaving Earth – Neville didn't really count. At least not technically. But despite burning with questions, Guy knew it wasn't the most appropriate time to ask them. So he merely stared at the Detector, whose face had just turned a shade paler.

"You're kidding, right?" Nelis said in a hopeful tone before taking another look at Max's grim expression. "You're *not* kidding."

"Wish I was," the Caynin said.

"But … why … how?"

"You sure you want to know?"

"No, but I suppose it's too late now. Lay it on me."

So Max laid it on him, pretty thick, and with each heavy layer the human's shoulders slumped a little more.

When Max was done, Nelis pulled himself up straight, although his face remained stuck in a state of disbelief.

"Geez, old friend, you *have* been through a lot."

He looked over at the Salamans standing to the side. "And by the sound of it, so have you."

Guy and Neville didn't know what to say, so they just gave him an awkward smile.

"So, what now?" the Detector addressed Max once more.

Max gave him an unreadable look. "I don't know," he said. "You tell me."

"What do you mean?"

"Well, I just told you that I might have assassinated the Presidor, so I suppose it all depends on what *you're* going to do."

Nelis rubbed his chin pensively. "Do *you* believe you did it?"

"I don't think so," Max said.

"I didn't ask if you thought so, Max. Do you *believe* it?"

"No, not for a second."

Nelis shrugged. "Then neither do I."

"Thanks, Nelis," Max said, looking relieved, "it really means a lot."

"It had better. It's not every day I pass up an opportunity to round up a suspect. I take it you have a plan?"

"Yes, but it's not a good one."

"Why?"

"Because we're going to Unyun."

Guy and Neville exchanged puzzled glances.

"I thought you said Unyun was too hot for us to go to!" Neville said angrily, taking a step forward.

"Yeah," Guy said, also stepping forward, not knowing what else to do.

"I'm with them on this one, Max," the Detector said. "It's too risky."

"Believe me," Max said, "it's not something I want to do, but we *must*. There are no other options left."

"You can turn yourself in," Nelis ventured without much confidence in his own words. "If it will make you feel any better, *I'll* take you in. I'll make sure you're kept safe until I can get to the bottom of this."

"Come now, Nelis, you heard what I said. Do you really think we'd be *safe*? No, my friend, there are some high-stakes players in this game, and we don't even know how many players are involved. On top of that, we don't have a good hand to deal with. In fact, we don't have *any* hand to deal with at this stage without the Salamans' real memories. You know I'm right."

Nelis sighed. "I do. But at least let me go with you. Between the two of us, I'm sure we'll be able to sort things out in no time."

"As tempting as that sounds, I can actually do better with a friend on the outside; one who's still … clean."

"Fine," Nelis said with a reluctant nod. "But I don't like you having to go it alone."

"I won't," Max said, indicating Guy and Neville. "I've got these two to keep me company."

"And me," another voice filled their minds.

They spun towards the entrance as a big Veagin entered the tent, only to find himself blinking at the weapon that had appeared in the Detector's hand faster than he could say *"What the …?"*, which he did in any case.

"Whoa!" Guy said, holding up his hands pleadingly. "He's okay! Really!"

"He is," Max confirmed. Nelis gave him a puzzled look, but holstered his weapon once more.

"What are you doing here, Cortex?" Guy scolded his friend.

"I suspected *you were going to disappear on me again,"* the Veagin said, *"and I wasn't about to let you get away with it a second time. You're not going anywhere without me this time around."*

Guy folded his arms. "Well, I cannot let you do that," he asserted. "I don't think it's a good idea."

"Well, I don't care what you think, I'm not *taking no for an answer,"* Cortex contended, returning the resolute stare his friend was trying to give him, before addressing Max. *"Besides, you might find the assistance of a telepath quite useful."*

Max paused before giving a nod. "He's right, Mr Leather-man."

Guy looked at the Caynin in distress, then turned the look on Cortex. "But what about the circus?" he tried. "You can't leave the circus!"

"It will take a while to get everything up and running again, so I have some spare time on my hands. Besides, I've already spoken to Rimmy and Kola. They agree that you need one of us to look after you. So, in short, I'm coming, whether you like it or not."

Guy wasn't sure whether he liked it or not, as he was at a loss for words.

"Well, that's settled then," Max said, turning to Nelis.

The human sighed. "I know that look. What do you need?"

Max shrugged. "Oh, nothing much. Just a few things."

CHAPTER 42

Spaceships weren't supposed to look cute. They were supposed to be mean-looking, sleek-looking, nimble-looking or, at the very least, spaceship-looking. Nelis's mom's ship, which the Detector had affectionately dubbed *The Mothership*, was far from spaceship-looking. It looked cute.

And that didn't sit right with Guy.

"We're going in *that* thing?" he moaned, his mind frowning along with his eyes as they swept over the pink ship. It just sat there like a big, pink ladybug, blending in with its surroundings like a pimple on a makeup model's forehead.

"Why?" Max said, walking past him. "It's *perfect*."

"If we were ladies going to a tea party, maybe," Guy mumbled unhappily, following Max to the side of the ship. The Caynin tapped the card Nelis had given him against a panel. The hatch opened, and a ramp with a handrail came down to rest on the blueish soil.

Guy's frown deepened as he eyed the handrail. "Not only is it a *lady* ship; it's … it's an *old-lady* ship."

"Which is why it's perfect," Max said as he walked up the ramp.

"Doesn't *seem* perfect," Guy muttered at his feet as he plodded up the ramp like a petulant child who'd gotten a knitted jersey instead of a gaming console for Christmas.

He bumped into Max, who'd stopped and whirled around to glare at the little Salaman.

Guy bounced back with a start.

"Look," Max grated, "if you don't like it, fine. But stop whining about it! I would've had to dump the stolen ship in any case; we were already pushing our luck with it. We can be thankful that we were *given* a ship that's not hot, because we won't have to use the less-reputable spaceports – which, I can *assure* you, will be teeming with eyes and ears all too eager to make a quick buck from reporting anything out of sorts to The Man. A general port won't be as closely watched as the others, and even if it is, a pink *old-lady ship* will not draw any unwanted attention for more than a second. Which is *why* it's perfect. So why don't you rather show some appreciation towards my friend instead of complaining about things you know nothing of!"

"Okay, geez," Guy said, holding up his hands. "Sorry I said anything."

Max cast him a hard glare before continuing up the ramp with a harrumph.

Guy looked at Neville, who gave the shrug of someone who clearly didn't want to be involved, so Guy just rolled his eyes and made his way through the hatch without another word.

Inside, he was grudgingly impressed with how clean everything was. The open-plan kitchen and living-room area was quite pleasant, aside from the pink mat at the entrance, the pink sofa and the pink coffee table. A narrow, short passageway led to the cockpit where Max took a seat to prepare the ship for takeoff.

Entering the cockpit, Guy froze when he spotted the pink, fluffy material covering the seats, complemented by two pink, fluffy cubes hanging just inside the window. He carefully sat in one of the seats, fearing that the colour would rub off on him if he moved too much. Not surprisingly, Guy was not a fan of pink. He however decided to keep it to himself to avoid another lecture.

"Uh, speaking of Nelis," he said instead, shifting carefully, "when is he coming?"

Cortex and Nelis had left earlier to pick up some things Max needed from the nearest Protector Station.

Before the Caynin could answer, Guy spotted a trail of dust heading their way. "Never mind," he said.

It didn't take long for the blue-and-white Protector buggy to skid to a halt. Nelis had acquired it for "Detector purposes" from two Protectors at the circus who'd been all too unhappy to oblige. It also didn't take long for the human and the Veagin to come walking down the passageway. At least, Nelis walked, while Cortex scraped down it sideways like a claustrophobic crab. They shuffled around in the confines of the cockpit until Nelis sat Cortex down on an extra-wide seat made for extra-wide people. The bug sat motionless to avoid knocking anything or anyone over.

"Comfy?" Nelis asked him.

Cortex nodded. *"Yes, thank you, sir."*

"Good," Nelis said, turning his attention to Max.

"Sorry about the cramped quarters," he said. "I wish I had more time to organise something better. I still can, if you're willing to wait a bit longer."

"No, thanks, this is *perfect*," Max said, shooting a quick yet meaningful glance at Guy. "And the other stuff?"

"All neatly packed in a container in the living area," Nelis said. "And here's a little something extra, just in case you need to reach out."

He handed a galphone to Max, who took it hesitantly.

"I don't want to get you in deeper than you already are, Nelis," Max said.

"Hey, you know me," Nelis said, flashing a grin. "I like the deep end. And from my point of view, I'm not in deep enough. But you know what you're doing, and if there's anyone who can sort this all out, it's *you*. But promise me you'll get in touch if you need anything. Whatever it is. I'll be ready."

The Infiltrator looked the Detector in the eye.

"Thanks for this, Nelis," he said. "Thanks for everything."

He pulled the human in for another quick embrace and pats on the back.

"No problem," Nelis said, turning to walk down the passageway.

He halted, and without looking back, added, "But if you get one scratch on my mom's ship, being branded an assassin will be the least of your problems. Cool?"

"Cool," Max said.

Without another word, the Detector exited the ship, and Guy could swear he caught a glimpse of a bit more moisture than normal in the Caynin's eyes.

CHAPTER 43

They flew in silence for a while as Grassi Nole rapidly shrunk behind them.

"So, er, Nelis," Neville said after a while had passed, taking a seat next to Max.

"What about him?" the Infiltrator said, staring ahead.

"You guys seem pretty close?"

"Yep."

"But you never see each other."

"Nope."

"Yet you remain tight?"

"Yep."

"How does a friendship like that *last*?"

Max glanced over his shoulder at Guy, who still seemed to suffer from some residual upset after the scolding he'd received earlier.

"Would absence prevent *you* from being friends?" he asked.

"No," Neville said. "But Nelis; he's … *human*."

"So? Interspecies relationships have come a long way since the Federation was founded. Got a problem with that?"

"Oh, no," Neville answered the daring flash in Max's eyes. "No, I didn't mean it like that. I just meant that he's *human*. I didn't know there were other humans out there."

"Oh, *that*," Maxed said, relaxing. "Humans are actually quite common throughout the Federation."

"I thought I'd seen a few on Unyun, but I wasn't sure. I thought my eyes were playing tricks on me, or that they were just very human-looking. But how did it happen? I thought most aliens were small, grey or full of tentacles."

Max sighed.

"I sometimes forget you're actually human," he said. "Just a word of advice, though: don't call people *aliens*. It just makes you seem like you're from a Dumb Planet."

"Well just for the record, I *am* from a Dumb Planet," Neville said, slightly irritated. "And, just a word of advice: we don't appreciate it being called a Dumb Planet. We prefer *Uninformed* Planet."

Max gave him a calculated look. "Fair point. Noted."

"So where *did* they come from ... you know, the humans?"

"From Earth, of course. While there are plenty of other humanoid species – some almost identical to you – humans have been abducted from Earth for millennia."

"I knew it!" Neville exclaimed, causing Guy to jump in his seat. "I've *always* known there had to be some truth to all the claims of abduction. You know, where there's smoke ...? But why, though?"

"Well," Max said, "long ago, mostly for experimentation. However, shortly after the Federation was established, a bill was passed to make the practice illegal."

"But it's still continuing," Neville said, looking at the Caynin conspiratorially.

"Yes," Max nodded. "As with any other law, this one gets broken. Most are taken for human-trafficking purposes; they're generally sold off as slaves in remote systems."

"That's sick!" Guy said from the back. "Can't anyone stop them?"

"You have similar sick practices on Earth, don't you?" Max said over his shoulder.

"Er, yes," Guy admitted.

"And have you been able to stop them?"

"Er, no."

"Well, there you go then," Max said. "If you cannot even stop it among your own species in a confined space like Earth, how much more difficult do you think it is to control throughout whole systems and galaxies? And that's just *within* the Federation – I'm not even talking about non-Federation worlds or undiscovered systems outside the Charted Universe. The Federation does what it can, but it's never enough. I've infiltrated and brought down a couple of these syndicates myself, but as soon as you get rid of one, another springs up in its place – or more, for that matter. The universe is teeming with evil people and evil intentions, Mr Leatherman. Earth isn't special in that regard."

Neville nodded reluctantly. "You said *most* are taken for those purposes. What about the others?"

"Usually for fun."

"Fun?!"

"Yes, generally by kids who think it's hilarious to abduct humans and drop them off at some remote location, all while recording the whole thing to share on social networks. They get plenty of Loves and ratings for it."

"But that's just … wrong!" Guy cried.

"That it is," Max said, "but at the same time it's also just kids being kids. We usually apologise to your governments whenever possible and return the abductees, if we can, after wiping their memory."

"*Our* government knows?" Guy said, astonished.

"The more prominent governments most definitely know. There'd be chaos if they didn't."

"But why not just tell people?" Neville said.

"Because there'd be anarchy if everybody else knew, wouldn't there? Getting a Dum— sorry, *Uninformed* Planet ready for integration takes time and patience. You're now only in phase one, which we call The Introductory Phase, where we gradually introduce ourselves to a select few, both governmental and non-governmental. We also introduce some of our technology through select channels."

Guy and Neville stared at him in disbelief.

"Think about it," Max said. "Do you really believe you went from inventing the first aeroplane to landing on Mars within less than a century without any outside help?"

"You mean to say that everything we have comes from out there ... I mean out *here?*" Guy said.

"Not at all. Humans can be quite clever and inventive, and once you were given the right tools, you advanced at an amazing pace. Some of your inventions have even been adopted throughout the Federation, like the popcorn-maker and the skateboard. Genius in their simplicity, but genius nonetheless. Oh yes, and apricot jam. It's become the most widely sold jam in the Charted Universe – one of *my* favourites, actually."

"Popcorn ... skateboards ... jam?" Guy said flatly. "*That's* the extent of our contribution?"

"Oh, no," Max said, noticing the glum look on Guy's face. "There are some other things, but these are the ones that stood out the most."

"But what about people who've been abducted and cannot be returned to Earth?" Neville interjected, more worried about the fate of his fellow man than man's contribution to food and recreation. "What happens to *them?*"

"They get sent off to a planet for Acclimatisation, after which they can decide what they want to do."

"And if they want to return to Earth and end up telling other people about their experiences?"

"We give most a memory-wipe; the others we're not too worried about."

"Why?"

"Have you ever heard people on Earth telling their stories of alien sightings and abductions?"

"Of course," Neville said firmly.

"And do other people believe them?"

"Uh, yes," Neville said less firmly. "Well, *some* do."

"And what happens then?"

"They make documentaries."

"And then?"

"Er, we watch them and talk about it now and again over drinks, and ... oh, I see. But what about the ones that go through rehabilitation?"

"Acclimatisation," Max corrected. "They're sent to a planet – much like Earth – that's been allocated to serve as the official Federal human homeworld, where they're gradually introduced to other species, technologies, foods and such. By the time they're deemed Acclimatised, they're given the option of staying or returning to Earth. You'd be surprised how many choose *not* to return to Earth."

"Not as surprised as you'd think," Guy grumbled.

"So what's the name of this … homeworld?" Neville said, ignoring the remark.

"Earth Too," Max said.

"Earth Too?" Guy said. "Earth Too! *That's* the best they could come up with?"

"Hey," Max said, "naming the planet almost led to a civil war among humans. To keep the peace, the naming was left to human kids under the age of ten, and the public got to vote on it. So when an eight-year-old girl from the farming village of New New Zealand came up with Earth Too, nobody took it seriously … until they saw her naming-motivation video and decided that Earth Too was actually quite endearing. So the majority vote went to her, and Earth Too it was. She was *really* cute."[*]

A peeping noise redirected Neville's train of thought onto another track. "What's *that* for?"

"That, Mr Andersman, means we're approaching an Orifice," Max said. "They were built to keep wormholes from collapsing."

"Huge" didn't even begin to describe the size of the structure they were nearing. Neither did "gigantic", nor "colossal" or any other synonym. Such words would have been better suited to describe the size of the larger ships entering and emerging from it, some of which could easily have swallowed thousands of pink *Motherships* with room to spare.

---

[*] The runner-up name came from a five-year-old boy who was even cuter, but the general consensus was that his cuteness would eventually fade over time, while the rest of the humans would be stuck with the name Poopypants Kill Robot forever.

No, there were no words to define the staggering size of the Orifice, which is why neither Guy nor Neville had any. All they could do was watch the Orifice grow bigger as the ship drew closer. The highly reflective surface of the ring mirrored the space around it as well as the green and red light from the green and red grids that divided the black mouth of the wormhole in two. It almost looked like a split-personality traffic light – albeit the biggest one in existence.

"What's the grid for?" Neville whispered like an excited golf commentator.

"That's a positioning grid," Max said. "The green grid at the bottom controls where ships enter the wormhole, and subsequently also where they'll exit, which is always at the exact same opposite position from where they entered. The red grid prevents solid matter from entering from the wrong side. They're flipped at the opposite end, and do a brilliant job in preventing collisions and alleviating traffic jams."

"Incredible," Neville said, enraptured.

Guy knew that his traffic-cop friend was relishing every moment of this, as opposed to Guy himself, who didn't really want to be reminded of traffic in any shape, form or size.

Max also picked up on Neville's reverence. "You like this, don't you?"

"Like?" Neville said. "No, *like* doesn't even begin to describe it. It's *stupefying*!"

"Well, that's good, because we're going in."

The little pink ship entered a sector of the green grid and was soon swallowed up by the black mouth of the wormhole.

•••

Guy couldn't decide if he was slightly disappointed or slightly terrified. He then realised he was feeling a bit of both, but only the opposite of slightly.

He'd seen a lot of movies and shows where people travelled through wormholes, surrounded by swirls or streaks of light of various colours, or at least one colour, as if they were travelling through some fantastic lightshow. So this is what he'd expected to experience. He was therefore extremely disappointed when he saw that this was not the case. At the same time, he was extremely terrified, because instead of dazzling light of any shape or colour whatsoever, they were surrounded by a complete absence of light.

It wasn't the same absence of light that Guy had experienced numerous times when the power company back home had conveniently forgotten that their main role in society was to actually supply power to the millions of households that relied upon them. It was much more than that. It was an absence of, well, everything. Even when he'd been cooped up in Kelp's pitch-black container, he had at least known that he was surrounded by *something*. But here it felt as though the ship was engulfed by a whole lot of nothing that seemed to stretch into infinity.

"Where has the light gone?" he said, staring anxiously at nothing. Even Neville looked uncomfortable.

"Oh, don't mind that," Max said calmly.

"How can I *not* mind *that?*" Guy said, pointing a trembling finger at the window.

"Don't worry about it," Max said. "It's quite natural."

"Natural my arse!" Guy countered. "There's … nothing! Nothing at all!! That's *far* from natural!!!"

Cortex woke up with a start.

"What's going on?" he said.

"Nothing, Cortex, *nothing*!" Guy wailed.

"What were you expecting," Max said, "a lightshow?"

"As a matter of fact, yes!"

"Well, sorry to disappoint," Max said, fiddling with the screen. The hum of the engines died with a *whooom*.

"What are you doing *now*?" Guy cried, as the weight of the silence inside the ship was added to the weight of the nothingness outside, crushing the last of Guy's fragile spirit.

"I'm powering down the engines," Max said, unbuckling himself.

"Why?" Guy prodded, not prepared to let it go.

"Because we don't need them, and I don't want to use the ship's engines more than necessary."

"But how are we going to get anywhere?" Neville asked uneasily.

"Engines don't make any significant difference in how fast we travel in here," Max said. "So it's useless to keep them running."

He noticed their dubious expressions.

"Look," he sighed, "it's simple. *Everything* travels at the same speed in a wormhole, even light; that's why you can't see it. No form of propulsion will make any significant difference. Engines or not, no matter where you go in the Charted Universe using a wormhole, nowhere takes less than an hour or longer than a day to reach."

Satisfied that he'd explained it to their satisfaction and ignoring the visible fact that he hadn't, Max said, "Now, if anyone wants to join me, I'm going to make some coffee."

With that, he left to make some coffee. Cortex, who was quite used to this type of travel, got up too, and enthusiastically squeezed his way down the passageway in anticipation of a hot mug of pick-me-up after his nap.

Guy and Neville just sat there for a while, then got up to follow the other two, because coffee sounded like a much better use of their time than staring at nothing for who knows how long but not longer than a day.

CHAPTER 44

Contucious Bragson arrived at work, bright and early – or at least early – ready to tackle another day at *Bragson Weaponry & Ordnance Providers*.

BWOPs, aka Beewops, have for centuries been the most popular weapons in the Charted Universe, known for their reliability and robustness. They're a favourite not only among law-abiding citizens but also the Militorate and the Protectorate, who regrettably also have to deal with the other end of the weapons, as they're also a favourite among enemy forces as well as not-so-law-abiding citizens.

Take for instance the newly released BWOP 459 flasher gun. As widely advertised, it's small and light, yet it packs a powerful punch. You can squeeze an impressive twenty-five shots from its improved battery clip, where similar flasher guns usually manage less than twenty before you have to re-load. And, yes, although not as widely advertised, all of this comes with a heftier price tag. But who can put a price on one's safety/income? Well, BWOP can, and they do.

In spite of his name, Contucious Bragson wasn't an owner of *Bragson Weaponry & Ordnance Providers*, nor was he management – not even middle-management. He was just a simple worker who'd started recently, yet it was the longest job he'd ever held. And he was confident he would hold on to *this* one.

Despite his normal worker status, though, Contucious's name *was* important. He was the son of Desmond Bragson, a Ronian who came from a long line of extremely successful,

wealthy Bragsons. The first in this line of successful Bragsons had been one of Desmond's ancestors, Tal Bragson,
who had prospected on Kilihiri for Kilihiri blue diamonds,
which were extremely high in value. Everyone thought she
was crazy to prospect for diamonds in that specific location,
and that she would fail miserably.

Everyone had turned out to be right. She had indeed failed
miserably in finding Kilihiri blue diamond; not even one. But
the failure became null and void when she accidentally
struck a vein of tenantium – the strongest and most valuable
metal in the Charted Universe.

However, with tenantium mining literally being a cut-
throat industry, Tal had kept the find a close secret, and sold
the tenantium off-world. She used the proceeds to buy up
more land, and more, and more, until she ended up with the
most lucrative tenantium mine in the history of the Charted
Universe. Tal then proceeded to buy out most of the other
smaller tenantium and diamond mines on Kilihiri, and later
most of the bigger ones too.

Although the mining sector remained one of their biggest
business strongholds, Tal's descendants have throughout the
centuries expanded their business interests into various sectors, such as technology and weaponry. Now, many of the
top hundred companies in the Federation were either owned
or partly owned by *Bragson Industries*.

Desmond Bragson currently ran the holding company
along with his two brothers and three sisters, although he was
the main shareholder. But while Desmond fully lived up to
the Bragson name, Contucious did not, thanks to a terrible
incident involving a less-reputable magazine and a power
socket in his early teens. For obvious reasons, nobody ever
talked about "the mishap".

The incident had left Contucious only half of what he'd
been in the upstairs department, and nobody wanted to talk
about what had happened downstairs either. Despite all the
money thrown at it, there wasn't any procedure that could
help Contucious regain full mental capacity. He'd simply
never be the biggest asset to society.

However, being a Bragson and a Ronian, Contucious's father believed in working hard for your money, and had been securing jobs for Contucious for years now. Maybe *secure* wasn't the best term, as Contucious kept getting fired because he could never grasp or remember what to do. But although Contucious's reputation had spread far and wide, no one refused when Desmond Bragson asked them to employ his son. On the flipside, Desmond also never got upset when employers "had to let Contucious go" – he couldn't really blame them.

But *work* he had to, if Contucious wanted to keep his penthouse and his gaming console, which he did. However, he *also* wanted to make his father proud, although that was a tough task if you couldn't keep a job for more than a few days … or hours. It was a no-known fact that Contucious was the most "let go" person in the Charted Universe, and everywhere else for that matter.

Which is why Contucious was now extremely happy and proud to have kept this job for almost a month. Sure, he only had to turn in a small screw on each weapon, but he did that really well as far as he was concerned. And the fact that he hadn't been fired yet just confirmed this, didn't it?

As he passed under the big, green-lit *Bragson Weaponry & Ordnance Providers* sign above the entrance of the black factory, Contucious was indeed filled with pride. His new-found positivity was painted all over his pale face, which housed two rusty-orange eyes and was adorned with a sharp nose and pointy ears that were a bit smaller than those of the average Ronian. His head was topped off with the same rusty-orange hair, which was quite dishevelled and contrasted sharply with his blue coveralls.

After following the ritual security procedures, Contucious walked just as proudly onto the factory floor, where hordes of machines, robots and people were diligently assembling the tools of control, pain and death. Reaching his workstation near the end of the assembly line, he sat on his stool, picked up his small screwdriver, and screwed in the small screw on the side of a brand-new BWOP 459 flasher gun.

He was about to do the same on the next gun when a message bot rolled over to tell him that the floor manager wanted to see him "right now". Contucious told the bot that he just wanted to finish screwing in the screw, upon which the bot yelled "No!!!" in alarm, and then proceeded to say, more calmly, that it would be better to just leave everything as is and proceed to the boss's office.

So Contucious reluctantly left his station and followed the rolling robot to the boss's office. Through the office window, Contucious could see the Ronian, Mr Brin, pacing up and down, speaking loudly to himself and occasionally throwing his hands in the air.

The robot knocked on the door and ushered in a hesitant Contucious before leaving again, closing the door behind him.[*]

Mr Brin turned around, red in the face, yet sporting a smile that seemed painfully in contrast to the rest of his face, which also sported a popping vein between his thin eyebrows.

Contucious had seen this look before. Plenty of times.

•••

As Contucious trudged out of the factory, he didn't look back at the sign, because he didn't want to see the Bragson name right now; a name he *most definitely* wasn't living up to.

Mr Brin hadn't yelled at him. No boss ever did. Instead, he'd explained the reason for his concern in a calm, quivering voice.

Apparently, *Bragson Weaponry & Ordnance Providers* had received numerous complaints about how the new "supposedly" super-reliable BWOP 459 flasher gun had failed to fire. After a thorough investigation, the company found that the fault lay with the small charge-connector screw that hadn't been fastened properly. Not on all of them. Just on some of those that had come from one specific line during specific assembly times that coincided with the specific times Contucious had been on duty. Mr Brin had specifically

---

[*] Not all doors in the universe open and close automatically, so if you're a doorman, there's no reason to panic.

wondered, through the clenched teeth of his fixed smile, how it was possible for someone "to get such a small task so incredibly wrong". The smile hadn't touched the boss's eyes as he explained, amidst heavy breathing, how the company's reputation had taken a knock, and that they'd now have to recall *all* the BWOP 459 flasher guns. He then politely asked Contucious to leave and never return.

Contucious had heard *those* words before, plenty of times, just as he'd done this walk, plenty of times.

And a few minutes later, like plenty of times before, Desmond Bragson ended a call on his office commpad, telling him that his son "unfortunately had to be let go".

Again.

Desmond didn't even ask *why* anymore.

After giving a sigh he'd given plenty of times, he continued puzzling over the drop in shares that *Bragson Weaponry & Ordnance Providers* had experienced in the past twenty-four hours.

CHAPTER 45

Guy awoke on the pink sofa and treated himself to a well-deserved stretch. He'd fallen asleep while Max was telling a rapt Neville about darkdrives; the main ship-propulsion systems used to travel to not-too-distant places that weren't accessible via wormholes. The drives utilised the respective push and pull of dark energy and dark matter, which enabled long-range ships to travel at mindboggling speeds. Of course, Neville had wanted to know more, and Max had been all too happy to elaborate, while Guy, who's tired mind had been boggled too much by that stage, had been all too happy to abandon wakefulness on the sofa – in spite of its colour.

He got up just as Max walked in from the passageway connected to the cockpit.

"Are we there yet?" Guy yawned, trying to rub the grainy dryness from his eyes. It felt as though he could sleep for another decade or so.

"Almost," Max said. "As a matter of fact, it's why I came to fetch you. Neville says you've never seen Unyun from space either. Come on, you're just in time for the show."

Guy ambled after the Caynin and slumped into one of the cockpit's seats. He looked at Neville, who was eagerly watching the window, although everything was still blacker than black outside.

"What are you looking at?" Guy asked with another yawn, but got no response.

"There's nothing out there," Guy tried and failed again; Neville's eyes remained fixed on the window.

A faint alarm went off, and Max muted it by pressing something on the control screen in front of him.

"We're nearly there," he said from the pilot's seat.

"Well, I still can't see—" Guy started, but stopped as light suddenly seared his eyes and fulfilled this prophecy.

"Aargh!" he wailed, covering his face.

Apparently they'd exited the wormhole.

"Sorry, just a moment," Max said, pushing a button to darken the windows.

Sight returning, Guy lowered his hands and squinted at two stars in the distance. He didn't know how big they were, but they somehow felt bigger than those of Grassi Nole.

"Freaky," he breathed.

"Freaky indeed," Neville confirmed.

They stared at the suns until they disappeared from view as Max changed their course and headed towards a spherical object that looked like a moon. Surrounding it, at various distances, were numerous shimmering Orifices like the one they'd just exited, swallowing and spewing out ships like the chain-smokers of commerce. The tendrils of traffic all flowed to and from the moon, which itself looked … odd. As they approached, though, Guy couldn't quite pin down its exact colour.

"Freaky moon too," he said.

"That's no moon," Neville said with more than a note of awe. "That's Unyun."

"It's too big to be …" Guy started and then stopped, as he suddenly felt like a bit of a rip-off for some reason.

Besides, the size of the constructed planet went beyond words. It would have dwarfed Earth's moon; even Earth itself, most likely. It was babblingly big.

"What are you babbling about?" Max said.

"Not … it's … couldn't," Guy caught himself saying, and realised that he'd probably have to string some more words together to convey a more coherent message. "It's … not possible. It's … too big. People *couldn't* have built something like that."

"Oh, but they did," Cortex said. *"Unyun was, and still remains, the symbol of what can be achieved when species combine hard work, determination and unity to reach a seemingly impossible goal."*

"And lots of money," Max added.

"Sure, that too," the Veagin said offhandedly, as if the latter merely got in the way of the things he truly admired about the accomplishment.

As the planet grew even bigger before them, so did Guy's amazement. He was familiar with soccer balls, and this definitely looked like one, albeit a very strange one. He realised why he couldn't make out the planet's exact colour before – because there wasn't one. Although the hexagonal sectors generally also sported other colours, each had its own primary colour, ranging from blues to browns, greens, and even reds and white, depending on the sector's prevailing landscape and atmosphere.

The Mothership, however, headed for one of the grey pentagonal sectors. Unlike the coloured sectors surrounding it, the sector had no outer atmosphere. Countless ships of various shapes and sizes moved to and from the sector in invisible lanes, entering from one side and exiting on the other.

"That's one of Unyun's spaceports," Max said in answer to the unasked question on Neville's face. "Along with the Orifices, they're the lifeblood of the Unyun Federation."

As they neared the continent-sized spaceport, ships started diverting in all directions. Max waited for an on-screen instruction, then manoeuvred *The Mothership* down and left. This happened several times until they finally stopped to hover next to a metal wall that stretched kilometres above and below them, dotted with a myriad of docking stations.

Max let go of the controls and sat back while *The Mothership* drifted towards one of the smaller docking stations.

Noting the wordless panic on Guy's face, he said, "Automatic docking beams. Nothing to be concerned about."

Neville didn't appear to worry, but Guy did. He didn't trust machines doing the work without people controlling them. He then thought about what he'd just thought, and thought about people's driving skills in general, and relaxed a bit. The ship stopped moving with a slight jerk accompanied by a dull clang.

"Well, that's it," Max said. Unbuckling himself, he got up and made his way down the passageway. Guy and Neville quickly followed suit while Cortex followed suit more slowly.

In the living area, the Caynin unlatched the big container Nelis had brought on board. He opened it and reached in to take out bundles of folded, bright-yellow material.

"Here, put this on," he said, tossing a bundle to each of them and taking out one for himself.

"What's this?" Guy said, unfolding the material, and held it up to reveal the answer. It was a bright-yellow hooded cloak made from rough yet sturdy bright-yellow material.

"Our disguises," Max said, eyeing his cloak.

"It's a bit big," Guy frowned.

"Give me that one," Max said, exchanging it for the one he was holding, which was way too small for the Caynin. He donned the exchanged cloak, which fit perfectly.

"It's also a bit ugly," Guy said, grimacing. He took a whiff of the stuffy-smelling garment, which didn't improve his expression.

"It's not a fashion show, Mr Leatherman," Max grated.

"You can say that again," Guy said, but donned the cloak anyway, and frowned at the bottom of the long garment lying crumpled on the floor. "It's still too big."

Max marched over to the kitchen, rummaged through the drawers, and came back with a pair of scissors.

"Hold still," he said, cutting the bottom of the cloak until it hung just above the floor.

He did the same with Neville and stopped at Cortex, where he realised that a pair of scissors wasn't going to do the trick. The cloak didn't even fit over the Veagin's shoulders, and hung down his back like a lonely curtain.

Cortex gave him a bashful smile.

"Oh," Max said, putting the scissors down on the coffee table. "This isn't going to work. Take that thing off."

He looked at the container and sighed.

"It's time for Plan B."

CHAPTER 46

Neither Guy nor Neville liked Plan B, and it wasn't any consolation whatsoever that Max didn't like it either. This was the second time Guy found himself locked inside a box, and while the container was much bigger this time around, it was also crowded by two other occupants.

"Move your foot, will you?" he hissed in the darkness.

"Shhh!" Max replied.

Guy didn't like to be shushed, but he also didn't like to be caught, so he kept the rest of his grievances to himself while hoping that the invading foot didn't press harder into the vulnerable area it was currently pressing against. Pushed by Cortex, the container silently moved forward atop the a-grav trolley they'd put it on. Guy heard hatches opening and closing and, shortly thereafter, the trolley stopped.

"Small ship for a Veagin," said a muffled female voice outside the container.

"…"

Guy couldn't hear the reply, which meant Cortex was probably directly addressing whoever had stopped them and had forgotten to mentally include his stashed companions in the conversation.

"Your mom?" the voice enquired. "Well, I suppose that explains the colour."

"…"

"No, no, I have nothing against pink. Just saying."

"…"

"Yes, I know guys can like pink too, but … what's in the container, sir?"

"…"

"Shoes? Er, I didn't know Veagins wore shoes."

"…"

"No, sir, I wasn't aware of the new trend."

"…"

"Yes, sir, I will check it out. But still, such a big container, just for shoes?"

"…"

"No, sir, I wasn't saying that your mom has big feet. I'm sure they're completely normal for a Veagin—"

"…"

"No, sir, I'm not implying that all Veagins have big feet. It's just … fine, shoes it is. However, I still have to look inside."

"…"

"Oh, I'm sorry to hear that, sir. There's a new cream on the market for that. She should try it. But despite the smell and health risks, I still need to have a look."

One of the container's three latches was unlatched, causing all inside to stiffen.

"…"

"Don't worry, sir, we're well-trained in this. I promise I'll treat her belongings with the utmost respect."

The second latch opened, sending another jolt of silent dread through the container's occupants.

"…"

"Thank you, sir. Your concern for my wellbeing is duly noted and appreciated, but I've got a job to do, so I'll just have to take the risk."

The final latch was opened and the lid lifted, revealing a blond-furred (all over, except for the scalp of course) uniformed female Stortian holding an electronic checkpad.

She stared into the container while three pairs of wide eyes stared right back up at her. She started reaching down, but her hand froze as a slight look of revulsion passed over her face and clung to her nose, which scrunched up involuntarily. She retracted her hand slowly before dropping the lid back into place. This was followed by the sound of latches being latched.

Despite not being able to see one another, Guy threw a flabbergasted glance at his fellow stowaways. He was sure they were doing the same, as it just seemed like the natural thing to do.

"It's an … impressive collection," said the muffled voice of the Stortian customs officer.

"…"

"Yes, I'm sure she'll be okay once she starts using the cream. Well, goodbye, sir, and enjoy your stay on Unyun."

The container started moving again, which would have brought great relief to all inside if they weren't so perplexed.

•••

"What happened back there?" Max asked Cortex, breathing heavily as he got out of the container. He was just as sweaty as the two Salamans he hoisted out into the deserted alleyway.

"I told you to just bribe a customs official and get it over and done with," he added, hunching over with his hands on his knees while trying to catch his breath. Guy and Neville sat down hard on the ground, panting, and tried to rub some of the pain from their recently contorted muscles.

"She was a Stortian, " Cortex said.

"So?" Max said.

"She was a Stortian, *"* Cortex repeated.

Max picked up on the emphasis.

"Oh, yes, of course," he said, taking another deep breath. "Sorry, being cooped up in this box is still playing on my senses a bit."

"What does being a Stortian have to do with it?" Neville asked, confused.

"They tend to be very pedantic about the duties bestowed upon them, " Cortex said, *"and they usually don't take kindly to bribes. So I had to improvise. "*

"Good thinking," Max said. "You did very well in trying to put her off, but she still looked inside the box. I mean, she looked straight at us! How could she miss three people hiding in plain sight?"

"Because she didn't see people. She saw shoes."

"But how?"

Cortex looked somewhat ashamed. *"There aren't many Veagins who can delve deep into people's minds, and even fewer who can ... impart thoughts."*

"You can *make* people do stuff?" Guy gasped. "I didn't know you could do that!"

"No one does," Cortex said. *"And it's not really making people do things. Depending on the species and the individual, I can only make people see, smell or hear things. They then do whatever they need to in reaction to that. But I don't like doing it. As with reading minds, it's very intrusive – even more so – and not very ethical. So I've only done it a couple of times – and only in* extreme *situations. It also takes quite a lot of mental energy. My head's spinning a bit."*

They hadn't noticed it before, but the bug did seem to sway somewhat.

"Shouldn't you sit down?" Guy asked concernedly.

"No, thanks, I'll be fine," Cortex said. *"Fortunately it wasn't a very complex illusion. A few small inanimate objects like shoes are okay, but making someone see an oncoming bus would likely knock me out for a bit. Projection takes a lot of detail to make it believable, and the more detail it requires, the more strain it puts on the mind."*

"Impressive!" Max said with an expression that supported the statement. "But can you walk?"

Cortex gave a weary nod.

"That's good," Max said, "because we've got a lot of walking to do."

CHAPTER 47

Max hadn't been joking when he said they'd have to walk far, which was good, as Guy's feet weren't laughing. Not even the previously remarkable sight of The Hub's massive buildings, nor the respective buzz and bustle of vehicles and people, was enough to keep Guy's mind distracted from the aches that built up with every step.

"My feet are killing me," he moaned, walking with the grace of swan on a bed of electrified nails. Neville didn't seem to fare any better, whereas Cortex and Max didn't appear bothered in the least.

"Why can't we just take one of those?" Guy said, pausing to cast a resentful glance at one of the busses gliding past above the street's surface.

"Because public transport has cameras," Max said, walking on. "We can't take the risk; not even in disguise."

"Speaking of which," Guy continued his gripe session, "this cloak weighs a ton. And isn't yellow a bit *attention-grabbing?*"

Max turned about, glaring at the whining Salaman. "Does it *look* like we're grabbing any attention?" he grated.

Guy looked about at the hordes of people passing by. It wasn't exactly as if no one saw the hooded figures. The passersby were more like lazy waiters going through great lengths to avoid the attention of those trying to get their attention.

"No, uh, I guess not," Guy admitted. "Why are they avoiding us?"

"Because *this*," Max replied, tugging at his cloak," is worn by the Knights of Absolute Avoidance. People tend to avoid them."[*]

He then walked on as if the question had been answered, and Guy limped after him like someone who didn't think so, raising a querying finger as he opened his mouth.

Neville saw it coming and, picking up on the fact that Max's annoyance threshold might just be exceeded by one more query or complaint from Guy, he decided to interject.

"So, the assassination—" he started, returning Guy's glare.

Max spun around once more. "I'd suggest you *don't* say those words out loud in public," he hissed, looking about them. "People are keeping themselves blind to us, not deaf."

"So what words should I use?" Neville asked.

"If you *insist* on talking about it now," Max whispered, using quotation fingers, "how about 'The Planet', 'The Vehicle', 'The Event', 'Number One' and 'Number Two'?"

Catching the gist of it, Neville nodded as Max walked on. "So, The Event," he tried again. "What happened?"

"As far as I could ascertain," Max said, "Number One was going to a meeting of Federal and non-Federal leaders on The Planet. It would have been the final round of talks surrounding the independence of certain species and colonies who don't want to form part of the Unyun Federation any longer. For some reason, Number Two was also on The Vehicle."

"Strange that the Presidor and Vice-Presidor would both *be on the ship when it was destroyed,"* Cortex said, not caring about the secret code, as no one else could hear him.

---

[*] This is true. The Knights of Absolute Avoidance pride themselves on avoiding attention by making themselves as visible as possible in public. Only by attracting attention to the fact that you want to be avoided can you truly achieve Absolute Avoidance. If you'd like to know more, you can visit the KAA's headquarters – if you can find it – where they'll avoid answering any queries you might have until you inevitably go away.

"Aren't there protocols in place to keep them separated, especially on such occasions?"

"Yes, there are," Max said, "and it's been gnawing at me too. They *shouldn't* have been together. Even Number Three stated publicly that they were investigating why Number One and Number Two were aboard the ship at the time of The Event."

Neville frowned. "Number Three?"

"Cortex?" Max hinted.

"Oh, yes," Cortex said, *"that would be Acting Presidor Don Tinckles. He was third in line after Presidor Harild Dooka and Vice-Presidor Julin Resis."*

"Yes," Max continued. "Someone must have organised for Number One and Number Two to be in the same place at the exact moment The Vehicle was crippled, allowing for The Event to be carried out successfully."

"Could it have been The Man?" Neville asked.

"Oh, The Man's definitely involved somehow. But it would take someone much higher up to pull off The Event in such a way. That's why we can't trust *anyone*."

The group walked on in silence before Max halted, causing everyone else to halt except for a still-brooding Guy, who walked past while irritably adjusting his cloak for the umpteenth time.

"Hey!" Max shouted after him. "Over here!"

Guy turned around. "Over where?" he said, giving the cloak another irritable tug.

"Here," Max said, pointing at the building in front of them. "The *Life Spectacular* head office."

CHAPTER 48

The reflective, egg-shaped building was, as part of its name would suggest, quite spectacular. The building's smooth, light-blue glass surface gleamed with a gleam that put some strain on the eyes. Fortunately, the beautiful green landscaping surrounding the building gave the eyes a rest. The darker-blue-lit glass letters above the big, rounded entrance read *The Life Spectacular Corporation. A division of Bragson Industries.*

"Spectacular," Guy said, forgetting his sore feet for a bit.

"Can we sit down, please?" he said after a bit, and didn't wait for anyone's permission before taking a seat on one of the benches dotting the serene vegetation.

Neville also took a seat on the opposite bench, and studied the people entering and exiting the building. They suddenly seemed to prefer taking the long way around, keeping away from the central landscaped area. A preoccupied Grey walking out of the entrance looked up at the yellow figures, looked down morosely at the lunchbox and thermos in his hands, and walked back into the building with slumped shoulders.

Neville stroked his cloak with a grin. "These things work like a charm."

"Yes," Max said. "Nelis is a genius."

Guy still wasn't convinced but didn't voice his opinion. "So, now what?" he said instead, massaging his feet.

"Our disguises work well in public," Max said, "but we cannot parade into the *Life Spectacular* offices with them on.

We don't want to arouse any suspicion, or panic. We need to send in someone who's a little more … normal."

He looked at Cortex, who'd been standing casually to the side while casually scratching an itch on his top-left arm with his bottom-right arm.

"What?" the bug said as all signs of casualness fled from the attention he suddenly commanded.

•••

"Are you sure he'll be okay?" Guy asked as Cortex's bulky shape disappeared through the building's round entrance.

"He'll be fine," Max said. "He proved himself to be very resourceful at the customs check, so I'm sure he'll be able to handle himself in a corporate lobby."

Guy knew the Caynin was right. Cortex had certainly been impressive, but Guy's nerves refused to settle down. A while later, though, he sighed with relief as his friend came strolling out of the building as if it was just another day at the office – albeit not his own office.

"And?" Max said as the bug joined the cloaked figures. "Did you ask them what I asked you to ask them?"

"Yes," Cortex replied. *"I spoke to the receptionist. Mr Gray definitely isn't here."*

"So, he hasn't returned yet?" Max said.

"No. As you said, he hasn't been in for months now. No one knows where he is. In fact, he's presumed dead."

"Dead!" Guy gasped, jumping up. He suddenly felt lightheaded and wasn't sure if this was because of the gasp, getting up too quickly, or the shock of the news. To eliminate one of the possible causes, he sat back down.

"Yes. Unfortunately, the receptionist wasn't very forthcoming with any further information. She's a Ronian, so I thought there might be a possibility that she's a speciesist."[*]

---

[*] Some people have joked that every person is either a speciesist or a closet speciesist, which is something most other people have said could only be said by a speciesist. Some people have subsequently stopped saying it.

"Quite likely," Max said worriedly. "So that's it, then? Another dead end."

He noticed the others staring at him uncertainly.

"Oh, come on," he objected. "You know I didn't mean it like that!"

"No," Cortex said, *"I'm sure you didn't. But all might not be lost. I did manage to read her thoughts."*

"I thought you didn't like reading people's minds without their knowledge," Neville said.

"Usually, no," Cortex replied. *"But, in the circumstances, it seemed prudent to do so. Besides, I detest speciesists, so it's no hair off my back."*

"What hair?" Guy joked, suddenly hopeful. "So, what did you get from her?"

"That she definitely is *a speciesist,"* Cortex said. *"I'd rather not repeat what she was thinking. But I probed a bit deeper and got the name of someone who worked with Mr Gray."*

"And?" Max said after a pause.

"And then she told me to stop staring at her and go away."

Max gave him a flat stare. "The name?"

"Oh, yes. Her name is Ms Beatrix. Even better, I got her address."

Guy slapped Cortex on the back. "Have I ever told you that you have your moments?"

"Not really. Still think it was a mistake to drag me along?"

"Hey, nobody dragged you anywhere," Guy said in mock defence. "And no, my friend, the mistake was all mine."

CHAPTER 49

Guy stared at the tall brown building where Ms Beatrix supposedly resided.

"How much longer do we have to wait?" he grumbled.

Max looked at him flatly. "People's movements aren't an exact science, you know?"

For Guy, no science was exact. There were just too many variables to keep up with. On Earth, rocks fell back down after you tossed them into the air. Water boiled on fire, and water extinguished fire. Frankly, the basics were good enough for him.

"Wait," Cortex said, pointing towards a Grey exiting the building. *"I think that's her."*

Like all the other Greys Guy had seen, this one wore no clothing except for a purple handbag tucked under her arm. He wondered why being naked never bothered them, although he suspected it had something to do with the species's lack of visible genitalia, which left much to the imagination. This was not a good thing, so he squashed his imagination and followed the others as they approached the Grey.

When she saw the group advancing in their Knights of Absolute Avoidance garb, the small grey figure pivoted and started walking in the opposite direction at a much faster pace.

Cortex stopped and focused. The Grey halted and stood there for a while, before she eventually turned around and approached them hesitantly.

"So you're not *KAA?"* she said telepathically with a feel of relief, which promptly transformed into worry. *"What's this about Mr Gray? Have you seen him?"*

"That's actually what we wanted to ask *you*, Ms Beatrix," Max said.

"No, I haven't seen him since before his last-minute job on the Dumb Planet, Earth."

Max clamped a hand over Guy's mouth and shot a warning glance at Neville.

"Did he at least make contact?" the Infiltrator continued.

"Not a word, I'm afraid," Ms Beatrix replied. *"I'm terribly worried about him. It's not like Mr Gray to just leave like that. He's usually very reliable."*

"Do you have *any* idea where he could be?" Max said.

"No, I don't. The Detectors investigating his disappearance already asked me that, and searched his apartment. Nothing. They've even stopped staking out the building, because he never returned there either. The last person to see him before he went missing was Donz, one of our trainees. It was he that bungled up that last job. He has, of course, been relieved of his duties. But as far as I know, the Detectors had already questioned him too."

"Where does he live, Ms Beatrix?" Max asked. "Maybe he can shed some new light on things to help us locate Mr Gray," he added quickly, noting a hint of suspicion crossing her face.

The Grey looked at Cortex, and they seemed to share a moment. The suspicion faded, and she sighed.

"His place isn't far from here," she said, pointing down the street. *"It's just three blocks down that way, then two more up right, in Hope Street. It's the last building on the right, called* Hope's End – *not the best-looking place in the neighbourhood. You can't miss it. He's in 342."*

She wrung the handles of her handbag. *"Just find Mr Gray, will you? He's ... special to me."*

"We'll try our best, Ms Beatrix," Max said. "And thank you."

She nodded, but as they were about to leave, she added, *"Oh, yes, before I forget, apparently there were also some Vahltans looking for Mr Gray at the office. The receptionist didn't like the look of them, so she sent them away. Okay, she doesn't like the look of most non-Ronians, but still, I don't like the sound of it."*

"Neither do I, Ms Beatrix," Max said. "Thanks for the heads-up."

With that, they quickly started making their way up the road, driven on relentlessly by a now-very-edgy Caynin.

CHAPTER 50

Although they were still killing him, Guy didn't complain about his feet, because Max wasn't listening, setting a pace more appropriate for a million-dollar dog-sleigh race. But as they neared their destination, the Caynin slowed down and stopped at the corner of Hope Street to peer around the corner.

"Anything?" Neville asked, taking a peek himself.

"No," Max said tentatively. "But just to be on the safe side, keep your faces covered."

They drew their hoods as low as they could.

"Cortex, you stay here and let us know if you see anyone or anything suspicious."

The bug nodded and watched as the trio walked off.

"So, the Vahltans Ms Beatrix mentioned," Neville said as they neared the end of the street. "The Man's men?"

"Undoubtedly," Max said.

"You think they're in there?"

"I don't know, but let's rather assume they are. So be ready."

When they reached the building they'd been looking for, Guy understood why Ms Beatrix had said they couldn't miss it. The skew-hanging rusty sign with the barely visible letters *Ho.. 's End* was in much better shape than the rest of the big building, which gave the word "rustic" a more apt meaning. Patches of rusted metal peeked through the peeling, fading yellow paint, and if the building had any unbroken windows left, they couldn't be seen from this side.

At least gaining entry to the building wasn't a problem, because the security gate protecting the property wasn't doing a particularly good job of it. In fact, it was doing no job at all, and neither was the open, automatic door, which tried its best to open a bit farther but only managed a screeching inch before giving up with a rueful *thunk*.

They entered cautiously and, after seeing the state of the elevator – or what was left of it – they made their way up three flights of dilapidated stairs, which creaked in a way metal shouldn't creak. At the top of the last flight, Max motioned the two Salamans to stop, and surveyed the hallway running left and right. Satisfied that all was clear, they went left.

The trio stopped in front of a rectangular object that at one stage must have been a solid white door, neither of which it was any longer. Max took out a device and connected its cable to a keypad next to the door. He was about to punch something into the device when the pad fell to the floor.

The Infiltrator glanced down at the keypad and decided to try something. He turned the doorknob, and the door creaked open not so silently. Gun in hand, he edged the door open and gestured for Guy and Neville to remain where they were. Neville, without any weapon, and Guy, without any courage, obeyed without protest.

Gun raised, Max silently entered the apartment, even though the creaky door had most likely already alerted anyone inside to the presence of an intruder. Guy and Neville waited apprehensively for something to happen, and were relieved when Max finally emerged from the doorway without his gun.

"Get inside," the Infiltrator said, and closed the door behind them.

The interior of the apartment left a lot to be desired, especially if one desired it to be clean. Clothes and trash were strewn about the cramped studio along with dirty, broken dishes.

"This place has been tossed," Max said.

"You sure?" Guy said, seeing as his apartment on Earth rarely looked better. Neville grinned knowingly but said nothing.

"Yeah," Max replied. "I don't think Donz would have received any medals for cleanliness, but it's certainly been tossed by someone too."

While Max proceeded to search the place, Guy walked about, trying to see if he could spot anything of importance. Knowing that he probably wouldn't know if he spotted anything of importance in any case – even if the place *had* been spotless – he wasn't surprised when he found nothing of importance. Neville didn't have any luck either.

"If there was anything here before, it's not here anymore," Max said, giving up his own search. "We've got nothing."

Tired and depressed, Guy felt the need to sit down. He warily eyed the torn, scuffed and stained sleeper couch, and instead took a seat on the square side table next to it, which comprised a metal frame with glass surfaces.

He rested his chin on his fist. "Great. Nothing, again."

"Don't give up hope, Mr Leatherman," Max said, seeming as though he was trying to convince himself more than his gloomy companion. "We'll just have to find Mr Gray some other way."

"Hello, would you kindly mind getting off me?" Guy's buttocks replied. It took a second for Guy to leap to his feet after he realised that, as far as he could remember, his posterior couldn't speak.

CHAPTER 51

ompletely bewildered, Guy rubbed his buttocks as if he'd just received a thorough hiding.[*] Neville stared at it as if it had sprouted horns, while Max had played the now-you-don't-see-it, now-you-do trick with his gun, with which he now scanned the apartment, ready to pull the trigger at a moment's notice.

"How can I help?" a voice said.

Three heads and one gun barrel snapped towards the side table, which started to emit a friendly baby-blue light. A square, white, smiling emoji appeared on each of the square glass sides facing the stunned figures in their yellow cloaks. The emoji facing Guy was partly covered by a brown stain, which he sincerely hoped was spilt coffee.

"Sorry about the coffee stain," the side table said, much to Guy's relief. "It's been there for ages, and I can't wipe it off myself."

Three confused glances met one another before turning back to the side table.

"Er," Guy said, before running out of words.

"Did …" Neville started, then followed Guy's lead.

"… that side table just speak?" Max finished the question. "I believe so," he replied too, as no one else seemed willing to do so.

---

[*] Those who've never received a thorough hiding might be relieved to hear that this is quite a natural thing to do.

"Well, some people say that seeing is believing," the side table said with a happy voice and the emoji to back it up. "What, you've never seen a robot before?"

"Uh, not one like you," Max said.

"It's also very likely that you never will again," the side table said with a sad, square emoji before the happy one returned. "But I've made peace with it. In fact, I've come to enjoy the notion that I'm unique – not like those other poor cans that get rolled off the assembly lines in their billions."

"So, um, what are you?" Guy asked, his eyes darting between the side table and his companions.

"A robot," the robot replied.

"Yes, so you said."

"Then why did you ask?"

"I meant, what *kind* of robot are you?"

"A unique one."

Guy glared unhappily at the happy face.

Max jumped in. "What he actually meant was: what is your purpose?"

"I have no purpose," the side table said with a flat emoji. "Would you rather like to know what my *function* is?"

"Sure," Max said with an equally flat expression that could have been used as the template from which the emoji had been created, albeit not as square.

"Currently, I'm a side table," said the side table, before his emoji turned to a thoughtful one. "I guess, if you really think about it, that could be seen as my purpose too. Thanks for pointing it out. However, I was created to be any piece of furniture you require, as long as it's small and square. I *do* make a very good side table, though, which is probably why I'm currently a side table."

"Yes," Max said, "so I see. It … er, suits you well."

"Thank you. I was manufactured by *WelDone Robotics*. Pretty big name in robotics, you know? I was a concept model for a proposed new line of IF – or Intelligent Furniture, if you like – that could move itself."

The side table suddenly rolled backwards and forwards with a loud clanging that caused the others to jump.

"See?" the side table said, stationary once more. He didn't seem to notice the fright painted on the faces of the biologicals covering their ears.

"The line was to be called the Intelligent Furniture Range, or IFR, but it was eventually scrapped," he continued. "Fortunately for me, I got a Barely Passed rating, which saved *me* from being scrapped. Instead, I was rebranded as part of the Original Concept Design range, with the designation 3OCD2. I suppose you'd call that my name."

"What?" Guy said, still stunned.

"Well, uh, hello … 3OCD2," Neville said, not wanting to seem rude, although he wasn't sure if robots could pick up on such things.

"Hello," the robot replied. "You must be Guy."

"No, that's Guy," Neville said, pointing at Guy. "I'm Neville."

"Apologies, Neville. I haven't had much input on you guys. Hello, Guy."

"Er … hello," Guy said, still feeling slightly awkward talking to furniture.

"And you must be Max," 3OCD2 said.

"Yes, I am," Max said, frowning. "How do you know our names?"

"Mr Gray told me."

"Mr Gray?" the biologicals exclaimed, astounded.

Max recovered first. "You mean you *know* him?"

"Of course," the robot replied. "He's my owner … well, my current one. I've had quite a few. Would you like to see him?"

The three biologicals gave baffled nods.

●●●

Upon request from Max, Neville fetched Cortex, who carried 3OCD2 down the stairs while the Caynin brought him up to speed.

Cortex put the robot on the metal sidewalk with a *clang*. *"He's quite … heavy,"* he said, breathing heavily.

"Sorry," 3OCD2 said.

"You can hear *me?"* Cortex said, astonished. *"I didn't know side tables could hear telepaths."*

His expression stated that there were a few things he didn't know about side tables, and this was one of them.

"Well, telepaths have furniture too, you know?" the robot said. "And how would furniture be able to follow a telepath's instructions if they couldn't receive them? In fact, telepaths would have formed quite a big chunk of the Intelligent Furniture market, especially Greys. I mean, have you *seen* their arms? That's why *WelDone Robotics* installed telepathic receivers into all concept units."

"But why are *you so heavy?"* Cortex said.

"Oh, that would be my motor. It accounts for more than ninety percent of my structural mass. But don't worry, I'll take it from here."

The robot started clanging down the street in the direction they'd come from, but was soon stopped by Max, who glanced anxiously at the passersby who had suddenly dived behind cars, garbage bins and anything else they could find that provided cover, and from behind which they were now peeking in alarm.

"This isn't going to work," the Caynin hissed. "He's drawing way too much attention."

"Don't look at me," Cortex said, holding up four tired arms. "I can't carry that thing around the whole time."

"Well, we can't let it go about by itself," Guy said, trying to extract some residual noise from his ear with a finger.

"No, we can't," Max agreed.

He looked down the street and took off without a word.

"Where are you going?" Guy shouted after him, louder than intended, as he still couldn't hear too well.

"Just stay here!" Max shouted over his shoulder. "I'll be right back!"

He trotted down the sidewalk and disappeared into the first alley. Guy looked at Cortex, who just shrugged, rubbing his sore arms. A while later, Max returned with an a-grav trolley that hovered silently above the sidewalk.

"I grabbed this from a truck parked behind a restaurant," he said. "Cortex, would you please?"

Cortex didn't look pleased, but bent over to pick up 3OCD2 with a grunt. The Veagin heaved the robot onto the trolley, which shifted slightly but maintained its elevation above the sidewalk.

"Thank you," the robot said pleasantly before it suddenly displayed an angry emoji. "But could you *please* also pick that up?"

"What?" Cortex said, staring in the general direction the emoji was looking. He couldn't see anything of interest.

"That!" 3OCD2 yelled, his square emoji eyes narrowing as if – like a pointed finger – it would help to focus the attention of the other party on the object in question. It obviously didn't work, because Cortex continued staring in the general direction.

"The candy wrapper," the robot growled. "Could you please pick up *that candy wrapper*?!"

Cortex picked up the wrapper.

"Now could you please throw it into that bin?" the robot demanded as it looked at the nearest bin.

Cortex threw the wrapper into the bin.

"Thank you," 3OCD2 said, watching with satisfaction as the wrapper was discarded in the proper manner for the piece of trash it was.

"Are we done here?" Max asked flatly in the tone of someone who didn't have time for this, which coincidentally was also what he was thinking. He didn't wait for an answer as he started pushing the trolley down the street.

CHAPTER 52

The group walked quite far, turning wherever 3OCD2 said they should turn and stopping regularly to pick up more pieces of trash at the robot's stubborn insistence.

On more than one occasion, a thoroughly irked Max considered covering 3OCD2 with something to prevent him from spotting any more garbage. However, they needed the robot's directions, so with every stop he just had to grin and bear it without the grin.

Eventually, they came to a bar where 3OCD2 told them to stop. The *Posh Pub* was anything but posh, looking almost as *rustic* as the apartment building they'd left earlier.

"He's in *here?*" Max frowned.

"Well, it's mid-afternoon," the robot said cheerfully. "So, yes, he should be."

The group approached the rusty, yellow door, which opened with a non-effortless *sssschwoooooop*, and entered. It wasn't a very big bar, and it didn't have many patrons. And those who were there didn't look very happy to be there. Yet they seemed happy to sit and wait for happiness to pitch up. Maybe with the next round.[*]

The barman, resting his elbow on the counter and, in turn, his cheek on his fist, was a bit slow to notice the yellow-

---

[*] They say you can't find happiness at the bottom of a bottle. While this might be true, some bottles have a little worm at the bottom, which is pretty neat.

cloaked figures that had just entered his not-so-fine establishment. But once he *did* notice them, he quickly managed to find something to do under the counter.

Max approached the spot where the bartender's head had disappeared. "Hey," he said to the empty space. "I'm looking for a Grey."

"Er, there are many Greys out there," the nervous voice replied from under the counter. "Maybe you can go look for them ... outside?"

Max ignored the hopeful plea. "Are there any Greys *in here*?"

A reluctant hand came up slowly and pointed a shaky finger towards the back of the room before swiftly disappearing again.

"Thank you," Max said, and walked off without waiting for a reply. Not that there was one.

At first, none of the few tables in the back corner seemed to be occupied, until the group came closer and spotted a small grey figure with its head slumped on the table.

"See, I told you he'd be here," 3OCD2 said with a smile that disappeared as soon as he looked at the table. "Would you mind giving those glasses a wash?"

Having reached their destination and itching to do something he'd wanted to do for some time, Max grabbed a dirty tablecloth from a nearby table and, with a satisfied smirk, threw it over the robot.

•••

As they stood staring down at the unmoving figure of the Grey, Guy had flashbacks of his own times spent passed out drunk at tables. Seeing it from an outside perspective, it looked kind of ... unappealing. He glanced at the half-empty glass of white liquid standing half-touched next to the Grey's limp fingers. Several other glasses, all with dried, white residue clinging to the sides, stood or lay scattered about the table.

"Think he's alive?" he asked.

"Not sure," Neville said, and poked the Grey's cheek with a finger, eliciting a soft groan. "I guess he is. Barely."

"Geez, what's he been drinking?" Guy asked, studying the glasses from a safe distance.

"Milk," Cortex said.

"Milk?" Guy said with a frown. "How can milk do *that* to someone?"

"Greys are lactose-intolerant."

"So?"

"When Greys have dairy, they build up a gas that's absorbed by their bloodstream, causing intoxication. The stronger the dairy, the worse the effects."

"What about ice-cream? Or cheese?"

"Good heavens, no!" Cortex replied. "Especially *not* cheese. It's like taking drugs. I once saw a Grey who got caught snorting grated parmesan. It took four Protectors to subdue him."*

"That's horrible!" Guy said, looking truly horrified, because a life without cheese just wasn't kosher.* "How do we get him to sober up?"

"Coffee," Cortex said, and noticed the look on Guy's face. *"Hey, it works the same as for most other species, but much faster. Just without milk, of course."*

So, without further ado and with something to do, Guy strode over to where the bartender was supposed to be standing and asked the counter for a big mug of black coffee. From his low vantage point, he noticed the door behind the counter opening and closing without seeing anyone going through, although anyone taller would also have had difficulty spotting the crawling barman.

A short while later, a hesitant hand appeared and placed a mug on the countertop before retreating without any further sign of hesitation. Guy reached up to fetch the hot mug, then turned around. Only then did he notice that the rest of the bar had mysteriously emptied. Apparently, no amount of alcohol could keep anyone in the same room as Knights of Absolute

---

* Not that kosher makes any difference to Greys hooked on cheese. They'll take anything.

Avoidance. With a shrug, Guy returned to the table where the others had taken a seat.

Pulling back his hood, Max shook Mr Gray until the small figure lifted his big, heavy head with a groan. The Caynin took the mug from Guy and exchanged it for the half-empty glass of milk, which he put on the table behind them.

"What ... what's going on?" Mr Gray emitted with glazy eyes. *"Is it happy hour yet?"*

"Almost," Max said, helping the Grey to bring the mug to his mouth. "But first you have to drink this."

"Ooh, coffee!" Mr Gray said, taking a sip. Jerking back his head, he eyed the brew as if it was about to jump out and strangle him. *"Hey, where ... where's the milk?"*

"No milk," Max said soothingly. "But if you finish this one and the one after that, the next round is on me."

This seemed to encourage the Grey, who started drinking the hot liquid as quickly as his mouth allowed. While he was busy, Guy went back to the bar to order another mug from the hand and brought it back to the table.

Some of the glaziness had already started fading from the Grey's eyes, which looked up at Guy as though they vaguely remembered something.

"Hey," he said, *"haven't I seen you before ... somewhere?"*

Guy thought it better not to answer and left to fetch more coffee. When he returned, he sat down and patiently watched the Grey slurping the hot beverage. As soon as he reached the bottom of the second mug, Max handed him the third one.

Mr Gray looked up at the Caynin. *"I'm* not *getting any milk, am I?"*

Max shook his head, and the Grey's shoulders sagged.

"Just as well, I suppose," he said, and after taking another sip, a thought seemed to hit him at the same time as the caffeine. *"Max?"*

The Caynin nodded.

"Ugh," the Grey said, holding his head as if it was about to explode. *"I'm glad you're here."*

He didn't look all that glad, but Max gave him time to take a few more sips. Guy was amazed at how quickly the coffee sobered him up.

"What took you so long?" Mr Gray said halfway through the third mug.

"I'm sorry, Mr Gray," Max said. "I got held up a bit longer than I would have liked."

"I didn't like it either," the Grey said. *"I thought you were dead."*

"Nope, still around. But what about *you*? Where did you disappear to for so long? People think you're dead too."

Mr Gray had a slow slurp and sighed.

"I, too, got held up longer than planned," he said with the look of someone who was about to get into a conversation they'd rather not get into. *"After you contacted me, I searched for the nearest Dumb Planet, which turned out to be Earth. You said you had two subjects for transfer, so I checked for double hits on the* Life Spectacular *entries list. And, low and behold, there it was; a bit old, but still active – a double wish!"*

He looked at Guy, who looked at him perplexed.

"You see, Mr Leatherman, when you made your wish, you also wished for your friend here to join you. And as I needed two people for the transfer, it was the perfect match."

Guy tried to remember the wish he'd made, but couldn't recall all the details. Although it *did* sound like something he'd do. He looked apologetically at Neville, who merely shrugged.

"I thought the selection was supposed to be random," Guy continued, grateful that his friend wasn't as upset with him as he should have been.

"Yes, but I had to cheat the system – not one of my proudest moments."

The Grey glared at the Caynin as he said that last bit.

"Hey," Max said defensively, "you owed me a favour, and a huge one at that. You *know* you did. Without me, your head would be adorning a spike on Wahyoo VIII, or worse. You were lucky I bumped into you when I did, because if the headhunters chasing you hadn't caught you, the cannibals you were about to run into would have."

Mr Gray sighed. *"Of course, you're right. In any case, yes, I cheated the system, and you guys 'won'. So, after contacting Bezam and Lenny to make arrangements, I did your human-consciousness transfers to the profile boxes, and sent my assistant, Donz, ahead to complete the transfers with the Salamans. He should* never *have done it while they were awake, though – very dangerous. I also contacted a colleague of mine, Ms Beatrix, to handle Neville's consultation while I did yours."*

"Never happened," Neville said, folding his arms.

"I know," Mr Gray said. *"Ms Beatrix was supposed to help you through the process, but she had to cancel because her mother fell ill. I asked Donz to find someone else to do it, but he conveniently forgot."*

"You're one to talk!" Guy cried. "You were supposed to return to the circus, but you never did!"

"I know," the Grey repeated sombrely. *"Another one of my ... less proud moments. With all the pressure of having to do everything so quickly, not to mention my dishonour at having to cheat, I needed to take the edge off with some Earth milk."*

"Earth milk?" Guy said. "When did you go to Earth?"

"Well ... see ... the thing is, I didn't quite correct you when you thought you'd been teleported across galaxies, Mr Leatherman."

Guy stared confusedly at the cringing figure. "What do you mean?"

"Well, you can't really teleport people over great distances; not safely anyway. I met up with Donz on a company ship near Earth, and we teleported you aboard."

"So?"

"Um, I just thought, while I was there, why not go all out and grab a cow?"

"You seemed pretty sober when I saw you at the circus."

"Oh, I was, pretty much. But when I found out exactly what Donz had done with your transfers, it kind of sent me

over the edge. So, after seeing you, I had a few more glasses ... and a few more and, well ... I kept on drinking and flying about until ... well ... until the cow died."

"It died?!"

"Yes, well," the Grey said defensively, *"I didn't exactly know how to keep it alive.* [*] *And I wasn't exactly in the right frame of mind to think things through, you know?"*

Guy looked shocked, and didn't know what to say, so he just hoped his face said enough to cover all the bases. If the look on his companions' faces was anything to go by, it did.

Mr Gray seemed to get the collective message, and sighed heavily before continuing.

"In any case, I knew I had to return home eventually, but I felt too disgusted with myself to go back to work. So, when I returned to Unyun, I spent most of my time inside bars, or outside bars in my car. However, I went home last night, and wished I hadn't. I tripped and fell over something as I walked in, and when I switched on the lights, it was a dead body ... shot. It was ... Donz."

He looked at their faces, which pretty much looked the same as they did a few moments earlier.

"I didn't do it, I swear," Mr Gray said. *"But someone certainly wanted the authorities to think so, because I heard sirens, and when I looked outside I saw Cup cars pulling up. I panicked and fled to Donz's apartment, only to find it ransacked. I saw my assistant, 3OCD2, which I'd lent to Donz but thankfully never got back. I figured that, should you ever return, I'd need some way of contacting you. So, not knowing what else to do, I programmed 3OCD2 to activate upon hearing Max's voice along with some keywords."*

He looked at Max. *"He was to bring you here, where I'd wait for you every afternoon. I never figured I'd see you so*

---

[*] Keeping cows alive in space is quite complicated. Some species tried this in their early days of space exploration, but simply gave up – partly because keeping the animals fed non-stop is a near impossible task, but mainly because the eventual non-stop digestive outcome was not that pleasant to live with in zero gravity.

soon, though, especially not after you've been gone for so long."

"Well, I'm here," Max said empathetically. "And if there's anyone who understands what it's like to flee persecution, it's me."

Mr Gray looked at him appreciatively.

"What about our human bodies and the profile boxes?" Guy asked, ignoring the moment.

"Your best bet would be the Life Spectacular *offices,"* Mr Gray said. *"I'm sure Donz would have taken the boxes there ... well,* reasonably *sure. Unfortunately, after last night, I won't be able to retrieve them myself."*

Max nodded thoughtfully. "Yes, the Protectors certainly would've gone there looking for you, so your colleagues will by now know that you're wanted in connection with Donz's murder. You'd undoubtedly be reported and detained within a matter of minutes after setting foot inside the building."

"So how do we get in?" Neville said.

Max pensively scratched himself behind the ear, but stopped mid-scratch as he caught sight of the square-shaped tablecloth.

"I think I have an idea," he said, "but first we have a stop to make."

CHAPTER 53

I t was a struggle to get Mr Gray onto his feet, and even more of a struggle to get him to give up his car's keycard. He insisted he was fine to drive while the others insisted he wasn't. The argument was resolved in favour of the others when the Grey walked into the wall next to the door. The coffee had apparently only helped so much.

The car itself, hovering about in a nearby alleyway, wasn't very new, but neither was it very old. The curvy vehicle had most likely looked a lot better not too long ago, but intoxicated driving had left its mark – quite a few of them, to be exact. The numerous dings and scrapes had transformed the once sleek body into something straight from an insurance broker's nightmares.

Mr Gray looked at it as if seeing it for the first time.

"Two months," he moaned, rubbing his large temples. *"Only two more months and she would have been paid off. Just look at her now!"*

Ignoring the Grey's financial woes, Max opened a door. "Get in," he commanded, which turned out easier said than done because, although it was done, it certainly wasn't easy.

The only place where Cortex could fit was in the front passenger seat next to Max, who subsequently had to sit leaning sideways to make space for the bug's bulky body and arms. And because there wasn't enough space in the baggage compartment for 3OCD2, the rest all tried to squash into the back seat. When this didn't work, they merely shoved a protesting Mr Gray into the baggage compartment. This created enough space for Guy and Neville to squeeze in on either side of the robot, and also helped to get rid of some of the sour-milk smell exhaled by the Grey. The rest of the smell, however, seemed to have become a permanent fixture in the car.

They drove on in silence, as no one really had much space to breathe, never mind talk. Besides, talking would have required more intake of air, which they tried to avoid in the odorous car. It didn't seem to bother Max too much, using the foul-smelling air as a good excuse to drive with his head stuck out the window. He seemed somewhat reluctant to get out after stopping at a tall, red building.

The Caynin opened the baggage compartment to let out a sulky Grey, who got back to his feet after tripping over one of them.

"Where are we?" Cortex asked, following Max, who'd locked the vehicle with 3OCD2 still inside.

"A safe house," Max replied as he stopped at the building's blue access door. He punched in a code, upon which the door slid open, and made his way to a metal staircase to the right.

"Can't we just take the elevator?" said Guy, whose feet still didn't want to walk farther than necessary.

"It's on the second floor," Max said, starting his ascent. "Easier to get out in a pinch."

Reaching the floor, they took the hallway to the right and stopped at the last door on the left. Here, too, Max entered a code into the keypad next to the door, which squeaked open.

"You might want to oil that," Guy said as Max ushered them in.

"Actually, it's better this way," the Caynin said, closing the door behind them. "Makes it trickier for someone to sneak in unnoticed."

"Oh," Guy said, as much in response to the Infiltrator's statement as to the apartment's interior, which was fairly nondescript.

A door led to a bedroom, and the main living area they were standing in had a small kitchen, which only appeared bigger than it should thanks to the undersized two-seater table. The rest of the apartment featured a living room with a scuffed fold-out couch, a box acting as a coffee table, as well as a thin, small TV panel on the wall. It was flanked by two *very* colourful paintings of what seemed to be some sort of parrot – although that was just about all you could say about them.

"So, what do you think?" Max said.

"About what?" Guy said.

"About the paintings," Max said proudly. "Did them myself, you know?"

"Colourful," Guy said, blinking.

Realising that Guy wasn't going to say much more, and noticing that Max's face suddenly sagged a bit more than usual, Neville jumped in.

"It's really … vibrant," he said.

"Yes, very … lively," Cortex backed him up, trying his best not to let his real thoughts slip out.

Max cheered up slightly.

"It makes my eyes hurt," Mr Gray said.

Cheer lost again, Neville tried something else.

"I think he just needs some more coffee," he said.

After shooting the Grey a quick glare, Max marched to the kitchen, got a mug out of a cupboard, dropped two extra-strong coffee pills into it, filled it up with water, put it in a device and removed it five seconds later, steaming hot.

"Sugar?" he grated.

"Yes please," said an oblivious Mr Gray.

A vengeful smile crossed Max's face as he shoved the mug into the Grey's hands.

"Good," he said, "because I don't have any."

"So," Neville said after an awkward pause, "you want to use the robot to go into the offices?"

"That's right," Max said. "After all, he was Mr Gray's assistant. Isn't that so, Mr Gray?"

"Yes," the Grey said, staring at the coffee as if he could mentally make it weaker and sweeter. Taking a sip, his face attested that this hadn't worked.

"He should *still be authorised to go in, "* he said as his left eye started twitching slightly. *"He's however pretty ... particular about certain things; rules being one of them. And going in unaccompanied is against the rules. You can try, but I doubt you'll have much luck."*

"Well," Max said determinedly, "he'll just have to do it."

CHAPTER 54

Three of the car's yellow-cloaked-and-hooded occupants drove in silence and then stopped in silence across from the *Life Spectacular* building. They were silent because, thanks to the fourth occupant, they couldn't get a word in edgeways.

"So that's why I'm *not* going to do it," 3OCD2 finished with its angry emoji turning away from everyone.

"But you *have to*!" Guy pleaded.

"I don't *have to* do anything," replied the now-solid-white square forming the back of the emoji's head. "Do I have to go over it all again?"

"No!" the biologicals cried in unison.

Guy buried his face in his hands and growled in frustration. Using every bit of reasoning they could think of, they'd tried their utmost to convince the robot that he had to go into the *Life Spectacular* offices, but to no avail. Even stating that it was a matter of life and death hadn't worked. Such matters didn't interest side tables. The more they'd tried, the more 3OCD2 resisted.

Neither Cortex nor Mr Gray had tried, because they weren't there. Both had opted to get some much-needed sleep for different reasons.

A sudden knock at the window scared Guy's face out of his hands.

"*Hello?*" emitted a figure, peering through the window.

It was a worried-looking Grey, whom Guy recognised as Ms Beatrix, if only because of her purple handbag.

"Ms Beatrix?" Max said, rolling down the window. "What are you doing here?"

"I work here, remember?" she said.

Apparently, Max did, and looked ready to drive off at a moment's notice.

"Er, yes, of course," he said, keeping his voice calm. "What can we do for you?"

"Did you find Mr Gray?" she asked with a feel of deep concern.

"Uh … Ms Beatrix, I don't think we should be talking about this," Max said. "We wouldn't want to get you into trouble."

"What, more trouble than Mr Gray being wanted for murder?" she said.

"So, you know about that," Max said, his hands clenching tighter on the steering wheel.

"Of course I know. Once reception *knows about something, it never takes long for everyone else to know."*[*]

Ms Beatrix picked up on Max's restlessness.

"Oh, don't worry," she said, waving a hand. *"I'm not going to get you into trouble either. All I care about is whether Mr Gray is okay."*

Max appeared caught between a rock and a hard place without knowing how hard the hard place actually was.

"He's alive," he sighed eventually.

"Thank goodness!" Ms Beatrix said in relief before concern returned. *"Still, he's a murder suspect, which I don't believe for a second! Is there anything I can do to help?"*

"I don't think so, Ms Beatrix," Max said, then threw a thumb over his shoulder at the robot on the back seat. "Unless you can get our *friend* here to go in there and get some info we need."

"Oh, well, I'm afraid he won't go in without an authorised supervisor. Very much stuck on protocol, that one."

"So I've gathered," Max grated. "More than once."

---

[*] If there's one thing any true receptionist is better at than reception, it's transmission.

"So why don't you just let me *take him in?"*

Max gave her a surprised look that, had he looked behind him, would have served as a perfect example in a go-to guide on synchronised expressions.

"You'd do that?" he said.

"If it will help Mr Gray out of this pickle he's gotten himself into, absolutely! Now, what information do you need?"

• • •

Ms Beatrix carted 3OCD2 away on an antique wheelchair that had previously been used to transport the robotic assistant around the office. Apparently, no one else had much love for the robot's self-propelled racket either, so Ms Beatrix had organised the wheelchair to help Mr Gray keep his noisy assistant both in the building and in one piece.

The others remained in the car without much to do other than hope for the best. Which, through recent experience, didn't mean much.

"So," Neville said in an attempt to alleviate the tension, "you think she and Mr Gray ...?"

"She and Mr Gray *what?*" Guy said, not sure that he was following, as confirmed by his frown.

"You know ..." Neville tried again, hoping his friend would catch on. But judging by the frown that remained in place, this didn't seem likely.

"I mean," he elaborated, "do you think they have like ... *a thing* going?"

A look of comprehension crossed Guy's face, only to be replaced by one of revulsion. "Ah, geez, Nev!" he said, rubbing his head as if trying to erase something from it. "Why would you *say* something like that? Why would you want me to think about ... *that?*"

Neville shrugged. "Maybe because I didn't want to be the only one."

"Well, sharing *isn't* caring," Guy grumbled.

"I think Mr Andersman is correct," Max opined from the front without taking his eyes off the Grey pushing the wheelchair into the building. "There's definitely something going on there – at least from the viewpoint of *one* of them."

"Which one?" Guy asked without thinking. Not that it would've helped if he had been thinking – he'd never been good at picking up on romantic signals, even if they were flashing and accompanied by alarm bells. And the few times he *had* picked up on such signals, even a little, he usually tried to duck under a table, not knowing what to do with them.

Neville decided to let it go, partly because of Guy's reluctance to talk about it, but mainly because he realised that he, too, didn't really want to think about it.

So they continued to sit there in silence, trying not to think about anything … especially *that*.

•••

Ms Beatrix finally emerged from the building, pushing the blocky robot to the awaiting vehicle.

Max rolled down his window. "So, did you manage to find out anything?"

"I don't know," Ms Beatrix replied. *"I kept my colleagues busy while 3OCD2 accessed the system, and we came right back as soon as he was done."*

"And?" Max said, directing the question at the robot resting quietly on the wheelchair.

"Oh," 3OCD2 said after a pause, "you're talking to me."

"Yes."

"And, what?"

"And, what did you find out?"

"Well, since the last time I was here, Ms Pinkleson was promoted to Assistant Call-centre Manager, and Billy got fired for sexual harassment because he kept on—"

"I mean, what did you find out about the bodies and the profile boxes?" Max snapped, cheeks flapping.

"Oh," the robot replied. "You'd be happy to know that the bodies are completely safe."

Guy and Neville slowly exhaled the tense air they'd been bottling up.

"But I'm afraid your profile boxes are gone," the robot continued.

Guy and Neville gasped the tense air back in.

"What do you mean they're gone?" Neville demanded, saving Guy the effort.

"Well, in simple terms, they're *not there*," the robot stated.

"I know what *gone* means," Neville said irritably.

"Good," 3OCD2 said, "because that's where your profile boxes are."

Ms Beatrix noticed Neville's red face reddening some more.

"I'm sure they've just been misplaced," she said. *"It's not as if someone can just walk in and take them. They're in the top section of the building. Very secure."*

"That's right," 3OCD2 said. "But according to the system log, someone walked in and took them."

"Say again," Ms Beatrix said, perplexed.

"That's right," 3OCD2 said. "But according to the system log, someone walked in and—"

"Yes, yes, I heard you the first time," Ms Beatrix said, *"but who?"*

"Oh, Mr Chase," the robot replied.

Even with her big eyes, Ms Beatrix appeared surprised. *"Mr Chase?"*

"Yes, Mr Chase. He collected them just this morning and didn't even bother to follow procedure. He removed them without getting authorisation from the Operations Director."

"Who's Mr Chase?" Max asked.

"Uh," Ms Beatrix said, frowning, *"he's our Department Manager. A Grey. Not the most likeable person these days, and certainly not the most trustworthy. Constantly late for work, that one;* if *he pitches at all, that is. But we actually prefer it when he's not there, as it's less work for the rest of us. We always have to fix his mistakes or redo his work from scratch. Rumour has it that he has some ... bad habits on the side, but I don't think it's just on the side. I'm sure I saw a cheese wedge in his top drawer last week before he slammed it shut."*

"Why would *he* take the profile boxes?" Max said.

"Who knows, but you never know with that one."

"So, now what?" Guy asked.

A blocky, angry emoji projected across all of 3OCD2's surfaces. "We must retrieve those profile boxes from Mr Chase," he said. "They don't belong to him."

CHAPTER 55

The three biologicals struggled to get the heavy robot out of Mr Gray's car and onto the wheelchair. Fortunately, the damage they did to the vehicle in the process blended in perfectly with the damage that had already been done before.

They were parked across the street from a building that had long ago seen better days but had since gone blind. It was more or less – although perhaps a bit more – in the same shape as the late Donz's apartment building. It was of the same cookie-cutter design, and it looked as though the same rusted cookie cutter had been used in its construction.

"Are you sure this is the right place?" Max asked, surveying the rest of the neighbourhood, which didn't look much better.

"Why, do you think my memory banks are failing?" 3OCD2 asked worriedly. "This is the last-known address for Mr Chase, which I downloaded from the system when I saw the breach in protocol. However, glitches are possible from time to time, so I can run a quick diagnostic check if you'd like. It will only take a few min—"

"No," Max said quickly, "that won't be necessary. It's just strange that a Department Manager would live in a place like … this."

"I'm afraid I wouldn't know why," the robot said. "I don't concern myself much with the state of biologicals' habitats, regardless of their professional status."

"Well, I suppose we'd better go knock," Max said as he pushed the robot to the building's access door, which was locked with a keypad. Just as he crouched down to inspect the device, the door opened. A man came stumbling out on his way to – it could safely be deduced – any place that sold alcohol or any other substance that would keep him stumbling in the same fashion for a while longer. Not surprisingly, he didn't seem too fazed by the three figures slipping in through the door behind him, pushing a side table.

They made their way to the elevator across a litter-strewn floor.

"Would you mind—" 3OCD2 began saying when Max said something.

"Before you start going on about trash," he said, holding up a warning finger, "I suggest you don't."

"But—"

"No buts," the Infiltrator said firmly. "If we spend all our time picking up litter, we won't be able to get the profile boxes. And what's the more important protocol to follow at this stage: the trash, or retrieving the boxes?"

3OCD2 contemplated this conundrum for a second.

"Retrieving the boxes, I suppose," he finally relented.

"Wise decision," Max said. "Now, why don't you stay down here and keep an eye out for us?"

He marched off without waiting for an answer, followed by Guy and Neville. The robot had no choice but to remain in the wheelchair, casting fearful glances at the garbage surrounding him like a pack of trashy wolves.

• • •

The trio stepped into a metal elevator adorned by graffiti, some of which were expletives that were so explicit they should rather not be repeated, even to those burning to know what they were.

As they jerkily ascended in the metal box, Guy gave a gulp that he wasn't sure was because of the expletives he'd just read or the fear of plummeting to his death. Fortunately, the elevator came to a stop with a final jerk and without anyone dying.

They stepped out into a hallway that was covered by a moss-green carpet. At least Guy hoped it was carpet, and not actual moss. Judging by the look of it, it could have been either, but he just decided it was carpet and left it at that. The walls bore more colourfully worded graffiti to greet both residents and visitors with a warm unwelcome.

"Here," Max said, stopping halfway down the hall at a door that could only be described as such because it separated one area from another, to some degree.

The door had no keypad; just a worn handle. Max reached out to test it, but his hand froze when faint voices emanated from inside the apartment. Taking out his gun, he eased his ear against the door to hear more clearly. However, his head barely touched the wood when a desperate yell caused him to jump back. Without hesitation, he stood back, lifted his leg and, with one mighty kick, the door violently remained in place. The Caynin's leg, however, was stuck in the hole it had just created.

Assisted by Guy and Neville, Max managed to dislodge his foot from the rotten door. Then, taking a couple of steps back, he charged forward and rammed the door with his shoulder, causing the weak barrier to shatter. Not expecting the door's sudden disintegration, the Infiltrator stumbled and nearly lost his footing, which in all likelihood ended up saving his life. A blue-white bolt streaked through the space where his head would have been and punched a smouldering hole in the hallway outside.

Unbalanced, Max squeezed off two shots of his own. While both missed their mark, they caused his would-be killer to duck and another to swivel his gun away from a Grey's head towards the intruder. Max barely regained his balance before he had to roll sideways into a small kitchen to evade the next three shots, which left three smoking holes in the opposite wall.

Although he'd only had a second to do so, the well-trained Infiltrator established that he was up against two armed Vahltans. To even the odds, he leaned around the corner to blow off the arm holding the gun nearest to him. With a shriek, the Vahltan jumped back, clutching the stump where his wrist used to be. The other Vahltan looked back at the spot where he'd held the Grey at gunpoint earlier and, realising that his target wasn't there anymore, he turned to run. Before disappearing beyond the corner, he fired another wild shot in Max's direction, forcing the Caynin to duck back into the kitchen.

Max heard a sliding grind and cautiously started advancing, but immediately had to flatten himself against the wall as another two shots hit his corner cover. He waited another few seconds before rolling into the small living area, and rose from behind a couch, ready to blast the next thing that moved. This, however, turned out to be tattered curtains, which moved lightly in the wind despite attempts by years of accumulated grime to weigh it down.

The Infiltrator cautiously approached the open window, gun raised. He hazarded a quick glance outside, and then glanced out a bit longer when nothing happened. A few flights down, two figures rapidly descended the metal fire-escape; one carrying a black bag that swung outwards at every turn. Max was about to climb out in pursuit when he heard frantic yelling from behind.

"Max! Maaaax!!"

He glanced back, then looked down the fire-escape once more. The two fleeing Vahltans had already descended more than halfway to the alley below.

"Maaaaaaax!!!"

With a cry of frustration, Max slammed his hand down against the sill, before he spun around and rushed to the hallway where the yelling had come from. A few metres from the door, two Salamans wrestled a Grey who struggled with all his might to escape the hands, arms and legs trying to constrain him. He almost managed to break free when the Caynin's big hand closed around his scrawny neck, yanking him back with a croak.

"Now where do you think *you're* going?" Max grated, twisting the neck so that the Grey could get a good look at the muzzle of the weapon pointed at his face. As in most normal situations where a gun is pressed to someone's head, this had the desired effect. When the Grey went limp, Guy and Neville stepped back, panting.

"Nowhere, " the Grey emitted as his fingers grappled feebly at the powerful hand squeezing his throat.

"Good to hear," Max said with a deadly calm. "Because if I let go and you try to run, you will indeed be going nowhere, permanently. Understand?"

If the words weren't enough, the muzzle of the gun tapping against his skull carried enough emphasis for the Grey to force out a fearful *"Yes "*.

Max released his grip and stepped back, keeping the gun trained on its target, who wheezed like a rubber duck tied to the wheel of a slow-moving car.

"Are you Mr Chase?" the Caynin asked. His glare clearly stated that lying would not be advisable.

"Yes, " the Grey said and gave a cough that sounded like a sneeze. *"Yes, I am. "*

Max looked down the hallway, where doors slammed shut before the owners could be spotted; owners who were, in all likelihood, about to call the authorities.

"Marvellous," he said as his glare returned to the Grey, whose terror-filled eyes darted about. "I think it's time we get going, don't you?"

"Where to? " Mr Chase said anxiously.

"To talk, Mr Chase," Max said with a steely expression. "Just to talk."

CHAPTER 56

Mr Chase wasn't having a very good day, and while he'd had his fair share of bad days, this one ranked right at the top of days that should rather not be repeated if time travel ever became a reality. But the day wasn't over yet. He was reminded of this fact when the cold barrel of a gun prodded him into an apartment, followed by the Caynin holding the gun, the two Salamans who'd foiled his escape earlier, as well as the clanging robot that used to irritate him to no end at the office.

As he trundled in, the first thing Mr Chase saw was a big Veagin frowning at him as he got up from the couch. Mr Chase didn't know him. The second thing he saw was a Grey who turned from the window, looking just as surprised as Mr Chase felt. *This one* he knew.

"What are you *doing here?"* Mr Chase said, looking like someone who'd just been punched by a ghost wearing a knuckleduster.

"I could ask you the same thing," Mr Gray replied, looking like he'd just witnessed someone being punched by a ghost wearing a knuckleduster.

"I thought you were dead."

"And I thought you were ... at work."

They stared at one another until Mr Gray turned to Max.

"No, seriously, what's he doing here?" he demanded.

So Max brought Mr Gray up to speed, very slowly, not only because the Grey still seemed a bit hung-over, but also because he was asking a lot of questions in between.

When Max finished, Mr Gray turned his stunned face to Mr Chase.

"Why would you take the profile boxes?" he asked.

"Well, that's a long story," the other Grey replied.

"Then keep it short," Max growled deeply.

Mr Chase glanced nervously at the Caynin, then nodded meekly and sat down at the small table with a sigh.

"My life has been a bit ... chaotic of late," he said. *"It started a few months ago with a bit of harmless fun at the casino with my wife—"*

"Shorter," Max growled even more deeply.

"Well, let's just say I got a bit carried away and ended up losing all our savings – which I didn't tell my wife about, of course. That next morning, at work, Billy asked me what was eating me, so I told him. He then told me about a Vahltan he knew called Sammi, who could fix me up with a quick loan. So I contacted the guy, and we met at a bar. He told me he'd be happy to help, but that the interest on the loan would be high. However, I was desperate, so I accepted the money.

"On my way home, I had second thoughts, but I also knew I needed the cash. I started panicking, so I stopped at a cheese shop and paid a Stortian kid to go in and buy me some processed cheddar wedges. Just some light stuff, you know, to take the edge off."*

As this clearly hit close to home, Mr Gray lowered his head and shifted uncomfortably.

"I kept the money," Mr Chase continued, *"but within a couple of months I had spent it all on gambling and cheese. When my wife eventually found out what I'd done, she kicked me out of our apartment, so I moved into the apartment you found me in."*

"The boxes, Mr Chase," Max said impatiently. "What happened to the *profile boxes?"*

---

* It's illegal to sell cheese to a Grey, so don't do it. It's okay to sell cheese to kids, unless they're Grey kids, in which case you *really* shouldn't do it.

"I'm getting to that," the Grey replied quickly. *"Late last night I received a visit from Sammi, who'd brought along one of his 'associates'. They said I was late on my payment, but I told them I didn't have the money at the moment.*

"The associate said late payments wouldn't be tolerated under any circumstances, and took out a gun. I was sure my time was up! However, Sammi told him not to be too hasty, as the matter could be resolved without resorting to drastic measures. He said there might be another way for me to pay off my debt. Apparently, they had a problem with two guys who owed their boss much more money than I did, and if I helped to bring them *in, my debt would be cancelled.*

"He said finding the guys wasn't the problem, but rather getting to them. And that's where I'd come in, because the guys they were looking for were currently part of the Life Spectacular Life-Enrichment Programme *and needed to be extracted. I told them they were crazy; I couldn't just remove people and profile boxes from the building – I'd be fired! But Sammi made it clear that being fired would be the least of my problems if I didn't comply, and that I'd better make a plan. Of course, seeing as I didn't have any other option, I agreed to do it. But they warned me not to double-cross them or try to run, because their boss would find me wherever I go. They said not even the authorities would be able to protect me. I've seen, read and heard enough stories about their boss to know they weren't exaggerating.*

"When I arrived at work this morning, I heard someone had killed or been killed by someone. Everyone was talking about it. I couldn't care less about who it was at the time, but it created enough of a distraction for me to grab the profile boxes. I tried to think of a way to get the bodies out too, but then I overheard someone saying something about Protectors questioning people in the building. I panicked, realising that I wouldn't be able to get the bodies out with that much heat around. So I left in the hope that the boxes would be enough to get me out of the mess I was in. It wasn't. When Sammi and his associate returned, they were furious that I

couldn't deliver the bodies too. I suspect they were about to kill me, when you guys showed up."

"So where are the boxes now?" asked Max, who'd been listening attentively.

"*I gave it to them, of course.*"

"You just *gave* it to them?" Guy said.

"*Well, it's not like I had a choice,*" Mr Chase protested.

"Still—" Guy began, but was interrupted by Max.

"This boss the Vahltan was talking about," the Caynin said apprehensively, "who was it?"

Mr Chase swallowed hard. "*Manni Karpachio. The Man.*"

CHAPTER 57

Max had known the answer before he'd even asked the question. He'd also known that, while he had not really wanted to hear the answer, the question had to be asked and unsatisfactorily answered, like when you ask your doctor if it would be better if you quit smoking.[*]

"The Man," he grated. "*Of course* it's The Man."

The Caynin took a seat on the couch and stared at the floor while the others stared at him.

"We have to go back, don't we?" Neville said, also knowing what the answer would be.

"Yes," the Caynin replied.

"Back where?" asked Guy, who definitely didn't want to hear the answer, because most of the places he had visited recently weren't places he wanted to revisit.

"The Mansion," Neville said quietly.

"The Mansion!" Guy said, looking at Neville as though he was crazy. "Are you crazy?"

He turned to Max. "The Mansion? You can't be serious. We barely got out alive last time!"

"We have to, Mr Leatherman," the Caynin said.

"No, *we* don't have to do anything. Just call the authorities – get *them* to round up The Man and his cronies. We have evidence, and witnesses."

---

[*] Many doctors have shared a good laugh over this ridiculous question during their smoke break.

Max shook his head. "We don't have nearly enough; and it's all circumstantial, at best. Nothing directly ties him to the assassination. Karpachio has avoided prison with *far* more evidence against him. And even if there is enough evidence at The Mansion, we still don't know how high up this thing goes. Any official move against him by the authorities will undoubtedly reach his ears long before *they* do. And by then, both he and the evidence will be long gone. Besides, as you may recall, I'm still a wanted man, so I'll most likely end up rotting in a prison cell, while you end up worse. More importantly, your bodies won't last much longer. We need to retrieve your profile boxes to perform your reverse-transfers as soon as possible. The Mansion isn't just our best shot, it's our *only* shot."

"He's right, Guy," Cortex said.

"Maybe," Guy conceded after a pause. "But I still don't like it," he added, just in case anyone had missed his body language.

"Neither do I," Neville said. "It's the last place I want to go. But unless you have a better plan, it's our only shot, like Max said."

"Yes, yes, I get it," Guy said, turning to Max. "Speaking of plans, what *is* the plan, then? Because for some reason, I don't think we're going to waltz in and out of there like last time, when they'd practically let us go."

"No," the Caynin said thoughtfully, "I don't think so either. The Man will know that this is our only play; he'll be prepared."

"It certainly isn't fair play if one of the teams doesn't have enough players," Neville muttered.

"Good point," Max said, getting up and walking into the bedroom.

"Where are you going?" Guy asked.

"To get some more players," the Infiltrator replied as he took out a galphone and closed the door behind him.

•••

A few minutes later, Max reappeared from the bedroom. The others, who'd been waiting in anticipation, got up.

Avoiding eye contact, Max walked to the window and sat on 3OCD2, who started to protest until he was silenced by the Caynin's boot.

"Ahem," Guy said, looking at Max looking out the window.

"Sorry guys," the Infiltrator said, not taking his eyes off the sunset outside. Orange light reflected lazily off the surfaces of shiny buildings as if it was just another day, or rather the end of one. "I had hoped to get us some decent backup, but it's not looking good."

"You mean we're on our own?" Cortex said, as each pair of eyes seemed to add more weight on the Caynin's shoulders.

"It seems as though we might just as well be," Max replied sombrely.

He sat there for a while, then rose with a determined expression. "We'll just have to make do with what we've got and be as careful as we can. Mr Gray, you stay here with Mr Chase."

Mr Gray shot a displeased glance towards his fellow Grey. *"But—"* he started before being glared into silence by the Infiltrator.

"And Mr Chase," Max said with a pre-emptive glare that had the desired effect, as the other Grey lowered his finger and kept whatever he was about to say to himself. "You might figure that this gives you the perfect opportunity to make a run for it, as there won't be anyone around to stop you. *However*, there are two things you should keep in mind. If you *do* decide to run and we fail, The Man will find you and silence you in ways you cannot imagine. And believe me, whatever you can imagine, it will be ten times worse. He won't keep any loose ends flapping in the wind. Your safest bet is to stay here and hope to Zolt that we don't fail."

"And the second thing?" Mr Chase asked hesitantly.

"If you run and we *don't* fail, I will make it my personal mission to hunt you down wherever you go. I'm *very good* at it. I trust you believe me?"

The lack of response from the Grey's stricken face confirmed that he did.

"Good," Max said, and turned to the other three. "Now, gentlemen, I hope you're ready."

Guy mustered up all the courage he could to say, with absolute conviction, "Not really."

CHAPTER 58

Captain Phealix strode purposefully down the long hallway, which was painted red by rotating emergency lights and filled by the blare of an alarm. It had been triggered by the security guard now lying unmoving on the white floor behind her. She shot another guard in the back as he tried to flee the advancing group of pirates that had appeared from nowhere.

"How far?" she asked Franki, who blasted one of the security cameras monitoring the hallway. It wasn't really necessary, but she allowed him his fun.

The Vahltan glanced at his handheld monitor. "Almost there, Captain. Up the next hallway; third door on the left."

As they rounded the corner, a Grey had just enough time to widen his eyes before he closed them again quickly, as he knew what was coming. The stunner shot that hit him made it unlikely that he would open his eyes any time soon, so he scored some points for being proactive. He'd frantically been trying to open the door Franki had indicated, and most likely would have succeeded if he hadn't been so frantic in the first place. However, judging by the lab coat he wore, no one could really blame him for not being used to people with guns bearing down on him.

The door had a hand scanner, so with a nod from the captain, Franki picked up the Grey's limp body with one arm and used the other to place an equally limp Grey hand on the scanning panel. As the door slid open, Franki dropped the Grey, who hit the floor like a sack of Buffalo wings.

Doop entered first and blasted another white-lab-coated Grey who'd been trying to keep the door shut. Captain Phealix entered the large room behind Franki, who continued down a row of pods, checking the numbers before disappearing around a corner. The captain waited patiently while the dull sound of gunfire continued elsewhere.

"Found it!" Franki shouted a short while later.

Two Vahltans each grabbed an a-grav trolley, which they promptly pushed in the direction of his voice. They returned shortly thereafter with two strapped-down stasis pods.

Captain Phealix motioned the Vahltans out the door and followed without a word. They made their way up the stairs, with the specially designed trolleys gliding effortlessly up the incline.

"Call back the others," the captain commanded as they reached the rooftop exit.

Franki relayed the order over his commlink and opened the door, revealing the rooftop with the huge football-kebab shape of the *Jolly Dodger* hovering expectantly above it. The ship reflected its surroundings so effectively that it would have been hard to notice by anyone not knowing what they were looking for. As the procession made its way up the ship's ramp, the rest of the Vahltans came streaming out of the rooftop door.

When they were all on board, Cap's voice sounded over the commlink. "Orders, Captain?"

"Get us out of here before the Cups wake up from their naps," the captain said.

She glanced at the two metal pods whose frosted glass panels hid their contents, although she knew exactly what lay beneath.

"On our way, Captain," Cap said as the ship lifted off with barely a jerk. "Shall I plot the course so long?"

"No," the Faylin said, "we have one more stop to make."

"The Man's not going to like any delays, Captain."

"Don't worry, Cap," she said. "I just need to pick up a gift for him. I'm sure he'll understand when he sees it."

CHAPTER 59

Guy and – to his relief – his now-un-yellow-cloaked companions alighted from *The Mothership*, which rested semi-pinkly in a ship parking lot outside the town of Schmol. The small town was home to a small community of traders and small-town businessmen, as well as an agricultural cooperative that served the local farmers.

A long row of elliptic metal silos on the edge of the town towered proudly above the smaller buildings, and eagerly awaited the rows of a-grav tractors pulling a-grav wagons laden with agricultural products. The silos, in turn, were ready to distribute the products to destinations where hungry people were waiting to chow down on their favourite meal, before chucking the rest into a waste bin after realising they hadn't been as hungry as they'd previously thought.

While Irik was mostly an arid planet, it also boasted giant oases where farms thrived, producing enough products for both local use and export. Towns like Schmol were scattered throughout these oases, providing enough work to keep the local populace and bars happy.

Guy sneezed from the red dust, which was still settling on the ship and his face after being kicked up by *The Mothership's* engines upon landing.

"Bless you," Max said as he locked the ship's hatch.

"Thanks," Guy said. While his well-filtered nostrils kept most of the dust out, it could only do so much, as Neville also proved a second later.

After another ritual blessing and the obligatory gratitude for the blessing, Max instructed them to wait, and left to secure some transport.

With nothing else to do, Guy sat cross-legged in the shade of *The Mothership* and gazed at the town. Everything seemed so tranquil, as if nothing was wrong in the universe; as if four people weren't about to walk into what was, most likely, certain death. He envied the people walking about, bantering, laughing, and basically just going about their daily lives without a care. He envied their blissful ignorance of the sinister activities unfolding not so far away in a place that none of them would ever wish to see the inside of. A place of nightmares. A place he and his friends were heading to; not because they wanted to, but because they *had* to.

Guy looked at Neville and Cortex sitting in silence a few metres to the side, possibly sharing the same thoughts. They looked back at him, said nothing, and returned their gaze to the people around them as if cherishing the feeling of normality for the last time.

A shiver of guilt hit Guy as he watched them watching the town's activities. He felt responsible for dragging Neville into this mess against his will through *wishful thinking*, and for befriending Cortex to such an extent that the bug felt obligated to help him. If anything happened to either of them, he wouldn't be able to forgive himself. He wished he could undo everything, but knew that the *Life Spectacular* programme wouldn't be able to grant his wish this time.

How long they sat there, Guy didn't know, but their final moment of peace was disturbed by the electric whizz of an open, light-brown buggy with big fat tyres that skidded to a halt in a cloud of dust.

Max hopped out with a grin. "Like it?"

"Beats walking," Neville said with a smile as they got up.

"Sweet ride," said Cortex.

"It's okay," Guy said, trying to inject some positivity into his gloomy state of mind, only to realise it had been a placebo. "Did you 'appropriate' this one too?"

"If you're asking whether I *stole* it, the answer is no," Max said, brushing off the accusation. "I had a lot of money stashed at the safe house, so I paid the owner double the value. He was more than happy to part with it. It's not pretty, but it should get us to The Mansion without a hitch."

Guy noted how Max had *not* said "to The Mansion *and back*", but kept it to himself.

The Infiltrator retrieved the big bag he'd left with Cortex earlier and chucked it into a cargo box affixed to the rear of the buggy, before hopping back in behind the steering wheel.

"What are you waiting for?" he shouted.

He waited patiently until Cortex climbed in next to him and the Salamans clambered into the back seat, then jammed his foot down hard on a pedal to send the vehicle spinning away.

As the dust settled, *The Mothership* stood there forlornly, with hints of pink peeking through the fine particles of red grit enveloping most of its hull. Had the ship been fitted with an AI control unit, it would have calculated that it needed a serious wash. It then would have calculated the chances of the four dwindling biologicals in the buggy returning to perform this task. It eventually would have realised that its time would be better spent calculating something that was more likely to yield a positive result, like that snowball's chance in hell.

• • •

Apparently, The Mansion wasn't that far from Schmol. Max had opted to land at the town rather than near The Mansion, as The Man would expect an aerial approach – he'd be watching the skies above his compound like a portly hawk.

The four drove on without a word, each with his own mixture of emotions, ranging from hope to hopelessness and, mostly, the regret of not having what might have been one last beer.

Schmol was situated on the edge of an oasis, so it didn't take long for the greenery to give way to the prevailing arid, rocky countryside. The buggy bounced over the uneven road as it passed by sparse clumps of brown grass and trees that were either dead or dying, awaiting the first and infrequent rains that came with the change in season.

Max's definition of *not too far* wasn't shared by everyone. After less than an hour, it felt to Guy as though they'd been driving forever. Not that he was in a hurry to get to The Mansion, of course, but the bumpy ride soon got tedious, and the stress began to weigh down on his eyelids. He was about to nod off, when the buggy suddenly decelerated. Forcing himself up straight, he peered through the dusty windshield. At first, Guy couldn't determine the reason for their reduction in speed, until he noticed something gleaming ahead.

As they came closer, the source of the gleam became apparent; it belonged to the window of a buggy similar to theirs. It stood immobile in the middle of the road, facing the oncoming vehicle. The buggy wasn't alone; flanked by a buggy on either side. The three vehicles were unoccupied because their occupants were standing in front of and behind the vehicles. The hands of the non-occupants were however occupied by rifles that were trained on the buggy coming towards them.

"Crap," Max breathed as he brought the buggy to a stop, close enough to get a good view of the uniforms worn by the armed figures ahead.

Guy had seen these uniforms before; uniforms which clearly indicated that they had just driven themselves into a Protector roadblock.

CHAPTER 60

Weapons raised, four Protectors advanced on the buggy that had stopped in front of them. Splitting up, they flanked the buggy, covering the sides while the others maintained position behind their blockading vehicles.

Guy eyed them nervously, and then glanced even more nervously at Max's hand as it carefully slid towards the gun strapped to his leg.

"I wouldn't do that if I were you," said a fifth Protector as he approached their buggy through the settling dust.

Guy recognised the voice, and so did Max, whose hand relaxed along with the rest of him.

"Good thing you're not me then," the Caynin said.

"For that, I thank my lucky stars every day," Nelis said as he reached the vehicle and casually leaned against the hood.

"Going somewhere?" he added, inspecting his fingernails.

"We're off to a party," Max said, getting out, followed by the others. "I sent you an invite, but it must have gotten lost in the mail."

"No, I got it. I just wanted to be … fashionably late, but it seems you beat me to it."

"Better late than never," Max said, looking at the other Protectors, who lowered their weapons and sauntered over to the vehicle. "I see you brought more guests. I thought you said I currently didn't have many friends."

"Oh, you've got *some*," Nelis said, waving over three Caynin Protectors who stepped closer and took off their caps. "You remember Rorke, Jenny and Rex?"

Max stepped forward.

"Fingers? Munchy? Sniffles? Who could forget?!" he said with a disbelieving smile, shaking each by the hand and giving them a courteous sniff, which was politely returned. "Glad to see my hard work in training you maggots wasn't for nothing."

"Good to see you too, sir," said Sniffles, aka Rex. He had darker, thicker fur than Max, and was a bit shorter. But what he lacked in height, he made up for in muscle. His stocky body seemed capable of flipping the buggy over with everyone inside, and his teeth looked sharp enough to chew through a cannonball.

Max eyed them sternly. "I appreciate the help, guys, but are you sure? You know I'm not the most ... popular person in law-enforcement these days."

"Nelis briefed us on everything, sir," Jenny said.

"And you still want to put your careers – no, worse – your lives on the line?"

"Well, sir," said Rex, "we figured if *you* are on the wrong side of the law, then we on the right side *must* be on the wrong side."

Max patted the stocky Caynin on the shoulder.

"And them?" Max said, redirecting his attention to the other Protectors, who all appeared to be human.

"They either trained under me or worked with me," Nelis said. "They also know that two humans from Earth need their help, which provided some extra incentive for those who were a bit hesitant at first."

"Not that they were *too* hesitant," he added quickly, seeing the flitter of doubt crossing Max's face. "I trust all of them implicitly, and vice versa. Besides, I promised that, if it turns out that you *were* responsible for Presidor Dooka's death, I'd arrest you myself. They know I'll keep my word, should it come to that."

"So do I," Max said, and nodded at each of them as Nelis made the introductions.

"This is Jon ... Dirk ... Vernon ... Selma ... Kristof ... Shorty ... Mike ... Sleek ... and Margot."

Guy caught himself ogling the last woman Nelis had introduced, and realised he wasn't the only one; next to him, Neville seemed smitten by the blue-eyed blonde strolling seductively over to them. She bent down, partially revealing an area that both Guy and Neville – and most guys, for that matter – generally found quite appealing.

"You'd better be worth it," Margot said. "I only signed up in case one of you turned out to be a looker in your human form."

She patted Neville on the cheek, which turned redder than Guy could have thought possible, before strolling back to her colleagues.

"You done, Margot?" Nelis said flatly.

"For now," she replied, shooting a wink towards the Salaman-humans, who weren't sure if this took away some of the nervous knots in their muscles, or added new ones.

Nelis shook his head, and turned to Max. "I'm sorry I couldn't bring more, but I had to keep the circle tight. I also thought it best, in the circumstances, to only bring Caynins and humans. Hope that's okay?"

"More than okay, my friend," Max said with a grin. "I've always thought a baker's dozen to be a good number. So, shall we?"

"So we shall," Nelis said, and nodded for everyone to return to their vehicles, which sped off in a cloud of dust soon thereafter.

At first, Guy thought he wouldn't be able to wipe the grin off his face, but the farther they drove, the more it faded by itself. Although the odds were now better, they were still heavily stacked against the small group. And if the stack fell the wrong way, they would certainly be crushed. As the big red sun started its final plunge towards nightfall, he could only hope they had enough going for them to get through this alive. *All* of them. However, his realistic side *knew* that such idealistic hopes had no place in the chaotic realm of the real, while his idealistic side sincerely hoped the other side was wrong.

CHAPTER 61

It was dark by the time seventeen shadowy figures scouted the area below from atop the ridge of a rocky hill, most of them lying flat to avoid detection.

"I count six guards patrolling the perimeter, and another eight in the gardens on this side alone," Nelis said, handing Max another high-magnification, night-vision zoomer.

The Infiltrator took his time to reconnoitre the lush terraced gardens surrounding The Mansion. "Make that ten," he said. "Two more just popped up from behind that bush. I didn't know The Man allowed hanky-panky on duty."

"You can report them later for bad behaviour," Nelis said. "I see eight more on the wall. They appear more focused on the sky than anywhere else. I guess you were right; The Man expected you to attack like a desperate maniac from above, otherwise there'd be more of them outside. It also explains the dim lights."

Max nodded. "Yep, he wouldn't want to make aerial targeting easy, now would he? By the looks of it, your secrecy has paid off, too. If he had any inkling that there were more of us coming, this place would have been crawling with itchy-finger Vahltans."

"That doesn't mean there won't be more henchmen crawling out of the woodwork once the fire is lit. I hear Karpachio has a small army at his command, and I suspect he's brought most of them here to keep his hide safe. If not *all* of them. I bet the rest of his men are either inside the main building or holed up underground somewhere, waiting to come running at a moment's notice."

"I wouldn't wager against it," Max said. "I think we can take out the guards patrolling the gardens without raising the alarm, but the ones on the wall will be a problem once we engage the main buildings."

"Not for me," Margot said, smiling broadly. She clicked a large scope into place on the large weapon she'd been assembling.

"A rail rifle with sonic suppression," Max said, impressed. "I hope you know how to use that thing."

"I'm a terrible cook, but *this* …" she said, patting the rifle with a fond smile, "… this is my favourite spatula. I'll flip any egg you point me at."

"Margot here is the best shot I've ever seen," Nelis said. "She'll not only flip an egg but scramble it too, just for good measure."

"Welcome to my kitchen," Margot said with a grin as she slapped a large magazine into place, before lying prone to scope out her unwitting targets.

Where Neville had looked googly-eyed before, he now seemed completely and utterly love-struck. Guy gave him a knowing nod; knowing Margot was entirely out of his own league but perfect for Neville, who appreciated a woman who could handle herself, let alone a weapon.

"Glad to see you brought some decent fireworks," Max said, oblivious to the love interest blossoming behind him.

"Oh, I brought even more," Nelis said, opening the bag next to him and taking out a sleek, compact rifle with a small scope. "I couldn't come to the party without bearing gifts."

He handed the rifle to Max.

"An APR50 plasma repeater," the Caynin said, checking the weapon. "Aww, you remembered."

"And a little something for you as well," Nelis said as he produced two handguns, which he handed to an appreciative Neville and an uneasy Guy.

"What am I supposed to do with this?" Guy asked, holding the weapon between two fingers like a dead rat.

"You point and shoot," Max said patiently.

"But I don't want to kill anyone!"

"And you won't," Nelis said. "It's a stunner. Non-lethal. Knocks a target out cold without doing any permanent damage. But from the way you're handling it, I suggest you only use it in a real emergency … preferably when I'm not nearby. You see that green light? When it goes yellow, you only have five shots left; red, you're out of power. So use it sparingly."

Guy's face stated he wasn't planning on using it at all.

"Oh, crap, I almost forgot," Nelis added as he opened yet another bag. "I thought you might need something to keep you safe. Or at least a bit safer."

He took out some bundles and tossed them at Guy, Neville and Max. He nodded towards a nearby bush, behind which the three disappeared and from which they reappeared a short while later.

Like the rest, they now wore head-commlinks and armoured Protector uniforms, which fit Max perfectly, but not so much the two smaller figures.

Neville rolled up his sleeves and pant legs, and looked down proudly at the sagging garment. Guy looked down uncomfortably, but followed Neville's example in rolling up the excess material drooping over his extremities.

"Apologies," Nelis said, "but that's the smallest I could find at such short notice."

He looked even more apologetically at Cortex.

"Sorry, my friend," the Detector said, "but I'm afraid I couldn't find anything that would fit you – not even remotely. But I do have another stunner you could use."

"Oh, no," Cortex said, holding up his four arms and shaking his head furiously at the weapon presented to him. *"No guns. I'm fine.* Really. *But, uh, thanks."*

Nelis shrugged and turned to Max, who was filling the clip holders on his armour with fully charged battery clips.

"You know more about the insides of this pigsty," the Detector said. "So, what's the plan?"

Max used a stick to draw in the soil, and took them through the basic layout as well as their tactical approach.

He kept going over it until he was satisfied that everyone knew what they were supposed to do – except Guy who, after several attempts, was told to just follow their lead. After a quick commlink test, the group took a moment of silence to gather themselves.

"So, everyone ready to party?" Max asked, putting the moment to bed.

"Let's get it started," Nelis confirmed.

The group commenced its quiet descent down the hill towards the foreboding buildings. Strictly speaking, everything outside Guy's head was quiet. Inside, however, he was screaming.

CHAPTER 62

Five teams converged on The Mansion from four sides. They'd decided to split into smaller groups to ensure they take care of all the garden patrols, and to divide the fight should they be spotted.

Nelis's team, comprising himself and the three Caynin Protectors, took point on the approach to the main entrance, taking out any guards they encountered. Bringing up the rear, Max led the Salamans and the Veagin past guards that wouldn't get up again soon but had been tied and gagged nonetheless. While the intrusion team knew that fatalities were unavoidable during a mission like this, they still didn't want to use deadly force unless absolutely necessary. This suited Guy just fine, because he didn't want to see any dead bodies unless absolutely necessary.

He also didn't want to see the Vahltan who'd just stepped out from behind a bush, pulling up his pants' zipper, but by the look on his face, the Vahltan didn't want to see them either. He tried to make a point of this as he fumbled for the gun at his hip. Max leapt forward and punched the guard in the stomach with the butt of his rifle, which he then brought down on the bent-over head. As soon as the Vahltan dropped, Max hog-tied him with some straps before fastening a muffler strap tightly over the henchman's mouth. The Caynin proceeded forward in a crouch. They passed two more guards missing the company of their consciousness.

Near the wall, they met up with Nelis's team crouching behind what, in different circumstances, could have been called a pretty hedge. Nelis was peeking over it when Max kneeled next to him.

"What do we have?" the Caynin whispered.

"Two guarding the portcullis," Nelis said. "I doubt we'll reach them before they raise the alarm."

Max risked a glance of his own over the perfectly trimmed greenery. "I suppose the time for playing nice is over. I hope you remember how to throw a knife. You take the one on the left. I've got the other one."

"And you three, cover our backs," he added to the other Caynins as he and Nelis took out matt-black knives that didn't reflect any light.

Checking that no guards were looking in their direction from the ramparts above, they were about to slip out of cover when Max pulled Nelis back.

"What are you doing?" the Detector hissed.

"The guards are coming this way," the Infiltrator replied, dropping his voice even lower.

"Great," Nelis muttered.

They gripped their knives tightly, ready to strike.

Strangely, though, just before they reached the hedge, the two guards suddenly dropped their rifles, sank to their knees, and held out their hands, wrists together. Max and Nelis looked at one another, flabbergasted. So did everyone else, except Cortex, who just stood there with a look of deep concentration.

"I'd hurry if I were you," he said with a wince. *"They think there are guns pressed to the back of their heads, but I can't hold it up much longer."*

The Infiltrator and the Detector tied and gagged the two Vahltans, and not a moment too soon, as the pair suddenly broke from their trance. They also seemed ready to break the silence by shouting a warning, but stopped trying when rifle stocks struck them against the side of the head, rendering them unconscious.

"Man, I'd love to have someone like you on my team," Nelis said.

"I thought I was on your team," the bug replied, confused.

"I mean back home at—" Nelis started. "Never mind. Let's go."

Keeping an eye on the ramparts, they rushed over to the portcullis where they flattened themselves against the wall. Max glanced around the corner before pulling back as two guards ambled by on the other side of the wall, patrolling the courtyard.

"Report," Nelis whispered over the commlink.

"At the wall, on our way," reported Dirk.

"On our way," reported Selma.

"We got two at the perimeter," reported Kristof. "Both alive but incapacitated. We then proceeded about fifty meters before we encountered another patr—"

"Not a *full* report," Nelis hissed. "Where are you?"

"Oh, er, about a minute out," Kristof said.

Nelis shook his head. Kristof was a superb Protector with meticulous attention to detail; just *too much* detail, at times.

"Set it," he said, indicating the portcullis. The Caynins, Jenny and Rorke, stepped up with what looked like a thin piece of rope, which they weaved through the iron grating to form a rough square of about two-by-two metres. They then connected a small black box with a blinking red light to the loose ends of the rope and backed away.

The other teams arrived shortly thereafter.

"Area secure," Dirk said.

"Area secure," Selma said.

"Uh, area secure," Kristof said as he noticed the warning glare cast at him by Nelis.

"Want to do the honours?" Nelis said, presenting Max with a small black device sporting a small red button.

Max took the device and looked at Neville, who in turn looked at him quizzically.

"*Me?*" Neville said as realisation struck.

"Only if you want to," Max said, presenting the device to Neville, who accepted the gift as if he'd just been handed a newborn kitten.[*]

---

[*] Those allergic to cats might react differently.

"Oh, I *want to*," Neville said with a boyish grin.

Max flashed him a smile before addressing the Protectors. "Remember, after this, there's no turning back. If anyone has any second thoughts, now's your chance to take your leave. No one would blame you."

"Well, I'm fresh out of leave," jested the Caynin, Rex. "Took my last few days to come here."

"My wife's been in a terrible mood since I came back home late from the bar last week," said the human, Sleek. "Frankly, I'm better off where I am now."

His face showed no sign of jest.

The others just shrugged, so Max nodded and took cover behind the wall. The rest followed suit on either side of the entrance.

"Well," Max said, looking over at Neville, "what are you waiting for?"

The Salaman-human took a deep breath before pushing the button, but he still seemed shocked as the controlled explosion sent bits of grating and stone flying inwards and outwards. He wasn't as shocked as the two patrolling Vahltans who'd noticed a strange blinking light on the portcullis as they made their rounds and, after closer inspection, realised what it was; just a tad too late.

CHAPTER 63

The blast was followed by a moment of silence, which was actually quite natural, as the armed force inside the walls needed a moment to wonder what was happening before realising what was happening and then reacting to what was happening.

Guy had seen many old war movies, and the scenes that stuck most in his mind were the ones where soldiers alighted from their landing craft to be met with bombshells and gunfire, with invisible bullets and loud explosions felling the men around the hero while he bravely pressed forward.

This, however, was *nothing* like those movies. Firstly, the streaks and bolts of energy were far from invisible. Secondly, Guy didn't feel like much of a hero as he crawled on all fours, trying to evade the streaks and bolts. Lastly, and most importantly, unlike those movies he used to enjoy watching from the comfort and safety of his couch, this was *real*. And it became even more real when a small chunk of wall dropped onto his back after being hit by a streak or bolt – he wasn't sure which, as his eyes remained firmly fixed on the cobblestones over which he was crawling.

While Max and Nelis took out the guards in the courtyard, the others fired back at the guards who were firing at them from above, but the Vahltans were too well protected by the battlements, and kept the group pinned down inside the passage. If reinforcements arrived while they were trapped in the choke point, things were bound to turn ugly, fast.

Whap!

The sound in Guy's ears startled him, and did so again seven more times, albeit with a slight drop in startlement each time. And, each time, the sound was also accompanied by a drop in the severity of the weapons fire from above. After the final *whap*, a Vahltan body smacked onto the stony courtyard like a wet T-shirt, causing Guy to freeze in place along with his expression of horror.

All shooting from above had ceased for some inexplicable reason; a reason that quickly became clear when Margot's voice crooned over the commlink.

"I hope you wanted your eggs to go," the sniper's voice said pleasantly. "But I have no further visual – you're on your own from here on out."

"Thanks for the support, *chef*," Max said, then spotted the first Vahltan reinforcements charging towards them. He assisted one of the guards in crossing the River Sticks[*] with a shot to the head.

"No problem," Margot said. "Good luck."

Guy looked over at Neville, who was grinning from ear to ear. Guy wasn't sure if this was because of the action, or because his friend had just reached a higher level of infatuation, or both. Probably both.

"We need to push inside!" Max shouted to Nelis. "We're sitting ducks out here!"

To prove this point, a bunch of duck-hunting Vahltans arrived from nowhere to take cover behind a fountain, so Nelis tossed a plasma grenade that helped many of them depart back to nowhere.

"Dirk, Selma, Kristof!" the Detector yelled. "Cover us and follow as soon as we're in!"

The three teams lay down covering fire as Nelis's and Max's teams sprinted towards The Mansion's wooden doors. Guy sprinted a bit haphazardly, struggling to see past his arms covering his head.

---

[*] It's similar to the River Styx but, according to Caynin mythology, much more fun.

Arriving at the doors, Max and Nelis didn't waste any time in placing a circular disc on each door. The discs attached themselves with anchors that shot through the wood, and the pair stood back as each device set off two rapid, consecutive blasts. The doors swung open, revealing a smoked-filled hallway littered with unmoving Vahltans. Apparently, the first blast had ripped away the locks, while the second had employed shotgun-like devastation to clear the immediate area of attackers along with a cloud of smoke to screen the team's entry.

Max and Nelis entered swiftly with their rifles raised to cut down any attackers left standing beyond the doors. There were none. The other Caynins followed to cover the hallways running left and right, while Nelis and Max advanced up the centre hallway. They only got about halfway when four red-armour-clad figures emerged from the far side of the hall-way, firing green bolts that slammed into the walls where the two had stood before diving for cover behind the base of a statue. The red figures activated shimmering, energy-absorbing blast shields and started advancing on the intruders.

"Elite Guards?" Max shouted. "What are *they* doing here?"

"Beats me!" Nelis shouted back, ducking as the red figures opened fire. The Detector fired back, striking one of the shields with no effect. "But they're definitely *not* friendlies. Those shields ... they're too strong!"

"We'll see," Max yelled, pulling the pin of a plasma grenade and tossing it with pinpoint accuracy to land between the Elite Guards. The men had just enough time to utter some un-elite words before they were sent flying through the air.

"And I thought *my* aim was good," Nelis said.

"I can teach you if you'd like," Max replied.

"Maybe later," Nelis said, waving the rest of the group over to join them before moving forward again.

As they entered the huge exhibition area, the two nervous Vahltans guarding the elevator seemed unsure about whether it was better to stand their ground or run and be put into the ground later by The Man.

"Halt!" the one on the left shouted with a demanding croak before glancing at his companion – whom Guy recognised as Gabbi – whose raised gun shook just as much as his own.

"Wait, don't shoot," Cortex said, stepping in front of Max and Nelis. *"I've got this."*

The bug concentrated on the pair who, after a few moments, gave one another a reluctant nod and dropped their weapons. They retreated warily yet hastily before disappearing among the exhibits.

"What did you do?" Guy asked.

Cortex smiled wearily. *"I merely showed them two possible immediate futures: one where they were playing poker at a casino on Vegon, and one where they were being autopsied by a coroner."*

"I guess they were smarter than they looked," Guy started, before his amazed expression transformed into one of concern. "Uh, Cor, you don't look so well."

"Just a bit tired," the bug said. *"Don't worry, I'll be fine."*

Before Guy could say anything, more yelling and gunfire erupted from the courtyard. Some of the Protectors started entering the building, and turned to cover their teammates.

Max rushed forward to press the elevator panel.

"Get in!" he commanded as the curved doors slid open.

After Guy, Neville and Cortex stepped in, Max followed suit.

"Will you be okay in holding them off?" he asked Nelis.

"Better than you in holding off scratching yourself behind the ears," the Detector replied with a grin, before taking cover behind a statue of a man who wasn't dressed for the occasion, or at all for that matter.

With a rueful smile, Max touched the panel to close the doors, and the cylindrical tube ascended quickly but silently up its glass shaft. As it came to a halt, Max raised his rifle, ready for whatever lay beyond the opening doors.

As it turned out, he wasn't completely ready.

Sure, he'd expected some adversaries, although not nearly as many. He had also expected the white-and-gold-robed Manni Karpachio, who held up two smooth metal boxes with a sneer. What he *hadn't* expected was the man standing next to The Man, although it did explain the presence of the now-ex-Elite Guards.

Facing them among the sea of other faces was a Ronian dressed in a long, red, perfectly tailored tunic, with long black hair framing a sharp, pale face with deep-set eyes, which belonged to someone who appeared slightly less dead than reports had made him out to be.

CHAPTER 64

Max's moment of shock didn't last long.

"Take out the Veagin!" yelled The Man, who must have observed Cortex's abilities on his security system.

Two weapons swivelled in the bug's direction, but Guy, in spite of his aversion to violence, didn't hesitate to whip up his own gun to fire off a shot.

In the unlikely event that everyone in the room were to ever sit down and discuss the event over a friendly round of drinks, they would have unanimously agreed that the speed with which Guy had acted was quite remarkable. However, they also would have agreed that speed wasn't always everything, and that waiting a split second longer to take some measure of aim might have been the more prudent thing to do in this particular situation. Guy would have agreed too, and indeed did so now as Cortex's heavy body crashed to the elevator floor from the unexpected shot in the back.

Horrified, Guy dropped the stunner as if it was a viper, and felt even more horrified when the weapon landed with a *whack* on the bug's head.

"Sorry!" he wailed, but no forgiveness was forthcoming from his unconscious friend.

"Thank you for the assistance," the Ronian man said with a smirk. "Your friend might also want to thank you later for saving his life … or at least for extending it a little while longer."

"You!" Max exclaimed, still dumbfounded.

"Who's that?" Guy said, finding himself even dumber; a feeling that was heightened after another guilt-ridden glance at the fallen Cortex.

The Ronian put on a taken-aback look. "What, you don't recognise me? Oh, yes that's right. You're one of the monkeys from that Dumb Planet, aren't you?"

Guy didn't even try to voice his offence at the derogatory terms, not only because the Ronian seemed likely to revel in any offence taken, but also because it seemed a bit frivolous in the greater scheme of things. Especially when those things included the muzzles of numerous weapons pointed at his face. The weapons also gave whoever was facing the same direction as the muzzles the power to order the opposing side to drop theirs.

Which is why The Man calmly said, "I suggest you drop those."

Which is what Max and Neville did, albeit reluctantly.

Two Vahltans picked up the discarded weapons, before motioning the trio out of the elevator and forcing them onto their knees. They however left the heavy, unconscious Veagin right where he was.

"No, really," Guy said from the side of his mouth, "who *is* that?"

"That," Max sneered, "is Vice-Presidor Julin Resis."

"Who— oh, um, Number Two?" Guy said perplexed. "I thought he was dead."

"So did I," the Infiltrator growled, glaring at the Ronian as if he would have been better off had this indeed been the case.

"And so did everyone else," Julin Resis said with a self-satisfied smile, completely unfazed by the Caynin's show of disdain.

"How is this possible?" Max said.

"Oh, come now, Max. In your line of work, I'm surprised at your surprise."

"And Presidor Dooka? Is *he* alive?"

"Good heavens, no! He's still cruising through space in various directions simultaneously."

Resis and Karpachio chuckled, followed promptly by the Vahltan guards, and then stopped, followed promptly by the Vahltan guards, as was Standard Operating Procedure.

The Ronian studied Max's grim face. "Oh, that's right," the not-dead Vice-Presidor continued in mock sympathy. "You were *friends*. Besties! My sincere condolences."

"Why kill him?" Max scowled. "Why do *any* of this?"

"Ah, yes, you don't remember, do you?" Julin Resis said, then glanced at his watch. "Well, I suppose we have a bit of time to kill before the rest of our guests arrive. And, I guess with you joining poor Harild soon, it doesn't really matter if you know the whole story. Besides, I reckon it's only fair for a man like you to understand why he's about to die."

• • •

"For the benefit of your *Dumb* friends here," Vice-Presidor Julin Resis started in a history-teacher tone, "I'll tell the story from the very beginning. The Ronian Empire had once been magnificent; we ruled most of the Charted Universe with impunity. But those we ruled over were too blind to realise that they were much better off under our strict guidance and protection. And when those ingrates stood up for themselves along with the help of other meddling systems, it led to the Ninety-nine-and-a-half-year War, which ended with the Great Treaty and, ultimately, led to the founding of the Unyun Federation.

"We saw this as an opportunity to rebuild and expand the Ronian Empire in a different way. We would take positions of power in politics and business, and shape the Federation to our will. But while we thought that others would eventually see the wisdom of letting Ronians lead the way, the Federation became more lovey-dovey with each generation. Even Ronians started losing their sense of identity, forgetting their *true* heritage.

"*I'm* not one of them," Resis spat, his face contorting with disgust. "Deserters, traitors, cowards, the lot of them! And people like your precious Presidor Dooka were making things worse, bestowing more and more freedoms on those too stupid to know how to handle it. What, you don't want to be part of the Federation anymore? Sure, go ahead; just sign here and off you go. No problem! And what's *this*, a perfectly habitable planet ruled by a bunch of apes bent on destroying it? Let's protect them with laws and give them the technology to destroy themselves even further, instead of invading them and showing them how things are *meant* to be done! And let's not forget the lawlessness that's been eating away at our way of life like a cancer without end. Let's just allow it to spread, instead of cutting it out for the disease it is!"

"Pretty ironic, I'd say," Max interjected, casting a glare at The Man, "considering the company you keep."

Julin Resis glanced at the curly-"haired" Vahltan beside him. "Oh, don't be a fool, Max. You *know* we'd never be able to rid ourselves of *all* the rot."

He ignored the brief-yet-hard look the Vahltan gave him. "My esteemed colleague and I have an arrangement. In return for his services, he'd be allowed to expand his criminal empire beyond his wildest dreams."

"Hypocrite," Neville snorted, not able to stop himself despite their situation. "You abhor crime, yet fuel its flames."

"Crime can never be stopped, little man," the Ronian said. "But it *can* be controlled. I'd rather maintain control over one large criminal organisation that, in turn, controls the smaller ones. Much easier, and much more effective. Mr Karpachio has a bright future ahead of him; a bigger empire with no real competition and a great deal of Federal protection."

The Man shifted, as if he wasn't so sure about this future, especially the part where *he* was to be controlled. But whatever doubts he had, he kept to himself.

"But people like Dooka cannot be controlled," Julin Resis continued, "because they have no control themselves. In fact, he and his group of simpletons were about to relinquish control over several valuable systems during the talks on Grassi Nole. Ridiculous!"

"But why kill him?" Max said. "Surely you know that others like him will keep opposing your extreme views."

"I do," Resis said. "But as Presidor, I'll be able to sway those who can be swayed, and get rid of those who can't. Ultimately, I'll be in a position to change and manipulate the laws and people as I see fit, until no one can do anything about it. Under *my* rule, the Unyun Federation will become the strongest force in the universe. Under *Ronian* rule, as it's meant to be."

Max shook his head in disbelief.

"You're deluded!" he said. "And apart from that, you're supposed to be dead, remember?"

"That's true, but fortunately *you* provided me with the perfect plan that would see me return as a hero."

Max eyed the Ronian warily. "Me?"

"Yes, you," Resis continued. "You see, I had been struggling to come up with a solution for the problem of not only ridding myself of dear old Harild, but also of how to make myself come out looking the better for it. Then, one day, while Mr Karpachio and I were brainstorming this conundrum, we were interrupted by a commotion. Two of the guards came dragging in your unconscious body. It seems you'd been investigating Mr Karpachio for illegal arms dealing and had infiltrated his compound, only to overhear our conversation. Very rude, that.

"At first, we were shocked and angry, and my colleague here understandably wanted to dispose of you quickly and quietly. Fortunately for you – or maybe rather *un*fortunately – I had a better idea. With the help of Mr Karpachio's brilliant physician downstairs, we wiped the previous year's memories from your mind. Or let's rather say, we *relocated* them. You presented the perfect scapegoat for our plan."

"That's absurd!" Max said. "No one who knows me would *ever* believe me capable of killing Harild. And what would be the motive?"

"Oh, that was the easy part," Resis said. "Love."

"Love?" Max exclaimed. "You're mad!"

"No, Max, you're the one who's *madly* in love."

"With whom, pray tell?"

"With Captain Phealix, of course."

"Phealix?" Max said, looking even more shocked than his companions, who were already displaying a fair amount of shock. "The *pirate*? Are you *insane*? No, wait, you don't have to answer. You're *completely bonkers!"*

"I'm afraid not, Max," Julin said. "You see, we politicians like to keep tabs on our rivals and those closest to them, which is how I came across this interesting tidbit of information. I don't know exactly when, where, or how it started, but you'd been seeing each other for quite a few months, at the very least. You tried your best to keep it a secret, and not many, aside from me, knew about it. Not even her own crew had a clue."

"That's … impossible," Max said incredulously.

"Not at all. Yes, you *are* on opposite sides of the law. And yes, both Caynins and Faylins *would* frown upon such a relationship, no matter how liberal many of them might think they are. But hey, love conquers all, doesn't it?"

"You're lying," Max grated.

"Oh, believe you me, it's perfectly true, although I did lie to her when I provided her with some false information that you'd betrayed her. I think she's quite … upset with you. Ah, when love goes wrong, things can really get ugly. Of course, no one will know about *that* part. They will, however, know about the relationship, and how Presidor Dooka prohibited you from seeing her, which sent you over the edge."

Max forced himself to calm down. "Fine, let's play along with your little fantasy. Why would he have done that?"

"Because he couldn't have his Caynin Infiltrator friend and confidant running around with an outlaw, now could he? Bad for the career. Especially seeing as it was with a Faylin, too – bad for the already strained relationship between your species."

"Harild had nothing against Faylins," Max countered.

"No, he didn't, but the public will be told otherwise."

"No one will believe you!"

Resis grinned. "*Of course* they will. You see, my incredible fabricated story and the subsequent scenario will go like this: When the ship was blown up, I was in a section that had remained intact but had been propelled away by the explosion. Fortunately, I was picked up shortly thereafter by some Drifters who didn't know me but took care of me on their ship – bless them. Out of fear, I couldn't return to my life, and stayed in hiding until the Presidor's real assassin – that would be *you* – was found and brought to justice. After all, *I* could have been your original target. When I heard you'd been killed in a firefight with law-enforcement, I knew it was finally safe for me to emerge from hiding.

"So, upon my miraculous return, I will launch a full investigation, which will reveal the unfortunate events that had led to our speciesist Presidor's demise. Tensions between Caynins and Faylins will flare up, which will inevitably cause political instability throughout the Charted Universe. Which is when I, the hero who survived the assassination, will step in to save the Federation from imminent collapse. To do that, however, I'll *unfortunately* have to declare Martial Law, giving me the perfect opportunity to reshape the Federation within a very short space of time. When people finally realise what's really going on, it will be too late. But eventually they'll understand, *and* they'll be grateful. I'll take back control over breakaway systems. I'll *make* systems join that never wanted to join, and our enemies will bend the knee or be wiped out.

"And Dumb Planets? They will quickly find out they're not alone in the universe, the hard way – no more of this weaning-them-in nonsense. They'll do as they're told or face destruction. Although I *do* prefer the latter, because I don't really have the patience to raise their pathetic little existences up to Federal standards."

He sneered at Guy and Neville. "Maybe I'll start with that miserable little rock *you* come from."

"You can't do that!" Guy exclaimed. "Earth has done nothing to deserve this!"

"Oh, really?" Resis said, raising an eyebrow. "War, hate, poverty, planet-killing pollution? Any of those ring a bell? And there are plenty more bells to ring. Judging by your face, I see I've touched on some painful truths. Pretty soon, I will be able to do whatever I want, and I think subjugation or annihilation is *exactly* what you monkeys deserve."

"You won't get away with this," Neville growled.

"Ah, but I will," Resis said. "Everything's in place. There are only a few loose ends to take care of."

The doors of the elevator closed and the tube descended.

"Speaking of which," the Vice-Presidor said. "I think those ends have just arrived."

When the elevator came back up, The Man ordered the guards to turn the captives around to face the doors, which finally opened to reveal Captain Phealix, Cap and Franki, along with two frosted pods standing side by side on a-grav trolleys. As the newcomers stepped out, Cap and Franki pulled the pods out with them.

Max looked at the pirates with murder in his eyes, knowing that his men downstairs must have been overrun for these three to have made it to the elevator. He tried to get up, but was forced back down by the muzzle of a gun pressing hard against his skull.

Captain Phealix glared down at him with an equally hard expression, although, for a moment, Guy was sure he'd also caught a glimmer of sadness. Max, however, didn't notice anything other than the face of the person responsible for murdering his friends.

Brushing off the hatred radiating from the Caynin's eyes, the Faylin gestured towards the pods and stood aside with a slight bow. "As ordered, Mr Man," she said.

The girthy Vahltan stepped closer and, producing a white handkerchief, wiped the frost from the glass of each pod to reveal the faces inside. Guy's heart jumped. After so many months, he almost didn't recognise himself. He glanced at Neville, who apparently felt the same.

"Splendid!" The Man smirked with satisfaction as he eyed the bodies inside. "I hope you didn't experience too much trouble in acquiring the items."

"No, sir," the captain said. "Even substandard banks have better security than the *Life Spectacular* building. Resistance was minimal."

"Good," The Man said, walking to the back of the pods to inspect them further, when he noticed a third pod that had originally been hidden from view by the pods in front.

"What do we have *here*?" he said, raising an eyebrow as he ran his fingers over the unexpected pod.

The captain smiled. "Oh, just a little gift to show my appreciation for your business. Just press that red button next to the handle."

Giddy with anticipation, the Vahltan pressed the button. The light turned green, and the door pushed out a little before sliding open with a *whoosh* of cold, trapped air. He stepped back, not sure what to expect, then jumped back farther with a yelp as his surprise gift yielded a bigger surprise than he would have liked.

His surprise was shared by Vice-Presidor Julin Resis, as Acting Presidor Don Tinckles stepped out of the pod. And they shared even more surprise at the weapons now aimed at their heads by the three pirates, who grinned the grins that only pirates could grin.

CHAPTER 65

The shock that Max had experienced earlier was now plastered over Julin Resis's face, which had turned a shade paler, and his deep-set eyes suddenly struggled to keep themselves deep-set.

"What the fhark are *you* doing here?" he exclaimed.

Acting Presidor Don Tinckles strode out of the elevator, wearing a tunic similar to that of the Vice-Presidor, only blue with gold embroidery. The Faylin's dark vertical pupils stood out against his bright-green eyes, which in turn stood out against his ginger fur that, as with most Faylins, was immaculately groomed.[*]

"Well, I just *had* to see for myself whom I'm up against," the Faylin said as he stepped in next to Captain Phealix. "And I'm *so* glad I did."

Julin Resis shot confused glances between the Acting Presidor and the pirate captain.

"Hey, don't look at me," Captain Phealix said with a shrug. "I'm just doing what my *real* client asked me to do."

"But *I'm* your boss," The Man objected.

The Faylin raised her weapon slightly to point between the Vahltan's eyes.

---

[*] Apologies for interrupting the tension, but Faylins generally put a lot of effort into grooming themselves. To do this, they have to get up much earlier than most other species. It's a big sacrifice, and their efforts shouldn't be for nothing, so it would be most inconsiderate not to share this bit of information at this time.

"*Are* you now?" she said, amused. "Tsk tsk, Mr Karpachio. *No one's* the boss of me. Just ask these two."

Cap and Franki nodded, so in the spirit of Vahltan self-preservation, The Man decided not to press the matter any further.

Acting Presidor Tinckles shook his head sadly. "I must say, Julin, I'm disappointed. Not surprised, but disappointed nonetheless – more for Harild's sake, of course. He had such high hopes of eventually getting you on board. But *I* always had my doubts. It seems I was right all along, although I must admit I never thought you'd go *this* far."

With a deep breath, Resis regained his composure. "You've always been an ignorant fool, Don," he said, his face hardening. "Never able to see the bigger picture. Just like Harild. Good bloke, but way too timid to do what needed to be done. It doesn't matter, though. You won't live long enough to regret your decisions. As you might have noticed, you're somewhat outgunned."

Resis gave a nod, upon which four Vahltans rushed in to form a wall in front of their boss and the Ronian. With a sneer, the Vice-Presidor held up a hand to give the universal signal one would give to guys with lots of guns to get rid of guys with fewer guns.[*]

"I wish I could say it was good knowing you, *Don*," he said, nearly spitting the name.

"Same here, *Julin*," Tinckles said with surprising calmness before calmly pushing a button on his watch.

As far as buttons go, this one did quite a lot in a very short space of time. Firstly, it plunged the room into near darkness. Secondly, it set off an explosion that sent several Vahltans flying. And, lastly, it caused two dark shapes to drop from an air vent towards the back of the room.

---

[*] To be clear, the signal isn't always the same, and different species may use different body parts. But the guys with the guns usually recognise the signal for what it is when they see it. You don't stay employed long, or live long, in the criminal underworld without knowing such things.

As the two shapes unfolded, the shorter, rounder one turned to the other. "Dat were de signal, were it not?" it enquired.[*]

"Yes, that *was* the signal," the taller, thinner shape said flatly. It then blasted the nearest Vahltan shape before sending the next one twirling to the floor from the hard blow it had just received across the face from the same weapon.

"I's finked so," the rounder shape said proudly, then started laying down a massive barrage of blue energy balls from the massive shape in its hands.

Vahltans scrambled in all directions, trying to find cover behind the first thing they could find, which mostly turned out to be other Vahltans.

Max didn't wait for an invitation. Grabbing the hands of the startled Vahltan standing over him, he flipped the henchman even farther over him while wrenching loose his rifle in one swift, smooth motion. Then, after blasting the guard with his own weapon, the Caynin quickly herded his bewildered Salaman companions behind a sturdy desk and shot the panicked Vahltan who'd tried to follow suit.

Bolts and streaks of white, blue and green energy flew everywhere. Several shots hit the desk but failed to penetrate the thick wood, which is why Max and Guy were somewhat mystified when Neville suddenly toppled over into a foetal position, screaming in agony while clutching at his head.

Max crouched by the little Salaman to check if he'd been hit, but after a quick examination, he couldn't find any wounds.

Guy kneeled on the other side of his writhing friend.

"What's wrong with him?" he shouted in panic.

Max just shook his head and repeated the check, but again failed to identify the cause of Neville's sudden collapse.

"Was he shot?" Guy asked, wide-eyed.

Max frowned worriedly. "I don't think so. I can't see any wounds."

---

[*] Also to be clear, there are just some people for whom signals aren't always that clear.

"How can that be?" Guy said. "He wouldn't just fall over like this for no reason!"

"No, he wouldn't," Max affirmed with a stumped expression, which transformed into one of uneasy realisation. "The only thing I can think of …"

"What?" Guy cried after the short-yet-excruciatingly-long-feeling pause.

"The signal," Max said, then nodded in agreement with himself. "Yes, it *must* be the signal."

"What signal?" Guy said, and cringed as an energy bolt sent a shudder through the desk.

"The signal between Neville's body and profile box. Something must have gone wrong, or maybe his mind has started degenerating."

"How can you be sure?"

"I can't. But one thing I *am* sure of, is that we don't have much time. Whatever's happening, we have to do his reverse-transfer as soon as possible. Otherwise neither he nor Lenny will survive."

Another two blasts shook the desk, adding to Guy's panic over his friend, who had suddenly gone very still.

"What do we do?" he said, trying to make himself even smaller than he already was.

"We need to get those profile boxes, and fast," Max said. He fired two shots of his own, the first of which took out the Vahltan used involuntarily as a shield by another Vahltan, who in turn suddenly seemed at a loss without a Plan B. The second shot helped him out of his dilemma, and he quickly joined his ex-colleague on the floor.

"But where are they?" Guy said, looking about.

"I think The Man had them."

"You mean the boxes he'd been holding when we got off the elevator?"

"Yes."

"The boxes that he's now taking onto the elevator?" Guy exclaimed, pointing.

"Yes … no, wait, what?" Max said.

The Infiltrator peeked over the desk just in time to see Manni Karpachio ducking into the elevator, clutching the two silver boxes tightly, followed by Julin Resis and the Vahltan henchman Andi. The elevator doors closed silently as the battle raged on.

CHAPTER 66

Despite being too late to stop them, Max and Guy ran for the elevator down which their adversaries had fled. The Caynin vigorously punched the panel several times to assist the elevator in ascending faster.*

They however had to duck behind the elevator shaft when green balls of energy thudded into it. Max spotted Acting Presidor Don Tinckles, who'd taken cover behind a bar counter. Next to him was Franki, as well as a Vahltan who suddenly appeared much smaller than usual, curling into himself while covering his head with one normal hand and one robotic hand as shots slammed into the counter. Guy was astonished at how unimposing Cap suddenly appeared, compared to their first encounter.

The elevator arrived and opened its doors with an aura of urgency.

"Mr Presidor!" Max shouted, waving towards the elevator. "Over here!"

The Acting Presidor shook his head. "No, you go; we'll hold them off!"

"But—" Max started.

"I can take care of myself!" Don Tinckles yelled before getting up with the rifle that had originally belonged to Cap,

---

* Those who've tried this before, namely everyone in a rush, namely *everyone*, can tell you from experience that this doesn't actually work. Not that experience will count for much the next time you're in a rush – it just sort of … happens.

who clearly wasn't going to use it. The Faylin fired a spread of white streaks at a group of Vahltans crouched behind a huge couch. One Vahltan, who hadn't been crouching, didn't have time to regret it.

The Presidor took cover again and nodded at Neville's unmoving body. "Go do what you need to do!"

With that, the Presidor and Franki got up and squeezed off several more shots in the direction of some Vahltans who'd been thinking about breaking from cover. They thought about it again and ducked back behind their cover, which they didn't seem to want to break from again anytime soon.

Max and Guy used the opportunity to retrieve Neville's small Salaman body, which they dragged into the elevator while the Caynin lay down suppressive fire with his free hand. Just as the Infiltrator punched the panel for the doors to close, another shaped blurred into the space with them.

"*You*, get out!" Max demanded, having held off on squeezing the trigger at the last second.

Captain Phealix calmly turned around to watch the doors close as if she was on her way to a cocktail party in the lobby.

"Not a chance, pretty boy," she said, her eyes fixed ahead.

"You're *not* coming with us!" Max shouted angrily confused.

"Have I ever told you how cute you are when you try to argue with me?"

"I … er," Max said angrily abashed, "I wouldn't know."

"Well, now you do," the Faylin continued. "And if you hadn't had your brains scrambled – at least not more than usual – you'd also know there's no use arguing with me. I'm coming, and that's that."

Max was about to try a useless argument nonetheless, but was interrupted when the doors opened on the exhibition floor, where another fierce battle was raging. More of The Man's guards had apparently been aroused from the unsweet dreams they'd been having in their barracks. They didn't look happy.

Nelis and the Protectors, who were more alive than Max had originally thought, were holding their position, although this would probably not have been possible had it not been for the large group of Vahltan pirates now fighting by their side. Completely flustered, Max looked from the fighting lawmen to Captain Phealix. He was about to say something, but was interrupted as more Vahltan guards came streaming down the main hallway, which was already strewn with both writhing and unmoving bodies.

"Hey, Captain!" Doop shouted from behind a pillar. "Everything okay upstairs?"

"Just dandy, Doop!" Captain Phealix replied, staying in the elevator and laying down some fire while Max rushed over to Nelis. "Now stop yapping before you get your head blown off."

"Yes, sir!" Doop said and ducked back behind the pillar just as a shot nearly blew his head off.

Max slid in next to Nelis behind the base of a statue.

"So, how are things?" the Caynin asked casually.

"Oh, you know, just another day," the Detector replied, getting up to slim down a bulky Vahltan before crouching back down again. "Good thing those pirates showed up when they did."

"You let them through?" Max said, and fired a few shots of his own.

"Well, we didn't have much of a choice. It was either that or be overrun. And when they took out The Man's men in the hallway, the whole enemy-of-my-enemy thing came into play, you know?"

Max did know, but he also wasn't quite ready to accept it. He however had to let it go, as there were more pressing matters to attend to. "Did he come this way?" he asked.

"Who?" Nelis said, felling another Vahltan who tried to flank them.

"Karpachio."

"No, but we did put your Veagin friend over there. Found him passed out in the elevator. What happened?"

"Don't ask," Max said, looking in the direction Nelis pointed, and spotted Cortex's legs portruding from under some kind of ancient chariot parked nearby.

"Sorry," Nelis said, "we didn't have much time to look for a better place to stash him."

"We have another one down, in the elevator," Max said.

"Who?"

"Neville."

"Wounded?"

"No. I think the link to his profile box has been compromised somehow. We have to get those boxes, but Karpachio escaped with them."

"He must have gone to the lower floor, because he sure as hell didn't come this way," Nelis said. "I sent Jon and Rex down earlier to secure the lower level, but I haven't heard anything yet. There must be interference with comms down there. I was just about to send someone to check on them."

"I'll see if I can spot them while I'm down there," Max said with an urgency in his voice as he turned to leave.

"Hey, you're not going alone," Nelis said, and before Max could protest, he shouted, "Jenny, on me!"

The Caynin Protector nodded, and ran over in a crouch as multiple shots passed over her.

"Kristof!" Nelis yelled to the human Protector, who'd just taken down a Vahltan who had tried his luck in advancing up the hallway before the luck ran out. "Hold the fort! We're going down!"

"Yes, sir!" Kristof replied.

"And give us some cover fire!" Max added, nodding towards Cortex's semi-stashed shape.

As the pirates and Protectors pinned their foes down with a huge barrage of fire, Max and Nelis ran to the chariot. They each grabbed a leg and dragged the Veagin's big body into the elevator, where Captain Phealix closed the doors.

A distraught Guy looked up from where he sat cradling Neville's body in his lap. "Cortex!" he cried, now looking doubly distraught. "Is he okay?"

As they started their descent, Max kneeled to pat the Veagin's cheeks until he came to.

"What's ... where am I?" the bug said, staring up at the faces staring down at him.

"You're okay, my friend," Max said. "Can you get up?"

Cortex did so, but very slowly, and with some groaning assistance from Max and Nelis.

"What happened?" the Veagin asked, holding his head. *"Did I get shot?"*

"Well—" Guy started hesitantly.

"Yes, you got shot," Max interrupted. "But you're okay, and we don't have time for explanations right now."

To confirm this, the elevator came to a halt at its subterranean destination.

CHAPTER 67

As the doors opened, Max, Nelis, Jenny and Captain Phealix raised their weapons, only to be greeted by an empty hallway. They however kept their weapons at the ready as they led the way down the deserted corridor, making sure each hallway was clear before moving on. The walls along one of the intersecting hallways were riddled with blast marks, and muffled weapons fire could be heard farther down. Max was about to follow the sounds, but Guy stopped him.

"Wait," he said, with Neville hanging limply in his arms. "We must help him first."

"How?" Max asked, looking restlessly down the corridor where the sounds of gunfire was growing fainter.

"This way," Guy said, moving down the main corridor with as much haste as the Salaman body in his arms allowed.

Max glanced down the side-hallway once more before reluctantly following the rest of the group to a door at the end of the main hallway.

"In here," Guy said, standing back as Nelis opened the door. Max entered first, followed by the others.

When Guy stepped in, the touch of déjà vu left a bruise. They were in the white room where he and Neville had undergone their mind probes. The four bed-chairs were still there, as well as the pedestal. The latter now served as a very ineffective hiding place for a familiar dark Vahltan wearing white scrubs, albeit white scrubs stained with dirt and faint streaks of hedge sap.

"Get up," Max commanded, his weapon pointed at the Vahltan's head, which slowly emerged carrying a terrified expression. "Who are you?"

"Dr Snyer," Guy said flatly. "He's the one who tampered with our heads."

"I didn't have a choice!" the Vahltan said with a tremble in both his voice and his raised hands. "Are you here to kill me?"

"That depends on whether you're useful," Guy said with a growl and glare that surprised everyone in the room. It would have surprised him too, had he not been so perturbed by Neville's condition.

Looking at the figure in Guy's arms, Dr Snyer didn't have to ask what he was to be useful at. "Of course, put him over there," he said.

Guy gingerly lowered Neville into the indicated chair, which the Vahltan flattened into a bed at the push of a button.

"What happened to him?" the physician asked with what sounded like genuine concern.

"That's what we'd like to know," Guy said nervously. "He just collapsed, clutching his head. Max thinks there might be something wrong with the connection between him and his profile box."

After performing a quick examination, the physician looked up.

"I think he's right," he said. "If we don't reverse-transfer his consciousness soon, we'll lose him … and the host too."

"So you can help him?" Guy said with a glimmer of hope.

"Maybe," the Vahltan said. "Mr Karpachio had planned on restoring the Salaman-human connections to conduct other means of … questioning, had it been necessary. So this facility has everything I need, and I know everything I need to know to perform the procedure. I will do what I can to stabilise your friend, but without his human body and the profile box, there's no way of saving him."

Guy looked anxiously at Max.

"Leave that to us," the Caynin said, turning to Cortex. "Are you feeling well enough to fetch the bodies from the top floor?" he asked the hunched Veagin. "They're in two stasis pods near the elevator door. You can just grab them and come right back down."

Cortex glanced at Neville lying on the bed.

"No problem," he said without any hesitation, and pulled himself upright when he noticed Guy's worried expression. *"No, really, I'm right as rain. It'll be a walk in the park, as they say."*

Despite his concern for his Veagin friend, Guy nodded appreciatively.

Max turned to Nelis.

"I think it's time to call in the cavalry," he said. "And medical support. We're going to need it."

"I'm on it," Nelis nodded. "But what are you going to do?"

"I'm going to see a man about a box," Max replied with grim resolve.

"Not without me you're not," said Captain Phealix, shouldering her rifle. "And don't even try to argue – we don't have time for that."

Knowing she was right, Max didn't try to argue.

"Good," the captain grinned, "you're learning."

"What about me?" Guy said, looking ready to do something without knowing exactly what that something should be.[*]

"You stay here with Neville and Jenny," said Max, who turned to his fellow Caynin. "If Doc here tries to escape, shoot him."

The doctor suddenly looked as though he'd already been shot. "But I wasn't even planning on running!"

"Keep it that way," Max said. "And begin prepping for the procedure."

"Yes, er, sir," the Vahltan said, his eyes darting nervously between the two Caynins.

"So, what are we waiting for?" Captain Phealix said.

"Nothing," Max said curtly before marching out the door.

---

[*] It's also the must-have look for interns on their first day.

As the rest of the group filed out of the room, Guy felt the knot in his stomach grow tighter. He didn't know whether he would see any of them again, but he just clung to the hope that fate, for once, would not throw him another curveball. Because, frankly, he was tired of this game.

CHAPTER 68

Max and Captain Phealix hastened down the blast-marked corridor they'd passed earlier. And with more marks pocking the walls as they proceeded, it wasn't hard to follow the correct path through the maze of hallways. The facility was much bigger below ground than it appeared topside.

After a couple of turns, they found a body lying face-down on the floor. Max turned it over. It was the stocky Caynin, Rex, who had a hole in his chest where an energy blast had ripped through his weakened armour.

The Infiltrator kneeled to check for a pulse, but couldn't find one. "Dammit!" he cried, slamming the wall.

"He's gone, Max," Captain Phealix said, gently placing a hand on his shoulder. "There's nothing we can do. I'm sorry."

"What do *you* care?" he grated, shrugging her off. He rose with an expression that said there was a lot *he* could do, and that the people on the wrong side of what he could do would be better off not knowing what it was.

He raised his weapon and advanced down the hallway with a cold, purposeful gleam in his eyes. He only paused briefly to inspect a blood trail leading off towards the sound of gunfire, which steadily grew louder as they followed the red smears. When they rounded the next corner, they watched as a blast took down the human Protector, Jon, at the far end of the corridor.

Max rushed to the spot where the human lay gripping his leg in agony. However, instead of going to the Protector's aid, the Caynin Infiltrator kept his weapon raised and rounded the corner quickly to blast the surprised look off the face of the advancing Vahltan, formerly known as Andi. He waited a moment to make sure that no one else was coming up the hallway, then grabbed the wounded Protector's collar to drag him around the corner, and sat him against the wall.

"You okay?" the Caynin said, removing the human's belt and wrapping it around his bleeding leg before strapping it tight.

"I'll live," Jon groaned, wincing, then looked up dolefully. "But they got Rex."

"I know," Max said, trying to keep the anger from his voice.

Jon threw a thumb over his shoulder at the now-lifeless shape of Andi. "It was *that bastard*. But not before Rex wounded the Ronian with them. Looked a lot like the dead Vice-Presidor."

"That's because it *was* him, but we don't have time to discuss that now."

The Protector's eyes went wide with disbelief, but nodded without fishing any further. Max helped him to his feet and glanced at the wound.

"Can you walk?" the Caynin asked.

"I can limp," Jon winced.

"That'll do."

"Then that's what I'll do."

"Good," Max said. "Just keep following the blast marks back to the elevator hallway. Turn left, and at the last door you can get some medical attention, understood?"

"Rodger that. And *you* just follow the blood trail. It should lead you right to those bastards."

Max nodded, but made sure that the limping Protector was well on his way before continuing the chase up the hallway, passing a slightly lighter Andi, who hadn't managed to stay out of trouble after all.

•••

Tracking the trail of blood, Max and Captain Phealix were about to round the corner of the next hallway, when they got the fright of their lives.

"Whose blood is that?" a voice suddenly rang out behind them.

Pivoting, the pair nearly blasted off the head that wasn't there, before looking down at the wide-eyed Salaman with expressions that ranged from being highly relieved to being extremely vexed.

"Oh, Guy, it's you!" Captain Phealix said, highly relieved.

"What the fhark are you *doing here*?" Max said, extremely vexed. "I told you to stay put! Don't you ever listen?"

"No," Guy said, folding his arms. "Not when Neville's life is at stake. I'm not going to sit around doing nothing while he's dying in front of me."

Max studied the small yet resolute figure. The number of stubborn people surrounding him these days was staggering.

"Fine," he said, "but stay close. We don't have time to go looking for you if you get lost."

Guy merely nodded and followed closely as the Caynin and Faylin recommenced their hunt along the blood trail. As they rounded the last corner, they spotted a limping Ronian leaning awkwardly on a short, round Vahltan, who stopped to open the door at the far side of the corridor. It was strange seeing The Man helping someone other than himself.

"Stop right there!" Max shouted, taking aim.

The pair froze in place.

"Now turn around, slowly."

Adding the impairment of injury to the demand, the pair turned like a defective garden sprinkler.

At the last moment, Max saw the gun in the wounded Ronian's hand, which was now pointed in their direction. The Caynin threw himself at Captain Phealix, knocking her out of the way, but wasn't fast enough to avoid the green energy bolt from tearing a searing gash in his side. He grunted in pain as he and the Faylin slid across the floor and crashed into the wall by Guy's feet.

The Faylin wriggled herself out from under Max, who was lying very still. She cradled his head in her lap and caressed the fine fur covering his face.

"Is he okay?" Guy said anxiously.

"I don't know," the captain replied with tear-filled eyes. As she checked the wound in Max's side, he emitted a slight groan.

Breathing a sigh of relief, the Faylin cupped the Caynin's cheek. "Hey, you alive?"

Max gazed up at her through his blurred vision and brought a hand to his head.

"Ow!" he flinched, then put his other hand on his side. "Ooowww!"

"He must have bumped his head," Guy said, also relieved that Max was awake, but his forehead creased with worry as he eyed the wound in the Caynin's side.

"It's just a scratch," Max said as he sat up slowly and raked his rifle closer with a grimace. "Where are they?"

"Down the hall," Captain Phealix said.

The Infiltrator started to get up, but the Faylin pushed down on his shoulder, keeping him in place.

"Where do you think you're going?" she said.

"After them," Max growled, brushing her hand away before getting up unsteadily.

The Faylin looked annoyed, but helped him up. "You can hardly stand, let alone walk, you oaf!"

Max's scowl might have been more effective if he hadn't swayed so much from the bump to his head. But he seemed to think it had done its job, and marched off like a brave soldier who'd just woken up after hip-replacement surgery.

With a click of her tongue, Captain Phealix rushed over and used her shoulder to prop up the groggy Caynin, who seemed to have trouble figuring out what was more important to hold on to: the weapon in his hand, his head, the wound in his side, or the wall.

Max clearly was in no condition to go anywhere, but it was also clear that nothing, or no one, was going to stop him.

CHAPTER 69

When their pursuers dived down the other corridor in their attempt to evade the blast from Julin Resis, Manni Karpachio took the opportunity to drag himself and the Vice-Presidor through the door, which he promptly closed behind them.

They were now in a large chamber surrounded by a tiered seating area carved into the subterranean stone, overlooking a small, round arena. The metal fence atop the lowest tier separated the seating area from the arena floor, on which the Vice-Presidor now lay groaning and squirming in agony.

Things hadn't gone the way Manni had planned. And he'd planned everything so carefully. This whole fiasco certainly wasn't *his* fault. He put the blame squarely on the unreliable Ronian in whom he'd placed his misguided faith. Why did he do that? He *never* did that!

He'd broken his own primary rule: If you want to save your skin, save it from the inside. Never trust anyone outside your own skin! But he'd been seduced by promises of ultimate criminal power and political protection. Hah! It had been the biggest load of camelhorseshit! Why did he fall for it? It must have been the delusive venom spewing from the Ronian's mouth that had slowly poisoned Manni's common sense without him even realising it. Yes, that was it!

With this newfound revelation, Manni looked at the bleeding man on the floor, and tried hard not to glare. When things had turned sour earlier on, he thought he'd need the Ronian's help to get out of the hole he suddenly found himself in. But now, looking at the bloodied Vice-Presidor – who *wasn't* even really the Vice-Presidor any longer, mind you – he realised something else. Not only was this useless maggot incapable of helping himself, much less anyone else, but he was also hindering the Vahltan's escape. He was *so* close! He only had to reach the hidden underground ship hangars. Then he could easily disappear, and maybe even rebuild again later on; once the dust had settled. However, none of that was likely with this lying, pathetic, bloody ball and chain clutching at Manni's leg, staining his favourite white robes.

"I said help me up," Julin Resis whined through clenched teeth. "Why are you just standing there? Get me out of here!"

"I can't carry you any farther," the Vahltan lied, trying to look and sound even more exhausted than he felt. "I must go … to get some help."

"You're lying," the Vice-Presidor rasped, struggling to breathe. "You're going to … leave me here … aren't you?"

"I'd *never*!" The Man said with his best taken-aback look. "I need your help to save my empire."

The Ronian glared at the Vahltan and raised the weapon he still held in his hand, unsure if he should use it. However, if he did, he wouldn't know how to get out of here. His options were limited to one.

"Fine," Julin said, wincing in pain as he spoke, "but don't … even think … about trying … to double-cross me. You will … regret it."

The Man swallowed hard as the Ronian's finger curled tighter around the trigger, but he kept his expression composed. "I'll be back before you know it."

The Vahltan walked apprehensively towards the black door on the opposite side of where they'd entered.

"Remember," Julin Resis said from behind, "don't even try … to stab me … in the back."

"I won't," Manni said over his shoulder. "I promise."

Reaching the door, he opened it, walked through, and turned around with a sneer. "Gullible idiot!" he shouted, upon which the gullible idiot shot him.

• • •

Julin Resis watched with satisfaction as the backstabbing Vahltan spun from the blast and went down, but kept his weapon trained on the doorway, ready to fire at any sign of movement.

When he weakly lowered the gun again, feeling confident that his marksmanship had done its job in the most fatal way possible, the door slammed shut. The Man's face appeared in the door's glass viewing pane. The Ronian fired three more shots into the door, one of which hit the viewing pane, causing the Vahltan behind it to duck involuntarily.

None did any real damage, though, as the solid metal and glass withstood every hit. But he kept firing until the weapon's battery clip was depleted. When the smoke cleared, The Man's flabby face reappeared in the viewing pane, sporting a pained look.

"You *shouldn't* have done that," his voice echoed through the chamber via a comm system. "I had planned on leaving you here for our pursuers to find, but now I think you deserve something a bit more … special. So long, Julin."

The face disappeared, and so did most of the light. Julin heard the sound of scraping metal off to the side. Shortly thereafter, two shapes emerged, slowly yet purposefully. As the shadowy shapes circled him on either side, the Ronian got up unsteadily and tried to track their movement by painfully whirling in one direction and then the other.

He tried shooting one of the skulking shapes, only to be reminded by a soft *whmmm* that there was no power left in the battery. Why did he waste all those shots on a door he knew would withstand the blasts?![*]

"You will die for this, Karpachio!" Julin screamed as his nerves got the better of him.

---

[*] While the merging of anger and stupidity isn't as widespread as that of boredom and stupidity, its power should never be underestimated. Many a mobile phone would have attested to this if it only had more time to do so during its short flight between the hand and the wall.

He hurled the now-useless gun at one of the shapes, which snarled as the weapon hit the stone behind it and charged forward at incredible speed.

"Aaargh!" the Ronian screamed in terror as the shape leapt through the air and knocked him over.

Pinned down, Julin Resis looked up in horror as the shape, which clearly was a Le'u, opened its jaws wide. His horror was spoilt somewhat by a sudden childhood memory of when he was at the circus; when he thought that the act where the tamer put his head into the mouth of a Le'u was the most awesome sight ever. The memory, in turn, was then spoilt by the most gruesome sight ever as the jaws of the present Le'u closed over his face.

CHAPTER 70

Assisted by Captain Phealix, Max reached the door that his adversaries had fled through, and glanced through the viewing pane. The glance turned into a stare that remained fixed on the grisly scene playing itself out before his eyes in the dim light, which wasn't dim enough as far as he was concerned. The Ronian deserved to be punished – even to die – for all he'd done. But the current method of punishment was a bit too much to take in, even for someone like Max. He recoiled from the sight.

"What?" Captain Phealix said, stepping up to see what had caused the Caynin's reaction.

"Oh," she said with a slight cringe. "That's … not nice."

"What's going on?" Guy asked, too short to see.

"Believe me, you're better off not knowing," Max replied, looking a bit pale in the fur.

"Wait," Captain Phealix said. "They spotted me. It seems they don't like to share – they're taking their meal to go."

Max risked another peak, just in time to see the feet of Julin Resis's dragged body disappearing into a hole before the metal grating slid over it. Not wanting to go in, but knowing they couldn't waste any more time, he opened the door.

Entering cautiously, they passed a spot where Guy noticed a chunk of something or someone in a pool of blood. Max was right; he *was* better off not knowing what had transpired in here. With a shiver, he followed the Caynin and Faylin to a door riddled with superficial blast marks. Before Max could inspect it, Captain Phealix, raised her rifle.

"Allow me," she said, and blasted the access panel.

The door popped open slightly, and Max opened it all the way. He looked quite flustered when the captain shouldered past him to step through first.

"What?" she said, glancing back innocently. "I just don't want to pick you up every time you walk into a wall. My arms are getting tired."

Max's indignant expression was ignored, so he followed her with some indignant muttering.

After a backward glance at the gory residue, Guy followed in trepidation, which wasn't alleviated by the torch-lit blood trail running down the new passage. It clearly marked the journey of someone who wasn't going to make it far, especially not in a speedy fashion.

They soon reached the next chamber, which was much smaller than the one they had just exited and didn't have a seating area. It did, however, feature a sizeable round hole in the middle of the floor with a chain hoist suspended from the roof above it. On the other side of the hole, The Man was dragging his wounded right leg towards another door.

"It's the end of the line, Karpachio!" Max shouted faintly, levelling his rifle in unison with Captain Phealix. At least it would have been level if the muzzle of his weapon didn't keep bobbing up and down.

Despite his injured state, the Vahltan spun around with surprising speed to aim a gun at the Infiltrator, who was still feeling too woozy to react quickly enough. Without thinking – which, in retrospect, he probably should have done – Guy leapt sideways across Max's body just as The Man pulled the trigger.

The gun went *weewwww*.

Guy picked himself off the floor, feeling a bit silly after nothing much had happened – glad that he was still in one piece, of course, but a bit silly too.

The Man also felt a bit silly, staring in disbelief at the gun that had just gone *weewwww* without much else happening. He had acquired the weapon recently. It was the new BWOP 459 flasher gun. It was *supposed* to pack a powerful punch.

It was *supposed* to fire an impressive twenty-five shots from one battery clip. It was *not* supposed to just go *weewwww*.

"Drop it," Captain Phealix demanded coolly.

So, as the weapon clearly wasn't going to do its job, The Man dropped it. He tenderly limped around the edge of the hole and stuck his hands into his robes.

"Don't even think about it," Max said woozily, his finger tightening on the trigger.

"Oh, don't worry, I'm not armed," the Vahltan said, and carefully produced two silver boxes, holding one in each hand. "See, I come bearing gifts."

"The profile boxes!" Guy gasped.

The Man sneered at him before Max waved the Vahltan over with his rifle.

"Bring them over here," the Caynin demanded. "Slowly."

Wincing, The Man limped around the hole, where he halted. With a sinister look crossing his face, he held the boxes over the hole before anyone could react.

"What are you doing?" Guy cried, taking a step forward.

The Man held the boxes even farther over the edge.

"I wouldn't come any closer if I were you," he said, shaking the boxes. "I might just get too jittery to hold on to these."

"You've got nowhere to go," Max said.

"I *always* have somewhere to go," The Man said with a weak smirk. "And if you drop your weapons, that's exactly what I'll be doing."

"I can't let you go," Max said with a wobbly shake of the head.

"Well, if you *don't* drop your weapons, I might just drop *these*," The Man said with mock worry. "And I just cannot guarantee they'll survive the fall. And if *they* don't survive, *you* don't survive, isn't that right?"

Guy returned the glare The Man gave him with a flood of anger rushing through his body. Neville was dying while this bastard played games.

"Decide quickly," the Vahltan said. "My arms are getting a bit heavy."

Max and Captain Phealix looked at each other uncertainly.

The Man gave the boxes a fake almost-drop. "Phew, that was close!"

"Okay!" Max relented, lowering his gun. "We're putting them down."

"Why don't you rather throw them in there?" The Man said, glancing at the hole. "Just to be safe."

With a scowl, Max tossed his rifle past The Man. The weapon clattered over the stone floor before disappearing over the edge and landing with a strange *sssssss*. He looked at Captain Phealix, who greeted his look with a grim expression.

"We can't," the Faylin breathed. "You *know* what he's done, and what he'll do if we let him go."

"I do," Max said. "But I also know that I'm responsible for Guy and Neville. They're here because of me, and if something were to happen to them I … I won't be able to live with myself."

After an uncertain pause, Captain Phealix's expression softened. She reluctantly lowered her rifle and tossed it down the hole, where it landed with another strange *sssssss*.

"Excellent!" The Man said, hugging the profile boxes to his chest. "You've made the right decision."

Guy glanced at the Vahltan's bleeding leg.

"You know you're not going to make it very far," he said.

A burst of delirious laughter erupted from the Vahltan, whose face turned paler by the second. It ended as abruptly as it had started, and his mood became as cold as the glare he directed at the Salaman.

"Yes, I know," The Man grated. "But neither are *you*, you fharking little gnat. You've cost me … *everything*."

He glanced down at the boxes with a sneer. "I think it's time to return the favour."

With a mad giggle, Karpachio whirled and raised the boxes, ready to cast them down the hole with whatever strength he had left. However, he suddenly froze in place. Cocking his head, he lowered the boxes and slowly turned around with a confused expression.

His eyes widened. "No!" he gasped. "It can't be!"

He pointed at the three baffled figures standing before him. At least *they* thought he was pointing at them, hence their bafflement.

Manni, however, didn't even see them any longer, and kept his trembling finger pointed at the man now approaching him, or whatever was left of him. With bite and claw marks all over his body, as well as an unspeakable amount of blood oozing from his wounds, the man lumbered towards the Vahltan, leaving behind a trail of crimson death. It seemed like he was trying to say something, but couldn't, due to the gaping hole where his throat used to be. Missing chunks of cheek left his teeth and jaws exposed, creating the illusion of a permanent, ghostly grin, while a punctured eye dangled from its socket like a Halloween-themed Christmas-tree ornament. The shredded man was barely recognisable.

"Julin?" the terrified Vahltan cried. "It can't … it can't be. It … just *can't be!*"

The advancing man ignored the repeated denial of his existence and kept lumbering forward.

"I'm sorry," Manni pleaded. "I didn't have a choice."

As the disfigured figure of Julin Resis came within reach, it raised a mangled arm towards Manni, who flung his arms up in defence.

This led to three things happening.

The first thing that happened was that Guy, seeing the two profile boxes arcing through the air, dashed forward and dived to catch them. However, so as not to distract too much from the second thing that happened, it might be better to come back to the first thing later.

The second thing that happened was that The Man turned to lumber away from the apparition lumbering after him, when he realised something: he'd forgotten about the hole in the floor. He tried to change direction, but found this impossible to achieve mid-air. He did, however, manage to twist around at the last moment, only to find that Julin Resis had vanished. In his place were the three hated figures Manni had faced earlier, one of whom was now also flying through the air after the profile boxes. Manni realised that his own fall, which sent his gold wig flying, was likely going to end really hard. This proved to be semi-correct as he hit the semi-soft floor with a strange *sssssss*. It suddenly occurred to him that the strange *sssssss* wasn't so strange after all. It was, in fact, the reason the hole had been created in the first place. He would know, as he was the one who had ordered its creation.

However, the last thing Manni Karpachio ever expected was that the snake pit, into which he'd sent many a man and woman to become their final resting place, would also become his own final resting place. Strange how life worked. Or death, for that matter.

•••

Those wondering whether the third thing that was supposed to happen, had in fact happened, will be relieved to find out that it had. It would, however, be prudent to first return to the first thing that happened.

Guy sailed through the air with the speed and dexterity of a circus acrobat, which, thankfully, he was. He caught the lower-flying profile box with ease, spun in the air to land on his back, and shot out his hand to catch the second box just before it could hit the floor. He then immediately shot to his feet before – through force of habit – he pivoted and gave a deep bow, causing one of the boxes to slip from his hand. It landed on the floor with a wince-inducing clatter.

As no one really knew if the box was okay – not even a swearing-out-of-character Guy – it might now be a good time to proceed to the third thing that happened, which was this: Max and Captain Phealix didn't know what to keep their eyes on – Manni Karpachio plunging down the pit or Guy leaping after the profile boxes. The third thing ended as they eventually stared in shock at the box dropped by Guy. Given, it was not the most exciting thing that happened, which is why it was kept for last.

Fortunately, to assist in forgetting the mostly uneventful third event, a fourth thing happened behind them, calling attention to itself with a dull *thud*. It also explained Manni Karpachio's odd behaviour during his final moments. Max and Captain Phealix spun around to find the slumped shape of Cortex sitting on the stone floor, looking at it as if it was the only thing left in existence worth looking at.

Max rushed over and shook the dazed Veagin by the shoulders. "Hey, Cortex! Are you with us?"

"I ... good ... fine," Cortex emitted with his head lolling on his chest.

Guy alternated anxious glances between his friend and the profile boxes he now clutched tightly in his hands.

"We'd better get *those* upstairs," Max said.

"But what about Cortex?" Guy asked.

"I'm sure he'll be fine, but I think he might need some time to recover."

"We can't just leave him here alone," Guy said, torn between two concerns.

"He won't be alone," Captain Phealix said. "I'll stay here to make sure he's okay. I'll bring him up as soon as he's ready to walk. Besides, I don't think Neville has a moment to spare."

"You heard her, let's move!" Max said, hastening in the direction they'd come from.

Guy followed hesitantly, feeling wretched about leaving one friend behind, but picked up the pace as he ran towards another friend whose time was running out fast. If it hadn't run out already.

CHAPTER 71

If the way back hadn't been as gruesomely obvious as it was, it would have taken Guy and Max hours to reach their destination, if they were lucky. But the blood trails and blast marks led them straight back to the white medical room within a matter of minutes, although it still felt like hours to Guy. They walked in on a scene that made his heart stop, with Dr Snyer straddling Neville's small Salaman body.

"Pass me that injector!" the Vahltan shouted at Jenny, who hurried over with the pen-like device indicated by the physician. The doctor placed the injector against Neville's neck and injected its contents with a *tssssh*.

As he got off, Dr Snyer noticed the new arrivals.

"Good gracious," he said, racing over to where Guy stood cradling the profile boxes. "It took you long enough!"

Guy was about to say something, but didn't get around to it as the doctor gently but firmly removed the boxes from his protective embrace.

"We don't have much time," the Vahltan answered Guy's surprised expression and hurried over to the pedestal.

Guy pushed his surprise aside and approached the bed on which Neville lay with an oxygen mask covering his mouth and nose. A red, noduled cap also covered the top of his head. "Will he be okay?"

"I don't know," Dr Snyer said. He pressed a button on the side of the pedestal, from which slid out a receptacle, into which he placed one of the profile boxes. "I've never actually *done* a reverse-transfer, even in normal circumstances."

He rushed to one of the stasis pods standing to the side. "And damaged stasis pods certainly don't fall under the category of *normal* circumstances." He picked up one end of a cable, which he'd already connected to the back of the pod earlier, and hurried back to the pedestal, where he plugged it into the receptacle. "It looks like the pod was hit during your little skirmish upstairs. It could have been the life-support or the wireless profile link that got damaged. Whatever it was, I just hope we're not too late."

While Dr Snyer punched in commands on the pedestal's screen, Guy raced to the stasis pod and saw the scorched blast mark on the side. He turned around apprehensively.

"I'll do my best," the physician paused to answer the un-asked question, then resumed his work on the screen.

Knowing there was nothing else he could do, Guy slowly returned to Neville. Out of fear that it might interfere with the procedure, Guy didn't really want to touch his friend, but he couldn't help himself from laying a hand on his unmoving shoulder. When Dr Snyer didn't object, he kept his hand there.

"Come on, Nev," Guy said, wiping a tear from his cheek.

"Okay," Dr Snyer said, straightening with an unreadable expression. "Here goes noth— here goes."

He took a deep breath and pushed something on the screen. Nothing happened.

Guy looked up in alarm.

"I … I did everything to the letter!" the physician cried, staring at the screen. "He was supposed to—"

Neville suddenly began to convulse, his limbs yanking forcefully against the restraints holding him in place. Guy involuntarily jumped back with a yelp, and watched in horror as the spasms continued to rack his friend's body before stopping just as suddenly as they'd started.

Guy approached cautiously. He grabbed his friend's hand and squeezed it.

"Neville?" he said.

After what seemed like a lifetime, Neville's eyes fluttered open.

Guy sighed with relief. "Neville, you're okay! You *are* okay, aren't you?"

"What?" his friend said, bewildered. "What are you on about?"

"It's me, Guy."

"Er, Guy?"

"Yes, you know, Guy? *Your* Guy."

Then realisation finally seemed to hit Neville.

"Oh … uh, hey bro," he said, smiling. "I'm really flattered, but you *know* I don't swing that way. You're kinda freaking me out here."

"But Neville—" Guy started, looking perplexedly at his friend, who in turn started to look annoyed.

"Listen, bro, I don't know what weird fantasy you've got going on here, but please stop calling me Neville, and *please* let go of my fharking hand!"

Guy did so with a confused expression, before some more realisation hit him with a series of *thumps*. Feeling a bit sheepish, he looked up at the stasis pod, from which there came the sound of fists banging against glass. Along with Dr Snyer, Guy rushed to the pod, where Neville was banging his fists against the glass.

The physician pressed a red button, causing the door to pop out and slide open. Neville tumbled out and hit the floor hard, gasping for air, like the goldfish Guy once had for a very short time up until "the accident". Assisted by Dr Snyer, Neville finally got up, coughing.

Jenny, standing by the bed of the injured Jon, gave a cough of her own, followed by a wide grin. "Oh my!"

Neville looked down at what she was staring at, which was something that would normally be covered by the pants he wasn't wearing at the moment. Nor was he wearing anything else. Which is why he promptly wobbled for cover behind the very pod he'd just emerged from. Dr Snyer tossed him a set of white scrubs, which he quickly donned before re-emerging, red-faced.

"Nev, I thought I'd lost you!" Guy cried, running up to give Neville a hug. He stopped just short, though, realising that his head was now about eye-level with the area his tall-again friend had just covered up. Neville seemed to realise this too, and cleared his throat. So they did an awkward high-to-low five and left it at that.

Human once more, Neville stared at his hands before touching his face, just to confirm that what he thought might be real *was* in fact real. Having gone from being a Salaman caught in a firefight to being his old self in a different location, clearly raised some questions.

"How … what …?" he started.

"What's going on here?" Lenny interrupted from the bed, sitting up after Dr Snyer loosened his restraints.

"Bezam," he continued, rubbing his wrists, "what the fhark is going on here, and who the fhark is *that*?"

Before Guy or Neville could say anything, Lenny turned his attention to the door. "And what the fhark happened to *you*?" he said to the hunched-over Cortex, who'd appeared in the doorway, supported by an exhausted Captain Phealix.

Cortex paused for a bit, breathing hard.

"Lenny?" he said after a bit. *"Lenny, is that you?"*

"Of course," Lenny said irritably. "Who else would I be?"

Cortex ignored him and cast a querying look at Guy in his Salaman body.

"Nope, still me," Guy said.

Cortex merely shook his head and used his Faylin crutch to limp to one of the unoccupied chair-beds. He clearly wasn't in a condition to handle any further complications.

Dr Snyer, however, was ready to uncomplicate things.

"I suggest we get rid of any further confusion by getting you back to your old self too," he told Guy. "But I see your box got damaged. How did *that* happen?"

"I, uh, had a bit of a … moment," Guy said, slightly embarrassed. "Will it still work?"

"Only one way to find out," the physician said, gesturing towards the remaining empty chair.

Taking a seat, Guy watched nervously as Dr Snyer placed a red noduled cap on his head before lowering the chair.

"Ready?" the doctor asked in his best bedside voice.

"I suppose," Guy replied with a shaky on-bed voice.

"Good," Dr Snyer said, then injected Guy's neck.

The sting wasn't as bad as the previous time, and Guy soon didn't feel anything at all as darkness blurred everything away.

•••

When everything blurred back again, a blurry shape was staring up at Guy.

"Hey," the shape said.

The shape came into focus, revealing a relieved Neville.

"Hey," Guy replied, shaking his head.

"Welcome back," Neville said, smiling. He helped Guy out of the stasis pod as Guy's wobbly human legs tried to recall what they were there for.

"Careful, the first couple of steps are a bit tricky," Neville said, supporting Guy by the arm as they walked away from the pod. "But don't worry, it'll come back to you. It's like riding a bicycle."

"You know I can't ride a bike," Guy grumbled, but when Neville stepped away, he was surprised to find his lower extremities keeping him upright, even after a few unaided steps.

"Feeling up for a stroll?" Max said, heading for the door. He seemed anxious to get back upstairs.

"Er, I guess so," Guy said, and wonkily followed the group filing out of the room.

They left behind Cortex, who opted to catch an emergency nap on one of the beds. Bezam and Lenny didn't even notice the others leaving as they continued a quarrel over something no one else cared about.

CHAPTER 72

ack on the exhibition floor, all fighting had ceased. The first of the Protectorate and medical backup teams had already arrived, and Dr Snyer excused himself to see where he could be of assistance. The last of The Man's Vahltans that were left standing – in a manner of speaking – had surrendered and were now lined up face-down on the floor, sporting shiny magnocuffs behind their backs. The others were on a-grav gurneys, ready to be transported to the nearest hospital or morgue. But mainly the morgue.[*]

"It seems you have everything under control here," Max said, patting Nelis on the back.

"Of course – I don't need you to hold my hand, you know?" Nelis said with a grin that quickly faded. "Sorry, Max, I heard about Rex."

He shook his head. "We lost Selma and Dirk too. That fharking Karpachio."

Max placed a hand on the Detector's shoulder. "Don't worry, my friend. Their deaths weren't in vain."

"You got him?"

---

[*] Although it's tempting to feel sorry for morticians who suddenly have to give up their weekend golf plans to deal with a sudden influx of bodies, it's important to note that this doesn't happen all the time. But if you're still adamant about feeling sorry for someone, it might be better to shift your sympathy to wedding planners who haven't touched a golf bag in years.

"Let's just say the snake got the justice he deserved – the poetic kind."

"Good," Nelis grated.

"I trust you'll be okay down here?" the Caynin said. "I've got some business to finalise upstairs."

"Believe me," Nelis replied, looking about, "I've got enough business of my own to take care of down here."

Max nodded, before joining Guy, Neville and Captain Phealix in the elevator. As they reached the top floor, the doors slid open, revealing a scene of utter devastation. An antique light fixture gave up its will to hang on and crashed to the floor next to a pair of booted feet, one of which kicked a Vahltan who was trying to get up. The boot belonged to Acting Presidor Don Tinckles, who looked up from the now-unconscious guard with a satisfied grin.

"What took you so long?" he said. "You missed all the fun."

"Oh, don't worry," Captain Phealix said, "we had plenty of fun downstairs."

She looked at Franki, and then at Cap, who'd finally emerged from his hiding place when all was clear.

"Thank you, gentlemen," she said. "That will be all for now."

"But—" Franki started.

Cap nudged him in the ribs. "We'll, er, just go downstairs to help with, uh, anything that needs helping with, Captain," the big Vahltan said, ushering Franki into the elevator.

When the doors closed and the elevator descended, Don Tinckles turned to Captain Phealix.

"Good to see you in one piece, kid," the Acting Presidor said with a strangely affectionate smile.

"Same, Dad," Captain Phealix said, returning the smile.

"Dad?" exclaimed three gaping mouths.

"Keep it down," the captain hissed.

She looked around carefully to see if anyone was too close or conscious to hear. At first it didn't seem so, but then a shot rang out from one of the other rooms, and two figures emerged from the doorway.

"See, I's telled you dat guy were playing dead," Gacko said, slinging his massive weapon over his shoulder. "He are not playing anymore."

"No, Gacko, he's not," Kelp said with a smile that turned into an amused grin as soon as he saw Don Tinckles. "Well, this is a surprise, *Mr X*. I'd never have thought that someone like the Acting Presidor would one day require our services."

Don Tinckles ignored Guy's surprise.

"Come now," he said, "you've known politicians long enough to know that's not true."

Kelp shrugged. "As long as we get paid, it doesn't matter."

"You'll get paid handsomely. I'll even add a little extra – for your discretion, of course."

"Hey, our lips are sealed."

"And I trust they'll *remain* that way," the ginger-furred Faylin stated with a dangerous undertone. "Otherwise I'll make sure they're sealed permanently. Am I clear?"

Kelp, in general, wasn't the type to take threats seriously, be he seemed to make an exception with this one, judging by his expression.

"Perfectly clear," he said, and didn't waste any time in pushing the panel to summon the elevator. "Well, Gacko, I think it's time we take our leave and start spending our hard-earned creds. *The Wormhole*?"

"Dat sound like a well plan," Gacko said.

"*Good* plan," Kelp corrected as they stepped into the newly arrived elevator and turned around.

"Lady and gentlemen," he said with a brief nod. "We bid you farewell."

"Aren't it fair*good?*" Gacko asked, frowning.

"No," Kelp said flatly before the doors closed.

Max turned to Don Tinckles. "Okay," he said impatiently. "Enough of this. I want some answers, and we're not leaving until I get them."

So, after a deep sigh by the Acting Presidor, Max got them.

• • •

"I presume you've learnt quite a bit on your own by now, Max," Acting Presidor Don Tinckles said. "But I'll tell you what I can.

"As you, too, might have suspected, the events surrounding Presidor Dooka's assassination made it clear that someone high up was involved. Someone with the ability to not only get the Presidor and Vice-Presidor on the same ship, but also to organise the convenient *glitches* that had left their ship vulnerable to the attack. So, without being able to trust anyone – not even my own administration – I could also not trust an official investigation. I therefore had to rely on more … unconventional methods."

Captain Phealix didn't look happy. "I don't know why you had to get *those two* involved," she said, nodding towards the elevator Gacko and Kelp had taken.

"I needed a smaller, separate team, my dear," Don Tinckles replied. "As I taught you: don't keep all your milk in one bowl. Besides, they have their own special skills."

Captain Phealix still didn't look convinced, but didn't say anything.

The Acting Presidor looked at Guy. "Someone overheard a conversation between a Caynin and two Salamans in a bar on Grassi Nole. But tracking you wasn't easy, and once I had you, I needed to get you into my daughter's hands. She was the only one I could trust. I had to make it look like a coincidence, though. You see, not even her crew knows of our familial bond. So I got Gacko and Kelp to take you to *The Wormhole*, where the … *chance* encounter with Franki could be organised without raising suspicion.

"With you and your friend in her custody, Phealix attracted the attention of The Man, who'd been looking for you too. So we'd identified *one* player in the plot. But Karpachio was still too low-key to have pulled off the assassination by himself. That's why I had Gacko and Kelp stow away on the *Jolly Dodger*, from where they could easily slip into The Man's stronghold, to see what else they could find out."

"You could have told me about that," Captain Phealix said indignantly.

"We'll talk about that later," Don Tinckles replied to the face whose expression stated they would *definitely* talk about it later. "Like I said, Kelp and Gacko have their own special skills. Not only can they infiltrate just about any place you can think of, but they also have a knack to remain undetected once they've done so. I knew they'd come in handy where they were, so I asked them to stay put until they received further instructions. Apparently they'd also managed to acquire some extra firepower while they were waiting."

He gazed about the room that bore testament to this fact, as another piece of plaster fell off the wall.

"But how the heck can your *own daughter* be a pirate?" Max said, shaking his head. "I mean, you're the *Acting Presidor*, for goodness' sake!"

"Actually, I was the one who got her into piracy in the first place," Don Tinckles said.

Max stared at him, dumbstruck.

"To a certain extent," the Acting Presidor explained, "Julin had the right idea, but completely the wrong way of going about it. Yes, the lawlessness in the Federation has spun out of control, but you cannot regain control from the outside by using force. The more force you apply, the worse it gets. So you have to change things from the inside by using logic. Crime and rebellion will never go away completely, but you *can* control their prevalence and severity. Phealix started the process among the pirates, who are slowly but surely seeing the benefits of raiding without killing – literally keeping the income alive; a sentiment, we hope, will also carry over to other criminal enterprises.

"And the planets that want to become independent? Let them. They'll soon realise that, however imperfect the Federation's laws might be, they were better off being part of the system. They'll rejoin, eventually, and we'll welcome them with open arms. They'll be more loyal than ever.

"As far as Dumb Planets and other independent systems are concerned, invading them and forcing them into submission is a ludicrous idea. As history has shown us time and again, it never works for long with *any* world or system.

Eventually they rebel and, more often than not, you end up losing more than you gain.

"But it all has to start somewhere. That's why my daughter volunteered to become a pirate – to slowly change things in her own special way and to help protect the freedoms that make the Unyun Federation so special. You *know* this, Max."

The Infiltrator snorted. "No, I don't."

"Yes, you do. And so did Harild. That's why you got involved with the plan and – somewhere down the line – how you and Phealix got … involved."

"Nope," Max said adamantly, "I still don't believe it. Me and a pirate hoodlum? Not possible!"

Captain Phealix's expression darkened.

"It's the truth," the Acting Presidor said, "and you'd know it if you could only remember. But I might know a way of rectifying this."

He looked at the Caynin, who eyed him warily. "This place is where your memories had been taken from you, and this is where you can get them back."

"No way!" Max said, looking at the Faylin as if he was mad. "Do you really think I'll let anyone screw around with my head again after everything that's happened?"

"Well *that's* the problem, isn't it Max? You can't remember *everything* that's happened."

"Well, maybe it's for the best," the Caynin said, folding his arms stubbornly.

"Come now, Max. Can you honestly say you'd be content living the rest of your life with such a big hole in it?"

"No," Max said after a hesitant pause. "No, I won't. But how do I know I can trust you?"

"You remember me from *before* the hole, don't you? You also *know* that Harild trusted me, and you trusted *him*. So please, trust *me* now."

Max glanced at Guy and Neville, who just gave him the universal might-as-well shrug.[*]

---

[*] It's almost like the universal "whatever" shrug, but slightly different.

"Fine," he relented, "but I'm only doing this to prove you wrong."

The Acting Presidor merely nodded and gestured towards the elevator.

As they stood there, waiting for it to come up, Max dreaded knowing the truth almost as much as not knowing it. But Don Tinckles was right. He would *not* be able to live with such a big part of his life missing. Good or bad, it was time to put an end to this, once and for all.

CHAPTER 73

After fetching Dr Snyer from the exhibition floor, the group went down to the room where the reverse-transfers had been performed. According to the doctor, this was also where Max's memories had been "relocated", causing his memory loss. Of course Max couldn't remember this, which was kind of the point.

Mindful of the possibility that he might involuntarily divulge Infiltrator secrets during his memory reclamation, Max asked everyone else to wait down the hall. Bezam and Lenny, in turn, were asked to wait even farther down the hall, as they were arguing again, or still. In all likelihood, it was the latter, as the two seemed very comfortable with their bickering. The others, however, weren't, and would gladly have sent the pair upstairs if it wasn't for the fact that they needed to keep an eye on the Salamans. Fortunately, they were now far enough away that they didn't have to keep an ear on them too.

While the others were mostly standing or pacing around, Captain Phealix sat with her back against the wall and her hands clasped around her knees, staring at the opposite wall in silence. In fact, she hadn't said much for a while now, which probably had something to do with the downcast expression on her face, which in turn probably had something to do with Max's behaviour. Yes, it was definitely the probable reason.

Pacing nervously, Guy glanced at her, but she kept on staring broodingly at the wall. He didn't need to wait for Max's returned memories to confirm the relationship between the Infiltrator and the captain. He thought they were an odd match, though – not because Max was a Caynin and she a Faylin, but rather because she was *way* too hot for him. This was just his honest opinion. The fact that he felt more than a bit jealous had nothing to do with it.

The Faylin finally caught one of his lost-in-thought glances and shot back a glare that made him continue his nervous pacing a little farther away.

When the door finally opened, Dr Snyer came out, looking grave. Everybody converged on the physician, except for Captain Phealix, who continued her staring competition with the wall.

"And?" Guy said nervously.

"I'm afraid I have some bad news," the doctor said glumly. "I won't be able to return to my former hospital. I have to join the Infiltratorate and swear an oath of silence, which—"

"Max!" Neville said, annoyed. "What about *Max*?"

"Oh, I'll be fine," Max answered as he walked past Dr Snyer, giving the physician a stern look. "It beats going to prison, doesn't it, Doc? I know you didn't have any real say in what you were forced to do, but you still have a lot to make up for."

The doctor accepted his fate with a woeful nod.

Max ignored the other relieved faces and carefully approached Captain Phealix, who didn't look up.

"I'm, uh, sorry," he mumbled, wringing his hands.

"For what?" the Faylin grated at the wall opposite her.

"For ... everything," Max said, looking embarrassed. "For not remembering *us*. For not remembering all we'd accomplished together."

He didn't receive any kind of response.

"Uh, for not remembering ... that I, er, love you?" he tried, looking hopeful.

Captain Phealix rose with a steely glare.

"I know *that*, you jerk," she said, her glare intensifying. "No, *you're sorry* for calling me a ..."

Max stared at her confusedly.

"What are you talki—" he eventually managed, before realisation hit him with a sigh. "Oh, er, yes, I, uh … I'm sorry for calling you …" he cleared his throat, "… a hoodlum."

"A *pirate* hoodlum," she corrected.

"Well, technically, er, you are—"

"Just shut your yap before you say anything else you might regret," she said and leaned forward to shut it for him with a long, passionate kiss, which, after a brief moment of surprise, he returned with even more passion. It wasn't a pretty sight, which was why the others were extremely relieved when Don Tinckles stepped in.

"Sorry to interrupt," he said. "I know you two have a lot of catching up to do, but if you don't want to blow your cover, Max, I suggest you leave now. Preferably through the back door."

Parting reluctantly, Max nodded and walked up to Guy and Neville to shake their hands.

"Well, uh, I guess that's it, then," he said. "It's been … fun."

"Will we ever see you again?" Neville asked with a lump in his throat.

"Don't worry," Max said, "I'll be in touch once the dust has settled."

"And what are *we* supposed to do now?" Guy said, feeling somewhat lump-throated himself.

The Acting Presidor placed a hand on his shoulder and addressed the humans with a warm smile.

"You, my friends," the Faylin said, "can do *whatever* you want."

CHAPTER 74

A few months later, Guy sat in the back of a bus en route to his new job on Unyun. He hadn't quite managed to get a handle on driving a car yet, but he'd been promised a new one as soon as he got his licence. He wasn't in a hurry, though, as the thought of driving in the chaotic traffic of Unyun still freaked him out.

Neville was another story altogether. Not only had he already received his driver's licence, but he was also well on his way to getting his pilot's licence for flying smaller Class A spaceships. His new Trafficor colleagues called him a natural, and envied his ability to breeze through any test thrown at him. Although it was generally more admiration than envy. They all liked him, and Guy wasn't surprised. He also wasn't surprised that Neville and Margot ended up dating. She'd really been impressed when she saw Neville for the first time in his human form, and even said as much – and more, which had made Guy's face go as red as the face of his former Salaman body. He was just glad that Neville still managed to make time for his old Earth friend in between his love interests and hectic work schedule.

Not that Guy really felt alone during the times Neville was busy. He and Cortex shared the apartment the powers that be had gifted the human in appreciation for his services. Neville had also received a place of his own, and so had Cortex, but the bug struggled to adapt to city life after being in the circus for so long.

After everything that happened, the Veagin had opted to join his new best friend on Unyun. Besides, he realised he could do more with his gifts than entertain people; something more *meaningful*. He didn't know what yet, but he would know when he found it. Guy didn't mind having Cortex around, as it also helped him with his own adjustment. So, the longer his friend took to figure out what he wanted to do, the better.

Guy had also joined *Spacebook*. He generally wasn't a big fan of social media, seeing as he wasn't much of a social butterfly. But he was too curious about the others, and wasn't satisfied with the bits of information Neville passed on during his occasional visits.

Now, as he still had some time before the bus arrived at the office, Guy used the opportunity to check out the latest updates on his new galphone.

Nelis had been made Senior Detector, which he apparently wasn't all too happy with. Not that he didn't deserve it, but Neville said the Detector didn't like having to go along with the bent truths and lies the public had been told regarding the assassination. He knew the deceased Manni Karpachio had to be blamed for everything, because the political ramifications for the Federation would be too great if the Ronian Vice-Presidor's involvement ever came to light. But Nelis still didn't like it. He had also adopted 3OCD2, which he obviously regretted already – his latest post almost pleaded for anyone in need of a side table to contact him "URGENTLY!!!"

Captain Phealix was wanted anew for a raid on a trade freighter, during which no one was killed or seriously injured, but after which everyone had woken up with a serious headache.

There was nothing about Max. But with him being an Infiltrator, it wasn't exactly a major surprise.

Gacko and Kelp had just hunted down a big crime boss who'd escaped from prison only two days ago. The Monitaurs posted a photo of themselves with their rifles shouldered and the unhappy detainee lying face-down under their boots. If the size of the bounty awaiting them was proportionate to the size of the grins they sported, it had to be huge.

Bezam and Lenny were having an online squabble over something, so Guy simply skipped the post.

Acting Presidor Don Tinckles was officially voted in as Presidor of the Unyun Federation. Hospitals were making a killing from the treatment of Social-media Fractures, better known as SMF, to the fingers (or whatever the equivalent was) of both his supporters and detractors.[*]

Mr Gray and Mr Chase had recently been released from rehab. Remarkably, they'd gotten their jobs back, most likely in return for their silence. Mr Gray and Ms Beatrix had just gone on a date. She looked pretty chuffed with her new purple handbag, which looked almost exactly like the old one.

The rest of the updates, however, had to wait for later, as the bus stopped at Guy's new place of work, *The Unyun Weekly*.

•••

Just as he sat down at his new desk, Guy had to get up again when his new editor came over to greet him.

"Welcome, Mr Leatherman," said the red-furred Stortian, shaking his hand with a friendly smile.

"Thank you, sir, but you can call me Guy," Guy said, beaming.

"Not a problem … Guy," the man said with a friendly smile that turned into an awkward one. "But could you please do me a favour and get here on time tomorrow?"

"Sure thing," Guy lied with an awkward smile of his own.

"Good, good," the editor said, looking relieved. "I have another favour to ask of you. I know you signed up as an investigative journalist, but my brother has a story that might be the perfect ice-breaker for your first day."

"Whatever you need," Guy said. "I'm good to go."

---

[*] That's why nine out of ten doctors recommend healthy online debate. The other doctor suffers from SMF and cannot recommend anything for the next four to six weeks. At least not online.

"Splendid!" the editor said. "I'll send him right in."

As the Stortian walked away, Guy sat down once more and looked at his new computer, which he had no clue how to operate. He checked his desk drawers and was relieved to find a notepad and pen among the junk his predecessor had conveniently forgotten to clean out.

He looked up to find a Stortian, which he assumed was the editor's brother, hovering nearby. After introductions, Guy pulled up a chair that belonged to one of his new colleagues for the man to sit in. The colleague returned with his freshly brewed coffee, only to find that he suddenly had nowhere to sit. He glared at Guy in a way that stated, in no uncertain terms, what he thought of his new co-worker and their future together.

Guy looked at the editor's brother in a way that stated, in no uncertain terms, he hadn't noticed.

"So, how can I help you?" he said, flashing a smile.

"Well," the Stortian said, looking really upset, "I bought this bag of potato chips yesterday and found a potato in it! A *whole* potato! Can you believe it?"

As it turned out, Guy *could* believe it. Manni Karpachio had been right about the truth coming full circle. And life, Guy thought to himself, was the same. You just had to sit back, relax and let the same old things repeat themselves in order to enjoy the new things when they eventually came along. Which is why he now sat back, relaxed and listened to the boring story while taking boring notes.

As the man rambled on, Guy started feeling something he'd never really felt before. He felt … content. And it felt weird. However, immediately thereafter he felt even weirder when he realised that, in fact, for the first time in his life, he felt truly … happy.

EPILOGUE

The Nonexistent Observer continued observing the space above Grassi Nole where he'd witnessed quite an entertaining event some time ago. He had hoped to catch a glimpse of something else that would pique his interest, but apart from an oddly shaped comet, nothing out of the ordinary had presented itself.

Just as he started contemplating whether his time would have been better spent following the comet, another nonexistent observer popped in to see if there was anything worth observing, only to find his intended spot already occupied. Being curious, he drifted over to see what The Nonexistent Observer was looking at.

"Hey," the nonexistent newcomer said.

"Hey," The Nonexistent Observer said.

"So, er, what are you looking at?"

"Oh, nothing much," The Nonexistent Observer replied, staring at nothing much – the remnants of the destroyed ship had long since been cleared away.

"Oh," said the other nonexistent observer.

After what seemed like an appropriate amount of time had passed of looking at nothing before saying something, the other nonexistent observer said, "So, um, I heard about this new bar that opened in a galaxy not too far away. I'm actually heading there now for a quick beer. Wanna join?"

The Nonexistent Observer cast one final glance at the empty spot of space where it seemed nothing was going to continue happening for quite a while.

"Might as well," he said, adding the appropriate shrug for good measure.

So, leaving behind the big planet and the mostly nothing surrounding it, the pair blinked out of the existence they were never part of to begin with, to discuss the meaning of their nonexistence over a *quick beer* that, in nonexistent terms, lasted two weeks.

ACKNOWLEDGEMENTS

Firstly, a huge THANKS to Gero, Jane (no, not *that* one), Mark and Werner for beta-reading the story during your Christmas holidays, and for telling me what I needed to hear instead of what I wanted to hear … and for adding some things I wanted to hear. I'd like to extend my appreciation to Mahen Reddy for assisting with some of the cover elements despite your hectic work schedule, as well as to Lucinda and my family, friends and social-media peeps for your support through all the ups and downs. It was a wild ride!

And last but not least, thanks to you – yes, *you*, the reader. Without readers, authors are nothing more than popstars singing to themselves in the shower. I truly hope you enjoyed *A Life Spectacular*, and if you did, please feel free to check out my latest LightSide novel, *Happy Meals*, or sign up to my mailing list at **www.eatonkrone.com/contact** or follow **@EatonKrone** on Twitter or **Eaton_Krone** on Instagram for upcoming releases and other random stuff.

ABOUT THE AUTHOR

After hitting pause on his planned writing career, Eaton Krone spent more than two decades slaving away in the fields of journalism, PR/communications and advertising – the latter devouring three quarters of his career-history pie chart along with a sizeable chunk of his sanity. He's done nearly everything copy- and language-related, from writing and editing to translation and proofreading across a wide spectrum of media. His journalism and copywriting qualifications are in a box somewhere.

Although he's pleased to continue his journey as an author, Eaton denies being the author of his own life, as it's riddled with way too many errors and scenes that cannot be edited or (preferably) deleted. He lives with his unofficial other half in Cape Town, South Africa. His mind lives somewhere else.

www.ingramcontent.com/pod-product-compliance
Lightning Source LLC
Chambersburg PA
CBHW020914110726
47900CB00001B/131